About the Author

Richard Solly grew up in South East England but has spent many years working in support of Indigenous and farming communities affected by destructive mining operations. He has been deeply influenced by the Theology of Liberation. He is unmarried, but open to offers. He lives in London.

Dedication

A.M.D.G. and in grateful memory of

Antony Mahony
Bert White
Joe Fox, Sr
John Medcalf
Lorraine Sinclair
Randy Lawrence
Teddy Woodenthigh
and Thelma Two

Richard Solly

BRIGHT WINGS:

A LIGHT-HEARTED TALE OF DISAPPOINTMENT, DESTRUCTION, DESPERATION AND DEATH

AUSTIN MACAULEY
PUBLISHERS LTD.

A CIP catalogue record for this title is available from the British Library.

ISBN 978 1 78455 795 9 (Paperback)
ISBN 978 1 78455 796 6 (Hardback)

www.austinmacauley.com

First Published (2015)
Austin Macauley Publishers Ltd.
25 Canada Square
Canary Wharf
London
E14 5LQ

Printed and bound in

Acknowledgments

With many thanks for advice, encouragement and hospitality to

Carolyn Pogue Phipps
Carrie Small
David King
David Raby
Desiree Hellegers
Diana Mills
Diarmuid O'Murchu
Dominic Mahony
Henrietta Leyser
Jeannette Sinclair
Luisa Raby
Maggie Scrimgeour
Mike Rebeiro
Raglan Hay-Will
Rick Rees
and Rob Esdaile

PROLOGUE

In the beginning was the theory

The moon was full when the residents of Noname, on the plains of western Canada, emerged from their newly-built community hall one warm summer night in 1898, and headed home, the beer kegs and whisky bottles drained, the new pine floor marked with its first signs of dancing.

The bright moonlight cast sharp shadows around the scattered houses, built of logs and sod, that lay some hundreds of yards in every direction from the timber-framed hall, and made the tall prairie grasses shine like silver.

The small community of English anarchists who occupied this patch of rolling plains, lying southeastwards of the sand hills and several dozen miles north of the US border, refused in principle to lay out their new settlement according to the regimental grid plan dictated by the Dominion Land Survey. They decided, at the first community meeting held in their collectively built hall, to construct their street plan according to the erratic routes, still fairly clearly visible in the surrounding grass, which they had each taken home from their inauguration dance, the worse for weariness, aching feet and alcohol.

They also decided that 'Noname' was no name for a settlement. They chose a new name, out of affection for the revolutionary Russian anarchist, Peter Kropotkin, who had inspired all of them and whom many of them had met at his home in exile in Bromley, Kent, where he was experimenting with improvements in horticulture. Kropotkin was to be the name of their new settlement, their experiment in hope, sharing and liberty – Kropotkin, Great West Territory – and after the Territory was divided in 1905, and its two halves attained the status of Provinces, it became Kropotkin, Assiniboia.

They rejected out of hand the dreary logic of western New World street names, and chose instead – once the crooked paths were marked out and paved with packed dirt – names inspired by Kropotkin's own address in Bromley, 6 Crescent Road. These were names that combined the basic elements of street names in their native land and would render any attempt to navigate the settlement by reason and prediction futile: not only Crescent Road but Street Road, Road Street, Crescent Avenue, Street Lane, Road Road, Avenue Road, Avenue Street, Avenue Lane and Avenue Crescent. When they had finally exhausted all such combinations, they used Not Crescent Road, Not Street Road, Not Road Street, and so forth.

At the second community meeting held in the new hall, the residents, including men, women and all those children old enough to help till the soil and tend the livestock, confirmed the decision they had made before leaving England. They had decided that each family would have its own plot of land as well as working what the community held in common, because this would provide the necessary balance between collective production, individual liberty and the natural bonds of blood.

They also decided to seek close and friendly relations with the Native people who had remained in the vicinity since the colonial wars and since forced settlement had been imposed on them by their European invaders. No one in the community wanted to impose further suffering on unjustly treated people, when they themselves had fled the injustices of a class-ridden and unequal homeland.

Finally, they decided to welcome among them anyone who came seeking liberty and was prepared to work hard, play a full part in the shared life of the community and respect the ways and views of residents already there. This meant that they could not accept anyone practicing a religion. As far as residents of this community could see, those who followed a religion thought they were somehow better than other people and duty-bound to convert them to whatever faith they followed for fear that, otherwise, they would burn in hell. Furthermore, such people, obsessed with some illusory afterlife, had no practical interest in changing the oppressive conditions with which so many in the world were burdened.

Residents felt no need to reconsider this decision for the next one hundred years and when they did so, it was because of the unexpected arrival, under the most trying of circumstances, of several natives of the island from which the community's founders had come.

EAST

the direction of new beginnings

One: Kerry receives the call

One afternoon, just over a hundred years later, in south-west London (the one in England, not Ontario), Kerry sat half-asleep in the launderette, made drowsy by the warmth and by the drone of the tumble dryers. He watched his jeans and acrylic sweater churning back and forth in the washing machine in front of him, blue legs tangling with green arms in a confusion of foam and underwear. He looked out at the grey, drizzly spring day, stretched out his legs, leaned back against the dryer behind him and closed his eyes.

"Excuse me, love."

The woman who worked in the launderette had returned. Kerry opened his eyes and drew his feet up under the bench so she could pass. "Sorry to disturb you, love," she said, "but I've got to get to the office."

"Sorry to be in your way," said Kerry.

"That's alright," she said. "You look tired."

She went into the small office at the back of the launderette and put down her shopping bag. "I just nipped to the shops for a few things, while it was quiet," she said, emerging from the back room with a service wash, which she began loading into one of the machines. "Not working today, then?" she asked.

"No, I rarely work on Mondays," replied Kerry. "The library's shut on a Monday and my other work is a bit unpredictable."

"Do you work in the library, then? I rarely go in there. Not much of a reader."

"Oh, you can get CDs and DVDs in there, too," said Kerry. "All sorts of stuff."

"Perhaps I should have a look," she said. "Have you got any country music? I like country music. It's relaxing. A bit sad, usually, but quite relaxing."

"I think so," said Kerry. "There's all sorts of music in there. It's much cheaper renting than buying stuff. Do have a look."

"Yes, I'll do that, then," she said, and after a pause, "What's your other work, then?"

"I'm a translator. Mostly Spanish documents that need translating into English. Sometimes I do French or Portuguese as well. I work freelance. I thought there'd be more work but I haven't had that much since I finished university. That's why I took a part-time job in the library."

"You haven't lived round here long, have you? I've not seen you before."

"No, I've not been here long. I grew up round here, but my dad died when I was eleven and we moved down to Wessex to be close to my mum's sister. My mum died while I was at university, so I came back to London when I got my degree."

"Oh, I'm sorry, dear," she said. "Awful thing to have lost both your parents when you're still so young."

"Yes," said Kerry. "I do miss them."

They were silent for a few moments.

Then she asked, "Do you have to go to college to get a job at a library?"

"It depends what job you want to do there. You do to be a translator."

"Did you always want to do that?"

"No, I never had a clue what I wanted to do. I thought going to college would help me decide, but I still didn't have a clue at the end of it. Being a translator sort of avoids having to know my own mind. I just have to make one person's thoughts clear to another person. I don't have to have any of my own. But not much work has come my way. I knew I could deal with books, though, so when I saw the library job advertised, I applied for it."

"My son Kevin loved books," she said. "He was always reading. All sorts of stuff. It used to annoy my husband. He told him he ought to get out more, get himself a girlfriend, get a life. I couldn't see what harm there was in reading, though, if that's what he wanted to do."

"What's he doing now?"

"Singing with the angels, perhaps. He died six and a half years ago."

"Oh, I'm so sorry," said Kerry. "What did he die of?"

"In a road accident. He was away in his thoughts, as usual, on his way home from school, and stepped into the road without looking. The driver tried to stop, but he hit my boy and he was thrown sideways and cracked his skull against the kerb. There was nothing they could do, in the end. He was only fourteen."

Tears sprang to Kerry's eyes. "I'm so sorry," he said. "Was he your only child?"

"He was," she said. She was silent for a while. "It's very hard sometimes, *very* hard. I loved him so much. He was such a gentle boy. Not a moment passes without me thinking about him, even if I'm thinking about something else, if you see what I mean. I'm sure you do, with your parents passed away."

"But it's different to lose a child," said Kerry. "You expect to lose your parents, but to lose a child...I'm so sorry. It must be so painful for you. How has your husband coped with it?"

"Oh, he didn't cope well at all. He was gentle too, inside – just tried not to show it too much in case people thought he was soft. He blamed himself for not making Kevin more practical, and then again, he blamed himself for nagging him, and especially for always telling him to get a life, and then he dies, like that. And my husband didn't have faith to keep him going, like I do. I talk to Our Lady a lot, because she knows what I'm going through. It does help."

"Are you a Catholic, then?"

"Yes – not a fanatic, but it means a lot to me."

"Me, too."

"Oh, really? Well, you'll know what I mean, then. My poor husband didn't. He pined away, you know."

"He's no longer with you?"

"No, he died two years after my son."

"Oh, I'm so sorry. Sorry to make you talk about sad things."

"You didn't. I started it. I don't usually talk about it now. You learn to live with these things. You go mental if you don't. Sometimes, I meet someone who just seems easy to talk to, and I talk to them."

"Oh, well, then," said Kerry, "I'm glad you can talk to me."

They were silent for a while. She looked lost in thought. Kerry's wash cycle came to an end and the machine fell silent too.

"I'm Dawn, by the way," she said.

"I'm Kerry," he said.

"Lovely Irish name," said Dawn.

"I think one of my great grandfathers came from Kerry," he said. "My mother loved the name."

"I've worked with the public all my life," said Dawn. "Before I worked here, I worked in a travel agent's for years. I've met so many people, I can usually guess what they do for a living. If you hadn't told me you worked in the library, I'd have guessed you were the local Church of England curate. You've got a kind, sort of concerned look about you."

"Oh! Thank you!"

"Have you ever thought of being a priest? You're a good listener. Anyone can see you've got a kind heart."

"Me, a priest? Oh, goodness, I'm not sure about that. Some of the things the Church comes out with are, well, a bit difficult to understand."

"Ah, but you'd go to college to study for the priesthood and they'd explain it all to you, wouldn't they?"

"Well..."

"Mind you, I expect you'd break a lot of hearts in a parish, with that lovely fine blond hair and clear skin, and so slim with it."

"Oh," Kerry blushed. He very rarely gave any thought to his appearance. "Thank you!"

Dawn looked at him. "Lovely hazel eyes, too," she said. "Like my son."

"Oh..." Kerry did not know what else to say.

"I bet you had all the girls chasing after you at school," said Dawn.

"I went to an all-boys school," said Kerry

"Oh, I see," said Dawn.

Kerry wondered whether she did see.

"St. Thomas More Catholic School in Westhampton," he added.

"That's nice," she said.

It had not been all that nice to start with, he thought. There were a couple of boys there who said he looked like a girl, and pushed him around. He never retaliated. He had no idea how to handle it. But the school had an enlightened anti-bullying policy, and the trouble did not last long. One of the boys was expelled. Kerry often wondered what had become of him.

Then, there was the boy two years above him who, when Kerry reached the age of thirteen, always seemed to want to spend time with him during the lunch hour, and to walk home with him, even though his house was in the opposite direction. Kerry never asked him why. Then, one day, on the way home, the boy became terribly agitated and told Kerry he loved him. Kerry did not know how to deal with that, either. He did not want to upset the boy. In a way he felt flattered, but he never did understand what it was to be in love with anyone, whether girl or boy, so he thanked his admirer but said he did not feel the same way. The boy left the school all of a sudden, in the

17

middle of the year, and Kerry never heard what had happened to him, either. He could not even remember his name, now.

"I think you should think about it, you know," said Dawn. "Ask your parish priest about it. You go to Mass, don't you?"

"Yes, but..."

"You go and talk to your parish priest. He'll help you."

Kerry did think about it, off and on, for several weeks. Then, one early summer day, he went to see the parish priest.

Two: Kerry learns to pray

"Well," said Father Patrick Murphy in his soft Meath accent. "What do you think yourself?"

"I don't know," said Kerry. "I'd never thought of it before."

They sat in the elderly priest's high-ceilinged, brightly painted kitchen, its two tall, thin windows looking out into a small garden full of flowers and birdsong.

"You're a sensitive and kind-hearted young man," said Father Patrick. "You always were. I remember when I first came here fifteen years ago and you were in the youth club, you were always looking out for the others. If anybody was new or looked lonely, it would be you who befriended them. That's a good start. That's the most important thing. You have to care about people or you might as well not bother. You've been visiting some of the old people in the parish since you got back to London, haven't you?"

"Yes," said Kerry. "I got chatting with old Mrs Smith one day after Mass, and she was so upset about her husband's death, so I started dropping in on her once in a while to check she was okay and give her a bit of company. She asked me to visit some of her neighbours because she said they were lonely."

"They've spoken about you," said Father Patrick. "They really appreciate you going to see them, you know."

"Oh, good," said Kerry, not knowing what else to say.

"What about God?" asked Father Patrick. "Is God real to you?"

"Yes," replied Kerry. "Plenty of people have told me it's all a load of old rubbish, but God always seemed real to me, even if he's rather hazy and ill-defined."

"Who do you think God is?"

"Oh, I don't know. I haven't really got a picture of him in my head. He just feels like a great mass of kindness and love to me. Maybe he's a projection of my late father."

Father Patrick laughed, and scratched his grey beard. "Who knows?" he said. "If God's beyond our capacity to understand or imagine – as he must be if he's infinite – then, any idea we have of him is bound to be a projection of something, isn't it? Better have a projection that's pleasant rather than one that's horrible. As long as you realise it's not the whole story."

"Yes, I suppose so," said Kerry.

"You must like going to Mass well enough, because I've seen you every Sunday since you moved back. Do you pray when you're not at church?"

"Yes. But I'd like to learn more about that."

"Well, we can sort that out in due course." Father Patrick paused. "You're twenty-four now, aren't you?"

"Yes."

"And you haven't got a girlfriend or anything?"

"No."

"Do you think you could cope with never getting married?"

"I think so. I mean, that side of life has never been that important to me, I suppose."

"And do you have a strong desire to be a translator or work in a library?"

"No."

"Or anything else?"

"Not really."

"Well, I suggest you carry on with your visiting. If you want to do anything official on behalf of the parish, we'll have to get a criminal record check on you, I'm afraid."

"Okay. And what about the praying?"

"Well, if you like, I'll teach you the way I pray myself, and you can see if that works for you. And you could join the parish prayer group. It's a joint effort with the Anglicans. There's some champion prayers there, I can tell you. Lovely people."

So, in the weeks that followed, Father Patrick taught him how to meditate on passages from the Bible; how to deepen his sense of gratitude for life and the beauty of the Earth; how and why to pray for other people and for the state of the world. "You see," said Father Patrick, "part of the purpose of praying is changing ourselves, making ourselves more loving and kind and gentle, and then the world starts changing because we've changed ourselves. Maybe you pray that so-and-so recovers from an illness and instead she dies, but perhaps in the process you've become more loving and caring and so-and-so has felt that, felt more surrounded by love and kindness, and it's made her final weeks more bearable. The purpose of prayer is to deepen your compassion. Any form of prayer that doesn't is a waste of time."

The prayer group met in different people's houses at seven o'clock in the evening on the first Friday of the month. The next meeting was at Stella Coelho's house. Stella Coelho was a retired schoolteacher in her early seventies. She had taught religious studies, English and drama in the local girls' secondary school. She had never married. All her caring and nurturing had gone into her work. She was sad to leave her job, and filled the void with acts of kindness towards her neighbours and with work for the church, the friends of the local hospital, and various community organisations.

She smiled when she opened the door to Kerry, shortly before seven the following Friday evening. "Ah, you're Kerry, aren't you? Father Patrick told me to expect you. I think you'll probably halve the average age of this evening's gathering!"

She ushered him into the sitting room, a large room, well appointed with soft chairs, in which half a dozen women, all elderly, were already sitting. They greeted him warmly.

Others arrived, including two elderly men, and finally, a little late, the vicar. Stella served tea and biscuits, then sat down and asked, "Shall we introduce ourselves?" A dozen short introductions followed. Seven of those present were from Holy Redeemer Church of England parish and the rest from Our Lady of Lourdes Catholic church.

"I've been thinking about several news stories this week," said Stella. "There's climate change and the damage it's causing in East Africa, the expected loss of species; those terrible floods in the Midlands; that poor boy who was stabbed just outside the station here by a teenage gang, one of whom is Molly Doorley's oldest son, and she's beside herself with grief and guilt, as though it was all her fault for not bringing him up properly. Oh, now, I should say, Kerry, matters are often raised in this group which need to stay here, so please treat what you hear here as confidential, won't you?"

"Yes, of course," said Kerry.

"Well," said Stella, perhaps we can bear these things in mind during the first part of our prayer this evening." She picked up a Bible from the small table beside her chair, opened it, and read, "Psalm 24, verse 1: 'The Lord's is the Earth and its fullness, the world and all its peoples.'" She closed the Bible, replaced it on the small table, and closed her eyes. There was a general shifting of bodies in chairs and exhalations of breath. Kerry looked up. As far as he could see, everyone's eyes were closed. He closed his own. He could hear the ticking of the clock in the next room, the occasional vehicle passing in the road outside, the odd sigh or rumbling of the stomach, the slightly wheezy breathing of Charlie, the asthmatic former miner, sitting opposite him. He caught wafts of the vicar's aftershave, Mrs Lloyd's perfume and the slightly acrid smell of stale sweat from the rather plump Mr Edwards, sitting next to him.

He did not know what he was expected to do. He thought about the boy who had been stabbed, about the boys who had stabbed him, about Molly Doorley, whoever she was, in her sadness and shame. He thought about the people who had lost their homes to flooding in the Midlands, the people starving in East Africa, their animals who were dying for lack of grass, the grass which had died, and the soil dried out by the sun. He felt a great sadness come over him, and a great feeling of sympathy for all these people and animals and plants that were suffering. Tears began to stream silently from his eyes, which he had to keep mopping discreetly with his unpleasantly filthy handkerchief.

He thought about the words which Stella had quoted, trying to turn them over in his mind as he was learning to do with stories about Jesus in his daily morning prayer. How should he think about 'the Lord'? The only images in his mind were childish pictures. As a child, he had always thought of 'God' as looking rather like his father and wearing his father's green checked dressing gown, because his father had been such a kind and gentle man, and he imagined that was how 'God' was. But if 'God' was the creator and sustainer of the seemingly limitless universe, it did not seem appropriate to imagine him wearing a green dressing gown, or looking like a human being. And why 'he' rather than 'she'? And how did this figure relate to the figure of Jesus, whom Kerry had, as it were, encountered in his imagination during his meditation that very morning? And in what sense did the world and everything in it belong to this 'Lord'? And if it did, why had 'God' allowed these terrible things to happen?

He thought, if I were 'the Lord' and everything in the world were somehow 'mine', how would I feel about it? He felt a stab of compassion in his chest that almost physically hurt him, and he began to weep silently again as he considered the sufferings of created beings and what he took to be the grief-stricken love of the creator watching those sufferings and willing relief. Just as he knew he was going to have to blow his nose and disturb everyone, he thought, well, we who live in the world have to be the ones who make that love visible, because whatever 'the Lord' is, the only way he or she or it can make it visible is through physical beings like us; and then the clock in the next room struck eight o'clock, and Stella cleared her throat and said, "Perhaps we can share any

23

concerns that people have brought with them now, and pray for God's blessings and guidance."

There were matters of unemployment and financial hardship; sickness and bereavement; difficulties in marriages; problems with teenagers and problems faced by teenagers; an impending birth; the announcement of an engagement. After each concern was raised, there was a brief silence before Stella said, "Lord, in your mercy," and everyone replied, "Hear our prayer."

As the evening wore on, Kerry felt an atmosphere of intense kindness in the room. It was as if great waves of goodwill were being generated by the small gathering and being directed outwards over the neighbourhood and beyond.

Then Mr Edwards said, "I was listening to the radio the other day and there was this very bright chap on there – I didn't catch whether he was a journalist or a professor or what – but he was saying shocking things about Muslims and about us and all religious people. I wanted to say, 'you've got it all wrong, we're not all like that,' but it's no good speaking to the radio because they can't hear you. I felt all rubbed up the wrong way, but I thought, well, if the way we carry on makes people think that about us, we really need to set our house in order. But I didn't think it would help matters, stirring people up against one another the way he was, creating tensions when there don't have to be any."

"Perhaps we should pray that people of faith will behave in a way that doesn't give others cause for bitterness," suggested Stella, "and that people of different religions and none will make more effort to understand each other, and not to judge each other so harshly."

There were murmurs of agreement, and some moments of silence, and then she said, "Lord, in your mercy,"

"Hear our prayer."

The clock struck nine. Stella said, "Perhaps we should draw to a close now." She led the group in a final brief prayer, then served more tea before people left for home.

Kerry's Aunt Liza was disapproving. "It's all very well praying and helping people, but I see no reason why anyone should become a priest," she said when he asked her opinion on the matter. "I take a distinctly dim view of the Catholic hierarchy and I think it would be tragic for a good-looking young man like you to deny himself the joys of love, when there are other much more practical ways of helping people."

Kerry greatly loved his aunt and respected her opinion; but the fact was that his experience of religion had always been rather positive, and his views of the Catholic Church coloured by the ministry of kind and rather jolly priests. On the rare occasions that he read what Popes or bishops had said about things, he usually felt they were living in a different world from him, and therefore dismissed their pronouncements from his mind. As for the joys of love, he had always thought they were for other people, not for him.

Kerry's two closest friends from university were both rather struck with the idea. Chris was a fellow Catholic and had considered priesthood himself before pursuing a career in law. If Kerry went ahead and got ordained, he would feel better about the fact that he had put the idea aside, and married. Brett did not have a religious thought in his head, and decided it would be rather fun to be friends with a priest, as he had never spent any time with one. Kerry could always give it up if he didn't like it, he suggested.

Kerry did not wish to take the matter lightly. He knew people left the priesthood but considered it unwise to get ordained with the possibility of abandoning it in mind. He wondered what his parents would have thought about him becoming a priest. His father would have expressed no opinion, he thought – simply let him know that he would support him in whatever he decided. His mother would have done likewise; but he felt sure that if he had announced his decision to go ahead with ordination, she would have given him a big hug and whispered, "Oh, I'm so proud of you!", even though it would have meant the death of any hopes she might have harboured for grandchildren. He reflected on the matter for a few more weeks, and then went to see Father Patrick again and told him he would like to give it a try.

"Nothing ventured, nothing gained," said Father Patrick. "If God's calling you to be a priest, it'll become clear during the selection process and at the seminary, and if he's not, that'll come clear too, and no harm done. Some of the young lads coming out of the seminary these days have got their priorities all wrong. They're so devoted to the Church, they forget it's about people. You'd be a breath of fresh air, if they let you in. Why don't we get you an interview with the Vocations Director? He's a bit of a twerp, but there's no way 'round him, I'm afraid."

Three: Kerry is counted among the chosen

"Come in," said Monsignor Ed Case-Mendelman, with a rather joyless smile. Kerry went in to the Diocesan Vocations Director's small, dark office in the Archbishop of Lambeth's huge, decaying Victorian residence.

"Sit down," said the Monsignor, indicating a couple of identical armchairs. Kerry chose the one further from the door, and sat in it.

"No, the other one," said Monsignor Case-Mendelman, disconcerting him. Kerry stood up and sat in the other chair. Monsignor Case-Mendelman pulled a straight-backed chair out from under the table and sat on it, facing Kerry, several inches above him and just an inch or two closer than Kerry found comfortable. Kerry wanted to push his chair back a little, but the wall prevented him.

"Would you like a cup of tea?" asked Monsignor Case-Mendelman.

"Oh, yes, please. That's very kind of you," replied Kerry.

"Why do you say that?"

Kerry was a little taken aback. "Well, it's kind of you to offer to make me a cup of tea."

"But I didn't. I simply asked you whether you'd like one. You're reading things in to what I'm saying."

"Oh. Sorry."

Monsignor Ed Case-Mendelman stared unsmilingly at Kerry. Kerry felt himself blushing deeply.

"You're very tense," observed Monsignor Case-Mendelman. "Try to relax."

Kerry found it difficult under the Vocations Director's relentless gaze.

"We'll do a relaxation exercise," said Monsignor Case-Mendelman. He stood up and moved to the far side of the room. "Close your eyes and slow your breathing." Kerry did so. "Now, try to think of something peaceful, perhaps a quiet stream, a beautiful view, a piece of calm music – and concentrate on it. Breathe slowly and deeply – in – out – in – out – in...out... breathe s-l-o-w-l-y..." Kerry began to feel a little calmer.

Suddenly, there was a terrific bang, and Kerry physically jumped in the chair as his eyes flew open. Monsignor Ed Case-Mendelman screwed up the remains of the paper bag he had blown up and burst, and threw them in the litter bin in the corner.

"Good," said Monsignor Ed Case-Mendelman. "Good, clear reactions. Good. Now," he continued, suddenly forcing a smile, "what makes you sure you want to be a priest?"

"I'm not sure," replied Kerry. "It's other people who seem to think I should be one."

"Excellent, excellent!" exclaimed the Monsignor. "Too many of the few young men who come to see me are certain not only that they want to be priests but that God wants them to be priests. Insufferable arrogance! Your humility is refreshing."

"People tell me I'm kind-hearted and easy to talk to. I don't know."

"Well, priesthood is about much more than that. Intellectual docility to the Holy Father, acceptance of the Church's teaching, especially in matters that are difficult for people in our benighted culture to understand, are essential – otherwise our kindness can become mere sentimentality and leave people confused, lacking clear moral directives. But I can see that you are willing, and malleable, so assuming the psychological tests show that you are sane, and the criminal records checks show you aren't a child-molester, I'll send you to a selection conference for the regional seminary."

The Seminary of St Simon the Stylite, St Scholastica and St Christina the Astonishing stood on the side of a range of partially wooded hills, facing southwest towards a great expanse of drained marshes, from which rose a steep, solitary hill. The hill was surmounted by a tower, which was all that remained of a famous medieval abbey; a tower in which Henry VIII had hanged the last abbot of the nearby monastery in his struggle for absolute control of the national Church. The seminary was an enormous late Victorian edifice, faced with mellow Cotswold stone and built in the form of the letter H, its extremities consisting of the chapel, lecture rooms, common room and refectory, and the four storeys in the crossbar, diminishing in height of ceiling with the elevation of each floor, providing study bedrooms for both staff and students.

One autumnal afternoon, some years after the restoration of the Roman Catholic hierarchy in England and Wales, the Most Reverend Alphonsus McAleer, first Archbishop of Lambeth, had struggled up the then grassy hillside from the lane below, dodging sheep manure and thistles. He was accompanied by an architect and numerous Canons and Monsignors, coming to break the sod and begin the construction of the southern regional seminary. A wealthy benefactor from an aristocratic family, which had never broken its communion with Rome, had bought a hundred acres of land covering the entire hillside above the lane, and the plan had been to build the seminary at the top, thus dominating the landscape for miles around in an act of triumphant defiance of over three centuries of Protestant Establishment. But the Archbishop was a portly man, a lover of good dinners and fine wines, and he had eaten a large lunch. Despite the assistance of a stout walking stick turned in hornbeam by a local woodsman, who had converted to the Catholic Faith, and trembling with nerves and pride had presented his handiwork to the most reverend prelate as he had stepped out of his horse-drawn carriage in the lane, the Archbishop was out of breath before he had climbed half way to the top. "Build it here!" he ordered, striking the ground with his stick, and the architect blanched as he realised the extent of the redesign that would be necessary. It would not do, however, in those days, to question the decision of an Archbishop – not of that Archbishop, anyway – and so, the seminary was built below the hill-crest, on sharply sloping land.

The Archbishop was, unusually for the Roman Catholic bishops of the time, a Patristic scholar. He had developed a particular devotion to St Simon the Stylite, who was everything that the Archbishop himself was not – ascetic, exhibitionist and popular – while sharing with him an indomitable will, which St Simon used to impose discipline on himself, and which the Archbishop imposed on other people. St Simon, rejecting worldliness and property, had ascended an enormous pillar in fifth century Syria and remained on top of it for thirty-three years, praying and proclaiming the Christian Gospel to anyone who had ears to hear – particularly sharp ears, of course, especially when the wind was blowing off the desert and howling around the pillar and the surrounding ruins. Thousands flocked to see the famous ascetic and to receive some blessing from him, either by hearing his inspired words or, perhaps, by failing to hear them. The Archbishop insisted that the seminary be dedicated to this saint as a model of devotion, in order to inspire in the students sound habits of prayer and abstinence.

The Holy See, however, had made it clear that the dedication of the seminary should be to the studious sister of the great St Benedict, St Scholastica, in order to inspire in students a love of learning. This was in the hope that, with the help of her intercession, they might reach, by the end of their six years of study, at least the minimal standards of instruction which their Anglican counterparts might be expected to have achieved before entering their theological colleges in the first place.

Meanwhile, the Bishop of Wessex, in whose diocese the building was to be constructed, had been warned in a dream that the establishment was to be named after the little known St Christina, whose title had been earned by her propensity for climbing trees to avoid people, so offended was she by the odour of humanity. The bishop believed that the guidance that had been vouchsafed him was a clear sign that the students should be set apart in manners and morals from the world of seething vice and Protestant error surrounding them, and be ready to take firm action to avoid compromising their priestly integrity, even at the cost of misunderstanding and mockery.

Faced with these three proposed dedications, each jostling for supremacy, the Church authorities, being catholic, chose all of them, and in the chronological order of their suggestion.

Most twenty-first century seminarians were not enamoured of the dedication. Poncey bloody name, they thought.

A taxi dropped Kerry off at the upper gate of the seminary the Friday afternoon after Easter, the weekend chosen for the selection conference, because all the students were gone for their post-Easter break. Rain fell steadily from a dark, heavy sky, and Kerry was wet through by the time he reached the massive front door. He was let in by a cleaning lady, because he was early, and the teaching staff assigned the task of greeting candidates were not yet ready for him.

He went to the chapel to wait. The smell of Easter lilies still hung sweet and heavy in the neo-Gothic gloom, perhaps a little too sweet as the lilies began to decay, and the grey light of the wet afternoon filtered in through a massive depiction of the crucifixion in the great window over the altar. It was a window which, had the chapel been a genuinely medieval building, would have faced east towards the rising sun, but in fact, faced southwest towards where it set in midwinter. A flickering candle hung in a glass container in front of a small cabinet in the wall to the left of the altar, in which the Blessed Sacrament was reserved.

As Kerry's eyes became accustomed to the gloom, he could make out more of the decoration. The lower part of the walls was divided into squares set on their corners, the squares demarcated by slightly wavy gold lines which caught the flickering candle light from time to time. The wall space was divided by stone ribs which soared upward to form the pointed vaulting, holding up the distant roof. All the squares between one pair of ribs were red, and between the next pair, green, alternating all the way down the chapel from door to altar. A horizontal stone rib led around the wall, at a height of about six feet, above which were the windows, bearing stained glass scenes from the life of Christ, and between the windows were murals of what looked like various saints. The gloom prevented him from making out the paintings on the ceiling.

Kerry heard the door to the corridor opening, and turned round to see a cassocked figure approaching down the chapel's aisle. The figure drew close and Kerry saw a priest of about sixty, with copious grey hair and a welcoming smile. "Are you Kerry Ahern?" he asked.

"Yes, that's right," replied Kerry. "I'm afraid I'm a bit early."

"Never mind. Better than being late!" said the priest, chuckling gently. "I'm the Rector, sort of in charge of the place. Why don't you come and sit in the common room and have something warm to drink and some toast or something? Sorry, we didn't arrange decent weather for you. Very gloomy afternoon indeed, I'm afraid. Did you get wet? Oh dear, yes, you look wet through. Well, we'd better find your room first so you can change into something dry, before you go to the common room. Wouldn't want you to catch a cold. Follow me."

The Rector led Kerry out of the chapel and up several lengthy flights of stairs to the top floor. They went through a set of double doors and down a wide corridor. Half way down was a door bearing a label with Kerry's name on it. "Here you are," said the Rector, smiling and chuckling again. "Make yourself at home. Showers are at the far end of the corridor, toilets at either end, should be towels and everything you need in your room, and the common room's back down on the ground floor, the opposite end of the main corridor to the chapel. Keep your mobile on you in case you get lost! I'll send out a search party if I don't see you in the common room in half an hour!" He slapped Kerry on the shoulder in a hearty manner and made off back down the corridor.

Kerry went into the room. It obviously belonged to one of the current students, because the shelves were full of books and the walls covered in pictures. On one wall was a large poster of Che Guevara, black against a red background. On another, a textile hanging of a Latin American crucifixion, a black Christ hanging on a spreading tree, with images of oppression in sombre colours at the bottom of the picture – tanks, soldiers, prison cells, police – and images of liberation in bright colours at the top – children playing, farm workers gathering the harvest, schools being built and villagers discussing some issue under a tree. At the bottom of the bed, by the door, there was a large photograph of a path going into a beech wood. Around and between them were prints of Russian icons and photographs of people that Kerry took to be family and friends, with a number of pictures obviously taken in some tropical country, with smiling families standing outside wooden shacks shaded by mango trees, or what Kerry took to be mango trees from the appearance of their fruit.

Kerry closed the door and changed, laying his wet clothes over the wash basin in the corner, the radiator, and the chair by the desk at the window. He inspected the books on the shelf over the bed – *The Communist Manifesto*, by Karl Marx; *The Making of the English Working Class*, by E.P. Thomson; *Fields, Factories and Workshops*, by Peter Kropotkin; An Introduction to the Works of Antonio Gramsci; Karl Polanyi's *Origins of our Modern Age: the Great Transformation*; *Jesus Christ, Liberator*, by Leonardo Boff, and by the same author, *Ecclesiogenesis*; *A History of God*, by Karen Armstrong. There was a copy of the Qur'an and the *Bhagavad Gita* and selections of the works of Keats, Shelley, Gerard Manley Hopkins, Billy Childish and Bill Lewis.

Kerry made his way down to the common room, where, by now, a number of candidates had gathered, together with some of the staff from the seminary.

It was an awkward assembly. The candidates, including Kerry, were all nervous and felt insecure and out of place –

apart from one man, a Tony Conwell, who made himself the life and soul of the party, but who made Kerry feel profoundly uneasy. Thus began a strange weekend of multiple interviews, shared prayer and disturbing observed social interaction, by means of which the staff and invited experts aimed to make a judgement as to who was, and who was not, suitable for admission to the seminary and training for the Catholic priesthood in one or other of the dioceses in Southern England and Wales.

Undoubtedly, the most disturbing element was the interview with a peculiar priest who attempted to evaluate the nature of Kerry's sex life, such as it was. They sat on opposite sides of a large desk. The priest was a very straightforward Irishman, and Kerry sincerely wished he would beat about the bush a bit. He came, disconcertingly, straight to the point. "The Church insists that the clergy take a vow of celibacy, and keep it," he said. "Have you ever had sex with a woman?"

Kerry blushed deeply. "No!" he said, sounding shocked without intending to.

"What about with another man?"

Kerry felt that his face was about to ignite. "No, no, certainly not!" he replied.

"You sound a bit defensive about that. Are you sure?"

"Yes, I'm sure," said Kerry.

"Have you ever kissed anyone?"

"Well, yes, my mum and dad, and my aunty."

"No, you know what I mean – I mean romantic kissing, boy-girl kissing."

"No," said Kerry.

"You've led rather a sheltered life, haven't you?"

"I don't know. Have most candidates for priesthood had an active sex life before coming here?"

"Well, yes, as a matter of fact. It's an aspect of modern life, isn't it? People in and out of each other's undies from an early age. Sad fact, but there we are. We have to be sure that candidates for the priesthood understand the facts of life but are mature enough to stay faithful to their vows."

"To be honest, that side of things has never meant that much to me. I don't mean I look down on that aspect of life, but it's never occupied my thoughts much."

"Well, it's good to be chaste, but we need real men in the priesthood. Real men, not Nancy boys. Do you know what masturbation is?"

Kerry did not think it would be possible to blush any more deeply than he already was, but nonetheless, felt himself turn at least two shades darker.

"Yes, thank you, Father. I do and before you ask, yes I did do it once, and yes, I know that I shouldn't have done it, and yes, I went to confession about it."

"Oh. I wasn't going to ask you that. I do try to respect candidates' privacy."

Kerry wished that he could jump into a pool of cold water to douse the raging fire of his face and neck. He even felt his arms blushing. He had not realised it was possible to feel this embarrassed, not even during his hopeless attempts to dance with girls at teenage parties.

"Well, that'll be all," said the priest. "I commend you for your honesty."

Kerry was surprised to receive the letter saying that he had been accepted for training for the priesthood. He was much less surprised when, some while later, he read that the disturbing priest had been arrested at a municipal swimming pool for interfering with adolescents.

Four: Kerry goes to college

The seminary was constructed for at least four times the number of students that it housed in the opening years of the third millennium. If one had been so inclined, it would have been possible to spend weeks at a time inside the building, without going out at all. Everything necessary for the maintenance of physical existence and for the support of such studies as the residents were required to pursue was housed conveniently within that one vast edifice.

This was a shock to most of the students, Kerry included, arriving from a wholly different world – and indeed from a different sort of Catholic Church – from the one in which the institution had been established. Most were disoriented by a sudden sense of claustrophobia and isolation from reality, rendered more acute by the fact that some of what the students were expected to learn seemed scarcely relevant to the world in which they were to minister.

But much of it Kerry found absorbingly interesting. As a cradle Catholic, he had not thought much about the Scriptures before Father Patrick had encouraged him to read the Gospels, and he found it fascinating to learn how these hugely varying writings of differing antiquity had been brought together; how the opening books of the Bible had been collated from a variety of contradictory sources; how to distinguish between history, poetry, legend and myth within the texts, and how 'myth' did not mean 'lie' but a story conveying theological, rather than literal, truth.

He was particularly impressed by their theology lecturer, Father Donald Black. Father Donald was in his early forties.

He was a prison chaplain, as well as lecturing two days a week at the seminary, and although he was academically gifted, he did not come across in the same dry manner that some academics did. Kerry was drawn into the subject matter during the first lecture.

"Right," said Father Donald. "What's theology?"

"Talking about God," suggested Tony Conwell.

"Yes," said Father Donald. "So why would we want to do that?"

"Because then we can explain God to other people, who don't believe in him," suggested Kieron McKeogh.

"Well, now, that's quite a tall order, isn't it?" said Father Donald. "Maybe we'd better try to understand God ourselves, before we try explaining God to other people. What do you think?"

There was a general murmur of agreement.

"So, how can we explain God to ourselves?"

There was silence.

"Yes, indeed," said Father Donald. "Silence." He paused. "Think of some of the things we say about God. God is infinite, eternal, almighty, omniscient, omnipresent. How can we talk about qualities like these? How can we understand them? They are beyond our capacity to imagine or conceptualise." He paused again. "Just think about all the damage that has been done by talking about God. Think about all the bigotry, violence and oppression carried out over the centuries in the name of different concepts of God. It might be better not to talk about God, mightn't it?" He paused again. "What I would like you to do may be painful, but I want you to try. I want you to set aside all mental pictures, concepts, images, understandings of God that you have brought with you, however good and inspiring and helpful, on the grounds that they are inadequate to the task at hand. Whatever our understanding of God, if we cling to it, we've made it into an idol, because there is always, always a difference between God and our concepts of God. To suggest otherwise is to suggest that we ourselves are all-knowing – and we aren't."

Kerry felt his heart burning within him. "Yes!" he thought. "Yes, I knew that..." Perhaps his rather hazy sense of God was nearer the mark than the dogmatic certainties that often passed for Christianity.

Each student at the seminary was required to choose one of the clergy on the staff as a 'spiritual director', with whom he could discuss his relationship with God, his prayer life and any matters that might be disturbing him, and to whom he could, if he wished, make his regular confession. Kerry chose Father Donald Black. The man inspired him. The way he talked made the spiritual life seem like a most exciting adventure.

Kerry found life at the seminary highly structured but not unpleasant. Most weekdays they were expected to attend Morning Prayer at 7.15, Mass at 7.30, breakfast at 8.00, lectures from 9.00 until 12.30, lunch at 1.00, Evening Prayer at 6.30, supper at 7.00 and Night Prayer at 10.00. On Thursdays Mass was in the evening, before supper, instead of in the morning, and it was full of music. On Sundays it was at 11.00, when the celebration was very lively, and generally, attended by plenty of people from the local area. During the afternoons and evenings, they were expected to study in their rooms or in the library, to attend to whatever pastoral duties they were given and to perform their house jobs (Kerry's job was to clean the downstairs toilets). But they were also expected to spend some time in rest, recreation, exercise and socialising. Kerry enjoyed lengthy afternoon walks in the surrounding countryside. Saturdays were free and most students went away for the day, visiting friends or attending football matches, or whatever else they might have done at weekends at home. On Sunday evenings, after supper, the student bar was open, and most of the building's residents spent a pleasant evening chatting, joking and drinking – in the case of a few students, drinking rather too much. On such occasions, Kerry generally stuck to gin and tonic, and usually drank only three. More than that affected his capacity to think clearly.

Kerry discussed at length with Father Donald his inability to feel certain about anything. Donald seemed to consider this a potential strength, as long as it did not lead to inaction. Action was necessary – action to relieve suffering and to create justice. Kerry accepted this, but did not know what action he ought to take. Donald said that perhaps all that was being asked of him at present was to develop his evident ability to listen respectfully and empathetically to other people. Much suffering of spirit could be relieved simply by such listening.

Kerry pondered this advice and considered how he might find opportunities for putting it into practice. Donald suggested that he ask that his pastoral work, which he would need to begin by the start of his second term at the seminary, should involve visiting housebound people. They often struggled with great loneliness, and Kerry's gifts were particularly suited to relieving it. So it was arranged that each week, from the beginning of Kerry's second term, he would spend an afternoon visiting elderly, housebound people in the surrounding area.

There were only half a dozen students in the first year, and Kerry got on tolerably well with all but one of them. Two of them shared his view that priesthood was primarily an exercise in love – a pastoral love for human beings, which reflected the nature of the God they believed in, a God who was supreme and infinite compassion. They aspired to be good listeners, kind and understanding, bringing comfort to the afflicted and hope to the excluded.

Two others were very conservative. They considered their classmates 'woolly-minded'. They associated with a small clique of students in other years, who saw their role as policing other people's doctrinal orthodoxy. They attacked the prevailing air of tolerance in the seminary as 'threatening the Church's entire economy of salvation'. They tended towards misogyny. Their humour was barbed, snide and cruel. But at least Kerry knew where he was with them, and since he was adept at avoiding confrontation, he managed to co-exist with them in relative harmony.

The odd one out was Tony Conwell. Kerry did not know what to make of him. He was certainly not a conservative – indeed, in private he sneered at the Papacy and expressed contempt for traditional doctrine – but neither did he manifest the kind of pastoral concern exhibited by his 'woolly-minded' classmates. He seemed to think it important to appear cool and fashionable, and to enjoy the attention that being a student priest brought him in the Catholic youth movement, in which he was involved. But Kerry could not tell what kind of God he believed in, or whether that God was in any way distinct from his own inflated ego. He seemed to lack any understanding of the difference between truth and falsehood. Kerry had read somewhere that three to four percent of the world's male population was psychopathic, and lacking a developed conscience. They often made convincing liars, convincing enough to fool potential partners or employers, or quite clearly, those responsible for admissions to Catholic seminaries. Three to four percent; that meant that out of three dozen students, it was no surprise that one should be a lying, selfish sociopath, and as far as Kerry could see, Tony Conwell was it. He hoped the staff would come to the same conclusion before the man was ordained.

Kerry made closer friendships with three students in other years. He greatly admired Francis Neale, a fourth year student in his late twenties, a man of genuinely saintly demeanour who appeared incapable of harbouring an unkind thought about anyone and always looked for the best in everyone. He was particularly gentle to those in any kind of distress, and spent an afternoon each week volunteering at a local home for elderly people with learning difficulties, some of whose behaviour could be very trying. Kerry went with him once and knew that he would not have the patience for the task, but Francis never became irritated, never lost his temper or raised his voice, never talked down to the residents and never said anything unkind or disrespectful about any of them behind their backs.

Unlike Kerry, who was studying for the Archdiocese of Lambeth, Francis was studying for the Diocese of Aylesford and Ebbsfleet, usually known by its initials, A&E. This acronym, so well known in a medical context, was taken by most students to refer to the dire state of the Catholic Church in that diocese. Many of its clergy were mired in the past and very few young men were coming forward to study for the priesthood. Of those who were ordained, at least half left the priesthood within ten years. Mass attendance was falling steadily and its gentle, rather unworldly, bishop simply hoped that things might get better if he waited long enough. Any suggestions for change were greeted with the polite affirmation, "We don't do that sort of thing in this diocese." Students from the rather more lively dioceses nearby referred to it as 'the Dead See'. Kerry wondered how long Francis would survive.

Peter Steel was also in his fourth year of studies, and Kerry looked up to him as to an admired older brother. Peter was in his mid thirties and had been a teacher before entering the seminary. Like Kerry, Peter was well educated and middle class, but Peter was what Kerry was not – firm in his opinions, sure of himself, willing to fight for what he believed in, and convinced of his calling. For him, faith and politics were inseparable. Both were inspired by the words of Jesus' Mother Mary in the song known as the *Magnificat,* which the students recited every day at evening prayer, in which Mary says of God, 'He puts forth his arm in strength and scatters the proud-hearted. He casts the mighty from their thrones and raises the lowly. He fills the starving with good things, sends the rich away empty.' Peter was a convinced, militant libertarian socialist, and drew inspiration from the Latin American liberation theologians, whom the Vatican had spent thirty years trying to silence. Kerry envied him his certainties, his political passion, but found himself unable to share them. It had been Peter's room that Kerry had stayed in during the selection conference.

Mario Rankin, in his third year, though only a year older than Kerry, was from South London, and of Irish and Italian heritage. He had inherited his mother's Mediterranean looks. He boasted of his paternal great-grandfather's activities, fighting the British in the Irish war of independence, and like Peter, held the British Establishment in contempt. He was as sure as Peter of his calling to the priesthood, but as unsure as Kerry that he would actually get there. He looked up to Peter, too. He would often point at Peter while Peter was holding forth on some topic and mouth the words, 'brilliant' or 'brainbox' to Kerry; or he would wait until Peter had finished and then point at him and then at his own head and say, "Brains, see, that bloke's got brains."

Peter spent his vacations from the seminary working with the Association of Cortesian Refugees in London, assisting new arrivals from Cortesia, helping with Spanish-English interpretation, advising on how to get the benefits they were entitled to, visiting Cortesians in immigration detention centres and trying to stop deportations. "I utterly love it," explained Peter, "and at the same time, it makes me hopping mad, the way these people are treated by the Government and talked about in the media."

Mario worked with a local youth group during term time, but over the summer, he too had been working with refugees, volunteering with a visiting group whose members befriended asylum seekers in immigration detention centres. "Some of the blokes I visited never wanted to talk about anything to do with what had happened to them, or about their legal case or anything," he said. "One only ever wanted to talk about football. Another one talked about God all the time. Another one kept asking me about British history, which was more difficult for me because I know fuck all about history, except that the bloody ruling class and the Brits, in general, spent all of it oppressing other people."

"That's not a very nuanced approach to the subject, Mario," Peter objected.

"Well, it's a pretty accurate summary," retorted Mario.

Kerry was intrigued by the strength of the friendship between Peter and Mario, who were so utterly different from one another in so many ways. Mario smoked heavily, occasionally drank too much, peppered most conversations with expletives, and had, so far, found it impossible to give up sex, despite his more than two years in the seminary. Not that the staff knew this, of course. Had they known, he would have been 'invited to reconsider his vocation' and expelled. Only his close friends knew – and the young women with whom he had been intimate. Peter, on the other hand, had never smoked, never drank too much, never used foul language, and appeared to be so completely absorbed in pursuing a vocation, which was both religious and political, that he did not have the time or mental energy to devote to sex. Mario was drawn to Peter partly because of that very devotion. He envied it, because he shared the convictions that lay behind it.

As for Mario's hormonal drives, they amused Kerry. Even at the height of adolescence, he had never understood why sex was so important to so many people. He noted that this was the way most people – or, at least, most men – were, but he felt as though he were observing the fact from afar, or that he was a visitor from another planet. Sexuality was simply not important to him. He certainly did not consider celibacy a potential problem for him. He had no doubt that, if he did not become a Catholic priest, he would nevertheless remain a bachelor. He was vaguely aware that he may have been chatted up on occasion, both by women and by men, but he was never sure. He was not confident that he could tell the difference between a particularly friendly conversation and a veiled proposition. He had been told once, by an elderly gay colleague, that he was quite exceptionally 'pretty', but other than thanking the man for what was obviously intended as a compliment, he had not known what to do with the information.

The fact that Kerry spent so much time in the company of Peter and Mario meant that he spent relatively little in the company of Francis, despite his admiration for Francis' gentle spirit. For some reason, this very gentleness irritated Peter and Mario, and neither especially enjoyed passing time with him. Although Kerry was, by disposition, much more similar to Francis than to Peter or Mario, their very difference from him drew him to them, and he got to know them much better than Francis.

Kerry particularly enjoyed his pastoral work: his visits clearly meant so much to the housebound people he visited. It delighted him to bring joy to other human beings. One of the people he visited regularly had been a ballerina. She told him that he would know that he was following the right path, when he felt his spirit dancing. The thought both pleased and troubled him. Far from dancing, he felt that his spirit was wandering in some desert place, and he could not say that, by the end of that academic year, he felt any more certain of his vocation than at the beginning.

Nor did he find those aspects of official Catholic teaching that had always troubled him any easier to understand or accept, when the background to them was explained to him, albeit by kind and well-meaning lecturers. Gay people, for instance, were apparently perfectly acceptable to God and to the Church, but they were expected not to engage in any 'genital expression' of their sexuality. They were to spend their entire lives as sexually frustrated as the Catholic clergy. And he really could not understand why clergy should be unmarried; especially, as there were several married students at the seminary who had been priests in the Church of England and had, for one reason or another, become Roman Catholics. They were to be appointed priests in the Roman Catholic Church after a year of extra study, despite their married state. Then, there was the absence of women students, because women could not be ordained priests in the Roman Catholic Church. Why could women not be priests? The rationale was explained to him several times and it made no more sense to him for the repetition.

Back in London, he had some helpful conversations with Father Patrick, whose wisdom and compassion seemed inexhaustible. Father Patrick encouraged him not to give up. If he still felt no closer to certainty after another year at the seminary, perhaps then would be the time to throw in the towel.

So, that September, Kerry returned to the seminary to begin his second year, and spent a further term in much the same manner as his first year.

Five: Kerry suffers an injustice

The autumn term ended after breakfast on 21st December. The night before, Kerry's year group went out for a meal. The effort of being pleasant to Tony Conwell exhausted Kerry and left him rather depressed. After Night Prayer, he sought out Peter. At his knock, Peter opened the door of his room and beamed in delight. "Kerry! How lovely to see you, as always! Come in! Mario and I are discussing the term."

Kerry stepped into the smoke-filled room.

"Sorry about Mario's smoke," said Peter. "You know there's nothing I can do to stop him."

"Never mind," said Kerry. "It's just nice to have congenial company."

"Have you just been in uncongenial company?" asked Peter.

"I've been having supper with my year group, including Tony Conwell."

Peter rolled his eyes heavenwards, saying nothing.

"That bloke's a lying little tosser," said Mario.

"You have such a way with words," commented Peter.

Mario began to laugh, and had a fit of coughing.

"I say," said Kerry, "Do you think we could open the window? It's a little stuffy in here."

"Sorry, Kerry," said Mario. "This'll be my last fag of the evening."

Peter drew back the curtains and opened the window on to the darkened woods and fields below. A cool draft blew in and he shivered. "Cooh, it's parky out there tonight," he observed.

"I'll shut it again when the air's cleared a bit, if you don't mind. You must cut down on the fags, Mario."

"I'm already down to forty a day," said Mario.

"You'll have to cut down more. You're going to cough to death one day."

"No, no, I can't cut down any more. I'm stressed, man, stressed. Only one more year and I'll have to give up sex forever."

"You're supposed to have given it up already," said Peter. "You haven't fallen again, have you?"

"Only a bit, I couldn't help it. She was gorgeous. She virtually forced me to."

Peter sighed, and gave Mario an exasperated look.

"They make a bee line for me," said Mario, defensively.

"I can't think why," said Peter. "I mean, look at you. Short, squat, ugly little git."

"Fuck off!" replied Mario. "You don't understand what attracts women."

"I certainly don't understand what attracts them to you."

"A combination of sizzling good looks and magnetic personality," replied Mario, proudly.

"Well, for goodness' sake, try and control yourself over the Christmas break," said Peter.

"Yes, teacher," replied Mario, with mock humility.

Peter made a pot of tea. Kerry drank a cup of it and then went to bed. He slept heavily. But, some time in the middle of the night, he was woken by a gentle but persistent knocking on his door. "Who is it?" he asked, quietly. The door opened a crack and a sliver of dim light from the corridor fell across his blue carpet.

"It's Tony," said the silhouetted figure in the doorway, and entered the room.

Conwell.

"What do you want?" asked Kerry. "What time is it?"

"It's about three thirty," answered Tony. "I need you to do me a favour."

"At this time of night?"

"Yes, look, I'm in a bit of a bind. I've been helping this woman in the village, you see, who's got troubles with her husband. She comes up here to see me quite a lot, and I think the staff are getting a bit suspicious."

"Should they be?"

"I'm just helping her, right, and none of that. Well, not much of it, anyway. I've been ... helping her tonight, and it's too late to get her back to the village now."

"Too right. What do you want me to do about it, then?"

"Well, look, Kerry, it's like this. If she stays in my room and anyone sees her in the morning, they're going to put two and two together and make six. I'm going to get chucked out. Whereas, if she stays in your room, A, nobody's going to take any notice and B, nobody's going to give a flying fuck."

"How do you reckon that?"

"Well, look, if she goes nice and early, say, before six, nobody's going to see her, are they? Who's up before six?"

"The Rector. He gets up at five thirty."

"Well, yeah, but he's going to be praying, isn't he? He won't see anything. You see, they're bound to be watching me now, whereas you've got a clean record, haven't you? Nobody's going to be looking at what you're doing, are they? Can she sleep on your floor? Please? I mean, look, it's only a couple of hours."

"What are you, paranoid or what? Anyway, if you *have* been intimate with her, you really ought to take the honourable way out."

"Oh, come on, you're talking like some Vatican official. Please, Kerry. I'm only asking because you're such an obliging kind of chap."

"You mean, I'm too soft."

"Oh, come on."

Kerry said nothing in reply. Tony hovered in the doorway. Kerry began to feel uneasy.

"Oh, alright then," he said, more crossly than he expected. He felt cornered. "Send her along here, and sort yourself out, for goodness' sake, man."

"Oh, thanks, Kerry. Nice one, well wicked."

Selfish idiot, thought Kerry.

"Don't tell anyone, will you, mate?" urged Tony.

"No, alright, I won't tell anyone," agreed Kerry.

Tony slipped out, leaving the door ajar behind him. A minute later, a young woman in a pink silk nightie pushed it open, hesitating in the doorway.

"Kerry?" she inquired in a whisper.

"Just as well I am," answered Kerry quietly, "Otherwise, you'd feel pretty embarrassed, wouldn't you?"

She came in to the dark room and shut the door behind her.

"Look, I'm really sorry about this, Kerry, I really am," she whispered. "I was opening my heart to your wonderful, understanding friend Tony, and we didn't notice the passage of time."

"Well," said Kerry, "You'd better take the bed and I'll kip on the floor."

"Oh no, I can't do that!" she said. "It wouldn't be right. I'll sleep on the floor."

"No, I can't let you do that," said Kerry. "I'd feel inhospitable, then I wouldn't sleep. Please, take the bed."

"All right then. Thank you very much. I won't forget this," she said. Kerry feared that he might not forget it, either.

"What's your name?" he asked her.

"Carol," she replied.

"Sleep well, then, Carol," said Kerry; and, taking a cushion from his armchair to rest his head, he lay down on the floor to sleep. He slept so heavily, he did not even hear her leave the room just before six, as the Rector passed on his way to the showers.

At the end of breakfast, the Rector asked Kerry to accompany him to his study. Kerry followed him up the stairs to the high-ceilinged room overlooking the seminary forecourt.

"Do sit down," said the Rector kindly, indicating a high-backed leather armchair, arranged at exactly sixty degrees from his own, to promote non-confrontational dialogue. The

Rector leaned slightly forward and fixed Kerry with a firm but understanding eye. "I gather you're having problems with celibacy," he said.

"No, not at all," replied Kerry, truthfully.

"Hmmm," said the Rector. He regarded Kerry with slightly world-weary compassion. "I'm sorry to have to say this, Kerry, but I find that rather difficult to believe."

"Is there any particular reason for your misgivings, Father?" asked Kerry, fairly certain what it might be, but needing absolute certainty before admitting it.

"I was passing your room shortly before six o'clock this morning and saw a young woman leaving it," replied the Rector. "She looked a little startled to see me."

"Ah, I see," said Kerry. There was an awkward silence.

"The other thing was that Father Derek saw her going into your room at about half-past three this morning, when he was on his way back from the loo. He said she was wearing a rather fetching nightie."

Kerry listened for a while to the ticking of the Rector's carriage clock.

"I wonder if there's any explanation, other than the rather obvious one," said the Rector.

Kerry wondered what weight to put on the promise he had rashly given Tony. What was the value of an undertaking given while half-asleep and under pressure from a sociopath?

"She's been having some problems recently," suggested Kerry.

"So I understand," said the Rector. "Her husband phoned me only yesterday to tell me that he feels that the amount of time she spends in 'counselling' with one or more students here (and he wasn't sure who they might be) isn't helping their troubled marriage. That, at least, is the gist of what he told me, as far as I remember. It was a lengthy conversation and a rather difficult one."

Kerry regarded his knees for a while, then a patch of wall above the bookshelves. He noticed a patch of damp which was discolouring the magnolia paint. He wondered whether he should mention this to the Rector, but decided that it was probably not an appropriate moment and that, in any case, he probably knew about it already.

"Any thoughts?" asked the Rector, kindly.

Kerry decided that a promise given under pressure to a sociopath was almost certainly invalid, but he did not think the truth sounded plausible. He was well aware that scientific method demanded that the simplest logical explanation of a phenomenon should be taken as the valid explanation, and, while keenly aware that this may not hold in all circumstances, and knowing the unavoidable consequence of a failure to explain convincingly what had actually happened, he decided to accept it with beatific serenity.

"I don't think there's anything I can say," said Kerry.

"I see," said the Rector, regarding him with the deepest sympathy.

There was another awkward silence.

"You know, Kerry" said the Rector, "you may well live to see the day when the Church decides to ordain married men as a matter of course, and not only in the cases of married Anglican clergy who join us. I don't suppose I will see it, but you might. But it hasn't come yet, Kerry, and you did know that when you applied to come here. And even if the Church had already changed its discipline, the fact is that you and she are not married. Worse, she is married to someone else. Even if you were not in formation for the priesthood, that makes a liaison with her adultery, Kerry. I am stating the obvious just to satisfy myself that you fully understand, Kerry. Do you?"

"I do, Father."

"And you know that you must not see the woman again?"

"I do, Father."

"I'm very sorry this has happened, Kerry. I think you have the capacity to be a very kind and compassionate pastor. It may be, that in time to come, when you have clarified what it is that you want, what it is that God wants of you, you could try your vocation again. But I hope you'll understand that it's impossible for you to continue at this time. Perhaps it's a blessing that today's the last day of term, so your departure will be easier for you. I'll write to your bishop."

The Rector stood up. Kerry felt strangely light-headed as he rose from his chair.

"If there's anything I can do to help you as you seek the way forward, let me know," the Rector said. He smiled sympathetically. "I hope Christmas won't be totally overshadowed by this, Kerry. Will you have company?"

"I'll be with my aunt in Westhampton."

"Good. I'll be praying for you."

"Thank you, Father."

Kerry went straight to Peter's room to tell him what had happened. Peter was beside himself with anger. "You must go and tell the Rector what really happened!" he demanded.

"Do you think he'd believe me now?" asked Kerry. "And anyway, you know I always had my doubts about coming here in the first place."

"That's no reason to get chucked out for something you didn't do!"

There was a knock at the door and Mario entered, with his bags, ready for his lift into Westhampton in Peter's car. They told him the news. He threw his bag down on the floor with some force.

"Why is that *total tosser* such a *fucking arsehole of a wanker?*" he shouted.

"What, the Rector?" asked Kerry.

"No, you prat, I mean that bastard Conwell."

"Mario, keep your voice down, please," said Peter. "I think we should tell the Rector. Conwell's a deceitful, manipulative psychopath, who should be exposed and expelled as soon as possible."

"You're not suggesting we grass him up, are you?" asked Mario, incredulously.

"Yes."

Mario became agitated. He held his head in both hands and shifted his weight from one leg to the other repeatedly. "No, no, no, mate, you don't grass people up! Better to offer him a deal; you fuck off out of it right now, and we don't ram your smarmy, fucking, lying face up your festering, fucking arsehole."

"That doesn't address the problem of Kerry's expulsion, does it?" observed Peter, primly.

"Look," said Kerry, "I really appreciate your support, but I don't want this taken any further. Please. Just let it be."

"Are you serious?" asked Mario.

"Yes," said Kerry. "I need some time to think. Maybe it was a mistake to come here in the first place. I don't know. I can't say the prospect of ordination has made my spirit dance."

"I want to do some damage to that tosser Conwell," declared Mario.

"Don't," said Peter. "That's hardly a Christian response, is it?"

Mario glared at him.

"Sometimes, I wonder how *you* got in here, Mario," said Peter.

"God called me," replied Mario, with mock piety.

"Well, perhaps God's now calling you to refrain from shoving Conwell's head up his behind."

"He's so far up his own arse already, there's probably no point, anyway," observed Mario, gloomily.

"Let's all let it be, shall we?" said Kerry. "Maybe I can get another library job, or something."

"No," said Peter. Inspiration had struck. "No, I've got a much better idea! These people who persuaded you that you ought to be a priest did so because you've got a kind heart, didn't they? And you have. So use it. You're a translator, aren't you?"

Kerry nodded.

"Including Spanish."

"Yes."

"Good. That settles it. You can help the Cortesian refugees. People need unofficial interpreters to accompany them to asylum interviews. They need help understanding official documents. People in detention need visitors to befriend and help them. You'd be brilliant at that. Do it!"

"Do you think I could?"

"Yes!" affirmed Peter with enthusiasm. "I'll take you to see my friends in the refugee association right after New Year. They're bound to be able to use your help. And I'll take you to meet the detainee visiting group, too. They're crying out for volunteers!"

"Sounds alright, that," said Mario. "Good way to stick two fingers up to the British State."

"Quite," said Peter. "And to help some of the people it oppresses."

"Waste of time, anyway," said Kerry's Aunty Liza. "The Church is an antediluvian institution and the sooner it's consigned to the waste-basket of history, the better, in my humble opinion. I came to that conclusion when I was in the WRENs. I think Ivy opened my eyes to reality." At the memory of her recently departed friend, Aunty Liza paused and gazed at the Christmas tree for a while. She took another sip of her dry sherry. "Dear Ivy," she said. "The place isn't the same without her." She paused again. "This'll be the second Christmas without her. Still," she said, visibly pulling herself together, "You're here, dear boy, and I for one am delighted you've been expelled from that awful place, and I'm sure whatever comes next will be a damn sight better than what's gone before. Be of good courage!" She smiled. "More sherry?"

"Thanks," said Kerry.

"Was that sweet or dry?" asked his aunt.

"Medium," replied Kerry. "I couldn't quite make up my mind between the two extremes."

"You could make a definite choice for the middle path, you know. It's quite respectable. I just prefer the dry."

"Well, then, half a glass of medium, please."

"Happy Christmas!"

Six: Kerry learns about Cortesia

Kerry called in on Father Patrick, as soon as he got back to London the day after Boxing Day. "Ah, Kerry, it's good to see you. Come in. Now, before you mention it, the bishop phoned me before Christmas, so you've no need to break the news to me."

"I'm so sorry, Father."

"Well, don't be. Obviously it wasn't for you."

"But the reason for being kicked out…"

"Well, I was a little surprised about that, I must say. It didn't seem quite in character."

"It wasn't quite as it seemed, Father."

"I thought it mightn't have been."

"May I tell you what really happened?"

"If you'd like to."

Kerry explained.

"You've suffered an injustice," concluded Father Patrick. "Do you not want to put it right?"

"I haven't got the energy," said Kerry. "If I had really wanted to be a priest, perhaps I would have done, but you know I was always uncertain."

"You were," agreed Father Patrick. "And we only agreed that you'd give it a whirl to see if it was right for you."

"My Aunty Liza said she was glad, because the Church is an antediluvian institution which ought to be consigned to the waste-basket of history."

"Well, I can see her point – although, strictly speaking, it's not antediluvian. It's post-diluvian, just slow to change when it needs to. It's full of human beings, that's the thing, and you know what we're like. Trouble comes when people start treating an institution as though it's the equivalent of God Himself. So, what are you going to do now?"

"More of the same: library work and translation. But my friend Peter is getting me involved with helping refugees from Cortesia, so at least I'll be helping people."

"Wonderful! Well, then, we'll see what comes, won't we? But all will be well, you'll see."

The office of the Association of Cortesian Refugees in the United Kingdom was in a newly refurbished community centre in north London, in the area where most Cortesians had settled. It was conveniently close to the local tube station, but it took Kerry nearly an hour to get there from across the other side of the River.

The area was full of Cortesian cafés and food stores. These establishments were interspersed with others; a few North African restaurants, a Polish supermarket, a Portuguese café, a couple of run-down pubs, a betting shop, a pawn shop, a couple of money transfer agencies and a number of internet shops. A small mosque stood next to a large Catholic church, which advertised Mass in English, Polish, Spanish and Portuguese.

The community centre was shared with a dozen or so other groups – refugee organisations, a housing co-operative, an ex-prisoners' support group, a group working to help people to stop smoking. Kerry met Peter in reception. Mario and Francis had come along as well, because they said they wanted to know more about it, although they did not think they could help, as they did not speak Spanish.

The Association of Cortesian Refugees in the United Kingdom was on the second floor. The door, which bore the Spanish acronym 'ARCRU', was open, and Kerry could see a startlingly beautiful young woman, perhaps in her late twenties, sitting at a desk just inside. She stood up to greet them, and Peter introduced her as Mercedes. She greeted each of them with a kiss on each cheek, and when she learnt that

Mario and Francis did not understand Spanish, she switched into perfect English, with a slight North American accent.

"Thank you for coming to find out about us," she began. "I will tell you what we do and why we do it, and then I will answer any questions you have and we can discuss how you could get involved if you want to.

"I'm sure Peter has told you there is a civil war in our country, a very brutal war being fought against the majority of the population by a Government of the rich. It is supported by military aid from the US, and your country, to protect the interests of big British and North American companies, which are working in collaboration with the twenty families who have run our country since we won independence from Spain. They own more than half the national territory and they want to keep it that way.

"The guerrilla movement started as an attempt to bring social justice to our country, but it has been split into different factions by forty years of unequal war. Some of them commit atrocities. Meanwhile, the Government and the twenty families have organised unofficial death squads that terrorise whole areas of the country into submission. Then, when they have killed off most of the Government's opponents in an area and cowed the rest into silence, they call it peace and boast about the improvement in their human rights record. Some of the death squads are off-duty soldiers. When they are on duty, they take courses in human rights provided by British military advisers. It is a farce. But it makes the Government look good, as though it is trying hard to stop all the abuses being committed by the death squads and the guerrillas.

"There are well over ten thousand Cortesians in London, and they come here for different reasons. Some flee the death squads or the army and police. Some flee the guerrillas. Some just flee the war. Some come because there is so little work in our country, because the economy has been damaged by so many years of war. Others come to study here. Some come for a combination of reasons. Because of this, there are divisions in our community here. The people who use our services are mostly on the political left. Some are not political. But nobody on the Government side uses our services for long. If they come here seeking advice on asylum law or benefits or employment or housing, we tell them the bare essentials of what they need to know. But they don't come back, because they can see just from our office that we are against the Cortesian Government and they feel uneasy. And we feel uneasy with them. I hope that doesn't shock you. But when there is a civil war, feelings run high. We are not neutral here. If it does shock you, you would not be happy working here."

"It doesn't shock me," said Kerry. "I must say I have never really thought much about politics of any sort, but people are people and if they are in need, they deserve our help."

"Thank you," said Mercedes. "That is a good humanist approach. Mario and Francis, it would be difficult for you to help with our advice services if you can't speak Spanish, but if you wanted to, you could be part of the English-speaking support group.

"Anyway, this office is open five days a week for advice on all these practical matters. We also try to help Cortesians who are detained in any of the Government's Removal Centres, but we don't have enough time or volunteers to cover all of them. We have to rely on local visiting groups, like the London group, which sends volunteer visitors to detainees of all nationalities in the West London Removal Centre."

"I've been involved with them for a while," said Mario, "Mostly visiting Africans."

"That's good," said Mercedes. "We also have regular political meetings for the community, and sometimes we have public meetings for others who want to learn about our country and about what they can do to assist our struggle. There is quite a group of British people involved now, mostly because of their existing interest in Latin America or their commitment to socialism. That's the group you could be involved with, if you want to help, but can't speak Spanish.

"Finally, we have a lot of cultural activities, films, concerts and dancing. There is always plenty of food and drink because our people really know how to enjoy themselves even when life is difficult.

"So, have you got any questions?"

There was silence.

"Nothing at all?"

"There's a lot to absorb," said Kerry.

"Yes," said Francis. "This is all new to me. I think I need to process what you've told us, before I know what to ask you."

"When's the next dance?" asked Mario. "I wouldn't mind learning a bit of salsa."

"Come along on Saturday and I'll teach you," offered Mercedes. "It'll be in the meeting hall downstairs."

Mario looked crestfallen. "I'm supposed to be back at the seminary on Friday," he said.

"Well, another time," said Mercedes. "Kerry, your fluency in Spanish could be very helpful for us. If you want to help with our advice sessions, let me know. We need more volunteers who are fluent in both languages."

"Can I have a think about it?" asked Kerry. "I maybe need to sort out my paid work first, and then I'll know how much time I have."

"You let me know when you know," said Mercedes.

"I'll help him to know," said Peter. "It'll shorten the process."

Mercedes kissed them each again, twice, on the way out.

"Gordon Bennett!" exclaimed Mario as they left the building. "I wouldn't mind slipping *her* a length."

"I despair of you!" replied Peter. "My colleague gives you a wonderful potted summary of the appalling situation in Cortesia, and tells you how you can help, and all you can think of is how much you'd like to copulate with her!"

Mario looked hurt. "I'm not saying I don't want to offer my solidarity to the Cortesian struggle against British and US imperialism, I'm just saying that in addition to, and as an integral part of, my revolutionary proletarian internationalism, I wouldn't mind getting my leg over."

"Well, dream on, mate, she's spoken for. So, for once, can you get your tiny little mind out of your trousers?" Peter looked genuinely angry.

"Alright, boss, keep your hair on," said Mario, and fell silent.

"Where are we going?" asked Kerry.

"To the Portuguese café down the street," replied Peter. "I usually go to one or other of the Cortesian cafés close to the office, but I want us to be able to talk about things without a Cortesian audience right now."

Once they were seated and had been served their coffees, Peter asked Francis and Kerry what they thought of the visit. "But not you," he said to Mario. "We already know what you think, thanks very much." Mario said nothing.

"She's a bit full-on, isn't she?" asked Kerry.

"What do you mean?" asked Peter.

"Well, she's a bit militant. Very nice, of course, but a bit militant."

"Well, you'd be militant if your people were being oppressed and brutalised like hers are."

"Still, we have to keep the spirit of forgiveness," suggested Francis.

"Oh, for goodness' sake!" exclaimed Peter. "You're going to make me wish I hadn't taken any of you there! Of course, we have to have the spirit of forgiveness, whatever that is, but that doesn't mean putting up with people being driven off their land, deprived of their livelihood, driven to the brink of starvation, and killed or tortured if they complain about it."

"No, but there are ways and ways of responding to it, aren't there?" suggested Francis.

"Well, what ways? What are you suggesting?"

"That violence is always wrong, whoever does it and for whatever reason."

"Who's suggesting using violence?" demanded Peter.

"I thought Mercedes was," replied Francis.

"Well, you thought wrong," said Peter, hotly. "She simply pointed out that the guerrilla movement started as a response to a history of oppression and violence. She also said that some of the guerrilla groups commit atrocities. She didn't say she approved of them. As a matter of fact, she did used to be a supporter of one of the guerrilla groups, but she's been disillusioned by the way they've behaved in recent years. They've lost their focus. She supports the political opposition, not the military opposition."

"Oh, okay," said Francis. "I didn't mean to annoy you. It's just that I can't support violence, simple as that."

"But there's a world of difference between mindless, nihilistic violence and disciplined, revolutionary violence," declared Peter.

"People still get killed," said Francis.

"People are being killed anyway," retorted Peter. "Often in the most unspeakably brutal manner. Sometimes an armed response actually stops more people being killed and hastens a real peace, based on justice, and brings an end to the violence of inequality and oppression. So you're actually saving lives."

"Jesus said, 'Those who live by the sword die by the sword.'"

"And in another place, he actually suggests that his disciples bring swords with them."

"What about when he drives the money-changers out of the temple with whips?" asked Mario. "That was violent, wasn't it?"

"Aha, my ally has found his voice again," observed Peter.

"But Jesus didn't kill people," said Francis. "It doesn't even say he actually hit anyone with the whip."

"That's true," agreed Mario. "They probably legged it as soon as they saw he was cutting up rough."

"It was still a violent act," said Peter.

"It was an angry act, but it wasn't necessarily a violent one, and it certainly wasn't a murderous one," said Francis.

"The point is," said Peter, "we're talking about a people who have suffered appalling oppression and injustice for centuries, and have had enough. And some of them, in defence of their own dignity and for the sake of justice, have taken up arms to create a better society."

"Have they tried mass non-violent civil disobedience, like Gandhi?" asked Kerry.

"Not in any sustained way, no," replied Peter. "It's not part of their tradition. You can lay that at the feet of our own Catholic Church, if you want to blame someone for the lack of a tradition of non-violent struggle. It's spent five hundred years blessing armies fighting on behalf of conquistadors and oppressive elites in Latin America."

"There wasn't much of a tradition of non-violent struggle in India, either," replied Francis. "Gandhi helped to create it."

"Whether or not that's the case," replied Peter, "it's not for us here in London, where we are safe and well-fed, to tell people in Latin America what's the right or wrong way for them to bring peace and justice to their suffering countries."

"Maybe not," said Francis, "but surely in offering our support to them in their struggle for justice, we can't lose our own integrity."

"I don't feel I *am* losing my own integrity," said Peter. "I don't believe Christians have to be pacifists. If armed insurrection leads, in the long run, to a reduction in death and suffering, then it is a perfectly acceptable Christian response to support it. Look at Santa Maria – the revolution there took over ten years, but when it finally won, and the dictator was kicked out, things really did get better for the vast majority of the population. They introduced free health care and education, improved food production and distribution and enabled ordinary people to take part in decision-making for the first time in history – it worked. And those who didn't like it went and lived in Miami, and good riddance to them."

"Well, I can't comment on that because I don't know enough about it. I just know I don't agree with violence."

"What about the Second World War?" asked Mario. "Would you rather be ruled by the Nazis, than have the Battle of Britain?"

"I don't know," said Francis. "But we're not talking about that, are we? If we say violence is an acceptable way of redressing injustices, we're saying that IRA violence or suicide bombings are okay, aren't we?"

"No, we're not," said Peter, firmly. "That's why the Church has a history of talking about 'just war'. To say that violence is sometimes acceptable does not mean that any form of violence unleashed by anybody is acceptable. The guerrillas in Cortesia have never gone in for urban terrorism and they have never deliberately targeted civilians, only members of the military, paramilitaries and the police – at least, until they started fracturing into factions, which have ended up getting caught up in all kinds of unacceptable behaviour."

"Violence has its own logic," said Francis. "You start using it with good intentions, and then you start pursuing it for its own sake."

"My great grandfather was in the IRA," said Mario. "They had to fight to get the Brits out once and for all."

"Maybe if they'd carried on pursuing non-violence, they would have achieved the same goal in the end, and not had Ireland ripped in two over it," said Francis.

"Look," said Peter, "the point is that Mercedes is not advocating violence and nor is the Association. But if you're looking for condemnations of guerrilla violence from them, you won't get them, because whatever their misgivings are, they are not going to openly condemn people whose basic motivation is social justice. And they're not going to condemn revolutionary violence in principle, because maybe they think they may have to use it themselves before the struggle is finally won. The point is to find unity in working for justice and not argue about an issue that nobody we are talking about is involved with anyway."

"I see what you mean," said Francis. "But it makes me feel uneasy. I respect you and I respect Mercedes, but I don't think this cause is something I can get involved with."

"Well, that wasn't on the agenda, anyway, was it? You and Mario have got your own involvements."

"I might get involved somehow," said Mario.

"Yes, well, we know where that's going," replied Peter, with resignation.

"No, no, mate, I don't mean so as I can get my end off, I mean as a genuine act of solidarity with the struggle. Ireland yesterday, Cortesia today, know what I mean? I don't know what I can do, though. I spend half the year down at that gentlemen's country club in Wessex and I don't speak Spanish anyway."

"Well, what about you, Kerry? What do you think?" asked Peter.

"I don't know what to think," replied Kerry. "You know I'm not a political animal. I just wish everyone would be nice to one another."

Mario and Peter raised their eyes.

"Being nice to one another hardly provides a strategy for dealing with land theft on a grand scale, torture and assassination, Kerry," said Peter. "Are you going to help the Cortesian refugees or not?"

"I feel it's my duty to use my Spanish skills to help people who are suffering," replied Kerry. "I just don't know that I can cope with going into why they're suffering, or analysing their situation, or getting involved in political discussions. It's not that I'm against that, it's just it's not really me."

Peter sighed heavily. "I'd hoped Mercedes might inspire you all with her clarity and commitment, but clearly not."

"She inspired me," said Mario.

Peter gave him a withering look. "I meant, inspire your minds," he said.

"She did inspire my mind!" retorted Mario. "You misjudge me, boss, you undervalue my political commitment!"

"Well, time will tell," replied Peter. "Kerry, let's try you with visiting Cortesian detainees. If you meet people one on one, and all you're asked to do is befriend them, perhaps that will fit better with your apolitical spirit. Would you be willing to try that?"

"Of course I would," replied Kerry. He felt hurt, but he also felt irritated by his own inability to come down on one side or another of an argument or commit himself to any grand scheme. Most of all, he felt discontented at his inability to please his friend Peter, his older brother and mentor.

"Good," said Peter. "Then we'll drop in at the Detainee Visiting Group this afternoon, and tomorrow we'll visit the Removal Centre. The DVG usually insist that people attend some training sessions before providing them with the name of a detainee to visit, but I'm going to get you to visit a friend of the man I visit, who hasn't got a visitor yet. I'll also give you a concentrated induction session myself tomorrow morning. After that, as long as you feel you can keep up with the visiting, I'll pass you over to the group's tender care, because you'll need support and advice. Then, once the man you visit is either released or removed, you'll need the name of someone else to visit.

"After tomorrow, I'll have to leave you to it, while I clear off to the country club. Only two more terms and then I'll be back in London full time. Thank God."

Seven: Kerry comforts the afflicted

It took Kerry and Peter nearly two hours to get from central London to the Removal Centre, near the airport. Peter told him what to expect when they got there, the entry procedures and the kind of people who ended up detained in the place. He also told him all about the etiquette of visiting, what you do and do not do, what you say and do not say, what you can promise and what you cannot, so as to help keep hope alive without raising it unrealistically. He explained the asylum system, with its complicated categories of fast-tracking, safe countries and backlog clearance procedures; the many ways in which a system which purported to be firm but compassionate proved to be chaotic and cruel.

"There are men, women and children in there," Peter told him. "People who've been refused entry to Britain at a port or airport, or detained while their asylum claims are examined, which can take months. Some have been refused asylum, and have been picked up by immigration officers in the small hours of the morning and kept here, while arrangements are made to send them back where they came from. Some can't even be sent back, because their countries are so dangerous there are no flights there, or their government won't accept they're from that country so they won't give them travel documents. And these people are just left to rot in here, sometimes for well over a year, because the government wants to 'send a message' that Britain's not a soft touch – as if desperate people fleeing war, disaster and persecution are going to stop to think about that! It's an outrage! These people aren't even *accused* of any crime, let alone guilty of one. This pathetic government just wants to look butch for the redtop papers that want to persuade their readers that these foreigners are their enemies, so it'll distract them from the ever-widening gap between rich and poor, the dismantling of public services, the loss of democratic control to murky privatisation agreements, mass surveillance and continuous war."

In the faceless reception hall for visitors, they were both finger-printed electronically, and Kerry, because it was his first visit, was photographed. After three sets of doors, they reached the waiting area for the visiting hall, and were searched by scanner and hand, and everything they carried with them, even handkerchiefs, was put in lockers for collection on the way out. Kerry asked what he should do if he needed to blow his nose. He was assured that he could ask staff for a paper tissue. He could also ask them for notepaper and pencils, should he need them, though, as Peter told him, having the right to ask was not the same as actually getting.

They were accompanied through two pairs of automatic security doors. At each pair, one of the automatic doors had to shut before the other would open. They then reported to the duty officer, who checked their fingerprints against her electronic record from the main gate.

"It used to be much freer and easier than this," explained Peter. "They never used to take finger-prints or count people out. But one evening, shortly after they opened this new building, when visiting ended at nine, half a dozen detainees just walked out with the visitors. It was priceless. I hope they're still free. I helped to get them to central London. I think I could get fourteen years for that, so I'd rather you kept it under your hat."

"I rarely wear a hat," replied Kerry.

"Get one, then," said Peter.

"What do we do now?" asked Kerry.

"We sit in these fiendishly uncomfortable plastic chairs here in the waiting area until our names are called," replied Peter. "Then we get directed to a table, where the detainee we've asked to visit will be sitting. The detainee sits in the red chair and we have to sit in one of the blue ones. I deliberately tried swapping once, and sat in the red chair, and the guards got all bent out of shape over it. It's all for security. They treat these people as if they were dangerous murderers."

Peter's name was called. Kerry watched him walk to the far end of the visiting hall and sit down with a tall, dark-haired man who he assumed was Luis, the man Peter regularly visited. Twenty more minutes passed before Kerry's name was called. "Sorry about the delay, sir," said the officer on duty in the hall. "My colleagues couldn't find Mr Galeano for a while. He'll be here in half a tick. You can sit down and I'll bring him over."

Kerry sat in one of the three blue chairs bolted to the floor around the low table, halfway down one side of the large visiting hall. After a few more minutes, a slim man of medium height, with reddish-brown skin, jet black hair and large, dark brown eyes was led to the table. He wore a crimson tracksuit. "Here's Mr Galeano, sir," said the guard. Kerry thanked him, stood up and shook hands with the detainee. "Good evening," he said, in Spanish. "You are Aristides Borges?"

Aristides smiled nervously. "Yes, yes, thank you. I'm glad Your Mercy speaks Spanish. I didn't know you would. I can't speak English – only a few words I picked up in here. The guards all call me Mr Galeano. I keep trying to tell them, I am not Mr Galeano, I am Mr Borges, Galeano is my second surname, my mother's surname, but they never remember. We are all foreigners to them. Even the Indian guards, they're just like the white ones. We're all foreigners."

"My name is Kerry Ahern," said Kerry. "I'm a friend of Peter, who visits your friend, Luis."

"Kerry," repeated Aristides. "Thank you for coming to visit me. I wanted a visitor because I am going mad in here. I've got to get out."

"How long have you been in here?" asked Kerry.

"Six or seven weeks, maybe eight. I lose track of time."

"Have you claimed asylum?"

"Yes, but they refused me straight away. They told me I was lying."

"What happened?"

"One of my friends told me, 'when you go to Europe, don't tell them you're from Cortesia, or they'll send you away because they think we're all drug pushers. Go first to Tierramedia, get a false passport, fly from there and tell the Europeans you're from Tierramedia.' So I went to Tierramedia, like my friend told me, and I planned to go to Spain, but my friends there told me, no, the Cortesian Government has spies everywhere in Spain. They pay people to make your life hell there, or even kill you, so go to England, because there are not so many Cortesians there. You can find work there, and everything will be okay. So I got a flight here on that false passport, and when I got here, I claimed asylum, and the immigration officer told me 'No, Tierramedia is a safe country, we do not accept asylum claims from there. So I am going to detain you and put you on the first flight back to Tierramedia.' I said 'No, no, please, I am not from there, don't send me back there, I am from Cortesia, and I am being persecuted there and I need asylum here. Please, please do not send me back.' And he said, 'How can you expect me to believe a word you say, when you've already lied about your nationality?' and I said, 'Please, it is my right to claim asylum. I claim asylum, I am being persecuted.' Then, he said, 'I am going to fast-track you, and I am going to detain you while we consider your case.' And then they brought me here in a prison van, as if I were a criminal, and I am going mad."

"Have you got legal representation?" asked Kerry.

"Yes, she seemed to be a good lawyer, but if she is so good, why am I still in here?"

"I don't know," replied Kerry. "I am only beginning to learn about these things. I think perhaps things take a long time, even with a good lawyer."

"She says I am no longer fast-track, that they accept that I am from Cortesia."

"I think that's a good sign. I think it means they will have to consider your asylum claim properly."

"I feel like I want to change lawyers, because she always sounds angry with me when I phone her, and she has a funny accent."

"If you tell me her name, I can go and ask my friend over there about her. He knows a lot of lawyers and he may know whether she is good or not."

Aristides told him the lawyer's name.

"I shan't be long," said Kerry.

"Thank you."

Kerry walked over to Peter and politely interrupted his conversation. He told Peter the name of Aristides' lawyer and explained his misgivings.

"That woman's brilliant," said Peter. "She's a very good, hard-working lawyer. She *is* always irritable but that's because she's so conscientious and because she hates this system as much as anyone. She's one of the best asylum lawyers in the country. I think she learnt Spanish in the USA — that'll account for the funny accent."

Kerry returned to Aristides and recounted what Peter had told him.

"Thank you for telling me that," said Aristides. "Thank your friend, too. So, she is not angry with me. That's good. And now I know why she sounds like a cross between a Puerto Rican and a Mexican. I want you to phone her and ask her to be in touch with me again to let me know what is happening."

"I'll do that," said Kerry. "Now, would you like a coffee or something?"

"No, thank you, the coffee in this country is shit," replied Aristides. "I don't know what they make it out of, but it doesn't take like any coffee I ever drank at home."

"Do you mind if I have one?" asked Kerry.

"No, please go ahead," replied Aristides. "And please get me a hot chocolate. It doesn't taste like proper chocolate here, but I still like it."

Kerry went to the drinks vending machine in the corner and returned with a hot chocolate and an insipid black coffee.

"Now, I am going to tell Your Mercy what happened to me in Cortesia," said Aristides.

"You don't have to tell me about it if you don't want to," said Kerry, remembering how firmly Peter had warned him against intrusive questioning, especially into the details of what had happened to a person in their country of origin.

"No, I want to tell Your Mercy, so you'll understand. It was horrible, what happened to me there. My family is poor. I had to find work. I joined the police. Because I joined the police, I was put on a hit list by the guerrillas. I didn't think about the politics. It was just a job. The guerrillas threatened my father and my brother, told them they should make me leave the police. But in our area, the death squads are more powerful than the guerrillas, and they came to our house and told me they would protect my family as long as I stayed in the police, but that if I left, they would kill me as a guerrilla collaborator.

"Then one night, when I was on duty, one of my colleagues arrested a prostitute and told me he knew she went with a guerrilla and so he was going to kill her. I told him, 'No, you can't do that, that's against the law, and we're paid to uphold the law,' and he asked me, 'What's up with you, are you a guerrilla sympathiser too?' He told me, 'I am going to fuck that woman and then you can when I've finished, and then I'll kill her, later.' I said, 'No, I won't do that. I know her, we grew up together, and you should leave her alone.' He told me, 'go fuck yourself, then, while I fuck her, Saint Aristides,' and he took her to the interrogation room and raped her. And I heard her screaming and I didn't know what to do, and so I did nothing, and I felt ashamed of myself. When she came out of there, she didn't even look at me, and she ran into the street. And then my colleague came out of the interrogation room, doing up his trousers and smiling a big smile, and he said, 'That was fun,' and I said, 'You are a sick mother-fucker.' He grabbed my throat and held me up against the wall and said, 'You're going to regret you ever said that, you queer commie scum,' and when the sergeant came in, they talked in the back room and then came out and told me I was to go with the sergeant and pick up the commie whore who went with guerrillas, and shut her mouth for good. I knew what that meant, so when we went out to the sergeant's Jeep, I just ran as far and as fast as I could, until I was out of our neighbourhood, and then I walked to my friend's house on the other side of the city, and I got there just before dawn and woke him and told him what had happened. He told me, 'Aristides, now you must get out, now everyone will be after you. Don't even go home,' he said. 'I will tell your family you are leaving the country,' and he gave me his clothes to change into, and I stayed at his house a few days so I could grow a bit of a beard, and then I got a ride across the border into Tierramedia like he told me, and I don't even know what has happened to my family, or to that poor woman that I failed to defend..." and he burst into tears and held his face in his hands.

Kerry remained silent for a while. Then he said, "Aristides, I will speak to your lawyer as soon as I leave here. Don't give up hope."

Aristides wiped his eyes with his hands. "It is difficult to hope, when all around me people are being sent back to their countries, even though they're terrified of what will happen to them there. I don't even know if my family is still alive."

"Would you like me to see if someone can contact your family?"

"Who could do that?"

"Maybe someone from the Cortesian community, who's already in London."

"No, don't tell them. I don't know anyone here and I don't know who I can trust. Maybe people here like the Government or the guerrillas, but nobody will like me because of what happened to me and what I did."

"Maybe some other group could help – the Red Cross or the Church or someone."

"No. It would be best is if I could phone my friend in Cortesia myself and ask him. But I have no phone card and no money to buy one. It costs a lot to phone from the Removal Centre."

"Then I'll get you a phone card and send it to you. And I'll phone your lawyer. Then I'll phone you to let you know I've done it."

"Thank you. I'm glad Your Mercy came."

"You know, you don't have to use the polite form with me. You can use the familiar form."

"Thank you. That would feel more friendly."

"I've never actually heard the form 'Your Mercy' before now."

"I think it is only in our country that it is used. My friends from Tierramedia make fun of me for using it."

"Would you like me to come again next week?"

"Yes, please. If I am still here."

"Try not to give up hope."

"Okay."

"I'm going to go now. I'll see you next week – same day, same time."

"Okay. Thank you."

Eight: Kerry goes to court

Over the following weeks, Kerry began to develop a trusting friendship with Aristides. Kerry looked forward to his visits, even though there was little he could do to help, other than facilitate communication through providing phone cards and talking to Aristides' lawyer. What delighted Kerry was the evident fact that Aristides felt some benefit from his visits. He seemed calmer and more hopeful, better able to bear the sufferings that the asylum system was visiting upon him. Often, he did not want to talk about what had happened to him in Cortesia. He talked about his family, about the countryside around his grandparents' village, about the food that he liked to eat. He asked Kerry about England, about its history and geography and how it was governed, about its dances and songs. Very often, Kerry did not know the answer to Aristides' questions, and had to go and look them up.

Meanwhile, Kerry was looking for work. His old job at the library was long gone, though there was the odd vacancy in other branches. But he really hoped to get more translation work and use his degree. Peter made good on his promise of help. Through friends of friends of Peter's, Kerry heard about a couple of vacancies at agencies which were flourishing because of lucrative contracts with City financial institutions and corporate law firms. By the end of February, Kerry had steady, well-paid work with an agency in Clerkenwell. It made it more difficult to visit Aristides. But he made sure that, one evening a week, he left work early so that he could get over to the Removal Centre with a couple of hours to spare, before visiting hours ended.

Although Aristides' case had been moved out of the fast-track system, it was not long before he received a formal refusal of his claim for asylum. On his lawyer's advice, he appealed against the refusal. In early March, Aristides told Kerry that his appeal hearing would take place the following week, and asked him to attend it if he could.

Kerry took a day off work for the purpose. The Immigration Appeal Hearing Centre was in a new, purpose-built edifice on the other side of the airport from the Removal Centre, and it took an equally long time to reach it. Nonetheless, Kerry arrived early. The Adjudicator, a man of rather military bearing, who spoke in a refined but commanding manner, was hearing another appeal, from a Sikh activist from Punjab. The case was made that such activists were harassed by police wherever in India they went, such was the Indian State's determination to quell the independence movement in that region.

"Well, I reject your appeal," said the Adjudicator when the lawyers had made their arguments. "And I'm going to send you back to India."

"What about me? What's going to happen to me?" called out the activist's distressed wife from the public seats, in a heavy West Midlands accent.

"You can go back to India, too," said the Adjudicator.

"But I've never been to India," she said.

"Where are you from, then?" asked the Adjudicator.

"Wolverhampton," she replied.

"Well, your parents are from India, then!" said the Adjudicator.

"No, they're not," she answered.

"Well, you're a Sikh, aren't you?" he asked.

"No, I'm not,' she replied.

"Well, you're sitting among Sikhs!" observed the Adjudicator. "Look at him!" he urged her, pointing at the turbaned, bearded man sitting next to her. "He's as much a Sikh as ever I've seen!"

"Well, I'm not," said the woman.

"What religion are you, then?" demanded the Adjudicator.

"Muslim," she replied. "My parents are from Pakistan."

"Oh, well, alright, you can't go back to India, then," agreed the Adjudicator. "But I'm still sending your husband back there. I reject his case. The man's clearly not a credible witness. Come on, now, next case!"

"But we have further proof that Mr Singh will be persecuted if he is returned to India!" said a man who was obviously the activist's legal representative.

"Oh, come on, you're too late now!" retorted the Adjudicator. "You had your chance to present all your evidence! In any case, I simply don't believe you. I was born in India and it's still a perfectly decent country, despite what happened in 1949. Now, come on, next case!"

This did not bode well for Aristides.

"Sir, the next on the list is Mr Aristides Borges Galeano," said the clerk, "but he isn't here."

"Well, then, his case is automatically rejected," said the Adjudicator. "If he can't be bothered to turn up to his own hearing, he doesn't deserve to have one."

Kerry felt an overwhelming need to do something and an equally overwhelming reluctance to say anything in circumstances where he did not know whether he had the legal right to do so. He felt his face reddening. He broke out into a nervous sweat.

"What's the next case, then?" asked the Adjudicator, and the clerk began to look through her notes.

"Sir!" said Kerry from the back of the room, raising his voice.

"Be quiet!" demanded the Adjudicator. "You've no right to intervene from over there!"

"But Mr Borges Galeano is in detention!" Kerry called out.

"In detention?" queried the Adjudicator. "Is this true?"

The clerk looked extremely embarrassed.

"Sir, yes, I apologise. I was confused. I mislaid his notes. This means it is not his fault he isn't here."

"Clearly!" agreed the Adjudicator. "Who's presenting for the Home Office?"

The lawyer who had helped ensure the removal of the previous appellant nodded at the Adjudicator and limply half-raised a hand.

"Thank you, Mr Cataract," said the Adjudicator. "But then where's his own damned lawyer? Who's representing him, for God's sake?"

The clerk gave the Adjudicator the lawyer's name.

"Oh, God spare us," said the Adjudicator, as if intending it to be *sotto voce* but in fact speaking loud enough for everyone in the court to hear. "The arrogant cow! We'll be here all morning, even if we kick off right away. Where the hell is the woman, then?"

At that moment, a well-dressed young woman carrying a large bundle of files under her arm burst through the doors into the court, approached the clerk and conducted a brief, whispered conversation with her.

"You're bloody late, Miss Bateman!" complained the Adjudicator. "What the devil do you think you're playing at?"

"Sir, my apologies," said Aristides' lawyer. "I was attempting to sort out the confusion caused by the transport company taking Mr Borges Galeano to the wrong hearing centre this morning. He is currently in central London, but I am assured they will have him here by midday."

"Bloody idiots!" exclaimed the Adjudicator. "Somebody should have told us earlier. No wonder the system's in such a damned mess! Run by bloody idiots! Now, I'll take the next case, if he's here. I'll hear Mr Borges Galeano's case after lunch. Feel free to go, Miss Bateman."

Miss Bateman left the hearing room by the side door and Kerry made for the corridor outside the back of the room with the intention of looking for her. As he entered the corridor, he ran into the clerk coming round the corner. "Thank you very much indeed!" she said. "That mistake could have cost me my job!"

"I was worried it might cost my friend his life," replied Kerry.

"Yes, yes, I do apologise," said the clerk. "It's so hard to keep track of who's where. There are so many cases it's easy to get people mixed up. I had thought it was the next man on the list who was detained, and if someone isn't in detention, it's their own responsibility to get themselves to their hearing."

"That must be difficult for some of them, when they haven't got any money for bus or tube fares," observed Kerry.

"Well, they should have thought of that when they decided to come here," retorted the clerk.

"I'm not sure how well publicised London transport fare structures are in Latin America, Asia or subequatorial Africa," replied Kerry.

"There's no need to be sarcastic," said the clerk. "I'm sorry I made a mistake about your friend, but you don't understand the pressure we're under. So many cases to hear every day! It's very stressful. And when you've been in as many hearings as I have, you find it difficult to believe that anyone's genuine any more. People make up the most bizarre stories in the hope of getting asylum and being allowed to stay here. They just make it more difficult for the genuine cases."

"Why do you think they make up stories?" asked Kerry.

"I don't know," said the clerk, with some irritation. "I suppose it's what people do when they're desperate."

"You'd have thought that being desperate might be taken as a sign that they needed help," suggested Kerry.

"Most of them are probably only here for the benefits," said the clerk.

"It's quite something to feel you have to leave your home, your family and everything dear to you, in order to receive food vouchers worth less than Jobseeker's Allowance and get housed in properties that nobody else is willing to live in," replied Kerry.

The clerk looked at him with annoyance and disapproval. "I don't think you're even trying to understand," she said. She turned away and stalked off.

Kerry felt rather light-headed. He had expressed a view, and rather forcefully. He was sorry he had caused the clerk offence, but at the same time he felt rather proud of himself.

He found Miss Bateman in the entrance hall to the Immigration Appeal Hearing Centre, talking on her mobile phone. When she had finished, she introduced himself.

"Ah, nice to put a face to the voice," she said, and shook his hand "Thank you for coming. It'll be an encouragement for Aristides that you're here."

"What are his chances?" asked Kerry.

"I'm afraid they're fifty-fifty at best," replied Miss Bateman. "We just have to give it our best shot. I've asked the Professor of Latin American studies at Thames University to give his expert opinion about the pattern of human rights violations in Cortesia and the migration paths which refugees take out of the country. He's recognised as the leading expert on the subject. He can also deal with the conditions of Cortesian refugees in Tierramedia, so we can have an answer to the Home Office's contention that he should have stayed there as the nearest safe country. I've got country reports from Amnesty as well, and a press report from last week, dealing with Cortesian paramilitary reprisal attacks on Cortesian refugees living in Tierramedia. If there was any justice, Aristides would be a shoo-in. But the Home Office will argue that he lacks credibility, because he travelled on a Tierramedian passport, and claimed to be a Tierramedian when he first arrived. They'll also say that there are parts of Cortesia where he would have been safe, because the number of extrajudicial executions in some parts of the country has plummeted recently, which is true, but the reason is the success of paramilitary terrorisation of whole sectors of the population, cowing them into silence. If we win the argument on safe havens in Cortesia, I mean, if we show that there aren't any, then they'll say that Tierramedia is a safe country of refuge and he should have stayed there. And if we can prove that it isn't, they'll say he should have stayed in Spain, because he changed flights there. I think we might have a better than fifty percent chance with another Adjudicator, but this one is a dinosaur. He has the most sickening, negative attitude of any Adjudicator that I've ever had to deal with, and I think he has only ever once granted an appeal. The man's an out and out racist and shouldn't be in the job. If he does refuse, we'll go for a Judicial Review, but it's difficult to get one nowadays, and it has to be on a point of law, not a point of fact. Still, we'll do our best."

It was difficult to maintain hope when, that afternoon, Aristides was produced in the hearing room and the appeal hearing had begun. Aristides looked extremely nervous, but Miss Bateman elicited his story from him in great detail and with great clarity, with the help of a reasonable interpreter whose mistakes Miss Bateman was able to correct herself for the benefit of the Adjudicator. Nonetheless, the Adjudicator seemed unimpressed.

Kerry wondered what happened in cases where the interpreter made mistakes and there was nobody around to correct them; or even what might have happened in this case, if the interpreter had been drawn from an opposing faction within the Cortesian community itself. In the absence of anyone else who could understand both English and the asylum claimant's own language, the opportunities for deliberate misrepresentation were legion. An ill-intentioned interpreter could, under such circumstances, make up an entirely different story that bore no resemblance to the account being given by the asylum claimant, and cause irreparable harm to the claimant's case.

Occasionally, the Adjudicator, who appeared to be writing everything down, interrupted to clarify a point or ask a question of his own.

"So, you're openly admitting that you spent time in Tierramedia unmolested, and then flew to Madrid, before you took a connecting flight to London?" he asked at one point, with obvious irritation.

"Yes," replied Aristides. "But I have explained why I did that."

"I have to take into account the facts about the countries you passed through, not just your feelings about whether those countries were safe for you or not," retorted the Adjudicator.

"Sir, I intend to call Professor Cleary of Thames University to give expert evidence on this point," said Miss Bateman.

"Are you going to keep us here all afternoon?" asked the Adjudicator, grumpily.

"Sir, I hope to move us through the case as quickly as possible."

"Good. Get on with it, then."

Professor Cleary was called and invited to explain the current human rights situation in Cortesia, the migration routes out of the country taken by political dissidents, and the problems faced by Cortesians in Tierramedia and Spain. The Adjudicator continued taking notes, but asked no questions. When Professor Cleary had finished, the Adjudicator thanked him curtly and addressed the Home Office Presenting Officer. "Have you any questions for Professor Cleary, Mr Cataract?"

"None, sir."

Miss Bateman submitted written reports on both Cortesia and Tierramedia from Amnesty International. The Adjudicator flicked through them perfunctorily, then invited Mr Cataract to make the Home Office case for rejection of Aristides' claim.

The Home Office case was exactly as Miss Bateman had predicted. The asylum claimant's original contention that he was from Tierramedia and subsequent assertion that he was, in fact, from Cortesia went to his credibility, calling into question every subsequent detail of his story. The Home Office did not wish to question the legitimacy of Professor Cleary's evidence, nor counter Amnesty International's country reports *per se*, but the British Embassies in both Cortesia and Tierramedia reported that there were areas of both countries where Cortesians, of whatever political stripe, would be safe.

Miss Bateman was allowed to interrupt with a question. She asked how the British Embassy in Cortesia could possibly know this when the Embassy staff never travelled outside the prosperous neighbourhood of the capital where the Embassy was situated, for fear of the generalised violence in the country.

"Oh, for goodness' sake!" exclaimed the Adjudicator. "We simply have to trust the wisdom and integrity of our people on the spot! Certain things have to be treated as absolutes, and with all due respect to other sources, if the Foreign and Commonwealth Office says that something is the case, then we have no alternative than to accept that it is. Please continue, Mr Cataract."

Mr Cataract then made the case for rejection of Aristides' case, even if what he had said happened to be true, though he reiterated that the Home Office believed it unlikely that it was. There was no evidence to prove that Aristides' police colleagues really intended to kill the prostitute whom they had allegedly arrested, and in any case, by the claimant's own account, they had not in fact done so at the time that Aristides had fled the police station. There was no documentary evidence to prove that, in this particular case, Aristides would have suffered any negative consequences from refusing to take part in a particular operation on the grounds of conscience. In the event that he had, the British Government was satisfied that the employee grievance procedures, which had been introduced into the Cortesian Police Service at the suggestion of the British Government's Cortesian Rights Assistance Programme, would be sufficient to ensure that Aristides suffered no negative consequences. If he had witnessed the extrajudicial murder of the young lady in question by his colleagues, he would be able to take advantage of the whistle-blowers' rights charter, introduced as a result of the same British-funded programme. Mr Cataract noted that a number of cases were under investigation under this programme at present, proving both the efficacy of the programme and the good-will of the Cortesian Government, which was endeavouring to address legacy issues of poor governance.

Aristides, following the Home Office case one sentence behind all the time, looked incredulous. Professor Cleary could not contain himself. "The number of cases is six at present," he said. "One was rejected out of hand and five have been under investigation for three years without resolution and without anyone being punished!"

"Sounds like they're doing a damn thorough job, then," said the Adjudicator.

"And if there are only six cases," added Mr Cataract, "it proves that such incidents are extremely uncommon."

"It proves nothing of the sort!" exclaimed Professor Cleary. "It proves that people have no faith in a wholly inadequate system which spins investigations out *ad infinitum,* with no intention of finding the truth and punishing the guilty!"

"Professor Cleary," said the Adjudicator, "I must ask you to remain quiet or leave the room. You have had your opportunity to speak and we are grateful to you for coming today, but you must respect the integrity of this process and stop interrupting."

Professor Cleary exhaled loudly and began angrily rearranging the papers on the table in front of him.

Kerry felt sick with disgust.

Mr Cataract concluded by asserting that Aristides was clearly mistaken in his assessment of the level of threat that he faced in his own city; that if he were afraid, he could and should have sought safety in another part of his own country; that if he were still afraid, he could have sought out a safe neighbourhood in Tierramedia, the first country he entered after leaving his own. He also said that if he were truly convinced that he was in danger, and serious in his desire to seek asylum far away from home, he should have claimed asylum in Spain, which, notwithstanding the expert opinion kindly provided by Professor Cleary, was, in the Government's view, safe by definition because it was part of the European Union.

The Adjudicator thanked Mr Cataract and invited Aristides and his lawyer to add anything that they wished in response to the Home Office Case. Aristides looked utterly bewildered. He and Miss Bateman spoke briefly in low voices, and Kerry could not hear what they were saying.

"Come on!" demanded the Adjudicator after a couple of minutes. "We haven't got all day! It's nearly tea-time, damn it!"

"Sir," began Miss Bateman, "Mr Borges Galeano wishes to restate that his account is true in all its details. He wishes to add that he was fully aware of the whistle-blowers' charter but that neither he nor anyone else he knew took it seriously. It was assumed that it was introduced simply to ensure the continuation of British and United States military aid, rather than to redress any injustices or give effective protection to anyone who actually used it. He says that he heard of a colleague in a neighbouring police district who refused to take part in an extrajudicial killing, complained about it, and was killed by his commanding officer on the evening of the day that he lodged his complaint. The commanding officer is still in post."

"Thank you, Miss Bateman," replied the Adjudicator, "but you know as well as I do that I can't take this kind of hearsay evidence into account. You've presented no documentation on this particular case so I am not going to allow it to affect my decision on Mr Borges Galeano's claim. Is that all?"

"We have nothing more to add, sir."

"Mr Cataract?"

"Nothing to add, sir."

"Good!" The Adjudicator looked at the clock. "Good! We've made faster progress than I feared. Time for tea. I can't give you a decision now, because I need to read the documents Miss Bateman has submitted. You'll have my decision in writing in a week."

Kerry felt numb. He stood up from his seat and tried to catch Aristides' eye. Aristides looked thunderstruck, gazing around the room as if he were seeing nothing. He was led out of the room into the neighbouring holding cell by the private security guards who had brought him in. Kerry went out into the corridor leading to the entrance hall, and found Miss Bateman. "What happens now?" he asked.

"They'll take Aristides back to the detention centre and I'll prepare the paperwork for a Judicial Review application, just in case that ogre gives us the slightest grounds for doing so. As soon as I get the Adjudicator's decision, I'll let you know as well as Aristides. But things don't look good. You may have to help him come to terms with going back to Cortesia. If I can think of any way of preventing it, I will."

Kerry went straight to the Removal Centre to visit Aristides. Aristides could hardly speak at first. They sat for a long time in silence, Kerry attempting without success to begin conversations, which fizzled out after a brief monologue.

Eventually, Aristides spoke. He was convinced that his cause was lost, that there was no possibility that he would be granted asylum. Kerry tried to encourage him. "We aren't sure," he said. "There is no point in losing hope when everything may in fact turn out well."

"Do you believe we will win?" asked Aristides. "I do not. Perhaps I need to think about what to do if they send me home."

Kerry was silent for a while.

"Let's wait and see what Miss Bateman says," he said at last.

"I could kill myself here, instead of waiting for them to kill me in Cortesia," said Aristides.

"No!" exclaimed Kerry, alarmed. "You mustn't think that way! You have to hold on to hope!"

"It is easier for you to hope than for me. You are not facing what I am facing."

"All the more important that you don't give up hope! You need it more than me."

"If I kill myself, it solves everyone's problems. The Cortesian Government will be happy, the British Government will be happy because I am no longer causing them problems, I'll be happy because there is nothing more to fear."

"But I will not be happy, my friend! Nor will your family be, nor your friends."

"If they are alive."

85

"But you know they are alive! When you phoned your friend, he told you your family was alive!"

"And being threatened. And the last time I spoke to him was a week ago. Anything could have happened since then."

"Look, it's quite understandable that you feel this way, but you are depressed. Maybe the medical department here could give you some help..."

Aristides laughed bitterly. "Them! They will give me a paracetamol. One. That is their answer to everything. Even if they had the best psychiatrist in the world working here, what could he do? People in here are depressed not just because of what has happened to them in the past but also because of the things that are happening to them now and what will probably happen in the future. Drugs won't help. Counselling won't help. The only thing that will help is the certainty of safety, giving us asylum and letting us out of this prison that they call a 'Removal Centre.' That's why people are always killing themselves in here."

Kerry was shocked. "You never told me this before!" he said.

"I didn't want to talk about it before," replied. "There was no reason to. You were giving me hope. I wanted to talk about other things. But now there isn't any hope."

"While there is life, there is hope," replied Kerry.

"So you say," said Aristides, heavily.

Kerry grasped Aristides' hands firmly in his and tried to look him in the eye, but Aristides' eyes were downcast. "Please, please, my friend, do not give up. Do not give up hope." Aristides looked up at him. "I will phone you tomorrow," said Kerry. "I will come to see you next week. We will both think about what we can do. Please, please do not hurt yourself. If you do that, the enemy has won."

Aristides smiled. "You never talked like that before," he observed.

"Nor did you," he replied. "Now, I'll speak to you tomorrow, and see you next week."

"Okay," said Aristides.

Kerry left, unsure whether he would see his friend again.

As it happened, he did see Aristides again, twice. He visited the Removal Centre eight days after the appeal hearing, one day after the news of the rejection of Aristides' asylum appeal arrived. Miss Bateman had immediately applied, without much hope, for a Judicial Review of the decision, on the grounds that the Adjudicator had not adequately taken into account, in his written decision, the expert opinion provided by Professor Cleary. But she explained that, more than likely, the High Court would take the view that this issue was a matter of fact, not a matter of law, and that therefore a Judicial Review could not be undertaken. Nonetheless, and surprisingly, Aristides seemed in better spirits than the week before. "I've survived this far," he said. "And I'll do whatever it takes to survive if they send me back. If I hadn't come, for sure I'd be worse off than I am now."

The Judicial Review was not allowed. Removal instructions followed swiftly after the rejection of the JR application. Kerry was able to visit one more time before the removal date. He was in a more sombre mood than Aristides. In the end, it was Kerry who wept this time, and Aristides had to comfort him. "Come on, man," he said. "You can cope without me. You're going to be okay."

"It's you I'm worried about," said Kerry.

"I know," replied Aristides. "But you've done all you can."

"Will you let me know how you get on?"

"Of course, my friend. I'll call you as soon as I can, once I get back."

Aristides' flight was due to leave the next day. By the time it arrived in Cortesia, it would be nearly midnight in London. Kerry did not expect to hear anything that night, so he went to bed. He hoped he might receive a call from Aristides the next day, but he heard nothing.

Kerry mourned the loss of Aristides, as if he were bereaved.

"The secret is to face the injustice of it and to work to change it without becoming bitter," said Father Patrick. "Most people don't get angry about injustices, because they don't know or don't understand or even don't care about them. Then there are those who do know and understand and care, and they get eaten up by anger. They lose their peace of mind and their judgement is affected. They don't always do what's necessary to challenge the injustice, because they're acting from their anger, instead of from a clear-sighted analysis of reality. I suppose I'm reasonably placid by nature, and it's true, I haven't done much about all the terrible injustices in the world, so it's easy for me to talk. But I'm just saying that it's important to remember why we're offended by injustice in the first place, and the reason is love. A great love for people, which is affronted by injuries to people's dignity, but we have to try to keep the love in our heart rather than the anger, and remember that the oppressors are human beings too. Their dignity is also wounded by the oppression, so we have to challenge their wrong action without hating them."

"I'm not sure my friend Peter would see things that way," said Kerry.

"Well, I'm not infallible, and Peter knows things I don't know despite my years, but I still think we have to steer a middle course between retaining our serenity by doing nothing, which is clearly a violation of charity, and doing the right things while full of anger. Anger corrupts us and usually leads right actions down blind alleys."

"I don't know what to do to challenge the asylum system, anyway," said Kerry, gloomily. "I just see the grief it causes people who deserve kindness rather than cruelty."

"Then, maybe the best course of action is to continue your work of love which is the visiting. We don't know what's become of your friend, Aristides, but there must be plenty of other poor souls in detention needing the help and comfort of a friendly face."

Kerry tried to keep hold on the hope that Aristides was alive, but after several weeks, he gave up hope of hearing from him. Meanwhile, the Detainee Visiting Group asked him to visit the next Spanish-speaking detainee on the waiting list, and he started the process all over again.

SOUTH

the direction of energy and life

One: Kerry's comrades join the clergy and Kerry makes a helpful discovery

Peter, Francis and their year group were ordained to the diaconate in June. Kerry was invited, but did not go. He felt too embarrassed about the circumstances of his leaving the seminary. He was unsure how he would have felt to be there. At the time the ordination Mass was being celebrated, he paused in translating a particularly tedious legal text from Spanish into English in his friendly but rather gloomy Victorian office, and prayed for the well-being of these men, and those whom they were to serve, then pressed on with his own task, to which he did not feel called, but which paid his bills.

Soon afterwards, Peter returned to London to begin his pastoral ministry in the parish of St Margaret Mary Alacocque in New Westgate. It was, for Peter, annoyingly far from the ARCRU office and the Removal Centre, and a good hour by train and tube from Kerry's flat, but at least it was possible to meet up from time to time. Peter spent many of his days off at ARCRU, and often met up with Kerry in town afterwards for supper.

Francis was sent to one of the sleepy seaside towns on the Kent coast, as deacon to a parish priest renowned for his devotion to the Church of the 1950s and his inability to cope with change.

Kerry saw much more of Mario that summer, as he was home in London. He was working with the Lambeth diocesan youth team, but had plenty of time at odd times of the day to meet up with Kerry for a drink. He admitted that he had taken up Mercedes' invitation to take salsa classes with her. "She's gorgeous, Kerry, fucking gorgeous. I mean, there's some really stunning women at that refugee association, but she is just amazing. I think this time I have actually, really fallen in love – and she's out of reach, Kerry, she's out of reach. I think she knows I'm besotted, but I'm no competition for her bloke. He's well fit."

"What's happened to your magnetic attraction for women?"

"That's a good question, Kerry. Am I losing it? Is it only Cortesian women who can't see it? It's a wind up."

"Shouldn't you be trying to give it all up, anyway?"

"What a man should do and what he actually does do are not always the same thing, Kerry. That's why we have the sacrament of reconciliation. Nobody has used it more than me."

"Don't the priests you confess to get a bit upset that you're having sex with women, while studying for the priesthood?"

"You have to choose your confessor with great care, Kerry," said Mario. "There's no point in upsetting people unnecessarily. There are those who are so aware of their own failings that they avoid getting freaked out about mine."

The following February, Peter was ordained priest. The ceremony was nearly cancelled, after Peter had an argument with the Cardinal over the wording of the service booklet.

"He was beside himself," Peter told Kerry a few days before the event, "just because I altered the service booklet a bit. I put in a few extra prayers, the wording of which His Eminence found questionable, and included a little statement inside the front page, dedicating my life and priesthood to the oppressed revolutionary masses of Latin America. He phoned me last weekend, as soon as he found the booklet in his in-tray. 'What's this utter nonsense about dedicating yourself to the revolutionary masses in South America?' he says. 'It's an expression of my devotion to the cause of peace and justice, as contained in the social teachings of the Church, and of my aspiration to serve one day in the Archdiocese's missionary programme in Cortesia,' I tell him. 'Poppycock!' he says. 'It's a pretentious and insubordinate piece of posturing. And don't patronise me, I'm perfectly aware of the social teaching of the Catholic Church. It does not sanction revolution.' I try to tell him about the just war theory but he cuts me off. 'Don't interrupt me when I'm talking to you!' he says. 'If you expect me to ordain you, you'll dedicate your life and priesthood to the people of this Archdiocese, whether oppressed or not. And whether you are allowed to participate in the missionary programme is entirely up to me.' 'Presumably God's will might have something to do with it as well,' I say. 'God's will is something which is discerned through a process which culminates in you accepting what I decide,' he says. 'That's what the vow of obedience means – and may I remind you that you took that vow in June. Nobody forced you to take it. And if you want to be ordained to the priesthood, you're going to have to take it again.' 'Well, perhaps I had better not be ordained to the priesthood, Your Eminence,' I say, because by this time I am really angry, 'and that'll save you the trouble of coming all the way over to St Margaret Mary's on Saturday.' 'I'm going to ignore the whole of that last remark and give you until tomorrow morning to think it over,' he says. 'I am willing to ordain you on Saturday, if you remove the ludicrous dedication from the inside front cover of that booklet.' 'I've already printed four hundred of them,' I tell him. 'Then either print some new ones or tear off the front cover so that the booklet begins with the entrance hymn. Nobody'll be any the wiser. You will telephone me at ten o'clock tomorrow morning, and inform me whether or not you wish to be ordained to the priesthood. Good-bye.' So I phoned him the next morning and apologised, and got the booklets reprinted without the dedication on the inside front cover. I've had it printed on small prayer cards instead, so I can give them to everyone, except the Cardinal."

On the following Saturday afternoon, at three o'clock, Peter was ordained to the Catholic priesthood. This time, because the event did not take place in the seminary, Kerry attended. He wept, not because he regretted his own decision, but because he was so moved to see his friend and mentor make the commitment that had meant so much to him for so long. It was an act of self-giving, which, in Peter's case, Kerry did not doubt would bring him much joy, but also much suffering because of his struggle with power structures, both secular and ecclesiastical, and because of the evident depth of his compassion.

Kerry missed Francis' ordination. It was on a weekday evening down on the coast, and work commitments prevented Kerry from attending it.

Early one evening, in the August of the year after his priestly ordination, Peter phoned Kerry and asked him if he was free for a drink. Since he was doing nothing whatever, except reading a Spanish novel of indifferent quality and gazing out of his window from time to time, Kerry agreed to meet up at a relatively quiet pub not far from Marble Arch.

"The Cardinal's letting me go, at last," Peter told him when they had sat down with their gin and tonics.

"Letting you go?" asked Kerry, aghast. "What are you supposed to have done wrong?"

"Not 'letting me go' as in chucking me out!" explained Peter. "I mean 'letting me go' as in letting me go to Cortesia at last!"

"Oh, brilliant!" exclaimed Kerry. "I suppose. Not so good for us."

"You'll have to come and visit me! Yes, the Cardinal's not all bad," said Peter. "He's a pompous old so and so but he's got a kind heart really. Either that, or he's finally despaired of me ever refraining from preaching politics and just wants me to go and do it so far away that he won't have to bother about it."

"Do you know where you're going?"

"Well, yes, and that's the not quite so brilliant part. They want me to go to the Diocese of Arroyomachete, way up in the far north. It's really remote, cut off from the rest of the country by a sort of clump of enormously high mountains, and surrounded on three sides by the Caribbean Sea. I've never met anyone from there. Cortesians tend to look down on that province as being backward."

"Oh, dear."

"On the other hand, I'll be working with a priest who's got a reputation for total commitment to social justice, totally my kind of guy. Bill Cowley, his name is. I think he's in his sixties now, and he's been in Latin America for donkey's years. The local bishop's good, too. He's one of the few bishops in that overwhelmingly Catholic country who actually does anything about justice, rather than paying periodic lip-service to it like the others. That's why he was made Bishop of Arroyomachete – because it's a tiny little backwater in a province that nobody cares about, in the back of beyond, and the other bishops can forget all about him. Bishop Gutierrez, his name is – a Jesuit. There's a Jesuit college near the cathedral, and a community of half a dozen Jesuits who teach in the college and serve parishes in some of the farming villages 'round about. They, and the bishop, have all received death threats for publicly calling for land reform, but Bill says it's all bluster and they don't take them seriously."

Kerry was alarmed. "Are you going to be safe out there?" he asked. "I don't want you being picked off by some horrible death squad!"

"They won't touch me!" Peter assured him. "Bill says he's never been threatened, even though he works with the Jesuits and says the same things as they do. He reckons it's because he's a European, and the death squads want to avoid killing foreigners, because it makes their precious Government look bad."

Kerry knew Peter well enough not to attempt to dissuade him from going. Peter's sense of service was what drew him to the place, but Kerry knew that Peter had sufficient vanity to feel some vainglorious thrill at the prospect of becoming a hero. Telling him not to go because it might be dangerous would strengthen his resolve and increase his vanity. Kerry refrained.

"When are you off, then?" he asked.

"End of next month," replied Peter.

The parish would throw a big party for him, but Kerry and Peter planned a second party at the Cortesian refugee centre, a 'fiesta de despedida', which was attended by all of Peter's Cortesian friends. Kerry went to both parties, and Mario turned up late at night at the fiesta, in the sure and certain hope of joining nubile young women in dancing salsa.

They were able to keep in touch more easily than Kerry had thought. There were several internet agencies in the city of Arroyomachete, and the Jesuit college had internet access, and Peter was frequently in town, so they were able to keep in touch by email. It was easier for Peter and a lot less expensive than using the unreliable telephone in the parish house. Thus, Kerry learnt something of the geography, culture and politics of the province of Caribe, of which Arroyomachete was the capital, and a great deal about Peter's opinions on them. Kerry was relieved to learn that Caribe was so cut off from the national life of the country that the level of political violence was much lower than elsewhere. There were killings among families involved in smuggling (a good number of families near the coast made a living from smuggling Scotch whisky and domestic appliances into the interior), but the province seemed devoid of the armed groups of left and right that were at war elsewhere in the country. The main difficulty for Peter was the heat – an intense, humid tropical heat which was infrequently relieved by sea breezes or a wind from the mountains, the tops of which were perpetually snow-covered. Peter, the great activist, had perforce to slow down in every way, since it was simply impossible to maintain the same level of activity as he would find natural and easy in London or in the mountainous and temperate Cortesian interior.

The one great cloud on Peter's horizon was, as he explained in his first email, a cloud of coal dust. The parish of Nuestra Senora de los Remedios, where Peter was working with Bill Cowley, included the small market town of Romania, on the edge of a long, broad valley thirty kilometres inland from Arroyomachete. Ten kilometres beyond Romania, stretching along the valley, lay the enormous opencast coal mine of Valle Negro. From the hill above the town, looking across to the mountains, the mine lay like a great scar across the landscape, and from it rose clouds of dust continuously – coal dust, dust kicked up from the un-metalled mining roads by trucks, and acrid diesel fumes from the mining machinery. The farming villages around the edges of the mine, all of them within the parish of Nuestra Senora, were being suffocated by dust, their lands much reduced and their agricultural productivity declining, as a result of the expansion of the mine. Children suffered from asthma and skin complaints, and when they were able to receive medical care, the doctors working in local clinics would never diagnose coal dust as the cause of their ill health for fear of losing their jobs, or worse.

This was bad enough; but there was a rumour that the mine, fifty per cent of which was owned by the Cortesian Government, and operated by its other fifty per cent owner, Valle Negro Coal Company SA, was soon to be sold off to some multinational company based overseas, and then expanded enormously. It would, perhaps, eventually rival the Cerrejon coal mine in Colombia, the largest of such mines in the whole of Latin America.

So it was with more than his usual level of interest that one grey afternoon, five or six months after Peter's departure, Kerry found in his in-tray a set of documents to be translated urgently from Spanish into English. They concerned the prospects and expansion possibilities of the Valle Negro coal mine in Cortesia, and the customers who required the translations so quickly were two multinational mining companies based in London: Anglo Australian plc and North Atlantic Mining plc.

Kerry was well aware of the ethics of his profession, and aware too, that any breach of confidentiality, if discovered, would be followed by instant dismissal and the possibility of legal action. But this was too important to ignore. As soon as he got home that evening, he phoned the parish house at Nuestra Senora de los Remedios and left a message for Peter to phone him as soon as he could.

Two days later, when Peter got back from a round of pastoral visits in the parts of the parish farthest from Romania, he phoned Kerry in alarm, a phone message being evidence of something really urgent. Kerry was able to tell him that he may have the identity of the buyers of the mine. They decided there were now two further tasks, to find out more about the companies concerned, which was easily done online from anywhere, and to see whether Kerry could find out any more, through his work, about the proposed purchase, in addition to any plans the companies might have for the development of the mine.

As it happened, within a week, the illness of a colleague meant that Kerry was asked to translate a legal document from English to Spanish, which he would not normally do. The document concerned certain conditions which the Cortesian State mining authority would need to fulfil if the two British companies, who were acting together as a joint venture, were to proceed with the purchase. One of them involved clarifying disputed land title in part of the mining concession, where residents of the village of San Martin de Porres were refusing to sell their plots of land to the mining company, without an agreement guaranteeing reconstruction of their village on another site of equivalent agricultural value. Anglo Australian and North Atlantic Mining made it clear that the existence of this village on land within the mining concession was a problem which needed to be resolved before the sale could be finalised.

Kerry phoned Peter again. Peter was at home this time.

"San Martin? That's one of our villages! I know it well! They've been fighting the company for years to try to get justice for having their lives wrecked by that mine! This confirms our worst fears. They're going to get them out by whatever means necessary now, you can be sure of that. We need to sort out what to do now. Thanks, Kerry. That's really important information. I'll let you know what happens."

"Is there anything I can do to help from here?"

"I'll discuss that with the community. Maybe there is, but I don't know. My head's spinning right now. You'll let me know if you learn anything else, won't you?"

"Of course," said Kerry. But he never set eyes on any more documents concerning the matter.

Two: Kerry turns to crime

One hot summer evening, a year after Peter had told Kerry he was going to Cortesia, Kerry had just got home from work when the phone rang. The caller spoke rather diffidently in Spanish, asking if this were Mr Kerry Ahern. Kerry thought he recognised the voice. "Yes, that's right," he replied in Spanish. "And are you Aristides Borges Galeano?"

"Yes, yes!" replied the caller. "Yes, it's me, Kerry!"

"My dear friend, how are you? What's happening? You are safe?"

"I am safe, thank you, my friend."

"Where are you?"

"I am in Cortesia."

"Good heavens! Can I phone you back?"

"No, no, it's fine, don't worry."

"I have been worried about you. I didn't know what had happened to you."

"Things were pretty difficult for me when I got back. I was imprisoned for desertion of duty. That's pretty serious. In a way, I'm glad it was only prison. If I had gone home and the local paras had found me, I would probably not be speaking to you now."

"Where were you in jail?"

"In the capital, in La Esperanza."

"So, are you back home now?"

"No, no, it wouldn't be safe. I need to stay well away from there. I'm staying in La Esperanza."

"Do your family know you are there?"

"Of course. I contacted them as soon as I was allowed to after I got back."

"And are they okay?"

"They're okay, thanks be to God."

"How long were you in jail?"

"Over three years. They just let me out."

"That's appalling! Three years!"

"I was lucky, Kerry. Usually you get longer than that for desertion."

"My goodness!"

"So, are you still visiting the detention centre?"

"Oh, yes. I go every week still."

"You really helped me, Kerry. You kept me sane. I would have gone mad without you."

"Well, I must say that visiting you was a very special experience for me. It's never been quite the same since. The people I have visited are all wonderful, courageous people, but you were the first person I ever visited in detention, and I think I made a connection with you that was deeper than I've ever made with anyone since."

"Well, maybe you should come to visit Cortesia."

"Oh yes, I would love to! In fact, I plan to do so. A very dear friend of mine from my seminary days is working there now, in Caribe."

"Caribe? My God, what did he do to deserve being sent there?"

"He loves it there, I think – though he finds it a bit hot."

"Heat is the least of it. It is the back of beyond. It is a shit hole."

"Have you ever been there, Aristides?"

"Of course not! No self-respecting Cortesian goes there! It is uncivilised."

"Well, that's where he is, and I have promised to visit him."

"Well, I am glad, because that means we can meet up in L.E."

"Then I must arrange to visit as soon as possible."

"Yes, yes, that would be good, Kerry."

"Yes."

"Kerry..."

"Yes, Aristides."

"Kerry, I am really sorry to have to say this, but I need to ask you a favour."

"Do you need me to send you some money, or bring you some?"

"I do not want any of your money, Kerry. You did so much for me when I was in detention. I do not want to take anything more from you."

"I hardly did anything for you apart from listen to you and buy you a few cups of hot chocolate."

"And phone cards."

"A few. Anyway, it would be no problem, Aristides. I have more than I need. I have all that money from selling my dear departed mother's house, remember."

"No, Kerry, I do not want your money."

"What, then?"

"Kerry, when they let me out of prison early it was on condition that I help the Prison Governor and the district police superintendent from time to time. They said they would never tell me to do anything violent but they would need me to do whatever else they tell me whenever they tell me if I do not want to go back inside. They said they wanted me to use my foreign connections to help them in a little bit of business they are doing. I told them I haven't got any foreign connections but they chose not to believe me. You are my foreign connection. My only one."

"I see."

"Kerry, I need you to take delivery of a package from some business associates of the district police superintendent and bring it to me. But I need it quite soon."

"What's in the package, then?"

"Money, Kerry. Quite a lot of it."

"I see. But can't the police superintendent's friends send it or bring it to him themselves?"

"They are already under suspicion of money laundering. They cannot bring it themselves, because they need to stay away from Cortesia for the moment. It would not be very healthy for them there. If they were to send it by Moneygram, or bank transfer, or anything like that, it would attract the attention of the British authorities. Britain has quite strict regulations concerning sending money to Cortesia. If you send more than £500 at a time, you need to register all your details with the agency, so you can be checked out."

"Well, can't they send it in several smaller sums, so they stay beneath the radar?"

"It would take too long."

"How much is it, then?"

"Two hundred and fifty million pedazos."

"Good heavens! That's nearly a hundred and twenty-five thousand pounds!"

"Yes."

"Oh, dear! Oh my goodness! I ... I don't know what to do! I don't know what to think!"

"I am really sorry to have to ask you this, Kerry. You do not have to do it. Nobody knows that it is you who are my contact, so there will be no negative consequences for you if you cannot help."

"Thank you, Aristides. I'm really not sure. I..."

"Unfortunately, there will be negative consequences for me, if you do not help."

"You mean, you'll go back in prison?"

"For sure."

"Anything else?"

"It's hard to say. I suppose it depends what mood the police superintendent is in."

"Can I think about this for one night?"

"Yes. Shall I phone you at the same time tomorrow?"

"Yes. I'm sorry to be indecisive."

"I am sorry to ask you something difficult and unpleasant."

"No, no, don't worry. It's lovely to hear from you."

"We'll speak tomorrow, then."

"Yes. Bye for now."

Kerry did not sleep very well. Under ordinary circumstances, he would have referred anything concerning Cortesia to Peter for his guidance. Anything this vexing to his spirit would usually be discussed with Father Patrick or Father Donald. But he knew well what they would all say in this case, so he did not think it was worth bothering them with it.

That decided it. If he knew what they would all say, and was still hesitant, it meant that he had already decided what he had to do.

The phone rang at exactly the same time the next evening. Aristides asked whether he had made a decision.

"I will help you, Aristides, because I cannot bear for you to go back in prison again."

"Thank you very much, Kerry. You are a true friend and I will never forget this."

"But I need to ask you some questions."

"Of course."

"Why would the superintendent's London friends trust someone they don't even know?"

"Because if a single centavo goes missing, I will suffer the same consequence as if you refused to assist. So, they know that I will only ask people that I trust with my life."

"And will I have to do this again?"

"No. I will not ask you again. They do not want one person in London getting too involved, in case there are bad consequences for them."

"But then what happens next time they need your help in this way?"

"That's when they will discover that I really do only have one contact in London."

"But won't they send you right back inside?"

"Possibly. Or they may ask me to do some other task for them. In any case, I get a few weeks of freedom before they lock me up again."

"Two hundred and fifty million pedazos for a few weeks of freedom!"

"Or maybe longer. Who knows?"

"But if they are dropping off this package, they will know where I live! What else might happen to me?"

"They will not know where you live, because they will not drop the package off at your house. I made that my condition of helping. I told them that the superintendent's friends must not be given any contact details of my own contacts. They will only have your photograph and a false name. Once you have booked a flight, you will let me know the flight you are booked on and the date. You will check in normally, go through security with your own hand baggage and sit near the departure gate. When the flight is called and people begin queuing to get on board, you will be approached by an individual who will ask you if your name is Green. You will say that it is, and you will discreetly swap hand baggage – so make sure you have anything you really need in your pockets, not your hand baggage. Also, make sure that your hand baggage contains nothing connected with you, nothing even that makes it clear what nationality or sex the owner is, because when the other traveller arrives in L.E., they will for sure be searched. You will not be. Put a newspaper in there; a couple of recent bestsellers; some paper tissues."

"How will he get through security in London?"

"That is their problem, not yours."

"Do I get my hand baggage back?"

"Yes. When you arrive at Hernan Cortes Airport in L.E., you come through border control, pick up your other baggage, come through customs and then out into the arrivals hall, and I will be waiting for you there. You will give me your hand baggage. When the other traveller comes into the arrivals hall, I will retrieve your hand baggage from him or her. Then you can forget you ever had anything to do with this."

"But, Aristides, I can't understand why some money-laundering cartel has to go to such lengths for an amount of money that must be paltry to them. Surely, they can simply bribe all the necessary officials and not have to bother with potentially untrustworthy foreigners?"

"It is not a cartel. It is the district police superintendent. He is just doing it for himself, calling in some favours –

including from me – and in doing so, possibly trespassing on the turf of the larger operators. That is one reason why he doesn't want to involve anyone he doesn't know personally more than once."

"So, we could incur the wrath of some of the really big guns?"

"Not for two hundred and fifty million pedazos. That really is chicken feed to them. They will probably laugh at the superintendent's cheekiness, buy him a few whiskies and let him know what a shame it would be if he tried it again and something unpleasant happened to him. They will not start a turf war over such a small sum. Meanwhile, the superintendent will have enough money to retire on."

"How soon do I have to do this?"

"As soon as possible."

"How long have I got before it stops being soon?"

"Two months. The superintendent is a gracious man but I think anything over two months would try his patience too far."

Kerry emailed Peter to let him know that he had booked a whole month's leave from mid-October to mid-November, so that he could come to visit. Peter was delighted. He suggested that, if Mario were free, he should come too. Peter would come up to L.E. to meet them at Hernan Cortes Airport.

Mario had been ordained to the diaconate in June – another event which Kerry had missed. Kerry did wonder how he had managed to make it through to ordination, given his continuing 'falls' with a succession of young women, who had apparently 'thrown themselves' at him. But Mario was resolute that he wanted to be a priest and that he was going to take his vows seriously. Kerry wondered how he could possibly do so, but felt that it was not his place to tell his friend what to do.

Kerry told Peter that he thought it unlikely that Mario could get so much time off so soon after beginning his diaconal ministry in St Felicity's parish in East Cheam, but that he would ask him. In fact, of course, as much as he would love to travel to Cortesia with his good friend, he absolutely could not afford to have anyone with him while couriering laundered money.

Kerry also attempted to persuade Peter that there was no need for him to come up to L.E. just to meet him off the plane. He could easily get a connecting flight down to Arroyomachete. He did not want Peter witnessing his meeting with Aristides. It would make everything much too complicated. But Peter insisted – and if Kerry had dug in his heels, Peter would have become suspicious. Better to spill the beans and deal with his disapproval when the deed was already done.

Mario was really disappointed. He told Kerry he would love to come, but that he could not expect to get time off so soon. He would have to visit Peter the following year. He might be able to take some time off after his ordination to the priesthood.

Kerry booked a flight for 11th October. Peter was delighted. He said that this day was a day for commemorating the last day of Indigenous liberty before the arrival of Columbus and the Spanish imperialists in the Americas on 12th October 1492. Kerry's arrival on that date was deeply propitious.

Kerry certainly hoped so, but he had a most unpleasant feeling about it.

After two more telephone conversations with Aristides, both of them had all the details they needed. Kerry posted a small portrait photograph of himself to a post office box in Liverpool. He dreaded this whole venture, but he could not let his friend down.

It was after he had already checked in for Cortesaero Flight CA123, and gone through the security barrier to the flight side of airport departures, that Kerry had a most unfortunate surprise. Someone suddenly grasped his left shoulder from behind and put a sweaty right hand over his eyes. Kerry flinched, suddenly rigid with fear.

"Guess 'oo?" asked Mario, and laughed loudly before releasing his grip.

Kerry spun round. "Mario! You nearly scared the life out of me! What are you doing here? Have you come to see me off?"

"No, mate. Good news! I'm coming with you!"

Kerry was astounded. "But how can you? I thought you couldn't get the time off?"

"Yeah, well, that's the bad news, I'm afraid. I've got rather a lot of time off right now."

"Oh. What happened?"

"Same old, same old, Kerry."

"Who was it this time?"

"Youth group leader. I couldn't help myself. She threw herself at me."

"How many times?"

"That's a rather personal question."

"You're right. I'm sorry. I meant, is it a deep and meaningful relationship or just a fling? Are you in love? Is she?"

"I don't know, Kerry. But it wasn't a one-night stand, for sure. We've been seeing each other a lot. It just became too obvious. Rumours began. My parish priest got a bit upset about it. Then the Archbishop did too. Told me to take at least a month off to think about whether or not I really want to be a priest, and whether or not I can keep my vows. He needs an answer by Christmas, at the latest. If I can't give him a definite 'yes' by Christmas, he won't ordain me to the priesthood and he'll de-deacon me, if you see what I mean. So, I'll just be an ordinary person again."

"Laicise you? Already? Goodness, that was quick! You were only ordained deacon in June."

"The Arch says it was a mistake to ordain me, because I obviously don't understand what it's about."

"Don't you?"

"I do, Kerry. It's just this whole bloody celibacy thing that does my head in. Why's a priest have to be celibate? The Orthodox and the C of E get by with married clergy. Why do we have to be different, for fuck's sake? I mean, I do want to help people, be available to listen to their troubles, try to understand the Gospel better and share that with them, animate a community, lead it in prayer, celebrate Mass, work for peace and justice – all the stuff that a priest's supposed to do, but with a wife."

"Just the one?"

Mario looked hurt. "What do you take me for, Kerry?"

"Well, you have had sex with rather a lot of women over the past few years, haven't you? Would you be able to stick to just one?"

"You misunderstand me, Kerry. I'm hurt. Yes, alright, I have done a fair old bit of shagging, but it's the prospect of having to give it up that stirs me all up. I mean, if I actually had a proper girlfriend, a partner, a wife, I'd be loyal."

"Would you?"

"I would, mate, I would. I was before. When I was working, before I got into this seminary lark, I went out with a girl called Sharon and I was always faithful to her while we were together. That lasted more than a year, and it only broke up because I started feeling the call to the priesthood. So, she chucked me, which is understandable really."

"But we're all supposed to wait for marriage before we jump into bed with anyone, aren't we?"

"Well, that is the party line on the subject, true, and I have been spectacularly bad at living up to that."

"And what about her? What does she feel about it all? When does she need her answer? What does she feel about you suddenly legging it to Latin America?"

"We talked about it, Kerry. We agreed we maybe ought to cool down a bit, have some time apart, think about what we each really want in life. So, she agreed to this little jaunt. I wouldn't have come otherwise."

"Really?"

"Yes, really! Don't get on your high horse, mate! Don't judge me! I may be a bit highly sexed, but I'm not a bloody inconsiderate wanker! I don't just use women and then chuck 'em!"

"Well, look, Mario, I'm not here to condemn you or anything," said Kerry. He paused. "How on earth did you know what flight I was going to be on, anyway?"

"Peter emailed me when I wrote and told him what had happened. He said I should get away for a couple of weeks and come and see him. I managed to get a seat on the same flight as you. We decided not to tell you – let it be a nice little surprise. Stroke of luck, eh?"

"Well, yes," said Kerry hesitantly. Very bad luck, he thought.

"Mario," he said, "I'm afraid I've got to do something, which I can't tell you about now, though I can later. But, for now, we have to pretend we don't know each other, and we have to go on pretending that until after we've arrived in Cortesia, and gone through immigration and customs."

Mario looked confused. "What the fuck are you going on about?" he asked.

"I can't say."

"Have you gone mental or something?"

"No."

"Are you involved in something dodgy?"

Kerry was silent.

"You *are* involved in something dodgy," concluded Mario. "You stupid fucking tosser. I can't believe it. You *fucking tosser*. You're going to fucking Cortesia, land of fucking death squads and drugs and fucking money laundering, and you get involved in something dodgy. Thank you so much. Thank you, Kerry. *Tosser!*" Mario's face was twisted into an expression of utter disgust. He turned half away from Kerry to emphasize his point.

"I'm sorry, Mario. It's to help someone in need."

"Well, who else is going to be in need by the time you're finished? You? Peter? Me? I don't suppose you told Peter about it, did you?"

"Of course not."

"No. Of course not. And why? Because he'd have told you not to behave like a stupid fucking tosser."

Kerry was silent.

109

"Well, you're going to have to tell me now, aren't you? You expect me to get on that plane, when I know you're involved in something dodgy without knowing what it is?"

"You don't have to get on any plane, Mario. I didn't ask you to come. It's your own free choice."

Mario glared at him. "So you're telling me, basically, to fuck off."

"No, I'm not telling you that, and anyway I don't use language like that."

"Oh, I see, so it's okay to do deals with bloody death squads and drug traffickers, but not okay to swear?"

"I didn't mean that. I haven't done deals with drug traffickers and death squads, and I'd be really, really grateful if you would *keep your voice down*."

Mario paced up and down in front of Kerry for a few moments, periodically exhaling heavily. "I could do with a fag," he said. "Everywhere's bloody no smoking these days." After a pause, he said, "What are we going to do then, Kerry?"

"Right," said Kerry. "I'm going to tell you exactly what I'm doing, and why, and then you can choose what you're going to do, and you can tell me what you're going to do so I can act accordingly."

Kerry explained, carefully, fully, and in a low voice.

"You fucking tosser," said Mario when he had finished; but this time he said it with evident affection. He smiled. "You're risking your life and liberty for an innocent victim of British and Cortesian state oppression. I like that." He was silent for a while, looking at his shoes. Kerry watched him steadily.

"Well, I'll have to come with you now, won't I? You don't know how to look after yourself. See, you're a gentle soul – which is why you're doing this bloody stupid thing in the first place – whereas me, I'm a hard bastard. I can cope. You might crack up out there, see, whereas me, I can take whatever. I'll be there for you, mate."

"So…?"

"So. I'm going to fuck off and have nothing more to do with you till we've both met up with Peter in the arrivals hall at La Esperanza airport."

Kerry exhaled loudly in relief. "Thanks, Mario."

"How'd you know my name?" said Mario. "I don't know who you are. Fuck off." Mario turned and walked over to the nearby newsagent's and began perusing the daily newspapers.

Kerry was in a cold sweat as he sat by the departure gate. He kept his bag on his lap. The waiting area was crowded and noisy. A large, well-dressed, middle-aged man of Latin-American appearance sat down next to him, on his left, and began fiddling around with a mobile phone. There were two free seats to the right of him. A strikingly beautiful young woman, also of Latin American appearance, sat down in the further of the two seats and took out a copy of *Hello!* She began leafing through it. A thin, swarthy young man with a heavy moustache took the seat immediately to his right, leaned back and stared into space. Was this the one?

People milled around, some already queuing at the gate despite the fact that boarding would probably not begin for another ten minutes. Which of these people was his contact? Who was he endangering by this act of mercy? What would be the consequences for himself?

He could see Mario over the far side of the waiting area, reading his newspaper. Kerry looked away, for fear of making accidental eye contact.

Before long, boarding was announced for families with young children, people in wheelchairs (of whom there were none on this occasion) and anyone in rows 28 to 35. There was a gentle pushing and shoving, as those already standing in the premature queue gave way to those whose seats had been called. As the last of these were disappearing into the tunnel, rows 18 to 27 were called. The man to his right jumped up and moved into the queue. Kerry stood up slowly and looked around. The young woman two seats away looked at him and smiled sweetly. "Mr Green?" she inquired, in English. Kerry's mouth went dry. "Yes," he said. Her gaze moved from his eyes to his bag and back. Still smiling, she put her bag on the seat between them. He placed his bag on top of hers. She picked it up and put the long strap over her shoulder. "Thank you!" she said, cheerily, and turned away to join the queue. Kerry, his heart beating hard enough to burst his ribcage, picked up the young woman's bag, and carried it beside him at knee level, on to the plane, stowing it carefully under the seat in front of him.

Three: Kerry arrives in Caribe

The flight lasted eleven hours. The young man beside Kerry, a Cortesian travelling from London to visit his ailing mother in La Esperanza, slept for most of it. After the in-flight meal, Kerry felt the need to visit the toilet. He stood up, carefully stepped over his slumbering fellow traveller, and walked forward to the toilets in the centre of the plane. On the way back, he looked over to the far side of the fuselage and saw Mario deep in conversation with the young woman sitting next to him – the young woman with Kerry's hand baggage. Mario looked animated. He was laughing and clearly completely at ease, utterly in his element, effortlessly impressing an attractive young woman. Oh dear, thought Kerry.

Kerry spent much of the rest of the flight looking out of the window at the cloud formations below. As they entered the tropics, huge clouds with shapes unfamiliar to him sailed beneath them like flotillas of ships, casting shadows on the ocean far below, which sparkled in the bright sunlight. Kerry contemplated the beauty of sea and sky as if it were the last time he would set eyes on them, so convinced was he now of the probability of death at the hands of some enraged drug trafficker.

An hour or so before their scheduled arrival time in La Esperanza, the plane crossed the Cortesian coast. Far below them, Kerry could see the colour of the sea lighten through various shades of turquoise, and then a thin strip of sandy coast gave way to a broad valley between high mountains, a large river meandering through the valley, between what looked like forests or plantations of the most brilliant green.

So this was it, at last. Cortesia, the land named for the Conquistador Hernan Cortes, who had never set foot in it, but whose exploits inspired the Spanish colonisers of this part of the continent. With the stress moved one syllable to the right, with delightful accuracy, the country's name described, in Spanish, one of the chief qualities of its inhabitants: courtesy. This was a land famed for politeness, hospitality, generosity, joie de vivre and extreme violence, where the great majority of the inhabitants would put themselves to great inconvenience for the benefit of another, but where a privileged few would have those who stood in the way of their economic interests eliminated without pity. It was a land in which refined antique Spanish affected the self-expression of its people, to such an extent that even the death squads used the polite form of 'you' in their written threats: "We wish to inform Your Mercy son-of-a-whore communist lawyer that Your Mercy is a military target and will be slaughtered like a pig unless Your Mercy leaves the country within the week – cordially, the Central United Front of the Black Condor Self-Defence Units."

The plane followed the river valley upstream into the mountains, the valley narrowing with height, and after around forty minutes, the plane banked to the left, climbed into thick cloud and began to shudder with air turbulence. Passengers were requested, in two languages, to return to their seats, fasten their safety belts and expect some routine alpine turbulence as they approached Hernan Cortes International Airport. The temperature was seventeen degrees Celsius, the sky clear with scattered cloud, humidity was low and the wind was blowing from the south west at eleven kilometres an hour.

Mountain crags loomed periodically out of the clouds, alarmingly close to the plane. The plane rose, fell, banked repeatedly, shuddered, climbed, and finally emerged from the clouds into bright day again as the mountains suddenly fell away into another broad green high valley. This led up to another range of mountains, and the plane banked to the right and began a steep descent over farms, scattered trees and greenhouses, until suddenly, it was a few feet above a runway, on which it touched down heavily, braked fiercely and began taxiing towards the airport buildings. A ripple of applause rose from the Cortesian passengers in token of their appreciation of the captain's skill.

Kerry broke out again into a cold sweat. As passengers began to leave the plane, he did not know whether to hang back or make haste. He allowed himself to be carried along in the flow. At immigration control, he answered the official's questions without difficulty. He was here to visit an English priest friend working in Caribe, he would be in the country four weeks, he worked in London as a translator. The official congratulated him on his excellent Spanish, smiled and wished him a pleasant holiday in Cortesia and good health to himself and his friend.

Kerry picked up his suitcase in the baggage hall and passed through the green channel at customs, as instructed by Aristides, and then he was in the arrivals hall. There, in front of him, was Aristides, and a little beyond him in the crowd, Peter, waving cheerily to attract his attention.

Kerry went straight to Aristides, embraced him warmly, whispered in his ear that his friend Peter was also meeting him and that they would need to be a little discreet, and handed over his hand baggage to him just as Peter reached them. Kerry detached himself from Aristides' embrace and turned to embrace Peter.

"Who's your friend?" asked Peter, in English. "And where's Mario?"

"Mario's on his way," replied Kerry, in English, then asked him in Spanish, "Do you remember Aristides? You introduced us, in a way." He added, in English, "At the Removal Centre – the friend of the bloke you were visiting."

"Ah, yes!" exclaimed Peter, in Spanish. "Ah, and you kept in touch all this time! How lovely! And you've been okay, Aristides? No problems when you came back?"

"No, I've been fine, thanks."

They exchanged pleasantries for a while, but Aristides was beginning to look uncomfortable. "I'm sorry," he said, "I just have to go and do something but I will be back in a few minutes. Don't go away!"

"If I'd known you were going to be seeing Aristides here, I'd have booked the flight to Arroyomachete for tomorrow instead," said Peter. "We'll have to check in in another hour."

"Maybe I can spend more time with him on my way back through La Esperanza in a few weeks," suggested Kerry.

"Yes. Still, you should have told me, you silly Billy. What's happened to Mario? Didn't you come through customs and immigration together?"

"No, we got separated because we were sitting in different parts of the plane and I just got carried along with the flow. I didn't want to wait, because of Aristides."

"Still, Mario doesn't speak Spanish. It might have been good to stay with him."

"Sorry."

Peter asked Kerry a few questions about home, and began to tell him the news from Caribe, but he was ill at ease.

"I hope Mario's alright. You know, he can be a bit of an idiot at times. I wish you hadn't left him behind, Kerry."

I wish I *had* left him behind, thought Kerry.

They fell into an awkward silence, broken sporadically with inconsequential smalltalk.

After fifteen more minutes, Mario emerged from customs, looking around for his friends. Peter called to him. Mario walked straight towards him and they embraced.

"Fucking hell, that was a wind up," said Mario. "They gave me a right going over in there. The geezer at immigration could speak a few words of English and I showed him your invitation letter, Peter, and my ticket out of the country, but he seemed well suspicious. Then, at customs, they had me open up all my bags, turn out all my pockets, I thought they were going to do a bloody strip search or something. They went through everything. None of them spoke a word of English, they just pointed and gestured. Then they discovered my breviary and asked what it was, and I said, it's a prayer book, and put my hands together and closed my eyes just to illustrate, and they said 'Sasserdotay?' and I thought, that means priest, doesn't it, so I said yes, and did a little gesture to illustrate the old clerical collar. They had a good laugh then and said I could go. I wish that bird I was sitting next to on the plane had been able to stay with me. She could have translated for me. I lost her in the immigration queue. She had to go in the citizens' queue and I had to go with the foreigners." He lowered his voice conspiratorially. "Between you and me, I wouldn't mind conversing with her at any hour of day or night, in whatever bloody language. In fact, you wouldn't have to bother with words. Fwoar!"

"How comforting to see how little you've changed," said Peter.

"I haven't lost my touch. Still got the old charm, Peter. She and I are going to meet up on my way back from your place. She lives here in La Esperanza, so she said she can meet me at the airport on my way back and we can spend some time together up here. I can hardly wait."

Kerry was finding it difficult to breathe.

"Are you okay, Kerry?" asked Peter. "You look a bit peaky."

"I'm okay," said Kerry, unconvincingly.

"A lot of people suffer from the altitude here," said Peter. "We're up at about two and a half thousand metres and the air is much thinner than at sea level. When you're not used to it, it can make you feel breathless."

"That must be what it is, then," said Kerry.

Mario suddenly waved cheerily to someone behind Peter and Kerry. "Claudia!" he called out. Peter and Kerry turned and saw the young woman with Kerry's hand baggage emerging from customs. She blushed, waved at Mario, called "See you soon!" to him in English, and hurriedly veered off to her right.

"Well, that's nice, isn't it?" said Mario. "Where's she going?"

Kerry watched her making quickly for the exit to the taxi rank outside. Mario began to follow her, calling to attract her attention. Kerry began to follow him. "Don't, Mario!" he pleaded, but there was no stopping him. Kerry saw Aristides by the exit. As Claudia passed him, she handed him Kerry's bag and carried on out into the taxi rank. Mario followed her. Kerry approached Aristides.

"Sorry," said Kerry. "My friend doesn't know what's happening."

Aristides handed him his bag. "I thought you were travelling alone," he said, his face tense and preoccupied.

"So did I," said Kerry. "This was a surprise."

"Is your friend okay? I mean, he won't say anything?"

"I would trust him with my life."

"Good. Okay. Look, I'm going now, but we'll meet on your way back through L.E. The police superintendent has his money now. Thanks for helping. Now, have a good trip and good luck."

"Thanks, Aristides. Look after yourself."

Aristides made off through the crowd. Mario returned from the taxi rank, smiling broadly. "I've got her phone number now, and told her where I'm staying, so we can be in touch while I'm at Peter's," he said, enormously pleased with himself. "Here, what are you doing with her bag?"

"It's not her bag, it's mine," said Kerry. "Don't you recognise it?"

"Then what was she doing with it?" asked Mario. Realisation dawned. "Oh shit. Oh shit."

"Yes, Mario, you have just befriended the courier, who I'm supposed to have no further contact with, ever again, in my life. That's why you were given the going over in customs. She was under suspicion. They saw you with her."

"Fuck," said Mario.

Peter joined them. "What on earth is going on?" he demanded.

"Nothing significant," replied Kerry.

"Mario looks guilty," said Peter. "That's a sign that something more than usually inexcusable has occurred. Furthermore, I would like to know what's with this baggage caper. You gave a bag to Aristides, Kerry, which I assumed was a present for him."

"It was," said Kerry.

"Then Aristides goes off, reappears without it, takes delivery of another bag from the young woman, with whom Mario is currently besotted, and gives it to you. What's in it?"

"Just my things," said Kerry, opening it to show Peter.

"Then why was she carrying it?"

"We were only allowed one piece of hand baggage, and she didn't have any, so she kindly agreed to carry mine on board so I could carry the presents for Aristides."

"That was both very kind of her, and a little unwise, given that you didn't know each other."

"Oh, we got chatting in the airport. You know how Mario is."

"I do know how Mario is. Is that why she attempted to run away as soon as she saw you both just now?"

"Maybe I was a bit full-on with her on the plane," said Mario. "But it's alright now. I've sorted it."

"Good," said Peter. "Well, we'd better go over to domestic departures and check in for the flight to Arroyomachete."

Kerry and Mario followed him.

"Will it be okay?" asked Mario under his breath.

"I hope so," replied Kerry. "We'll find out, won't we?"

"We're alright," said Mario confidently. "I'm a hard bastard."

"Good," said Kerry. "Because whoever she's working for is going to know where we are."

As the plane began its final approach to Arroyomachete, descending steeply from the mountains, Kerry saw the Caribbean shining like liquid gold flowing from the huge reddening sun setting over the sea. When the doors were opened, he could feel warm humid air pouring into the cabin. As he stepped out of the plane, the heat was so intense it felt as if he were immersing himself in a hot bath.

"You may find it a little difficult getting used to the heat," said Peter, as they walked over to the airport terminal. "I find the best thing is simply not to think about it. But you do have to remember that you can't do things as quickly as you might at home."

"It's fine by me," said Mario. "Some like it hot."

"Good," said Peter. "But I hope the humidity has the effect of taking the edge off your libido."

Once their bags had been brought inside the building, they took a taxi to the Colegio del Caribe, the Jesuit school where they were to spend the night. "The roads around Romania can get a bit dodgy after dark now," said Peter. "There have been periodic roadblocks set up by various armed groups. They're usually only after money, but it can be a bit hairy, so it's better to stay overnight in the town."

A splendid supper, typical of the area, was provided as soon as they arrived at the college. It consisted of locally caught fish with rice, plantain and salad, accompanied by a variety of *frescos*, fruit pulped and mixed with water and sugar. Kerry particularly enjoyed the tree tomato.

Four: Kerry begins to fall in love

They were joined, for the journey to Romania the next morning, by an American woman in her early twenties. She was slightly shorter than Kerry, with fine, jet black, shoulder length hair, which curled inwards slightly at the ends, lightly bronzed skin, dark eyes and a ready, radiant smile.

"Hi!" she greeted Kerry. "I'm Hannah Ferraro. And you must be Kerry!"

Kerry agreed that he must.

"I've heard so much about you from Peter," she said. "I'm glad to meet you!"

Kerry felt a most unfamiliar fluttering around his heart, but was unable to identify the emotion that it signified.

"Was it good?" asked Kerry.

Hannah laughed. "Of course it was!" she said.

"It would have been better if you'd paid me more, Kerry," said Peter.

"You didn't tell me about Hannah, Peter," Kerry said, somewhat accusingly.

"Oh, I've only been here three weeks," said Hannah. "I'm working up in Romania as a volunteer, staying with the Sisters, who work with Bill and Peter in the pastoral team up there. The Sisters of Charity of Jerusalem, Massachusetts, have a volunteer programme for women who are interested in working with them. They're not getting many vocations these days, but they want to be able to carry on their work. So, they started this programme for those who might like to stay with them for a year or two, but not for a life-time. They're a good bunch of women. They feel a calling to the marginalized and oppressed – so they're in inner city communities across the US and in rural black communities in the Deep South, on Indian Reservations in the West and Midwest, and now, they are also in a few communities in Cortesia and the Central American Republic."

"They have very much the same outlook as Bill and me," added Peter.

"You're not planning to become a nun, are you?" asked Kerry.

"Oh, no," replied Hannah, with a laugh. "No, I want to be a human rights lawyer, maybe deal with immigration cases at home, and perhaps end up helping with cases in the Inter-American Court of Human Rights. Before going to Law School, I wanted some work experience in a country like Cortesia, where human rights are so often violated."

"Where are you from?" asked Kerry.

"I grew up right in Jerusalem, Massachusetts, so I've always been familiar with the Sisters. In fact, two of my school friends joined them and are working down South."

"How does the pastoral work here relate to human rights work?"

"Well, the parish team – that's Bill, Peter, Sister Patsy, Sister Alison and me – use a kind of model of pastoral work where we always link religious teaching with reflection on people's actual living situations, economic and political conditions, as well as their emotional and devotional lives. We always encourage people to think about the life of the whole community, not just themselves or their own family. So, whatever kind of religious discussion we're having, we'll always be thinking about things like, why don't most people in the community have secure work; why have they lost access to land that they used to work; why is it that land that everyone used to be able to use for free has been fenced off and patrolled by security guards? We encourage people to think about what it means to be made in the image of God, what this means for their dignity, their rights, their capacity for creative activity. We run literacy classes and use materials that start with the actual situation of people here in Caribe, and get them to think about how the community could be better in the process of learning to read."

"It really encourages people to stand up for their rights," added Peter.

"The other thing is, the pastoral work enables me to see all the ways in which people round here are denied their rights, and also the ways in which others have been encouraging them to insist on their rights under the Constitution. There's an excellent national organisation called the Congress of Black Communities, the Congreso de Comunidades Negras, or CCN, which has been running workshops in communities round here recently, simply informing people about what they're supposed to be entitled to under the Constitution. Communities of African descent, like most of the communities round here, are supposed to have community control of their land. That means that neither the mine nor anyone else has the right to be buying families out one by one, without proper consultation with the whole community, and a decision by the whole community. The Constitution is good on paper but the powers that be don't take any notice of it. If communities have the knowledge and the confidence to insist on their Constitutional rights, it can strengthen their bargaining position with the mining company and the powerful local families that control this province."

"You've seen all that in three weeks?"

"Yes!" Hannah laughed again. "The team didn't waste any time. The first week I was here, the CCN were running workshops in some of the communities round the mine. I spent the whole week there with the communities, seeing the interactions between them and the pastoral team and the influence of the CCN activists. It was totally inspiring, seeing people not just getting a better understanding of their own situation, but visibly growing in self-confidence to do something about it. It was good to have local people there from San Martin de Porres, too, because they've been fighting the mine for years. So, they're pretty confident and well organised, and that shows other local communities, who are next in line for removal, what can be done."

The road to Romania led through gently undulating mixed farmland, leading up to the foothills of the mountains to the south. Thin brown cattle, of a breed that Kerry had never seen, grazed in fields dotted with large shade trees. Here and there were small patches of woodland.

Kerry sat in the front of the Toyota Land Cruiser with Peter. Mario, predictably, was attempting to charm Hannah, with whom he sat in the back. Hannah was continuously cheerful and polite with him, but no more so than she was with Kerry and Peter. She repeatedly sought to involve everyone in the conversation, rather than simply falling into a *tete a tete* with Mario. Kerry noted this with approval.

There was more traffic on the road than Kerry would have expected. He did not know what he had expected, but it wasn't this. Perhaps he expected horses and carts, rather than Japanese four wheel drives and pick-up trucks.

"Is there normally this much traffic on the road?" he asked, "Or is it because it's a public holiday?"

"Oh, I think it's pretty normal," replied Peter. "They don't go in much for the *Dia de la Raza* in Caribe. For Indigenous People, it's a celebration by the victors of their conquest, so they don't observe it at all, except as an occasion for political protest in La Esperanza and the other big cities. Black Cortesians might use the excuse for a bit of a drink and a dance in the evening, but they don't feel attached to the event either, because Columbus and co enslaved their ancestors. In Caribe, it's only the few families who run the place that'll really be celebrating 12th October."

After nearly half an hour, the road reached the top of a gentle incline, and there before them, at the foot of the hill, lay the little town of Romania, at the side of a broad valley. Across the valley was the great dark scar of the Valle Negro mine, from which rose a great dust cloud like mist or smoke.

Romania was much like many small Latin American towns. In the centre was the town square, on the eastern side of which stood the church, and beside it, the priests' house.

Opposite the church was the town hall, and beside it, the police station. On the other two sides of this small square was a café, a petrol station (known alarmingly in Cortesia as a 'bomba', a bomb) and a few shops. Four, rather poorly looking, algorrobo trees grew in the square, one in each corner, but Romania's square lacked the statue of Cortes that usually graced – or defaced – the centre of larger and older towns. The town consisted of a grid of half a dozen straight streets running east-west and a similar number north-south. It was like a smaller, newer, less aesthetically pleasing version of Arroyomachete.

The Sisters lived in a small house behind the church on Calle 2 Este, Second Street East. Peter dropped Hannah off there, before pulling up in the square in front of the priests' house. Kerry was sorry to be parted from her. He found her intelligent, dedicated, courageous, admirable, cheerful, full of life and energy. Something in her manner lifted his spirits, made his heart lighter. And she was ... pretty, very, very pretty. Kerry rarely thought much about people's appearances. He was surprised and confused that Hannah's looks impinged upon his consciousness. She seemed to him altogether beautiful.

Now that they had stopped moving, there was no breeze to take the edge off the stifling heat. Kerry felt as if he were in a sauna.

"Hot enough for you?" asked Mario as he stepped out of the vehicle.

"Don't even mention the heat," replied Peter, sharply. "I survive it by steadfastly refusing to think about it."

"I rather like a little bit of warmth," said Mario.

"Good for you," replied Peter. "You'll enjoy eternity in the fires of hell, to which God will most certainly condemn you for being an irritating little twerp and getting on my nerves."

"That's not very nice, is it?" said Mario.

"It won't be, no, and I shall pray God to make sure you're stuck in the most unpleasant imaginable bit of it."

Further meditation on the nature of the fourth of the Four Last Things, and Mario's place in it, was cut short by their arrival in the front room of the priests' house and the pleasant necessity of greeting Father Bill Cowley.

Bill had thick grey hair and a short, but rather unruly, grey beard. He wore knee length, baggy, sandy coloured shorts, a stained white polo shirt, open at the neck, and open leather sandals.

"Aha!" he said. "The three wise men!"

"No," said Peter. "Two wise men and an idiot. And I'm not the idiot."

"How inspiring it always is to see true friendship," said Bill, as he shook hands warmly with Mario and Kerry, and clapped Peter affectionately on the back. "Now, Peter will show you to your room and you can put your bags in there. I'm afraid that one of the disadvantages of living in the tropics is that it's much too hot for anything more than a sheet to cover you at night, which removes the possibility of giving people apple pie beds, because you need at least one blanket to conceal the apple pie, so to speak. I used to enjoy giving people apple pie beds in England. Come to think of it, I used to enjoy apple pie as well, and that's something you don't encounter over here, for lack of apples. Never mind. Other things make up for it. Cortesian coffee is one of them. I've made a large pot of *tinto*, so when you've put your bags down you can come back in here and have a few cups while you tell me all about yourselves. Later on, we can start showing you around the parish."

Peter took his friends past a small bathroom and down a short corridor into the back of the single storey house, where they were to share a bedroom.

"Bit of a joker, that Father Bill?" asked Mario. "Bit of a humorist? Bit of a wind-up merchant?"

"Yes," replied Peter, "but of consummate sensitivity. He always knows when to stop, and when not to start."

"I thought he'd be very serious," said Kerry, "given his concern for social justice."

"I think it's that that necessitates the humour," said Peter. "We'd all go spare otherwise."

"But apple pie beds?" said Mario. "Bit public school, isn't it?"

"Well, I suppose being in the army, and then in seminary, is a bit like being at public school," said Peter.

"Army? So he's fairly hard?"

"In your terms, I think he'd count as well hard," said Peter. "Before he came to Cortesia, he was a priest in the Central American Republic during the counter-revolutionary war. The village where his church was, was attacked by the US-backed paramilitaries, trying to overthrow the revolutionary government, which Bill supported, because it was into land reform and literacy programmes and democracy in the workplace. A couple of his own priest friends were ministers in the government. Bill and his housekeeper held off the attack from the presbytery kitchen with a machine gun. He's a good shot, he had plenty of ammo, and the paras gave up and withdrew. Just as well. Bill told me about what they did to people in villages they took. They used chain saws. The only purpose was to demoralise people, to prove that nobody could stand up against Uncle Sam and his 'Boys', as they called themselves. Bill doesn't agree with violence, but in certain circumstances, he's willing to use some to prevent something much worse."

"He's well hard, then."

"Exactly," confirmed Peter.

"Good geezer," concluded Mario.

There was, as Peter had suggested, a dance in the town that evening. People gathered in the town square at dusk, and a local band played until far into the night. Fiery home-distilled rum was drunk and people ate roasted goat with yucca and plantain. But the people were not celebrating the arrival of the Spanish conquistadors in the Americas. They were celebrating one another and their life together, with all its joys and sorrows.

Peter advised Kerry and Mario to be careful to avoid water, or anything washed in water that had not then been cooked, as the water supply was not safe, if your system was not well used to it. Anyone who could afford to do so bought purified water in large containers from a truck that made weekly deliveries. But, unless you knew that the water was purified water, it was safer to avoid it if you wanted to avoid a stay in hospital.

Peter introduced his friends to many of the local people, but Kerry was too tired to make much conversation and somewhat distracted by a desire to spend time with Hannah, who for some reason was not in the square. He retired to bed about midnight, and Mario, who of course needed interpretation to be able to converse with anyone, returned soon after. They were tired enough to fall asleep, despite the sound of highly amplified accordion music wafting through the open windows from the square, and the town's leading singer lamenting, "She left me, she left me and my heart is breaking, my heart is breaking, life has lost its charm and I shall die of grief." Despite the words, the tune was so lively that only the most resolute melancholic could be sad.

Five: Kerry meets the Mayor

Hannah had been in San Martin de Porres with Patsy and Alison. The residents had invited them to their celebration, because they feared it might be their last before they had to leave their village. They had just learnt that the next week, they were to hand over their land, legally and formally, to the mining company, despite the fact that the company had still provided no alternative land to which to move.

Hannah and the Sisters returned to Romania the following morning, and came to the priests' house to explain.

Patsy was a tall, thin, grey-haired woman in her late sixties. She wore an expression of deep concern, but she smiled easily and her pale blue eyes were kind. Alison was in her mid-forties, short, solidly built, square-faced, with short, dark brown hair. She looked determined and efficient, and Kerry thought that she would be much better to have as an ally than a foe. They both wore knee length shorts and pale t-shirts, and each wore a small wooden cross on a cord around her neck.

"Juan Pablo's coming into town today to try to see the Mayor," said Patsy. "We should go with him to see if we can get them to delay this *entrega de tierras*. Juan Pablo's trying to get hold of Gabriel to see if he can try some legal manoeuvre to get it stopped."

"We'll certainly go with him to the Mayor's office," said Bill. "We can make out that Kerry and Mario have come specially from London because of this, and that there'll be international condemnation if they go ahead. It's stretching the truth a bit, but it might impress the Mayor. We need them all to think they're biting off more than they can chew.

"Kerry and Mario, Juan Pablo is the President of the Community Relocation Committee at San Martin de Porres. Gabriel's their lawyer," said Hannah.

"I'll go up to San Martin on Sunday and celebrate Mass," said Bill. "I was going to go to Santa Rosa this weekend, but maybe I can go there the weekend after. Peter, you'd better stick around here in town to do the Mass. Kerry and Mario might want to come with me to learn what's going on around here."

Juan Pablo Ramirez arrived at the priests' house around midday, together with Gabriel Garcia Araujo. Juan Pablo was tall and very dark skinned, with short hair and a wispy beard. He wore faded jeans, sandals and a blue cotton shirt open at the neck. Gabriel, whose European features and tawny skin proclaimed his mixed Spanish and Indigenous descent, was dressed in highly polished brown patent leather shoes, sharply creased beige trousers, a neatly laundered white shirt, bright blue tie and white cotton jacket. His thick, greying black hair reached his jacket collar at the back of his neck, and a luxuriant moustache covered his top lip. They both greeted Bill and Peter warmly, embracing them, and then shook hands with Kerry and Mario. "Delighted, my friends!" said Gabriel, with enthusiasm. "At your service, sirs," said Juan Pablo, with deeply courteous diffidence. "Now, I have greater hope," he said, "because you two English gentlemen can carry word back to England and to the world about what is happening to us, and then these English mining companies will make sure that we receive justice."

"Well, let's see, Juan Pablo," cautioned Bill. "None of us has a magic wand. We must do what we can."

"We need allies outside our country," replied Juan Pablo. "We are few, and poor, and the Government and the companies are powerful and rich. We need people to carry our voices to the places where these decisions are made, so that we will be heard."

They sat and drank hot, sweet *tinto,* while discussing what they should tell the Mayor. Gabriel had made an appointment to see him at 2pm. Around 1pm, they all wandered over to the café for lunch.

Some time after two, they crossed the square to the Mayor's Office, passing the armed guards on the door and announcing themselves at reception.

"Your Mercies are early," the receptionist told them. "The Mayor is at lunch."

"Our appointment was for 2pm," replied Gabriel, "and it is already a quarter past two."

"Your Mercies are early," repeated the receptionist. "Your Mercies will have to wait."

They took seats and waited.

Shortly after three, the Mayor returned with his two bodyguards. The Mayor was clearly of African descent, but was much paler than Juan Pablo, clean-shaven and dressed in immaculately pressed shirt and trousers like Gabriel, though without the jacket and tie.

"Your Mercies are very prompt," he said to Gabriel and Juan Pablo. "I am very busy today, so it is lucky Your Mercies are here already as I do not have much time."

"It is very kind of Your Mercy to make time for us," said Gabriel.

"We are much obliged to Your Mercy," added Juan Pablo.

"Allow me to introduce our delegation," said Gabriel. "The Fathers Bill and Peter you know. They have explained our situation to their fellow countrymen, and distinguished human rights organisations in London have sent their representatives to see for themselves what is happening here and make a full report of it to their government, and to the British companies seeking to buy the Valle Negro mine. I present to Your Mercy, Mr Kerry Ahern and Mr Mario Rankin."

The Mayor looked most uncomfortable, but shook hands politely with Kerry and Mario. "Delighted," he said, unconvincingly. "Permit me to introduce myself. I am Jorge Asustado Poltron, Mayor of the Municipality of Romania in

131

the Province of Caribe in the Republic of Cortesia. I am honoured to receive such a distinguished international delegation," he said, "and in order to show Your Mercies the respect which Your Mercies deserve, I am going to ask our municipal attorney to sit in on our meeting, as she may have helpful observations to offer. One moment, please." He retreated down the corridor leading off the reception area, knocked once on a door and disappeared from view. Two minutes later, he returned with a rather short and generously built woman of unmistakably European ancestry, wearing a knee-length turquoise dress, matching high-heeled shoes and a delicate gold necklace, bearing a small crucifix adorned with tiny emeralds.

"Allow me to present to Your Mercies our honourable District Attorney, Mrs Isabela Yosefina Alto Delgado de Moron."

"And of her three surnames, only that of her husband is appropriate," observed Bill in English out of the side of his mouth to Kerry, who struggled not to laugh.

"Good afternoon," she said, nodding to the visitors with a brief, cold smile and without offering her hand or indulging in the usual pleasantries.

The Mayor ushered them into his office, taking his seat behind a large, well-polished desk and indicating the seats around the edges of the small room with a delicate hand gesture. The room was air-conditioned, and the contrast in temperature with the world outside was so extreme that Kerry felt as if he had walked in one step from the tropics to the arctic. He shivered.

"Fuckin' 'ell," remarked Mario to Peter in a low voice. "Talk about freezing the bollocks off a brass monkey!"

"Well, no, I wasn't, actually," replied Peter, "and I'll thank you to watch your language."

"Well, they're not going to understand, are they?" said Mario.

"That's not the point," said Peter; then, in Spanish, he explained to the Mayor, "My colleague Mr Rankin will need interpretation, as he does not speak Spanish, so with Your Mercies' permission I shall interpret for him quietly."

"Your Mercy is most welcome," replied the Mayor. Mrs Alto inclined her head slightly, which Peter took to indicate consent.

"Your Mercies have asked to speak to me about the planned handover of the meadow known as San Martin de Porres to the Valle Negro Mining Company SA," said the Mayor. "Please explain your concerns."

Juan Pablo began. "As Your Mercy knows, San Martin de Porres is not a meadow, but a village in which our families have lived these past two hundred years since our ancestors fled slavery in the great cities on the coast. Many of us have written title to our land. We are willing to move to new land, if the company or the municipality is willing to provide us land as productive as the land we are being asked to leave. Until such time, we are not willing to leave, as we have nowhere to go and will be forced into a life of penury and desperation. For the love of God, and for the honour of our patron saint, I ask Your Mercy not to proceed with this handover of land."

Mrs Alto answered curtly. "You have all been offered financial compensation by the company, and most of the villagers have accepted it. It is only a hard core of recalcitrants who are insisting on land."

Gabriel jumped in. "With your permission, Juan Pablo," he began, receiving approval with a nod from his friend, "I must explain two fundamental legal issues, a financial matter and a matter of international convention. First, the fact that the land has been incorrectly designated a 'meadow' in the papers filed with the National Lands Office for the application for this handover of land invalidates the permission granted by that Office. Second, the community is demonstrably and indisputably a community of African descent. Therefore, it has the right, under the Constitution of this Republic, to a process of prior community consultation over any major project which affects its lands or livelihoods, before such a project can go ahead. No such consultation has occurred, rendering any handover of land unconstitutional. Third, the amounts of money offered to landholders within the village were very much below the true market value of their properties as productive farmland, let alone as land containing one of the most valuable coal deposits in the world. The company took advantage of residents' lack of knowledge of such matters to pressure them into accepting valuations that were, in fact, unacceptable. Fourth, it is internationally accepted best practice, that wherever a farming community is required to move because of a major development project, such as a mine, they must be provided with agricultural land of equivalent or better value in terms of its fertility. Financial compensation alone can never be offered as a substitute for this. Under current circumstances, if this handover of land goes ahead, it will undoubtedly be challenged in the law courts in this country and in international fora, and this would bring our noble republic into disrepute, a consummation which Your Mercies must surely wish to avoid."

"Your Mercy misunderstands," objected Mrs Alto. "The meadow occupied by the settlement of San Martin de Porres contains not only householders with written title to the land, but a large proportion of squatters, who never registered their landholdings and therefore have no rights either to the land or to compensation for that land. As for those who do possess some legal title to their land, it would be quite wrong for me – as it is for Your Mercy – to object to the level of financial compensation which they have accepted from the company. This would be to pry into matters confidential to the two parties concerned, and to imply a criticism, both of the integrity of the company and of the decision-making capacity of the householders, who I am sure are all most grateful to the company and highly satisfied with the generous compensation they have received."

"But Your Mercy," interjected Juan Pablo, "the families who have received compensation so far have not even been paid sufficient to buy houses, let alone land, and they have had to move into the already overcrowded homes of relatives and friends, wherever they can find a welcome, sometimes very far from us, on the coast or even in La Esperanza."

"And the company, in its generosity, has, I understand, paid for schooling for at least one of these families, now living in a civilised dwelling in the most beautiful city of Nueva Gibraltar," observed the lawyer.

"Indeed it has, Your Mercy. But the family has no money for clothes, or shoes, or food, or medical care for their sick baby. So, although the two older children are attending school at the company's expense, all the family's other expenses are being paid for by those of us still living in San Martin, and we have little enough for our own needs now."

"All the more reason to move to places of greater economic opportunity."

"If I may return to the matter of the handover of land, Your Mercies," resumed Gabriel, "I must insist, that given the legal irregularities involved, the municipality postpone it."

"This is not possible!" declared the Mayor, becoming quite flustered. "We have absolutely no power to postpone it! Our hands are tied! And why? Because the National Land Office would censure us! Because the Office of the National Inspector of Government Departments would censure us! Because the company would sue us! Because the foreign buyers of the mine may withdraw from the purchase! This, we cannot allow to happen, and why? Because, one, both national and provincial governments would lose a phenomenal quantity of money in overseas investment, and two…"

There was clearly no two. The Mayor simply petered out.

"Who is this fucking tosser?" inquired Mario. "He's asking for a fucking knuckle sandwich."

"Your colleague has a question?" asked the Mayor.

"He was just asking for clarification of what I had translated," replied Peter.

"Careful, Mario," whispered Kerry. "They'll understand the sentiment whether or not they understand the language."

"Well, the tosser's getting on my fucking tits," replied Mario.

"But surely, Your Mercies cannot intend the people of San Martin to be thrown into penury," suggested Father Bill, knowing full well that, even if they did not intend such an outcome, neither the Mayor nor the District Attorney cared what became of the villagers. "I certainly can't remain indifferent to it myself. I am their pastor, their parish priest. They are my parishioners and I have a responsibility to them."

"What you fail to understand, Father," replied Mrs Alto, "is that these people are primitive. They stand in the way of progress. We are actually helping them by removing them from their land. It is necessary for progress that this link between a man and his land be broken. Only then can he be free to move around and sell his labour in the market economy. The mine is progress for our province and for our country. It links us into the world economy. These peasants don't care what is happening with the world economy. They simply live off their own land, selling their small surplus in towns like this, and it doesn't matter to them whether shareholders in Europe or North America are making a profit on investments, as long as they and their families continue living well from their own ancestral land. It is a very selfish way of life that they live, uncaring about the needs of others. It would be unfortunate if the Church were to stand in the way of progress by siding with these misguided peasants. Regrettably, the Church has too often been opposed to progress."

"But Your Mercy," objected Juan Pablo, "without farmers, nobody would be able to eat."

"Mr Ramirez," replied the Municipal Attorney, "if you and your accomplices insist on working in agriculture rather than improving yourselves through education, you will want to support the provincial government in its ambitious plans for the agricultural sector. Of course people need to eat, but your form of agriculture is the way of the past. The government intends to develop *enormous* pineapple plantations where you, and thousands of others, will be able to obtain waged labour. The pineapples will then be exported to Europe and North America, and the company owners will be able to invest their profits in more and bigger plantations producing even more food for export. This is the way of the future."

"If we export all the food," said Juan Pablo, "what will we eat?"

"We will import food, of course, and you will be able to buy it with your wages! This will link you to our friends here from overseas! They will buy the pineapples that you produce and you will use your wages to buy the flour and butter and cooking oil that they produce."

"I fear Your Mercy may be a little behind the times," interjected Bill. "Pineapples are a little old-fashioned in Europe, I am afraid. There would be a better market for a variety of fruit and vegetables that were certified as being produced without agricultural chemicals by independent farmers or small agricultural co-operatives. In England they call this 'organic' and 'fair trade'."

Mrs Alto glared at him. "Very well. We shall sell only to North America, then."

"She's asking for a bunch of fives an' all," observed Mario. "What a couple of total fucking *wankers*."

"My colleague is disturbed by what appears to him to be a fundamental lack of respect for independent small-scale farming," Peter explained to the Mayor and the lawyer. "He points out that the Prince of Wales, heir to the British throne, is deeply concerned about the conditions of peasant farmers both in Britain and throughout the world, and will be particularly exercised if my colleague explains to him what is planned for farming communities here in Caribe."

"That's a rather free translation," observed Bill, in English. Peter ignored him.

Both the Mayor and Mrs Alto looked alarmed.

"Your colleague is a friend of the British royal family?" inquired the lawyer.

"He sees the Prince of Wales frequently and the royal family communicate almost daily," confirmed Peter, since he was confident that Mario often watched the News at Ten and sure that the various royals issued numerous press releases, albeit not aimed specifically at Mario, and without doubt, never seen by him.

"Forgive me, Your Mercies," interjected Gabriel, "but I believe we should return to the matter of the mine, the expansion of which is the reason for our meeting here today. My clients are not objecting to progress, or even to the expansion of this mine. They are simply asking for their rights under the constitution and for a relocation arrangement which will allow them to carry on their way of life as a community in a different place, where they will no longer be in the way of the mine."

"Indeed, indeed," agreed the Mayor, "but we have explained that the handover of land cannot be postponed."

"In any case," added Mrs Alto, "Juan Pablo and his fellow residents are worrying unnecessarily. As you know, Mr Garcia, handover of lands is a technical matter, involving the official recognition of change of legal ownership and control of a determined piece of land. It does not mean that the people of San Martin will have to leave the settlement next week, simply that the next legal stage will have been completed, so that the foreign purchasers of the mine will have clear legal title and know where they stand. I am sure that Juan Pablo and his fellow residents will have plenty of time to pursue negotiations with the mining company afterwards, so that they can reach a solution satisfactory to all."

"Your Mercy is most kind to reassure us in this way," said Juan Pablo, "but we find it difficult now to trust the company after it has deceived us so often and so badly. We will have to see what happens. I thank Your Mercies for your time."

As they began to file out of the icy office, Mrs Alto said, "Your Mercies, those of you from the civilised world must understand the heroic efforts that the more enlightened sectors of Cortesian society are making to modernise our country, which is held back by the prejudices and laziness of the poor, and by the way they have been cosseted for too long. Do not misunderstand us. Like you, we care deeply for the wellbeing of Juan Pablo and his fellow villagers, but their fears are misplaced. They are misguided. They do not understand the progress that they are being offered. Please do not stop them from attaining the level of progress that you have attained in your own country. Think of your own way of life – you all have a nice house, a fridge, a car, a television, you have big roads and high-rise apartment buildings. Most of you never even have to see the countryside, unless you really want to, unless you choose to. Don't deny Juan Pablo and his people the chance to become as you are. He and his fellow villagers are like little children, holding on tightly to their childish toys. It is for their own good that they grow up and participate in the adult world, which you and your people have created. Don't stand in the way of progress. I know Your Mercies would not wish to do so."

They emerged into the stifling heat of the Caribbean afternoon.

"Gordon Bennett, I need a fag before I explode," said Mario.

They returned to the priests' house to discuss the next move. Gabriel said he would attempt to file an injunction, preventing handover of the land on the grounds of administrative error and unconstitutionality. If it did go ahead, he would challenge it after the fact.

The English visitors were horrified at the patronising attitude of the District Attorney and her cavalier disregard for Juan Pablo. "This is how they always treat us," explained Juan Pablo. "Today, she was more polite to me than she normally is, because you were there. They treat us like beasts of burden. If we're bearing their burdens, they tolerate us, though they make sure they pay us as little as they can; and if we're not, we're just relics of the past, who are in the way of their beloved progress. And if we question their progress, we're called guerrilla sympathisers, and then we're targets for arrest or for the paramilitaries."

Gabriel and Juan Pablo left, because it was well on in the afternoon and they needed to be home before nightfall. Father Bill explained that he would visit the community on Sunday to celebrate Mass and talk with the community about what they had decided to do, and what they needed the Church to do to assist them.

Six: Kerry sees Mass at San Martin

The road to San Martin took a roundabout route, now that the mine had cut the original highway. What had been a fairly straightforward journey of twelve kilometres, much of it on surfaced roads, was now a journey of thirty kilometres, only half of it on surfaced roads. It was necessary to go around the end of the mine to the south west, and then back up the other side. Part of the way lay along wide dirt roads, along which massive mining trucks moved at speed, throwing up enormous clouds of choking dust. The final five or six kilometres were along a rutted mud road, which even the Land Cruiser could barely negotiate. It took well over an hour to get there.

At last, after half a kilometre of dry, straight track between hedges, their way turned suddenly to the left and into a spinney of large trees, then as suddenly to the right, fording a clear stream five or six metres across, at the far side of which was the village of San Martin de Porres. It was already nearly nine o'clock, and the heat was becoming intense.

The road was flatter and firmer in the village, and it curved up hill to the left, then to the right, and the land flattened out as they approached the centre of the settlement. Here was the little church and, opposite it, the school. A narrow dirt road led up hill to the left, and Bill mentioned that a small clinic and communications centre were up there. Most of the houses lay along a broader dirt road to the right, down which Bill turned, bringing the Land Cruiser to a halt in front of a small, solidly built single storey cement-block house, painted a brilliant blue, its windows edged with bright vermilion and with a yellow corrugated iron roof. A porch ran along the whole front of the house. Large fruit trees shaded the house behind; smaller ones were growing in the front yard. Hens roamed freely inside the property's wire fence, pecking at scattered grain.

Juan Pablo stood in the doorway, smiling in welcome. "At your service, at your service," he greeted them, shaking hands with Kerry and Mario and embracing Father Bill. "*Tinto?*" he asked them. "Or would you prefer *fresco?*" They all opted for *tinto* out of concern about the impact of unboiled local well water on visiting bowels, and Juan Pablo disappeared into the dark interior of the house, while they sat on plastic chairs in the porch waiting for his return.

"When we've drunk these, we'll go over to the church and get ready for Mass, unless Juan Pablo's got something he wants us to do beforehand," said Bill. "It'll take an hour or so for everyone who wants to come to get themselves over to the church, so there's no rush."

Juan Pablo returned with his wife, Carmen, who was carrying a tray with the cups of *tinto*. She smiled broadly at them all and greeted Bill with great affection. "Ah, Father, you've brought us allies now from your country! We'll be stronger now. They can carry our voice back to your country where those companies are that want to buy the mine. Now we can open a second front in this battle!"

They each took a cup of *tinto*. Juan Pablo raised his and said, "To victory!"

"To victory!" agreed Carmen, Kerry and Bill. Mario raised his cup before sipping his coffee, but did not quite catch what the others had said, so he remained silent.

"To victory!" Kerry explained in English.

"Oh, yeah, I'll go along with that," said Mario, and smiled broadly at Juan Pablo and Carmen.

"You don't speak Spanish?" Carmen asked him.

"What's she saying?" Mario asked Kerry.

"She says, you don't speak Spanish, do you?"

"Oh, no," said Mario.

"He says no," Kerry translated.

"Aha! So 'no' is the same in English as it is in Spanish," observed Carmen.

"Yes," confirmed Kerry.

"Good!" said Carmen. "Then these English companies will understand when we say, 'No'!"

They all laughed, including Mario, not understanding the words but grasping the sentiment.

"Father," said Juan Pablo, "we'll hold a community meeting at the church immediately after the Mass, to discuss what to do on Thursday. You'll stay for it?"

"Of course," said Bill. "That's why I came today."

"It means a lot to us, your support."

"What kind of a priest would I be if I didn't support you?"

They drained their cups and walked slowly back to the church. It also was built of cement blocks, a rectangular construction some six metres wide and twelve long, with a gently sloping roof and unglazed windows adorned with ready-made concrete tracery allowing for the greatest possible combination of ventilation, shade and aesthetic satisfaction. The external walls were painted white, but the inside was richly coloured, painted with what appeared to be scenes from the life of Christ set in contemporary Caribe. Behind the wooden altar was a large mural, showing an African Christ hanging on a great tree, with images of oppression – tanks, bombs, armed soldiers attacking farming people, well-dressed people in large cars driving past thin people dressed in rags – at his feet. Images of peace and prosperity were depicted above him on either side, rural people walking hand in hand under trees covered in fruit, children playing among flowers, a mountain cougar asleep beside a pair of goats. It was just like the wall hanging in Peter's old room at the seminary. To the right of the altar was a statue of St Martin de Porres, the freed slave, who was patron of the village, and to the left, a statue of the Virgin Mary, her skin as black as that of the villagers. Rough wooden benches stood in rows on the concrete floor.

"We built this ourselves," said Juan Pablo proudly. "My cousin Jaime painted it with the help of his sons. But we had to buy the statues, because none of us can carve wood."

"It's really beautiful," said Kerry.

"Thank you. We are pleased with it. We finished it just before they told us we were going to have to move. We keep it clean and tidy as a gesture of defiance."

Villagers began arriving for the Mass. Children ran in and out of the church, laughing and playing. Two young men, Juan Pablo's oldest son, Enrique, and Gustavo Castro, another member of the Community Relocation Committee, came in with a small accordion and a guitar, and began practicing the music for the Mass. Shortly afterwards, they were joined by two young women, Yildiz and Julia, who sang. After perhaps an hour, several dozen people had gathered, and Bill put on an alb and a brightly coloured stole, lit two candles on the altar and invited the musicians to begin.

The opening song had a haunting chorus, "I will follow you always, wherever you go." Kerry had heard it once before. It was a popular modern love song, but here it was applied to Christ.

When the song ended, everyone crossed themselves, saying, "In the name of the Father and of the Son and of the Holy Spirit, Amen."

Bill said: "Whenever we gather for Mass, we gather with joy, because we remember and make present the victory of Our Lord Jesus over death. But we gather today also with sadness and perhaps with trepidation, because we don't know what will happen this coming week. We need to be strong and united in the face of oppression. We begin the Mass by considering how we may have failed to offer each other the love and solidarity that God asks of us."

He was silent for a while, praying with closed eyes. Then he said, "For the times when we have hated those who do us wrong and wished to do to them what they do to us, we pray, Lord, have mercy."

The people replied, "Lord, have mercy."

"For the times when we have given in to the worse sin of inaction in the face of oppression, apathy in the face of the denial of our own dignity and that of our community, failure to stand up for our own rights and those of our people, we pray, Christ, have mercy."

"Christ, have mercy."

"For the times when we have committed the even worse sin of turning against one another, rather than standing together in the face of injustice, we pray, Lord, have mercy."

"Lord, have mercy."

"May the God who is just and compassionate forgive us our sins, strengthen in us our will to do what is right, enable us to stand united in the face of oppression, and bring us at last into the Reign of God."

"Amen."

The musicians sang a song from a Central American Folk Mass. "Jesus Christ," they sang, "identify yourself with us. Lord my God, identify yourself with us. Jesus Christ, offer us your solidarity; not to the oppressor class, which exploits and devours the community, but to our people, thirsting for peace."

Kerry translated for Mario. "Gordon Bennett!" exclaimed his friend. "Can you imagine them singing that at the seminary? It would give some of them jokers a heart attack!"

After the Bible readings, Bill invited Dona Isabela to share her thoughts. Dona Isabela was the oldest woman in the village and it seemed that she was viewed as a wise woman, sought out for her insights and her cures. Dona Isabela stood up and walked slowly to the front of the church, leaning on a walking stick. She turned around to face the people, standing in front of the altar.

"The Bible tells us all about how God led the people out of slavery into a Promised Land," she said. "That's what happened with us. Our ancestors were led out of slavery and they found this place, our Promised Land, fertile and healthy. The Bible also tells us about how God was born on earth with the help of Our Lady. Jesus was God on earth, and he grew up in a small rural town like ours, so he knew what it was to live from the soil and work with his hands. He was poor himself and he stood up for poor people like us against all the people oppressing them, religious authorities and state authorities, who treated the poor as beasts of burden and as if they had no intelligence. That's how we're treated here in Caribe. Jesus stood up for people's dignity, so the authorities killed him, and everyone was too scared to stick with him to the end, even his friends. We've suffered from divisions too, and some of us have given up hope and sold out, while others have stuck with the Relocation Committee, and it looks as though we're approaching some kind of crisis with this handover of land this week. But Jesus rose from the dead, and whatever they do to us, we will rise too. We are brothers and sisters of Jesus. We are children of our Father God and our Mother Our Lady. Whatever they do to us, we must stick together, and never give up hope, because if Jesus rose from the dead, we can reach a better future whatever they do to us. And we've got San Martin de Porres here praying for us, a freed slave like our ancestors, and Our Lady as well, so we're not alone. Isn't that right, Father?"

"That's right," said Bill, and Dona Isabela went and sat down. "Has anyone got anything to add?" asked Bill; but nobody spoke up. "Neither have I," said Bill. "I think Dona Isabela has said all that needs to be said, just now."

Another song was sung, and Bill continued with the Mass and the sharing of Communion. Children continued to run in and out of the church, and from time to time, an adventurous hen would strut through the open door, clucking with apparent disapproval at the lack of grain or worms on the swept concrete floor, and leaving again.

Kerry found himself weeping. It was almost as though he had never understood what the Mass was about before this hot, humid day, celebrating the rite among poor farmers, facing overwhelming odds in the struggle for their dignity and their independent way of life. He looked at Mario. His face, too, was wet with tears.

After the final song and the blessing, Juan Pablo walked to the front of the church and began the community meeting. He explained what had been said at the meeting with the Mayor – how he had refused to stop the handover of land, how the Municipal Attorney had assured them that it would not mean that they had to move yet, that it was only a legal formality, but that he did not trust her or the Mayor and did not know what to think. He also said that the village's lawyer, Gabriel, was trying to get the handover stopped, but thought he may not have enough time to do so.

Kerry could not translate everything that was being said, as the conversation moved too rapidly, and sometimes more than one person was speaking at once. Kerry could see that Mario's attention was wandering, but he needed to pay attention to what was going on.

"I'll summarise this all for you afterwards," he told him.

"Yeah, alright mate, don't worry," said Mario. "I'm going to have to learn the lingo, that's all there is to it."

Dona Isabela said, "We need to tell these visitors from England what the company has done to us, so they'll understand and can tell their people when they go back."

"Yes," agreed Juan Pablo. "Maybe you can start, Dona Isabela, and then everyone can take it in turns to say what they experienced – though we must all try to be brief."

"One day, five years ago," she began, "two guys in suits turned up in a flashy Jeep with tinted windows. They drove into San Martin, up what was then the main road, into the street down there." She pointed, indicating the street where Juan Pablo lived. "They stopped at the first house, old Don Rodrigo's house, and told him they were from the mine and that they wanted to talk to him. They bought him lunch at the café and told him that the mine needed to expand and that they would have to use some of the land where he ran his goats, but that they would pay him well for the privilege. They offered him a hundred thousand pedazos. That was more money than Don Rodrigo had ever seen or thought of in his life. He didn't know it was only a tiny fraction of the value of his property. The company men told him he just needed to sign a document they had with them, and then they could give him the money. He couldn't read, so he couldn't see that the document was an agreement to sell his house and land and his rights on common land. He told them he couldn't read, and they told him not to worry, if he could just confirm his name, they would write it down at the end of the document. They'd got an ink pad, so they told him he could just put his thumbprint by his name and it would all be legal. So, he did it. They handed him over all the money in one go, and he just about died of shock, seeing so much money in his hand. He was big friends with the mining company then, and those guys would stop by his house every time they came to San Martin after that, and drink his rum and *tinto*.

"But the next door neighbour, Gustavo, could read. When they came to his house, they sweet-talked him into accepting money for sharing his pasture, but when they brought out the document for him to sign, he said, 'Hey, that's an agreement to sell up! I'm not doing that at that price! You're joking! Clear off!' And they said, 'That's the market price. We've already established that. Your next door neighbour has agreed to sell for this price, so that's the market price. You don't get a penny more than that.' And he said, 'Then, I'm not selling,' and they said, 'You've got to. If you don't sell up, we'll get your property anyway, and you'll have nothing to show for it,' and when he still refused, they said, 'You'll regret this,' and a few nights afterwards, half a dozen big guys pulled up in another flashy Jeep and walked straight into his house and told him that if he didn't sell his property that very moment for the price they were offering, they were sure his widow would sell at that price the next day. So he sold up, and they left and went to Romania to live with his wife's sister's family. Before he left, he told old Rodrigo what had happened, but Rodrigo couldn't believe it. He carried on thinking he'd struck lucky.

"The bastards carried on like this day after day for a month. Some people thought these guys were angels in disguise, giving them all this money. Even if they could read, they didn't understand the sales documents. They were in technical, legal language and people thought they were just agreeing to share their pasture land, because that's what the suits told them. Others knew these guys were snakes in the grass and refused to sell, and they all got threatening visits, so some took fright and agreed to sell. Some left immediately.

Others stayed, but you could tell they were frightened. And some of us just refused to sell. When they came to my house, my husband told them to leave, because what they were doing was against the law and he would not talk to them without a lawyer present. They could see they'd picked a difficult one and must have thought they'd come back for him another time, because they just left and carried on through the village trying to persuade people to sell. My husband and I went 'round all the houses telling people what was really going on — we hadn't really understood before they came to us — and telling people not to agree to sell. There were still a few people who didn't believe us, but most people did and refused to sell even when threatened, and the suits stopped coming then. We found a lawyer, Gabriel, and he explained to us that the whole exercise really was illegal, because as people of African descent, we had communal rights. Of course, once the company got wind of that, they started denying that we were of African descent. As far as they are concerned, we are just farmers, so the Government refuses to recognise our legal status. But look at us! We're all different shades of black! Anyone with eyes can see we're of African descent!

"Anyway, then they started coming to take possession of the properties they'd bought. A working party just turned up one day and started putting up posts around the edges of properties they'd bought, and linking them up with plastic tape, red and white plastic tape. They started with Don Rodrigo's house. He was out in the fields at the time but he came back just as they were finishing. 'What are you doing in my house?' he asked them. 'It's not your house any more, old man, it's ours,' they said. Don Rodrigo was thunderstruck. He sat down there in the street and had a stroke right then and there. He never did recover. He only lived another six weeks. In a way, it spared him suffering. He had spent all the money they gave him, bought some new seed and livestock and other supplies. He didn't realise that was it, that was all he had to live on, once he'd lost his land. To add insult to injury, the company then bragged about how it had helped Don Rodrigo, that they'd taken him in their own vehicle to the hospital that they financed, that they did this and that for him in his final weeks and they were so kind, that they never even charged him for it – or his widow. They put all this in their glossy magazine that they come out with every month. His widow lasted another three months, then died of a broken heart. I was there when she died.

"After a couple more years, my husband died. I think he'd have lived a good ten years more if it wasn't for all the stress the company put us under. They killed him, just as surely as if they'd shot him."

In the end, it was decided that, even if the legal handover of land meant they were required to move out, they would all refuse. They would hear what the Municipal Attorney and the company had to say, but whatever it was, they would return to their houses and simply, peacefully, refuse to move out. Nobody would accept a payoff from the company, however much they were offering, until and unless there was the guarantee that the whole village could move to new, productive land. Even if the company brought bailiffs and threatened them, they would refuse to move from their homes, and would carry on tending their crops and livestock while Gabriel found another legal manoeuvre, and while the visitors from England found ways to make the English companies see sense. They would only move once new land had been bought by the company and a new community constructed there at the company's expense. Before that, they would not budge.

Seven: Kerry accompanies the community

On the day of the handover of land, the whole parish team and their English visitors left just before dawn to travel to San Martin de Porres. They arrived an hour after sunrise. The village seemed deserted. The two land cruisers pulled up in front of Juan Pablo's house. He came to his front door with his customary smile, and called a greeting to them as they stepped out of the vehicles.

"Where is everybody?" asked Bill.

"Everyone is in their houses," answered Juan Pablo, "ready to resist any attempt to remove them. Patricio from the CCN is staying with Gustavo. Gabriel is here in my house. He has not yet been granted an injunction, so he intends to mount a legal challenge here when the District Attorney and the company's lawyers arrive. We will stand firm, and see what they will do."

Gabriel emerged from the house in a state of sartorial disorder, drying his freshly shaved jowls with a small towel, and greeted them cheerfully. Carmen brought them all *tintos*.

"The judicial authorities have not refused my application for an injunction," explained Gabriel. "They have simply not responded. I imagine this is because they realise that it is sound and there is no legal reason to refuse it. They will, therefore, leave it until after the legal handover has been completed and then declare the injunction application out of time, because the handover has already occurred. I will, therefore, put the same arguments to the District Attorney today, and see whether she has the effrontery to refuse another formal application. If she does, we will appeal after the event. There is always something we can do."

"What should we all do?" asked Patsy.

"It would be good if you could each go to people's houses and stay with them," said Juan Pablo. "Then, if the company sends officials 'round to try to threaten people into leaving their homes, they will see that there are outside witnesses to everything going on. It may scare them into withdrawing."

This was agreed. Patsy, Alison, Hannah and Peter were to go to families living in the four extremities of the village, while Bill stayed with Juan Pablo, Carmen and Gabriel in the centre. It was agreed that Kerry and Mario should accompany members of the pastoral team, so Mario went with Peter and Kerry with Hannah, glad of the opportunity to spend more time with her.

Kerry and Hannah chose to go to Gustavo Castro's house at the south end of the village. They walked back up the main street past the church and the school, and up the hill past the clinic and communications centre, both of which looked empty and disused. "The Municipality closed them down last year," explained Hannah, "as a way of pressuring the people to leave. They withdrew funding for the school as well, but the teacher, Fidelia, decided to stay and work without pay, out of commitment to the community. She stays in the school and everyone brings her food, so she doesn't have to worry so much about the lack of money. Everyone helps to do cleaning and maintenance at the school, too."

Gustavo, his wife Chaio, their oldest daughter Celia, and Patricio from the CCN, were sitting on the porch in front of their bright orange cement-block house. They greeted Kerry and Hannah warmly, and Celia went indoors to brew fresh *tinto*.

"It brings me joy, that at least in this part of the country, the Catholic Church is with the people," declared Patricio. "In very many places the Church is indifferent or worse. But here, we are allies."

"It's a real shame when an institution, supposedly dedicated to following Jesus of Nazareth, ignores everything he stood for," replied Hannah.

"Religion has always been used by the ruling class to dominate the people," said Patricio.

"But there's usually been another religious current running alongside that, one of solidarity with the poor, even if it's only been practiced by a minority within the official Church," replied Hannah.

"You are right," said Patricio. "In any case, here we have the objective fact that you, the representatives of the Catholic Church, are in solidarity with the people rather than with the ruling class."

"Well, I wouldn't say we are representatives of the Catholic Church any more than Gustavo or Juan Pablo or Dona Isabela are. We all make up the Catholic Church."

"But you and the Sisters and the clergy are the official representatives of the hierarchy."

"Goodness, I wouldn't put it that way, either. But I see what you mean."

"Anyway, to me it is good when Catholics like you and people like me can work together in the service of the people. We need the greatest possible unity in the struggle for justice in this country."

Celia returned with the *tintos*.

"I don't really understand politics," said Gustavo, "but our community understands unity, and justice, and friendship, and loyalty, and courage, and we appreciate all the support that Your Mercies give us."

Chaio agreed. "Yes, sirs, yes, madam," she murmured, nodding.

"Ah, my friends, I have spoken to you before about this formal language. Just call me 'you'."

"Me too," said Hannah.

"But here is our friend from England, whom I have not met before, and I must show him the usual courtesies, said Gustavo."

"Please," said Kerry, "do as Patricio suggests. 'Your Mercy' is too grand for me. Let me just be 'you' as well."

"Well, we know you now," said Chaio, "so you can just be 'you'."

"Good," said Kerry. "Then I can relax!"

They laughed.

"Listen!" exclaimed Celia. "What's that noise?"

They fell silent. From the other end of the village came a low rumbling sound.

"Kerry, you and I should go check it out," said Hannah. "I don't like the sound of that."

"I will come too," said Patricio.

They began to hurry down the dusty street towards the school, unable to see the centre of the village for mango trees and bends in the road. People were standing in their front yards now, looking down towards the centre of the village.

Then, up the street, Juan Pablo's younger son Alberto came running, hot and breathless.

"Come now! All come now!" he called out. "The company has come with armed men and with bulldozers! They've started on the trees and crops at the far end of the village, just destroying everything!"

People hurried into the street and began to run together towards the centre of the village. There, in front of the church, was a line of four large new Jeeps with dark tinted windows, with a pick-up truck at each end of the line, in each of which sat half a dozen or so uniformed security guards carrying automatic weapons. Lining the main street, the street leading down towards the mine, were dozens of police with riot shields and large batons. A small table and chair had been set up outside the church door, and around it stood a group of people among which, as he came closer, Kerry could see Gabriel, Juan Pablo, Bill and Mrs Alto Delgado de Moron, together with two men in suits. At the table sat a man with a manual typewriter. Around this group of people, the residents of San Martin were beginning to gather quietly, drawn from their houses by the wholly unexpected arrival of machinery and armed police. Kerry and Hannah pushed as close as they could to the table in an effort to hear what was going on.

"...the invalidity of Your Mercy's application for an injunction," the District Attorney was saying. "The shortness of time meant, as Your Mercy knows, Mr Garcia, that Your Mercy should have applied for an emergency injunction, not an injunction, but Your Mercy failed to write the word 'emergency' on the application, so Your Mercy cannot be surprised that the judicial authorities have failed so far to consider it."

Gabriel was clearly flustered. "I should have thought that the fact that the application clearly referred to a legal formality planned for today's date would have made it obvious that it was an emergency application, even if I had failed to write the word 'emergency' at the top of the application, as is customary. In any case, the operations now taking place around us are most irregular. A handover of lands does not justify the presence of armed security guards, police and bulldozers, still less the destruction of the trees and crops at the far end of the village."

One of the men in suits spoke up.

"Mr Garcia, the company has lost patience with your endless legal manoeuvring, and as a result, my colleague and I, as the company lawyers assigned to this case, made an application to the District Attorney last night to clear the village on the same day as the formal handover of lands. The company is keen that this should take place as quickly and efficiently as possible, and with the minimum of distress to residents. Hence the need for sufficient security personnel to deter resistance."

"This is outrageous!" exploded Bill.

"And you are...?" inquired the company lawyer.

"The parish priest of this village!" replied Bill.

"Then I should inform you," said the other lawyer, "that as a result of a separate judicial application, the company has taken legal possession of the church already, with the help of officials at the Bishops' Conference offices in La Esperanza.

"Bishop Gutierrez would never agree to such a thing," declared Bill, aflame with indignation.

"Indeed," agreed the lawyer. "Which was why we took the precaution of going over his head. He will be informed today."

"But how can the Bishops' Conference give legal possession of the church to the company?" asked Juan Pablo. "We built it with our own hands and paid for it with our own money. It is ours. How can Church officials in La Esperanza give away our church?"

"I can assure Your Mercy that they did not give it to us," said the lawyer. "They sold it to us."

"At what price?" asked Bill. "Thirty pieces of silver?"

"Your Mercy is most amusing," replied the lawyer, and laughed coldly.

Kerry felt a hot anger rising inside him, but could see no way in which he could helpfully intervene.

Juan Pablo looked devastated. "How can Your Mercies clear the village?" he asked, incredulously. "Your Mercies mean to destroy our homes?"

"The company has made clear for a very long time that the community is occupying land which is part of a legally approved mining concession, and therefore needs to move, as numerous residents have done already," said the first lawyer. "The company takes no pleasure in this necessary operation, but the community has left it no alternative."

"This is irregular," said Gabriel. "The community and its legal representative have the right to be informed of applications affecting them. We should have been informed of the company's application to clear the land, so that we could oppose it."

"Your Mercy has now been informed," replied the first company lawyer.

"Then I apply formally to the District Attorney to refuse this application!" declared Gabriel.

"Your Mercy will need to put it in writing," said Mrs Alto.

"This will be difficult, given the shortness of time," observed Gabriel.

"Your Mercy may wish to use the services of the court stenographer," said Mrs Alto, indicating the official sitting at the small table.

"Your Mercy is most gracious," answered Gabriel, and began to dictate a letter to the District Attorney, opposing the company's application to clear the village on the same day as the formal handover of lands. He mentioned the issues which had been included in the application for an injunction to prevent the formal handover of lands; the administrative irregularities, the unconstitutionality of the purchase procedures and the failure to consult the community. From time to time, the stenographer read the text back to Gabriel, until Gabriel was satisfied that he had included everything that was necessary in the letter. He checked with Juan Pablo that the letter reflected the wishes of the Community Relocation Committee. Juan Pablo confirmed that, as far as he could understand legal terminology, it did. The stenographer removed the letter from the typewriter and handed it to Gabriel, who signed it, and handed it to the District Attorney, who surveyed it briefly.

"Mr Secretary, take a letter," she commanded, and the stenographer placed a fresh sheet of paper in the typewriter.

"To Mr Gabriel Garcia Araujo, Attorney at Law, re application for refusal to grant application by Valle Negro Coal Company SA for clearance of the meadow known as San Martin de Porres, on the same date as the formal handover of lands involving the said meadow. Since Your Mercy has merely rehearsed the same reasons to support Your Mercy's application – alleged administrative error and alleged unconstitutionality – which have been rejected by this office in the case of previous applications, Your Mercy's application is consequently rejected – Cordially, Mrs Isabela Yosefina Alto Delgado de Moron, District Attorney for the Municipality of Romania in the Province of Caribe in the Honourable Republic of Cortesia."

The Secretary read back the text to Mrs Alto, who expressed her satisfaction. He removed the letter from the typewriter and handed it to her. She signed it and handed it to Gabriel. "There!" she said, smiling. "Everything is now in order." To the company lawyers, she said, "Your Mercies may now proceed."

Kerry listened with cold disgust.

Gabriel said, "I would like it put on record, that I believe that District Attorney Mrs Isabela Yosefina Alto Delgado de Moron has acted outside her powers, and to note that I shall be appealing this decision to the Provincial Court of Appeal. I would also like to inform Your Mercies, that I intend now to telephone the Municipal Human Rights Defender's Office to ask him to attend immediately."

Mrs Alto said, "Your Mercy is most welcome to call the Human Rights Defender, but I wonder whether he will have anything to do by the time he gets here. The company is most efficient in achieving what it sets out to do. Your Mercy is also most welcome to appeal the decision, as Your Mercy has every legal right to do. As to putting on record Your Mercy's belief that I have acted outside my powers, Your Mercy is again most welcome to make use of the services of the stenographer, but I consider it important to inform Your Mercy, that if Your Mercy does choose to put this belief in writing, I shall most certainly sue Your Mercy for libel. As it is, I am minded to sue for slander, since Your Mercy was unwise enough to make the allegation in the hearing of third parties. But, as Your Mercy will be aware, the penalties for libel are considerably more serious than those for slander. Now, if Your Mercies will excuse me, I need to hold a private conference with the company's lawyers to clarify a few practical matters."

The two company lawyers and Mrs Alto climbed into one of the Jeeps and disappeared behind its tinted windows.

Kerry had never before felt murderous, but he thought he would be very happy at that moment if someone were to shoot the municipal attorney dead.

Gabriel was already on his mobile telephone, trying to get hold of the Municipal Human Rights Defender in Romania.

Juan Pablo called all the residents present, and their allies, to attend an impromptu community meeting inside the church. Kerry and Hannah followed the crowd into the building. People were in tears. Patricio suggested that they attempt to walk calmly to the north end of the village, where the bulldozers were, and to form a line to block the bulldozers' way into the village. There was an objection: surely the police would attempt to stop them? But nobody had an alternative suggestion, so it was decided to make the attempt.

Hannah told Kerry she was worried about Alison, who had gone up to the north end of the village earlier. By now, Patsy, Peter and Mario had joined them by the church, summoned by Alberto. But between them and the north end, there were the dozens of armed police.

The villagers moved out of the church and into the main street. This time, Kerry and Hannah were at the front of the crowd. The security guards in the pickup trucks covered the villagers with their automatic weapons. Juan Pablo and Dona Isabela moved to the north side of the crowd, and began to walk north along the main street. The guards sprang out of the back of both pickup trucks and began to fan out around the villagers. Simultaneously, the police in front of them began to coalesce and form a line across the street, riot shields in front of them, batons at the ready. The villagers came to a halt in front of the line of riot shields.

"Your Mercies," announced Juan Pablo, "we wish to pass by in order that those of us living in the north of the village can return to their homes, and so that we can check on our neighbours at that end of the village."

The commanding officer, speaking from behind the line of riot shields, answered, "I cannot allow you to pass." He dispensed with the polite form of address. "You cannot return to your homes. You must leave the village. Your homes are to be demolished. For your own good, I cannot allow you to pass this point."

"But Your Mercy must allow us to collect our possessions from our homes, even if we have to leave our homes."

"I cannot allow you to pass this point. You must leave the village by any of the roads out, except this one that leads to the mine."

"But what of our possessions?" objected Juan Pablo. "They are few enough as it is! We must be allowed to collect them."

"You have had years to collect your possessions and leave," replied the police commander. "The company has run out of patience. Turn around and go. We do not want any casualties here today."

From behind the police line came a sudden mechanical roar, and then screaming. Kerry could not see what was happening beyond the armed men and riot shields. The villagers, alarmed at what may be happening to their friends and families, began shouting, and some of them began beating on the riot shields with their fists or the flats of their hands. One policeman responded with a savage blow of his baton, catching Celia on her left shoulder. She staggered back, screaming and clutching at her bleeding shoulder. Her left arm hung limply. Others immediately gathered around her to protect her. "Her shoulder blade is broken!" shouted one.

Kerry turned to see what was happening behind him. He noticed Patricio with a small video camera, recording the scene. Gabriel, now off the phone, pushed his way to the front of the crowd and called out to the police commander. "Your Mercy, Police Commander! I am this community's legal representative, and I must inform Your Mercy that the Human Rights Defender is on his way and that he confirms the illegality of this operation. He was not informed of the plan to evict the villagers and demolish their houses today. This operation is in violation of the constitution of our republic."

"I am following the orders of the District Attorney, according to law," replied the police commander at the top of his voice, from behind the police line. "I urge Your Mercy to persuade your clients to withdraw so that they will remain unharmed."

"Your Mercy must allow my clients to return to their homes and collect their possessions," asserted Gabriel.

"I cannot allow that," replied the police commander, "as I believe that they would then refuse to leave their homes, and injuries would follow."

"If Your Mercy destroys my clients' possessions, a further legal matter is raised, as the order to clear the land does not encompass the theft or destruction of personal movable possessions. This can be checked quite easily in the Law Code of the Republic."

There was a moment of hesitation.

"I am willing to have my men load Your Mercy's clients' possessions in one of our trucks and take them to the police station in Romania. Your Mercy's clients can then come and reclaim their possessions from there. To prevent misunderstanding, all possessions will be handed over to Your Mercy and Your Mercy will be responsible for handing them over to Your Mercy's clients."

Gabriel looked at Juan Pablo, who nodded sadly.

"My clients accept Your Mercy's suggestion," called Gabriel.

"Then urge them to disengage," called the police commander.

"We cannot move," called out Juan Pablo, "until we know what has happened to our homes and our neighbours on the other side of this police line."

"My men are bringing your neighbours down to you now," replied the police commander.

A few moments later, the police line parted, and a line of villagers, some limping, others clutching wounded limbs, many in tears, were ushered through it. At the end of the line came Alison, covered in dust and bleeding from a wound in her arm. The police line closed behind her. Hannah and Patsy rushed to embrace her, demanding to know what had happened. "I'm okay," Alison reassured them. "I was in Florencio's house, the first one in the village. When they got done with bulldozing the crops, they told us to get out of the house because they were going to destroy it. We refused. They started bulldozing it anyway. Florencio got out quicker than I did. I just collided with some falling cement blocks. I'm okay."

"There are injured people here," Patsy called to the police commander. "Your Mercy must allow our parish team to use our two vehicles to get people to the clinic. Our vehicles are behind your police line."

The police commander agreed. Patsy and Peter were allowed to cross the line, retrieve the vehicles and return with them. As Peter climbed out of the land cruiser, Kerry called to him, "What do you want me to do?"

Peter replied, "Find Bill, stay with him, and do whatever he tells you. I've got to get these people to the hospital."

Alison, Celia and as many as possible of the other wounded villagers were crammed into the two land cruisers, and they drove off towards Romania.

Juan Pablo urged the other villagers who had just joined them to gather in the church. Others went with them, comforting the weeping and assisting the remaining wounded. Some of the villagers, enraged at what had been done to their neighbours and to their own homes further down the street, began again to beat on the riot shields, but the police stood solid as a brick wall. Kerry saw other villagers run off around each end of the police line, round behind the nearby houses and into the street beyond. He supposed they were going to see what they could salvage. Individual police officers pursued them, beating them with batons when they caught up with them and ordering them back beyond the police line again, where they staggered in to the church to join their comrades.

In the confusion, Kerry lost track of where his friends were. He assumed that Hannah, Alison and Patsy were in the church. Patricio had disappeared, and he had no idea what had happened to Bill or Mario. He followed the wounded into the church.

The statues of Our Lady and San Martin de Porres had been removed. One of the villagers said he had seen them being put on a flat bed truck with villagers' possessions.

Inside the church he found Bill, Hannah and Mario. Bill told him that Patricio was filming as much as he could of the destruction without getting himself shot. Kerry was alarmed, but Bill reassured him, "Patricio knows what he's doing. He'll be okay."

Mario looked badly shaken. "This is a fucking wind-up," he said, then, uncharacteristically, fell silent.

"I can't believe this is happening," said Hannah.

Those from the north end of the village were describing what was going on. There were at least six massive bulldozers, of the sort used in the mine, and they were just flattening everything before them; houses, fruit trees, gardens, fences. At first, they had flattened the houses with everything in them. Then, they had stopped for a while, while company personnel and police started going into the houses still standing, bringing out anything they found there and loading it onto a flatbed truck. The police had told villagers they would have to claim their possessions at the police station in Romania.

Despite Juan Pablo's best efforts, it was difficult to reach a consensus on what should be done. People were angry, demoralised and afraid. Of what use now were their years of resistance against the mine?

But Dona Isabela rallied them.

"These policemen are stronger than we are," she said. "If we attack them, we'll be beaten to a pulp. Where's the point? There have been too many injuries today already. Why torture ourselves? They're bulldozing our houses and we can't stop them. But have we lost yet? No! We've resisted this far – resisted while they divided our people by threats and bribery, resisted while they started stealing our pasturelands, resisted moving until this very day, years after they wanted us out, and we're going to go on resisting. They'll not defeat us! They may kick us out of our village, but we're still alive, so we can fight another day. They may have broken our houses but they won't break our spirit. We'll just have to resist them in a different way now, till we get justice for what they've done to us. There's no point us dying today. Then they've really won.

No, let's stay alive so we can go on with our struggle! One day, we're going to get justice. We must never give up hope. I say, let's make our stand here in this church that we built together. This is what we made together, a sign of our unity. Maybe they'll bulldoze this too, but let's make sure it's the last thing they get to in the village. People whose houses are still standing should go now and get their possessions out of their houses and on to whatever trucks these people are making available, because we've got no alternative. Then they should come back in here and join the rest of us. And we'll stay in here till they force us out or they leave."

Nobody dissented. Nobody had an alternative plan. People from the southern half of the village went off to their houses to clear them of their possessions. From the church door, Kerry saw the few who owned small vehicles loading them up with the remaining wounded and driving away. Possessions were loaded onto the company's flatbed trucks in the hope that they would be retrievable in due course from the police station. People remained at their homes until the last minute, but as the tide of destruction passed through the village, none wished to be entombed in the ruins of the homes that they had built. All, eventually, came hurrying to the church.

The Human Rights Defender arrived after an hour and a half. By that time, most of the houses in the main street, together with their fruit trees and gardens, had been destroyed. The District Attorney and the company lawyers had left. The Human Rights Defender, seeing the crowd, came first to the church, then approached the police commander, who was standing nearby. Kerry watched from the church door.

"This is most irregular!" the Human Rights Defender complained to the police commander. "This procedure should not have been carried out in this way!"

"Then, I advise you to make a written report for consideration by the District Attorney," replied the police commander.

"It is the District Attorney whom I believe to be at fault," replied the Human Rights Defender.

"Then, I advise making the complaint to a higher authority, the Provincial Attorney."

"The Provincial Attorney is the District Attorney's Father-in-Law," said the Human Rights Defender, "and I am not convinced that he will take an objective view of the matter."

"Then, I cannot advise Your Mercy," replied the police commander. "Your Mercy is free to observe this operation, but I advise Your Mercy to stand well clear of the bulldozers, in order to avoid injury."

In the church, the villagers sat in stunned silence until Juan Pablo was able to encourage them to give practical thought to where each family would go. After a few hours, Bill led them in prayers. Gabriel discussed with them his legal strategy.

By sunset, everything had been flattened apart from the church, and the air was thick with choking dust. The police commander came to the church door.

"You must leave," he said. "There is nothing here for you any more. The company needs to demolish this building."

"This building is the church that we built with our own hands," replied Dona Isabela, "and you have no right to destroy it."

"It belongs to the company now," declared the police commander. "You are trespassing."

"You would destroy a consecrated building?" demanded Bill.

"I am only following orders," replied the police commander. "We have no desire to see further injuries. Leave the building, or face the consequences."

"Where are we supposed to go at this hour?" asked Juan Pablo. "Most of us will have to go and seek places to stay with friends in Romania. We can't walk there at night. Let us stay here till the morning, when vehicles can come from town to carry the children and the old people, and the rest of us will, at least, have daylight for our walk."

"Stay, then," agreed the police commander. "But you must leave at dawn. The bulldozers will come first thing in the morning to destroy this building. You must be gone by then."

Gabriel phoned the priests' house on his mobile to inform Peter and, through him, the Sisters and the wounded villagers, what was happening at San Martin. He also asked that those with vehicles return from town at dawn to fetch those too weak to walk.

So, they stayed. They lacked food and water or any private place to relieve themselves. Without sufficient space to lie down, they tried to maintain their spirits by singing well into the night, but eventually, weariness forced them to fall silent. People dozed as they could, sitting on benches or on the floor. Kerry hardly slept at all, despite the extremity of his exhaustion. Hannah and Mario, sitting on the floor either side of him, seemed to doze intermittently.

Kerry's thoughts alternated between fierce anger at the injustice inflicted on the community and self-indulgent delight at his physical proximity to Hannah, who in her exhaustion had slumped against him.

By dawn, everyone was stirring, and people began moving outside the building to seek some shred of privacy in the surrounding wasteland to relieve themselves.

As the sun rose, Kerry heard once more the sound of an approaching bulldozer, and a pickup truck full of company security personnel drew up in front of the church. A security guard, armed with a machine gun, appeared in the church doorway. "You have ten minutes to evacuate this building, before it is demolished," he said.

Those villagers who were still inside the building filed out. Juan Pablo said, "My friends, as we agreed, we'll wait at the edge of the village for the vehicles to return from Romania, then, as many as can ride will do so, and the rest of us will spend the day walking."

Dona Isabela said, "We won't leave this place defeated. We'll sing as we leave. We'll keep our dignity." And she began to sing a song that started like a lamentation, but as the villagers took up the refrain, became a song of defiance, and they repeated it over and over as they walked across the ruined land towards the edge of the surviving vegetation. By the time they reached the trees, the church that they had built with their own hands was a pile of rubble, and a great plume of cement dust hovered over it until, as the sun warmed the morning air, a gentle breeze blowing up from the south west began to disperse it towards the north east, like the shining cloud, which in the vision of the prophet Ezekiel in the Bible, symbolised the Glory of the Lord leaving the Temple in Jerusalem.

Eight: Kerry encounters Claudia again

The day afterwards, the radio, television and newspapers were dominated by the exciting news that the sale of the Valle Negro mine to the two British multinationals had been completed, and the Province of Caribe could look forward to a time of unparalleled prosperity, as the expansion of the mine brought jobs and money flowing into the area. Coal for the world! Progress for Caribe! Privatisation and globalisation would soon bring their undisputed benefits to the province, and everyone would be happy. Bill turned off the radio in silent anger. Kerry read the newspaper and felt despair.

Peter took Kerry and Mario with him to visit the wounded in the clinic in Romania, which had benefited from a generous donation from Valle Negro Coal Company SA. Medical staff were attentive and effective in their treatment of the villagers from San Martin, but felt unable accurately to record the causes of injury. The number of 'domestic accidents' that had occurred in the village over the course of a few hours was extraordinary.

Peter confronted one of the doctors. "You know exactly why these people are injured and who is responsible!" he told him. "Why not write it?"

The doctor took them aside and told them, "If I did that, funding would be withdrawn and we would not be able to treat anyone, so it would be better to err on the side of caution."

Kerry moved on with his friends to the police station. The reclamation of villagers' possessions was as chaotic as could be expected, since San Martin's corporate looters had not troubled to label them, keep together items taken from one house, or separate those taken from different houses. Gabriel did his best to ensure that villagers retrieved what was their own, but it was an impossible task, and as the police chief had foreseen and intended, many villagers, whose possessions could not all be found, blamed Gabriel for his supposed inefficiency. He was deeply distressed, both by the injustice inflicted on his clients and the damage done to his relationship with some of them, because of the impossible situation into which he had been manoeuvred by the authorities.

But the worst of it, from Juan Pablo's point of view, was that the statues of Our Lady and San Martin de Porres were not released by the police, on the grounds that they did not belong to any villager and could, therefore, not be handed over. This caused massive offence among the people. "They have kidnapped our saints!" they said.

Not all the displaced villagers had relatives or close friends in Romania. At Bill's suggestion, they stayed for a few nights in the church, eating at the Sisters' house or in the front room of the priests' house. After a week, they were all gone – to relatives in Arroyomachete or further down the coast, or in some cases, to try their fortunes in La Esperanza.

"I don't know what to do," Kerry said. He was sitting with Bill, Peter, Mario, Hannah and the Sisters in the front room of the priests' house late one evening the following week. "Everyone from San Martin seemed to think that Mario and I could help them, but I don't know how to. I don't know anyone influential in England. I haven't a clue how to influence companies. What do they think we can do?"

"I fear they may have unrealistic expectations," said Bill. "You're from the country where the purchasers of the mine are based, and therefore, in their view, you must be able to help. They don't know how, but they assume that you do."

"I've told Mercedes what's going on here," said Peter, "but she doesn't know what to do either. The Association has no history of working with people from Caribe. To the best of their knowledge, there's nobody from Caribe living in

London. And she's so busy advising and helping refugees and low-paid workers there that she hasn't got time to think about how to influence the mining companies."

"In the States, there's an organisation that works on behalf of a whole range of religious organisations, like our Sisters," said Patsy, "and they spend their time trying to get corporations to clean up their act. Maybe there's something similar in England, and you could get in touch with them. You could even contact our colleagues in the States and see if they know of anything similar in England. Why not see what you can find next time you're in Arroyomachete at the internet café, or the Jesuits' place?"

"Of course!" cried Peter. "I mean, that's how we found out about these companies in the first place! There was that website we found with all that information about mining companies! They must know what we could do! Maybe they know of groups in London who could help! Let's go down to Arroyomachete tomorrow and see what we can find out!"

The next day, Peter, Kerry and Mario went straight to the Colegio del Caribe and found the website they had used to learn about the companies that had now bought the Valle Negro mine. Peter emailed the London-based Movement Against Destructive Mining, to ask if there was anything that they could do to help. Bill and Gabriel met them at the college. Gabriel had filed a lawsuit against the District Attorney for acting beyond her powers in allowing eviction and demolition of properties under the simple pretext of a handover of land. Bill had visited the Bishop, who had agreed to denounce the eviction to the local and national media. Gabriel had also spoken to the Human Rights Defender, who was writing a report, castigating the municipal authorities for unlawful collaboration with the mining company.

Kerry and his friends stayed at the Colegio that night, so they could check email in the morning. They received the reply they had been hoping for. The Movement Against Destructive Mining would do whatever it could to publicise what had happened, and try to find international allies. It would contact Members of Parliament and look into the possibility of legal action against the British companies which had now bought the mine. They just needed good and continuous communication from Caribe, so that they would know what was going on. Patricio's video footage of the eviction and destruction of San Martin would be invaluable. Posted on the internet, allies overseas could make use of it to prove what had been done.

Late the following afternoon, when the heat was so intense that Kerry thought the trees in the square in Romania seemed ready to expire and the air itself to explode, a battered taxi drew up outside the priests' house and Claudia stepped out, apparently unaffected by either the temperature or the humidity.

Kerry, feeling exhausted by the drama of the past few days and the oppressive heat, suddenly felt keenly alert. He sat bolt upright in the chair in the front room, from which he was observing the square.

"Your Mercy is certain that this is the house where the priest lives?" she asked the taxi driver.

"I am certain, Your Pretty Little Mercy," he replied.

"Thank you," she said, smiling fetchingly, and handed him a ten thousand pedazo note.

"Always at your service!" he replied, and drove away.

The door of the priests' house was open, as usual. Kerry darted from his chair and into the small bathroom, just off the corridor leading from the front room. He nearly closed its door and stood perspiring in the suffocating gloom, watching the front room.

Claudia called out, "Is anyone here?"

Bill emerged from his office. "Can I help Your Mercy?" he asked.

"I hope so, Father. I am looking for a gentleman from England, a Mr Mario Rankin."

"I am afraid Mr Rankin is away today and won't return until late evening. Can I tell him that Your Mercy called?"

"I have come rather a long way to see him," said Claudia. "All the way from the capital."

"From Arroyomachete?"

"No, from La Esperanza."

"Oh my goodness! That was, perhaps, a little unwise. How could Your Mercy be sure he was here?"

"I am afraid I had to make a decision rather quickly, Father. You know how things can be in this country."

"Ah. Is there some trouble?"

"I am afraid there is, Father."

"Of a personal or political nature?"

"Sometimes they are one and the same, Father."

"But what is the connection with Mario? He is a visitor. He has never spent time in La Esperanza."

"I met him on the plane from London, Father. We sat together. We became friendly."

"Ah, I see." Bill paused. "I am afraid, I have to ask Your Mercy whether Your Mercy's presence constitutes any kind of threat to my guest from London."

"It does not, Father. Nobody in La Esperanza knows of his existence, and those who have a quarrel with me have no idea where I am."

"I see."

"Would you mind if I wait for him here?"

"I would not wish to violate the laws of hospitality, Your Mercy. Please make yourself comfortable. May I bring Your Mercy water? *Tinto*? *Fresco*?"

"I would like a glass of water, please, Father. It is very much warmer here than in the capital."

"Today, especially," agreed Bill. "It is the kind of day when it is difficult to think, let alone work." Bill paused. "I assume that, if Your Mercy met Mr Rankin on the plane, Your Mercy is also acquainted with Mr Rankin's friend Mr Ahern."

"No, Father, I don't believe I have met him."

"Really? How peculiar! They were travelling together."

"Mr Rankin was sitting on his own on the aeroplane. Perhaps Mr Ahern was sitting somewhere else."

"Ah, that will be it. I mention it because Mr Ahern is in the house..." Bill looked around. "At least, he was in the house, last time I looked. Kerry!" he called, and paused. Kerry remained absolutely silent. "Well, evidently he has gone out. I thought he could perhaps keep Your Mercy company, while we await Mr Rankin's return. I fear I must attend to some paperwork. I shall bring you some cold water. Then, if Your Mercy will excuse me, I shall return to my office for a while."

Claudia took a seat, and Kerry, inwardly cursing the entire set of circumstances, resigned himself to a long stay in the bathroom, fervently hoping that Claudia would not need to use it before he had found a way of effacing himself, without being noticed.

Darkness fell swiftly around six, but the heat did not dissipate. Bill emerged from his office. Claudia was sitting in the dark in the front room.

"I am afraid I have neglected Your Mercy," said Bill. "Your Mercy need not sit in the dark. We have electricity here."

"I do not need light to think," replied Claudia.

"Well, it's time for supper, and we should eat," said Bill. "I will prepare some food."

"But I am causing you inconvenience, Father."

"I would be eating whether or not Your Mercy were here."

"May I help you, Father?"

"If Your Mercy would like to."

She smiled. Her brilliantly white teeth reflected the light coming from Bill's office. "Yes, of course. It would give me something else to think about. But before I do, I wonder whether Your Mercy has a bathroom that I could use?"

"Of course," replied Bill. "There is a small one just there in the corridor."

"Bother," thought Kerry. "Right, this is it." He shut and locked the door.

Claudia tried the door handle, but could not open the door. "Oh!" she exclaimed.

"Funny!" said Bill. The door handle rattled, and Kerry heard Bill's voice just the other side of the door. "Odd! The door seems to have jammed."

"Shan't be a minute!" called Kerry, realising that he was going to be discovered soon. anyway.

"What?" exclaimed Bill. "When did you come back, Kerry?"

"Er... just nipped in a few moments ago, Bill. Through the church and the side door."

"Oh, I see. You're okay, are you?"

"Fine. Slightly upset tummy, that's all."

"Oh, I see. Well, Claudia can use the back bathroom. That's okay."

Kerry heard their footsteps retreating into the back of the house. He considered whether he should leg it now or stay and face the music. He decided that, since the truth would emerge as soon as Peter and Mario returned later that evening, he might as well deal with the situation, without further delay. He unlocked the door and went and sat in the front room. Bill returned from the back of the house.

"Forgive me for saying so, Kerry, but you're behaving most peculiarly," he said.

"Really?" replied Kerry.

"You're not given to lying, yet you tell me you came into the house via the church and the side door, when the side door was locked from inside the house, and I had the only key to it in my pocket."

"Ah," said Kerry.

"You've been indoors all the time, haven't you?" asked Bill.

"Well, yes, I have," admitted Kerry.

"Hiding in the bathroom?" asked Bill.

"Yes," admitted Kerry.

Claudia returned. She caught her breath when she saw Kerry.

"Oh! Mr Green!" she exclaimed.

"Curiouser and curiouser," said Bill. "So, you two have met?"

"Yes," said Claudia. "But I did not know Mr Green was a friend of Mr Rankin's."

"Mr Green...?" said Bill, seeking further enlightenment.

"A little joke," said Kerry. "I didn't tell her my real name."

"So, you are staying here with Mr Rankin and the Father?" asked Claudia.

"Yes," said Kerry.

"And do they know about...?"

"Mario does, and Father Bill will soon," said Kerry.

"Oh," said Claudia.

"Don't worry," said Kerry. "The sooner we tell Father Bill, the better."

"Well," said Bill, "I can't begin to process whatever convoluted tale you're going to tell me on an empty stomach, so you'd better both come and help me get some supper."

Bill shut the front door. They went to the kitchen.

"Before we deal with how you two know one another," said Bill, as he began to gather ingredients for a pasta sauce, "Would Your Mercy feel able to talk to me about the troubles that have brought Your Mercy here?"

"I have fallen out with my father," replied Claudia.

"Ah," replied Bill. "I think this is not uncommon. Was it a dispute about a young man?"

"No," said Claudia. "It was a dispute about my father's money-laundering operations and corrupt misuse of his office, Father."

"I see," said Bill, rather uneasily. "What office does Your Mercy's father occupy?"

"He is a district police superintendent in L.E."

"Oh, dear. You disapproved of what he was doing?"

"I disapproved of what he was making me do. I turned a blind eye to his system of favours to criminals in return for favours to him. I even agreed to help smuggle money for him from England, because I thought, maybe once he'd got enough money for a comfortable retirement, he would give it all up. But it's made him greedier than ever, and now he wants me to smuggle money for him again, and I told him I won't. He got very angry, and told me that while I live under his roof, I will do as he says. So I left."

She began chopping onions. Kerry started on the tomatoes.

"Do you not think he will send someone after Your Mercy?"

"He doesn't know where I am. I left secretly, at night, and stayed with friends in L.E. for a few days, before flying to the south west, and then to the north. Then I got a bus along the coast to Arroyomachete. We have no relatives and no friends in Caribe. He has no reason to look for me here. I left him a note saying I was staying with old school friends in the mountains east of the city because I was feeling cross with him, but that I would be back in two weeks' time and that we could then have a discussion. That will prevent him bothering to look for me for another week, and when he realises I was not telling the truth, I shall have disappeared."

"But he is a policeman, my dear! He has contacts everywhere! Surely, he will send your photograph to every police station in the Republic, and then you will be found easily!"

Claudia looked crestfallen. "You may have identified a flaw in my plan, Father," she said. She sighed. "Then what can I do?"

Bill began frying the vegetables that Kerry and Claudia had chopped.

"We'll think of something, my dear," he said.

"I am glad you have stopped calling me Your Mercy, Father," said Claudia. "It was making me feel uneasy."

"Well, then," said Bill, "perhaps you would do me the reciprocal honour of not calling me 'Father'. My name is Bill."

"Veal," she repeated.

"Well, nearly," said Bill. "You know there is quite a clear difference between 'b de burro' and 'v de vaca' in English, and between a short 'i' and a long one."

"I know," replied Claudia, in English. "I studied in England for six months, but I still find certain sounds difficult to make."

"You speak the language of Shakespeare with consummate charm," observed Bill, in the same language. "Well, then, you go ahead and call me Veal, though it makes me feel younger than I am. 'Old bull' would probably be more appropriate, as in 'a load of'. As long as you don't call me an old cow."

Claudia laughed. "You are a joker, Father!"

"I thought we had agreed you would not call me that, daughter. And if you understand that joke, you're impressively fluent in my mother tongue."

"Thank you, Veal," said Claudia.

"Now," said Bill, "I am still in the dark about how you two met, but I confess that I am developing a suspicion, which I hope will prove to be unfounded. Can either of you explain?"

Claudia explained how and why she had met up with Mr Green.

"I fear my hope has been confounded, while my suspicion was well-founded," observed Bill. "Kerry, can you shed any light on your involvement in this matter?"

Kerry explained exactly why he had agreed to Aristides' proposal.

"Well," said Bill, "I am afraid you let your heart rule your head. What you have done was spectacularly unwise. You were probably unaware of all the possible consequences. Let's think, now. You yourself could be imprisoned for several years here in Cortesia, which would not be a pleasant experience. Depending on how the money was made in Britain, you could be subject to criminal proceedings there as well. Given that the police superintendent was acting independently of any of the criminal cartels that control both drug trafficking and money laundering, and that most of these have close links with members of the Cortesian congress, and even with several government ministers, you could perhaps be targeted by hit-men working on behalf of any of them, as a warning to those attempting to muscle in on the trade. Given that Mario innocently informed the main courier about your whereabouts, the rest of us could similarly be targeted for sheltering you, and now, for sheltering Claudia as well. Is that enough to be going on with for the moment? I may be able to think of other possibilities in due course."

"I think that's enough for the time being," said Kerry, quietly.

"I think that Peter may be a little cross with you, don't you?"

"Yes," replied Kerry. He sat looking dejectedly at the floor. Claudia was silent.

"Well, now," said Bill, "let's not be too downcast. Would you like to know why I don't think we're all going to be slaughtered?"

"Yes," they replied.

"First, I think Aristides was probably right that the amount involved was not sufficient to arouse the real animosity of the cartels, even if they find out about it, which they probably won't, because there's so much of this kind of stuff going on. And if they did get annoyed, they would be more likely to take it out on Claudia's father than on her or you."

"Oh, Veal, I hope not!" exclaimed Claudia.

"Well, my dear, I am afraid your father has been playing with fire," replied Bill. "Anyway, I am confident that nobody who might get annoyed has yet got any idea that you are here, rather than in the mountains close to L.E. Once they start looking for you, we may indeed have problems, but we've got a couple of days before that happens and I think we can work out some brilliant plan before then.

"As for legal consequences, I don't think an investigation into a money-laundering operation of this size is very likely, given all the other priorities the police are working on and the probable connections that your father will have with the relevant prosecutors. Otherwise, he wouldn't have risked it on his own account. The only problem will be if some well-placed personal enemy of your father gets wind of it, and starts sniffing around in the hope of causing him trouble. Even then, it's unlikely that you would be considered important targets, and you, Kerry, might get expelled from the country without imprisonment. Let's live in hope, anyway."

Kerry felt a great deal less hopeful than Bill seemed.

"What about Aristides?" asked Kerry.

"Well, Aristides is big enough to look after himself," said Bill. "I don't think further involvement in protecting him would be a helpful course of action, under the circumstances."

Nine: Kerry is concerned about Bill's plans for Mario and Claudia

They chatted for a while after they had eaten, but Bill wanted to visit some of the people displaced from San Martin, and Claudia was tired after her travels and clearly needed to rest. Bill phoned the Sisters and they agreed to provide her with a bed – or, rather, a hammock – for the night, so they walked together around the corner to the Sisters' house, where Bill left them. Claudia was shown the facilities of the simple house, and quickly retired to her hammock, giving Kerry a welcome chance to spend a while with Hannah. She was, of course, intrigued at the presence of the beautiful young Cortesian, but Kerry decided not to tell her everything just yet – he would await the formulation of Bill's promised brilliant plan.

Later on, on his way around the corner to the priests' house, Kerry ran into Bill, returning home from his visits. Peter and Mario were back after a day of visiting communities on the other side of the mine, beyond the former site of San Martin. Peter looked exhausted with the heat, but Mario seemed energised by their activities. They were in the front room, drinking beer. Mario, his back to the door, was in full flow.

"Who the fuck's Pik Bloemen, anyway?" he thundered. "Who the fuck does he think he is? I'll tell you who he is! I'll tell you who Pik Bloemen is! He's a *fucking cunt!*"

"I'm impressed with the lucidity and subtlety of your analysis," said Bill.

Mario turned round, and blushed. "Sorry, Father, I didn't hear you come in."

"Don't worry," replied Bill. "Is it wise my asking who Pik Bloemen is, or have I already heard all that I can expect to learn on the subject?"

"He's Anglo Australian's Vice President for Community and Public Relations," said Peter. "We met him today in Santa Rita. He was addressing a community meeting, telling the villagers about the great benefits they can expect from the company's involvement at Valle Negro, and how the company is looking forward to working with them as the mine expands. I'm afraid I wasn't as diplomatic as I might have been. I couldn't believe the man's gall. It's only a few days since the destruction of San Martin and here he is talking about the benefits of mining, about 'stakeholder involvement' and all manner of other euphemistic claptrap, when it's clear that Santa Rita's next in line for destruction."

"He was a wind-up merchant," said Mario. "Peter just told it like it is, explained to the villagers what had been done at San Martin."

"And Mr Bloemen became rather pompous," added Peter. "And said that he was confident that the handover of land had been conducted strictly according to the law of the Republic of Cortesia, that it would be completely out of order for him to comment on the laws of a sovereign state in which the company was a guest, that as he understood it, the people of San Martin had been offered very generous terms by the former mine operator, and that he regretted that they had not taken advantage of those generous terms. And that in any case, this was not the responsibility of Anglo Australian or its partner company, that it was a 'legacy issue', and that if we had concerns about it, we should take them up with the former mine operator and the appropriate Cortesian authorities. It made me sick. It's as clear as the nose on your face that Anglo Australian and North Atlantic knew full well what was going on at San Martin and encouraged the company to destroy the village because it would make it easier for them, when they took control of the mine."

"Those documents I translated certainly gave me that impression," said Kerry.

"Anyway, having ascertained that I was assistant priest in Romania, he told me that he was planning to visit you soon, as part of his programme of meetings with 'opinion formers and other leading stakeholders' in the area," said Peter.

"Goodness, that'll be something to look forward to," said Bill.

"I should tell him to fuck off, if I were you," said Mario.

"I may phrase it differently," said Bill.

"You may not need to," said Peter. "He's South African. They're not noted for their subtlety of expression."

"Let's avoid stereotyping, shall we?" suggested Bill. "I've met some very fine South Africans in my time."

"Sorry, Bill. Frightfully bad form," replied Peter.

"Well, while we wait in joyful hope for the appearing of Mr Bloemen, I need to tell you about a most interesting encounter that Kerry and I had while you were away today," said Bill.

He told them not only about Claudia's arrival, but about the content of their talk, diplomatically omitting information about Kerry's role. When he had finished, Peter and Mario looked white with shock.

"She's come to find me, then?" was all Mario could say.

"Apparently so," observed Peter. "Please tell me that when you told her you would be staying here, you did not know that she was involved in money-laundering. Or that her father was a corrupt police superintendent."

"I had no idea!" replied Mario, angrily. "What kind of an arsehole do you take me for? It was only after I'd told her where I was staying that Kerry told me that she ..." He trailed off.

"Told you that she what?" asked Peter, sharply. Mario remained silent. Kerry wiped the perspiration from his face with both hands. Peter looked at him quizzically. Bill maintained the half-smile of beatific serenity.

"I knew she was involved in money-laundering," said Kerry.

"How did you know?" demanded Peter. "And if you knew, why didn't you tell Mario?"

"I didn't know Mario would be sitting next to her on the plane! Or that he'd have charmed her senseless before we landed, and given her notice of his whereabouts!"

"Did you meet her through ARCRU?" asked Peter.

"Not directly. I met her through Aristides."

"I see," said Peter. "So that explains the peculiar behaviour at the airport. Is Aristides involved in money-laundering?"

"He was forced into it by the prison governor and the district police superintendent," explained Kerry.

"Who turns out to be Claudia's dad," added Bill.

"Yes," agreed Kerry. "But that is truly news to me."

"Now," said Peter, who appeared to have regained energy through shock and indignation, "there's one final loose end to tie up here. I recall a certain amount of bag-swapping at the airport terminal. Think very carefully indeed before you answer the next question, Kerry, because it is difficult to predict whether I shall be more angry if the answer is 'yes' or if the answer is 'no', and if this subsequently proves to be a lie. Were you also involved in couriering laundered money?"

Kerry hesitated.

"Thank you, Kerry," said Peter. "I take it that the answer is yes. Now, I am going to go for a breath of fresh air outside, because I fear the consequences of expressing the depth of my anger, both on my own physical health and on your continued physical existence. While I am gone, Father Bill will, I am sure, explain exactly what the consequences of your behaviour could now prove to be, not only for you, but for us. Thank you so much, Kerry. Thank you so very, very, very much."

Peter left the house, closing the door quietly behind him.

"I told you were behaving like a tosser," Mario reminded Kerry.

"I know," said Kerry. "And Bill has already explained the possible consequences."

"I also explained why I think they are unlikely to come to pass," added Bill.

"What are we going to do about Claudia?" asked Mario.

"You're going to go and see her in the morning," said Bill, "because she came here to see you. If I understood her correctly, she came here simply because it was a place to come to where she sort of knew somebody of whose existence her father is blissfully ignorant. However, I suspect she must be smitten with you, Mario, or she'd have thought of somewhere else to go and hide. I'm going to think about how we can help her, without hurting ourselves. Give me till midday tomorrow. Before that, please don't do anything rash."

Kerry and Mario retired to bed.

"Fuckin' 'ell, Kerry!" exclaimed Mario. "Fancy that! A really scorching Cortesian woman's come looking for me! See? I've still got the old charm!"

"Well, that'll be a comforting thought, when we're all being dismembered with chainsaws," replied Kerry.

"Don't say that! You heard Bill! That ain't going to happen."

"Let's hope he's right."

"Well, anyway, it's my duty to go and comfort the damsel in distress."

"Not now, it isn't. You'll have to wait till the morning."

They slept.

Around one o'clock in the morning, Kerry woke up and went to use the bathroom. He heard voices in the front room, and went to investigate. Bill and Peter were having a quiet laugh. They looked up when Kerry wandered in.

"Behold, the dead man lives!" exclaimed Bill.

"Peter, I'm very, very sorry," said Kerry.

"You're forgiven," replied Peter. "Though it did take three hours, two whiskies and a lengthy conversation with Bill."

"All shall be well," Bill assured them. "All manner of thing shall be well."

"I hope so," said Peter. "I do hope so."

"Oh ye of little faith!" said Bill. "Doubt no longer, but believe!"

"If you say so."

"I do say so. I also say, 'Whisky?'"

"Thanks," said Peter. "Another large one. With plenty of ice."

"Kerry?"

"Thank you. Small, with ice."

Mario went to fetch Claudia from the Sisters' house at seven in the morning, and brought her straight back to the priests' house. Bill greeted them warmly, and asked them to join him and Kerry in his office for a little chat. Peter was out visiting the clinic.

"I had some thoughts during the small hours about what we might do to assist you, Claudia," he said as they sat down. "But I realise that I need a good bit more information about your father, before we can decide on a definite plan. Is he a violent man?"

"No more so than most police superintendents," replied Claudia.

"That's not a very encouraging response," observed Bill. "Is he likely to do violence to you, or to us for helping you?"

Claudia was aghast. "Absolutely not! It is true that he has done away with a number of people who have upset him in the past, something which he knows I disapprove of very strongly, but he would never hurt me or people dear to me. He gets angry with me if I don't do what he wants, but he would never hurt me. He keeps telling me I am his queen, the light of his eyes. He has no other children, and since my mother died, I am his only family."

"Yet he would be willing to have you, effectively, arrested and returned to him by the police?"

"Yes, without doubt, because he would think he was doing me a favour, saving me from getting into trouble."

"But he is happy to risk you being arrested in London, or L.E., for couriering laundered money?"

"He was convinced there would be no problems, because he had sufficient contacts to avoid them. But it's true that his love of money rivals his love for me."

185

"There seem to be inconsistencies in his approach."

"Is that not true for most of us?"

"I suppose it is." He paused. "If you really refuse to get involved in your father's criminal activities, will he reject you?"

"No. He will get very angry and shout at me a lot. He will tell me I am a disgrace to his name and to my mother. He will drink too much whisky and sleep heavily. Then he will cry all over me and tell me I am his queen and the light of his eyes, and the only thing that makes life worth living for him."

"Not uncommon behaviour, I believe," said Bill.

"But he will keep on at me, thinking he can make me crack. Until, eventually, I either do as he says, which I am now determined not to do, or go clinically insane, or run away again. What I need is something to blackmail him with."

"Like...?"

"Well, it's no good threatening to expose him to the authorities. They are almost all involved in activities at least as disreputable as my father's, and most of those who had nothing to hide have now accepted favours from him, so they would not take action against him. But with my contacts in England, I could threaten to emigrate. It would break his heart if I did that."

"But you have not threatened it?"

"I did, once, but he laughed at me. He told me he was well aware of the difficulties of moving legally to England and staying there. He said the only way he thought I would ever do that, would be to marry an Englishman, and he knew what a pale, weak, sickly, effeminate bunch of scoundrels they all were. So he knew, he said, that I would never fall in love with one."

"That's a bit much!" exclaimed Kerry.

"Too right!" agreed Mario. "We're not all pale, weak, sickly and effeminate! I'm not, anyway!"

"No," said Claudia, looking him straight in the face.

"Mind you," said Mario, "I'm not really English. I just come from England. My roots are Irish and Italian."

"Suppose you were to tell your father that you were going to marry an Englishman," said Bill. "Would he accept it, or would he shoot him?"

"Oh, Veal, I have already told you he would not hurt anyone I care about! He would only shoot him if he upset me, and even then, he would spare him if I asked him to!"

"Splendid!" exclaimed Bill. "Well then, here's what I propose. You wait a few more days, until two weeks have passed since you left home. Then, you phone your father and tell him that while you were at college in England, you fell in love with an Englishman. You couldn't bear to tell your father, because you knew he would be worried, so you have waited to tell him until your beloved could visit Cortesia, which he has now done. You suggest that you introduce your beloved to your father, and say that your beloved wishes to ask your father's permission to marry you. Your beloved will then return to England to complete the necessary preparations for coming to live and work in Cortesia, so you can remain close to your father. Then you stress that once you are married, you could at any time go and live in England, and that if your father persists in pressuring you to run criminal errands for him, you will. Your English beloved is a scrupulous man and would be horrified to learn of your past involvement in law-breaking, and should you ever become involved in it again, he would most certainly disown you, thus breaking your own heart. Or something along those lines."

"He will not believe me."

"He will, when he sees your beloved."

"But I haven't got one."

"The Lord will provide. Indeed, the Lord has provided." He looked at Mario. Claudia blushed, giggled, and covered her face with her hands.

"Hang about!" said Mario. "You want me to get between Claudia and her trigger-happy father?"

"I thought we had just established that he wouldn't hurt her beloved."

"Unless he upsets her..."

"But you won't upset her."

187

"What happens when I don't marry her?"

"You'll be safely in England, where he can't get at you."

"But his contacts there could," said Claudia.

"There, see?" said Mario.

"But I could explain that it was I who had broken off the engagement, and that we are still great friends," said Claudia.

"But then you'd be back to square one, with nothing to restrain your father from pressuring you into criminality again," observed Kerry.

"It might buy a few months," said Bill, "and give Claudia time to think of something else. Or even convince her father that he really shouldn't get her to do his dirty work any more."

"There are other obvious snags," said Kerry. "Being married to a British citizen no longer gives a non-EU national the automatic right to live in Britain."

"Does your father know that?" asked Bill.

"I don't suppose so," replied Claudia. "I didn't know it myself. I just assumed, if you were married, you could always live in your husband's country, or your wife's."

"Not any more," said Kerry. "Immigration law is cruel."

"There is also the fact that I'm an ordained deacon," said Mario.

"What!" cried Claudia, visibly shocked. "You didn't tell me that!"

"So, it's unlikely that Claudia's father knows it," concluded Bill.

"You never told me that!" exclaimed Claudia. She sounded angry, and looked as if she were on the verge of tears. "Why didn't you tell me?"

"I... I didn't think it was important," mumbled Mario.

"Not important! Not important! Excuse me a moment," said Claudia, standing up and making for the door. As she hurried across the front room to the front door, Kerry saw her dabbing her eyes with her handkerchief.

"Oh, Gordon Bennett!" exclaimed Mario. "Now I really have upset her! I'll be back in a minute." He hurried after Claudia.

"Was it wise to plant false hopes in Claudia's mind, Bill?" asked Kerry. "Surely you could see she's smitten with him – like umpteen other women."

"Indeed, I could," replied Bill. "And that he's smitten with her."

"It'll pass," said Kerry. "It always does."

"Always?"

"Anyway, he's vowed to celibacy now."

"And from what Peter told me, he's about to be laicised for failure to keep that vow, even after a few months."

"Yes, you're right. But surely it was unwise to come up with the suggestions you made, when you could see they were interested in each other? And the whole reason he's here is that he got into a relationship with that youth leader in East Cheam, who's presumably waiting for him to return."

"Let's see," said Bill. "Claudia wants help to break free from her father. Mario obviously needs some kind of assistance in deciding what he is going to do with life. Perhaps this will clarify their thinking."

Their thinking obviously needed some time to clarify. They were gone for some hours.

Ten: Kerry witnesses a joyful engagement and a penitent's sorrow

Kerry invented some pretext to visit the Sisters' house and see Hannah, who invited him to breakfast. As he was returning, shortly after nine-thirty, a top of the range land cruiser, with dark tinted windows, pulled up outside the priests' house. It was closely followed by a pickup truck with two guards sitting in the back, cradling automatic weapons. A well-dressed Cortesian-looking man in his forties emerged from the back of the land cruiser, followed by a tall, thin, pale-skinned man of similar age, dressed in a light grey suit and dark glasses. The Cortesian knocked on the open door of the priests' house and called out, "Is anyone in?"

Kerry reached the front door from the square, as Bill appeared from inside his office. "At your service, Your Mercies," said Bill. "How may I help Your Mercies?"

"If Your Holy Mercy has a moment, Father," said the Cortesian, "may I introduce to you Mr Pik Bloemen, Vice President for Community and Public Relations for the Anglo Australian company?"

Pik Bloemen offered his right hand, which Bill shook, and a formal smile, which he returned.

"I take it you won't mind if we speak in English, padre," said Pik Bloemen, in English.

"Not at all," replied Bill, in the same language. "I speak it rather well."

"Good," said Pik Bloemen. "I don't speak much Spanish yet, and my colleague here can just about follow an English conversation."

"Come in," said Bill. "And you, too, Kerry." Kerry followed the men in to the house, introduced himself, and shook hands with them.

"May I offer you some *tinto*, or *fresco*, or anything to eat?" asked Bill.

"No, thank you, padre," replied Pik Bloemen. "We don't intend to stay long."

"Well, feel free to sit down, at any rate," said Bill.

"Thank you," said Pik Bloemen, sitting down on the edge of the chair nearest to him. His Cortesian colleague remained standing near the front door. Bill sat on the chair nearest to his office. Kerry sat beside him.

"I'll come straight to the point, padre," said Pik Bloemen. "You know that our company, along with our colleagues at North Atlantic Mining, has just taken control of the Valle Negro coal mine. We're planning to expand the mine about threefold. It'll bring many new jobs and a great deal of prosperity to the province, but of course, there'll be some temporary disruption to people's lives and livelihoods because some of the villages are going to have to be moved to new sites. It would help us to know we have your support in pursuing these changes, which will ultimately be to the great benefit of your parishioners. We see you as a key opinion former in this area, so you have the capacity to calm the unjustified fears which some of your parishioners have expressed, and help us to help them manage the transition from their current way of life to the new and better way of life which our plans will bring them."

"I'm afraid I'll take some convincing of that," replied Bill. "I was not impressed by the recent events at San Martin de Porres, at which I was present."

"It's highly regrettable that our predecessors, the Valle Negro Coal Company SA, an entirely separate legal entity from us, were forced into an action which they would far prefer not to have had to take," said Pik Bloemen. "Had the residents of San Martin been properly informed about the company's intentions, and their own options, I'm sure things would have come to a much happier conclusion. That's precisely why your assistance would be so helpful. Our intention is to come to reasonable agreements with residents of all the communities which will need to be relocated, so that the kind of actions which have been taken in the past will not have to be taken in the future."

"You speak as if recent events were distant history," said Bill. "They took place a matter of days ago – the very day before your company and your partners took ownership of the mine."

"Nonetheless, the operation at San Martin was undertaken by an entirely separate legal entity, over which we had no control. And although we are confident that everything took place strictly in accordance with the law, we have absolutely no legal liability for any mistakes or misjudgements that were made, or any infringements of the law that may have occurred."

"I see," said Bill. "Well, it's good to be clear about that."

"Yes, indeed, padre. In that context I must ask that you rein in your curate. I met him by chance in Santa Rita yesterday, and he made some immoderate – even, perhaps, inflammatory – statements about recent events at San Martin, and about our supposed moral responsibility for them. This kind of talk is most unhelpful. It sows distrust among local stakeholders, when I should have thought it was the duty of men of the cloth to sow trust. It sows fear, when people need reassurance. It sows hatred, when God's ministers should be sowing love."

"Well, I am grateful to you for your inspired words, Mr Bloemen," answered Bill. "I agree that it is our duty, not only as ministers of the Gospel but as human beings, to sow love – a duty which I find hard to reconcile with forced evictions and the violent beating of unarmed protesters. But I need to clarify that the words spoken at Santa Rita were spoken by an entirely separate clerical entity, over which I have no ultimate control."

"I am not sure that I appreciate your sense of humour, padre," said Pik Bloemen, his expression stony.

"Ah, I fear it is the curse of the British that our sense of humour is so obtuse as to be scarcely understood, let alone appreciated, outside our own shores. Alas, we are stuck with it."

"It's for you to decide what an appropriate form of guidance may be for your subordinates," continued Pik Bloemen. "But I advise that you counsel your curate to be circumspect in what he says, in case his meaning is misconstrued by persons who might be quick to take offence, even if none is intended. I understand that the laws on slander in this country are relatively strong, and usually interpreted quite generously."

"I believe you are right," agreed Bill. "On the other hand, those with good reputations to maintain in English-speaking countries may do well to bear in mind the possible impact on reputation of taking legal action against a British individual, who is expressing an opinion in a country where to do so requires a high level of courage and commitment in the first place, and where that opinion is based on direct experience of events which might not show the litigant in the best possible light. It might appear to be an unwarranted over-reaction."

Pik Bloemen stood up. "I had hoped for a rather more positive beginning to what will undoubtedly be a long and, I hope, ultimately fruitful relationship," he said.

"Ah, well," replied Bill, "nothing is beyond redemption. I'm sure that your company is determined not to repeat the mistakes of the past, so my parishioners should be assured that you will respect their wishes in full and operate to the highest conceivable international standards. I am happy to pass this assurance on to them, if you are willing to make it."

"I'm sure we shall talk again, padre," said Pik Bloemen, nodding to Kerry as he left.

When Peter returned to the priests' house, Bill had gone out. Kerry and Hannah were in Bill's office, sitting together at his desk, reading a copy of the International Finance Corporation's Operational Guidelines on Involuntary

Relocation. One of the parishioners, Magdalena, was in the kitchen, preparing lunch.

"Have you seen Mario?" asked Kerry. "I'm a bit worried about him. He's been gone for hours."

"I don't think you need worry," replied Peter, "I saw him sitting under a mango tree, at the edge of town, about an hour ago. He seemed fine then."

"What did he say? What was he doing there? And where's Claudia?"

"Well, in the order in which you asked the questions; nothing, snogging like there's no tomorrow, and half way down Mario's throat."

"Ah. They must have made up their differences."

"I suspect they are very much enjoying their differences. He seemed particularly enamoured of the differences manifesting themselves on Claudia's torso."

"Oh, my goodness. Your friend is a little forward," Hannah commented.

"A little? Have you a Master's in understatement?" asked Peter.

"I'm sorry about our friend," said Kerry.

"No need to apologise," replied Hannah. "Far be it from me to condemn young love."

"Well, what did he say when he saw you?" asked Kerry.

"As I said, he said nothing, and he didn't see me, and as far as I could see, he couldn't see anything but the visage of his beloved, and if he did see anything else, he wouldn't have cared about it."

"In a public place?" asked Kerry.

"Not very public," said Peter. "I was caught short after several *tintos* at different people's houses, and dodged into the bushes for a pee. Once I saw them, I dodged out again. Had to trot home double quick, then, so if you'll excuse me, I'll be with you in a minute." He moved towards the bathroom.

"Does Bill know this?" asked Kerry.

"That I need a pee, or that I'll be with you in a minute?"

"That Mario and Claudia are snogging in the bushes."

"Not unless he's seen them himself. I haven't seen him since I saw them. It won't surprise him though. He virtually engineered it."

"Yes," agreed Kerry. "I think you're right."

"A shrewd man, is our Bill," said Peter, as he disappeared into the bathroom.

Bill returned for lunch, followed shortly afterwards by the young lovers.

"Claudia and I have discussed your suggestion, Father Bill, and we've decided it's worth a try," said Mario

"Oh, good," said Bill. "It'll buy Claudia some time, and of course, once you go home to Britain, you can forget all about it, while Claudia carries on with the charade. Are you happy with that, Claudia?"

"Well, Veal, I am a little tired of all the play-acting my father made me do. I am not very happy about having to play-act any more."

"Oh!" exclaimed Bill. "So you're *not* going to pursue my little plan, then."

"Yeah, yeah, we are, Bill," said Mario, "but with our own little twist to it."

"We really are going to get engaged," said Claudia.

"Upon my word!" exclaimed Bill. "What a surprise!"

"Isn't this a little quick?" inquired Kerry.

"We'll have time to get to know each other better before we get married," said Claudia.

"But what if Mario decides against it, and upsets you? Then your father will shoot him."

Claudia giggled. "I am sure he will not shoot him. He wouldn't shoot an Englishman. It would undermine his honour."

"Anyway," added Mario, "I can cope. I'm a hard bastard."

"But how could you live in Cortesia?" asked Kerry. "You don't even speak Spanish!"

"I will teach him," said Claudia. "I am sure he will be a very attentive student."

"But what would you do here?" asked Kerry. "I assume you're going to ask the Archbishop for laicisation. What work will you do?"

"We talked about that this morning," replied Mario. "I'll get a qualification in teaching English as a foreign language."

"Good heavens!" exclaimed Peter. "Can you imagine how foul-mouthed your poor students will become under your tuition?"

Mario looked hurt. "As so often, you misjudge me," he said. "I shall be the soul of discretion in the classroom."

"Well, that's all sorted out, then," said Bill. "Now all that remains for us to do is to defeat the sordid machinations of the multinational mining companies, ensure that the former residents of San Martin de Porres receive adequate land and compensation, engineer a comprehensive land reform, expropriate the oligarchy and end the civil war. Whatever shall we do tomorrow?"

"How about, addressing gender inequalities and ending domestic violence?" suggested Hannah.

"Splendid plan!" replied Bill. "Plenty to keep us going for at least two days, then! Meanwhile, Mario and Claudia, feel free to use the telephone. It's working today, so it might be wise to take advantage of the fact. You may need to make at least one call each. Mario, just in case you hadn't memorised it or brought it with you, I managed to find the phone number of the Archbishop of Lambeth's office. Don't forget to add the international code."

Kerry sat with his friend while he made the phone call, and heard the unmistakable tones of the Right Reverend Monsignor Alec Smart, Secretary to the Archbishop of Lambeth. He sounded relieved. "It's undoubtedly for the best, Mario," he said. "The Arch knows you've struggled with celibacy, and it's better to resolve that struggle in this way now, rather than proceed to the priesthood and risk giving scandal to the faithful."

"Yes, Father, I certainly wouldn't want to give scandal to the faithful," replied Mario.

"I'll let the Arch know what you've decided, and as soon as you return to London, we can complete the necessary paper work. When are you planning to be back?"

"Within a fortnight, Father."

"Well, let me know as soon as you get back and we'll fix an appointment with the Arch. Don't feel bad about this, Mario. You're not a failure, even if it feels like that right now. Not all are given the gift of continence. Thank God that he has revealed your inward self to you, before it's too late. I shall pray for you."

"Thank you, Father."

Mario rang off, exhaled heavily and looked at Kerry with an expression of disgusted resignation.

"Patronising fucking wanker," he said.

That evening, over supper, Claudia told them that her father was not as angry as she had expected him to be. He had told her that her disappearance had caused him to reflect on the way he had been treating her. She was twenty-two now, and he should not expect her to follow him into the family business, if she really wanted to do something else. He was moved to learn of the kindness of Father Veal and the Sisters.

"But he was not so happy when I told him that I want to marry an Englishman," said Claudia. "'Light of my eyes,' he said to me, 'you make the task of being a father very difficult for me. There must be a hundred thousand eminently eligible young men in Cortesia. Why neglect them in favour of one of those pale, sickly, effeminate, cold-hearted, mean-spirited northerners? Is he especially rich?'

Mario looked affronted.

"I told him, 'He is poor, Papa, but he has a kind heart, and I love him. And he is not any of those other things you mentioned.'"

Mario looked relieved.

"'A poor man,' said my father, 'and English with it. Mother of God, what have I done to deserve this?' 'Well, Papa ...' I said, but he said, 'Don't tell me. I am well aware of my sins. I have been having very peculiar dreams since you left. I have received nocturnal visitations from St Scholastica and St Christina the Astonishing, and a vision of some crazed ascetic standing on a tall pillar, the possible significance of which I shudder to think about.' I told him, 'I wish you would be content with what you have, Papa, and I wish you would not misuse your office,' and he said, 'My little queen, I intend to retire from office. The last errand you ran for me will enable me to do so without any problems, and you are right to say that I should now be content with what I have.' So I told him, 'Your words make me happy, Papa,' and he said, 'And you would make me happy if you would come home to me, my little emerald.' When I asked him, 'Will you accept a visit from my Englishman?' he said, 'Just as soon as an aeroplane can bring him from the far, cold north to this happy land of sunshine, my sparkling little cut ruby.' And I said, 'But he is here with me in Caribe, Papa,' and then he became angry."

"Oh, dear," said Bill.

"'What!' he shouted, 'He is with you? Has he dishonoured you? I swear to God, even though he is a foreigner, if he has dishonoured you I will tear his manhood off and make him eat it fried with prawns!'"

Mario looked distinctly uneasy.

Claudia went on, "I said, 'He has done no such thing, Papa! I am staying with a community of nuns, and he is staying at the parish priest's house, with an English friend. Everything is in order,' and he said, 'But he has at least tried, I take it?' and I said, 'Well, he is a very passionate man, Papa...' and he said, 'Thank goodness for that! It would break my heart to think of my beautiful daughter marrying a cold fish, who did not have to be held at bay with her grandmother's hat-pin.' When I asked him, 'Shall I bring him to you, Papa?' he said, 'Certainly not! Travelling together unsupervised before marriage would cause a blot on our family's honour! What kind of a father would allow such a thing? No, I shall leave for Caribe on the next available flight and come and inspect the gentleman *in situ*.' So there we are. He is on his way."

Two days later, just after sunset, Kerry was in the front room when Hannah arrived at the priests' house, accompanied by a generously built, barrel-chested man in his late fifties, dressed in an immaculately pressed beige suit, highly polished crocodile skin shoes, a white shirt and navy blue tie. Bill came out of his office to greet them, and Hannah introduced the two Englishmen to Claudia's father.

"You also are North American, Father?" asked the police superintendent.

"I am English, Your Mercy."

"Ah. A fine race of men."

"As with all groups of human beings, we are a mixture of the good and the not quite so good."

"I trust that my potential future son-in-law is among the good, rather than the not quite so good."

"Your Mercy will be able to come to your own judgement in the matter, when the young man returns to the house."

"That is not the young man, is it?" asked Claudia's father anxiously, half turning to Kerry.

"No, no," replied Kerry, hastily.

Senor Gomez looked relieved. "He is not with my daughter?" he asked.

"I believe he is," said Bill.

"Unsupervised?"

"I believe they are taking their evening walk with my curate, Father Peter Steel."

"Another Englishman?"

"I am afraid so."

"I mean no disrespect, Father. Clearly, the English are particularly well-suited to the priesthood. A well-controlled, rational race of men, who do not allow their passions to rule them."

"I am ill-suited to give judgement on our qualities."

"Your Holy Mercy is too modest, Father."

"Please, take a seat," said Bill. Senor Gomez sat down with his back to the front door.

"Excuse me for a moment," said Bill. He turned to Hannah, still standing by the door. "I think Peter's in the church," he said, in English. "Would you go and ask him to find the lovebirds and warn them that the expected visitor is here? He may need to throw cold water over them or prize them apart with a crowbar. I don't think it would do for the visitor to see them locked in too enthusiastic an embrace. You might wish to keep an eye out for them too. It's quite important that they arrive here with Peter."

Hannah went out.

"Kerry," said Bill, still in English. "Go and make some *tinto* for our visitor, while I keep him occupied."

Kerry withdrew to the kitchen, from which he could clearly hear the conversation in the front room.

"I confess that I am glad that is not the young man in question," said Claudia's father.

"Your Mercy disapproves?" asked Bill.

"Oh, it is a small thing, not at all important!" replied the police superintendent. "I am perhaps looking at the young man with eyes too rooted in Cortesian culture. He seemed a little ... I mean, he does not seem ... quite as *vigorous* a young man as a Cortesian father might wish for his only daughter."

"Fear not, Your Mercy. Not all young Englishmen are the same."

Kerry felt slightly irritated by this exchange. He was perfectly aware that he was not the most masculine of young men, indeed, that he was what might be described as rather sexless. But he did not think it just to dismiss him, on that account, as unfit material for a son-in-law. He wondered what Hannah's father might think of him. It suddenly seemed very important. This whole matter of the engagement of his friend Mario to a Cortesian belle had intensified his awareness of his feelings for Hannah. But he took some pride in the fact that *his* feelings were so much *finer* than those of his friend. His growing love for Hannah was not, as far as he could see, rooted in such obviously animal lust as Mario's love for Claudia. No, he loved her for her personality, not just because she looked so beautiful – though she did, of course, and that was rather nice, when he thought about it. Perhaps he ought to tell her how he felt, but he was not yet sure of himself, and he did not want to scare her off. Anyway, he could not think of what words he might use, or on what occasion he might reveal the truth, or what might follow. What on earth did one do when one asked someone out? And why was Mario so good at all this kind of thing, while he himself was so completely at a loss?

"Father," said the superintendent, "I am aware that I owe Your Holy Mercy a great debt of gratitude for the kindness which Your Holy Mercy showed my daughter, when she came here to find her young man, and for the resolve and discretion which Your Holy Mercy has shown in ensuring that no impropriety has taken place between a beautiful young woman and an ardent young man."

"It is nothing," replied Bill.

"Father, I have been thinking very seriously about life since my beloved daughter left home, and I have been troubled by strange dreams of a spiritual nature. The fact that Your Holy Mercy and I find ourselves alone for a while seems to me an invitation extended from the Throne of Grace to make my peace with the Almighty, because I admit that my life has not been all that it might have been, and that there are matters which should rightly be discussed with a priest in the privacy of the confessional."

Kerry emerged from the kitchen with the *tinto* on a tray. Through the still open front door, he saw Mario and Claudia crossing the square towards the house, stopping every few paces to embrace and kiss each other. He realised that Bill had seen them too. Peter and Hannah were nowhere to be seen.

"I will happily hear Your Mercy's confession. I suggest that we go into the church to do so. Follow me. We can enter the church through the door at the back of the house." He took hold of the *tinto* as he passed Kerry, and led the police superintendent down the corridor.

Thus, Claudia's father did not see his daughter and her beloved arrive together unchaperoned. When he returned to the priest's house with Bill, over an hour and a half later, having discussed his sins – his many sins – at some length with his confessor, he found the light of his eyes in the company of not only her beloved, but of a priest and Sister, or at least, a woman whom he took to be a Sister. The sight of his daughter's radiantly joyful face, and the knowledge that he himself could make a new start in life, making amends for at least some of the wrong that he had done in the past, predisposed him in any case to be rather more forgiving than he might otherwise have been.

Indeed, guided by suggestions made by his confessor in response to his request for a penance, District Police Superintendent Gomez offered a considerable sum of money for the emergency relief of the displaced villagers of San Martin de Porres. He set aside a similar sum to enable his beloved daughter to train as a primary school teacher, and to assist her in establishing her own school for poor rural children, as she told him that evening that she wished to do. He also accepted his daughter's choice of spouse without objection, and with open-hearted generosity. This was assisted by his evaluation of his future son-in-law as a vigorous young man of fine features, who would give him healthy and pleasingly swarthy grandchildren, unlike his future son-in-law's delicate, and to his eyes, typically English, and therefore effeminate, young friend. In addition, he undertook to release Aristides from his obligation to assist him in his more questionable activities, an undertaking which naturally followed from having committed himself to abstain from them himself, and to ensure that the prison governor do likewise.

The police superintendent and his driver lodged overnight at Romania's one and only guest house and, in the morning, accompanied Claudia to Arroyomachete, from where father and daughter returned to La Esperanza. A week later, Mario followed them, paying his respects to his prospective father-in-law, before returning to England to begin the lengthy bureaucratic process of laicisation, and the slightly shorter one of obtaining a student visa for Cortesia.

Eleven: Kerry finds work, takes courage and experiences an awful shock

The urgent predicament of the former residents of San Martin, however, remained to be addressed. None was starving, but only because of the support of friends, relatives and well-wishers. Even when Senor Gomez's contribution arrived, it would not last for long. Juan Pablo, Dona Isabela, Gabriel, Bill and the Sisters were all perfectly clear that what was needed was not charity, but justice.

A few days after Mario's departure, the Relocation Committee met with their lawyer Gabriel and the whole pastoral team – including Kerry – in the front room of the priests' house. Patricio from the CCN had had to return to La Esperanza but had undertaken to remain in touch with Juan Pablo and the Committee and do whatever he could do at national level to publicise recent events and work to gain allies in the capital. The atmosphere in the priests' house was sombre. It was all very well for the pastoral team to speak of the importance of never giving up hope; it was not them who had lost their homes, land and livelihood.

Gabriel set out the steps that he was taking to challenge the eviction and the demolition of properties. But he was distracted by the legal action which District Attorney Mrs Isabela Yosefina Alto Delgado de Moron had initiated against him for slander. It was clearly a strategy for undermining his capacity to represent his clients. More was needed than the pursuit of a judicial remedy. "This is why we need international allies," he insisted. "We need to ensure that the new owners of the mine feel the pressure of publicity in the countries where they have their headquarters. It may be that the multinational owners are persons of greater integrity than the local managers, who are the same today as they were before the mine was sold. It may be that they are not, but it must be the case that they wish to avoid damage to their reputation in front of their own shareholders and their own government."

Peter said, "I confess to my own failures on this score. I have not been in touch with the mining campaign group in London, since the day we heard back from them. We need to ensure that Patricio's video is posted on the internet, and that we keep the groups in London informed about what is happening here. They are not telepathic and will not be able to build a campaign with real momentum unless we supply them with the information that they need. But our pastoral team also has a large and geographically extensive parish to run, with many villages requiring our attention, and if I, or any one of us, spends a disproportionate amount of time on the campaign for justice for San Martin, it will cause resentment among the other villages. We really need someone outside the parish team, who can devote some time to this. But I can't think of anyone."

"What about you, Kerry?" suggested Hannah. "When do you have to go home?"

Kerry's heart leapt. Did Hannah want him to stay?

"Well, I only took a month off work," said Kerry. "But my tourist visa gives me permission to stay here for six months. I don't have to go home yet."

"But if you don't, you'll lose your job, won't you?" asked Patsy.

"I could send them my notice today," answered Kerry. "I'm sure I could get another job when I get back home, however long I stay."

"I should think twice before jacking in a perfectly good job, Kerry," said Bill.

"But you could be really, really helpful if you stayed here," said Hannah. "Think what you could contribute to the struggle here."

That decided it for Kerry. Hannah obviously wanted him to stay. Did she feel the same for him as he felt for her? How he admired her commitment, her bravery, her cheerfulness, her clarity of thought, her faith! How often had he wished, since arriving in Caribe, that he could impress her as effectively as his friend Mario had managed to impress Claudia! Here was his chance! He would impress her with commitment to the struggle!

"I'll email work as soon as I can get on the internet in Arroyomachete," said Kerry. "I'll stay here for another five months and ensure good communication between here and London. I've got some money saved up, so I need not be a burden on the parish – I can contribute to my own food. But may I carry on staying at the parish house?"

Bill smiled. "You'd be a blessing to us," he said.

"Bless you, young man," said Dona Isabela. She began to weep.

"This means a great deal to us," said Juan Pablo. "I did not want to express my opinion in this discussion, because it is a very big thing to be away from your own country and I did not want to ask this of you, my brother. But when Hannah mentioned this possibility I hoped in my heart that you would say yes. Thank you."

Thus, it was agreed that Kerry would devote himself full time to working with the Relocation Committee, and with Gabriel and the CCN, to make sure that colleagues in London received full and frequent updates on all that was happening around the mine, that they were made aware of what the people of San Martin wanted, and that the people of San Martin learnt what was being done, as a consequence, by their allies in London.

The work gave Kerry a sense of purpose and of usefulness with which he was unfamiliar. It was true that he had not thought of the idea himself, had not sought it out. As usual, he was following the suggestions of other people. But it seemed to him that this work, more than anything he had ever done before, was worth something. It also gave him the longed-for opportunity to spend time with Hannah.

Indeed, Hannah seemed to seek him out. If ever she was visiting the villages around the mine, she asked him to accompany her. Whenever he was going into town, she would come too, if she was free. She even took time off for a few days to go with him to visit Aristides, Claudia and her father in La Esperanza.

Of course, Kerry was not forward enough to let Hannah know how he felt about her. He was so unfamiliar with love, he was taken aback by the increasing strength of his feelings. He knew it was not merely physical; desire played a much less important role than the profound admiration he felt for the nobility of her character. He did not quite have the courage to tell her yet, but was sure that in just a few weeks more, maybe a few months, he most certainly would...probably, at least, he might do. He really should. He would, quite probably.

When they were in L.E. together, Aristides encouraged him. "She's beautiful, my friend! Do you not love her?"

"Well, I, er...I..."

"You do! I can see you do! You are in love with her! You must tell her, man!"

"Please don't tell her, Aristides! Please don't! I must do so, but I need time to summon the courage! I have never been in love before, ever!"

"I don't believe you, my friend!"

"No, truly. It has never meant anything to me before. So now that I am in love, I don't quite know what to do, and I must take it slowly."

"Well, don't take it too slowly, my friend, or some other guy will take her away from you!"

Early one morning, a few days after their return from the capital, a top of the range land cruiser with dark tinted windows pulled up outside the priests' house in Romania, followed by a pickup truck with half a dozen armed guards in the back, and Pik Bloemen got out, preceded by his driver, who opened the cruiser door for him, and knocked for him on the open door of the priests' house. Bill and Kerry were in the office. They emerged to greet their visitor.

"Padre!" said Pik Bloemen. "We meet again!"

"Always a pleasure," replied Bill.

"Good morning, Mr Bloemen," said Kerry.

Pik Bloemen nodded. "Morning," he said. "Well, padre, I wonder whether you have had a chance to think over our little chat of a few weeks ago," said Pik Bloemen.

"I confess, I haven't had a moment to do so," answered Bill.

"Yes, I feared as much," said Pik Bloemen, "as I note that not only is your curate as indiscreet as ever, but you seem to have initiated some propaganda mechanism for purveying alarmist misinformation to our investors and the press in London. At least, I assume you're involved in this, as it obviously requires a fairly impressive level of communication and at least one person fluent in both Spanish and English. It wouldn't be you, now, would it? Or your curate?"

"Certainly not!" replied Bill. "We are both much too busy with parish work to be involved in anything of that sort."

"Nonetheless, the contagion appears to be spreading. Not only are unjustified criticisms being made about our supposed responsibility for the unfortunate, and wholly preventable, events at San Martin, but now, scurrilous attacks are being made on the nature of the relocation programme planned for other villages."

"Presumably, then, you will be suing whoever is responsible for these inaccuracies."

"There is a rather clever mind at work here, padre, which is one of the reasons I thought it might be you. Nothing that has been said or written is *factually incorrect*. It is the interpretation given that is so hurtful."

"You mean you can't sue, because your critics are telling the truth?"

"I hope that our relationship is going to improve, padre, as I cannot help feeling that we got off on the wrong foot, and as I explained before, I would hope to build a fruitful working relationship with you."

"I seem to remember that I was fairly clear about the necessary preconditions for such a relationship to be built."

"Nothing was particularly clear to me other than your understandable and wholly commendable devotion to your parishioners on the one hand, and on the other, your inexplicable belief that somehow our presence was not conducive to their well-being."

"I am looking forward to being convinced."

"I shall make it my business to convince you, padre. We shall meet again."

"Doubtless."

Pik Bloemen turned to Kerry. "I trust you are enjoying your stay, Mr..."

"Ahern," said Kerry. "Kerry Ahern."

"Thank you. How are you getting on with the language?"

"Oh, fine. I'm a translator by trade."

"I see. Most interesting. I don't suppose you'd like a job, would you?"

"Oh, I'm much too busy, I'm afraid. Anyway, I don't think I'd be allowed to take a job on my tourist visa."

"Ah. You are here on a tourist visa? Well, I'm sorry I can't offer you a job. I wouldn't want to cause you any difficulties with the authorities. I'll say goodbye, then, and wish you all a very merry Christmas."

"And to you to, Mr Bloemen. Goodbye."

Pik Bloemen returned to his land cruiser and swept out of the square, followed by his truck full of armed guards.

"I fear you may have sowed the seeds of a problem, Kerry," observed Bill.

"Oh, dear. What have I said?"

"Mr Bloemen was wondering who was behind the flow of information to London. Shows you've done a good job. But I am afraid he will now both realise it was you and inform the authorities. Discretion may have been the better part of valour."

"Oh, dear. What can we do?"

"Bide our time, and hope."

Not long afterwards, Peter took an excited phone call from Mario. He had obtained a student visa, and would begin his Spanish language course in La Esperanza in the new year. Claudia would begin her teacher training studies at the same time.

Christmas was exhausting. Each member of the parish team was busy in one or other of the villages encompassed by the parish of Nuestra Senora de los Remedios. Kerry stayed with Peter, who celebrated Midnight Mass in the church in Romania and another Mass there in the morning, before moving on to the nearest of the villages, Predio Nuevo, for a third Mass. By that hour in the morning, the heat was overpowering, and Kerry was glad of the fact that the settlement's church was nothing more than a palm leaf roof supported on posts, so that what breeze there was, could pass freely through the structure. The design also allowed for easier access by dogs, hens and running children.

By sunset, the whole team was back in Romania. They gathered in the back room of the priests' house – Alison, Bill, Hannah, Kerry, Patsy and Peter – together with Juan Pablo and his family. Carmen had prepared a Christmas dinner for them; roasted goat with yucca, plantain, potatoes and a salad carefully washed in bottled water.

Kerry sat next to Hannah. She was in the most delightful mood, full of laughter, making witty responses to what others said, always attentive to what others needed, whether it was a glass of water or an affirming word. Kerry, never before interested in romantic love, never drawn to it, never understanding what it was about, now knew, without doubt, that he loved this good, kind, sensitive, beautiful woman, and determined that soon – very soon – he was going to declare his love. He really was.

It was thoughtful of the local agents of the Department of Internal Security to allow Kerry to spend Christmas in Romania before detaining him, but they were not entirely heartless. As with most officials within oppressive systems, they sincerely believed that their work was conducive to some greater good.

So it was not until Boxing Day – a holiday nobody had heard of in Cortesia, or the United States, and therefore of significance only to the three resident Britons – that a land cruiser with dark tinted windows drew up before the priests' house, and two DIS agents stepped out, the priest's house reflected in the large mirror lenses of their character-concealing sunglasses. And since it was Boxing Day for local Brits, Kerry was indoors, not doing much of anything and not expecting there to be much good on the telly.

Luckily, Bill and Peter, being Brits on Boxing Day, were also in and not doing much of anything.

It was Bill who answered the door. Not that the DIS agents waited for anyone to answer it. It was, as usual, open, and they simply walked straight in. Bill was glad that he had not given them the occasion to break it down.

"I regret the disturbance to your morning, Father," said the senior officer, an obsessively cleanly shaven man in his early forties, who carried the knowledge of his state authority in the straightness of his spine. "I regret that an immigration offence has been committed by a foreign visitor, registered as staying at these premises, and we are here to detain the individual in question and ensure his departure from the country."

"An immigration offence?" queried Bill. "Of what nature?"

"We need to speak to Mr Kerry Ahern," replied the officer. "Is he here?"

To save Bill the trouble of engaging his fecund imagination in well-meaning subterfuge, Kerry, who had heard the conversation from the kitchen, called out, "Yes, officer, I am here," and he walked through into the front room.

"Your Mercy has violated the conditions of Your Mercy's tourist visa by working. This is against the law. As a mark of leniency, the Minister of Internal Security has decided not to imprison you, but to facilitate your immediate removal from the country."

"But Mr Ahern's 'work' has simply been to assist our parish team, out of the kindness of his heart, and for no financial consideration of any sort."

"Working, whether in a paid or voluntary capacity, while present in the country on a tourist visa, is a violation of the Immigration Act of 2002, section fourteen, subsection twenty-six. Your Holy Mercy may check it yourself."

"But, surely, we have the legal right to challenge this decision?" suggested Bill.

"Of course. According to the Law Code of the Republic, the decision can be challenged at any time within the next six months, providing that the person who is accused of the infraction is outside the Republic at the time the appeal is lodged, and remains outside it until and unless it is decided in his or her favour."

"How long does that take?" asked Bill.

"A decision could be rushed through in two years, if the correct procedures are followed," replied the senior officer.

Bill fell silent.

"What must I do?" Kerry asked the officer.

"Your Mercy may pack your bags under supervision, and then we will take Your Mercy to the airport at Arroyomachete, from where Your Mercy will be accompanied to La Esperanza and put on a plane to your country."

"May I not say goodbye to my friends?"

"If Your Mercy's friends are here in the house, Your Mercy may say goodbye to them. Your Mercy may not leave this building."

"Please, Bill," said Kerry, in Spanish, so that the DIS officers would not suspect some secret plot and react aggressively, "see if Hannah and Peter are at the Sisters' house, and bring them here right now."

"You have ten minutes," warned the senior officer.

Bill, aggrieved at what was happening to his young friend, but at a loss to know what to do to challenge it, hurried from the house. Kerry, accompanied by the younger officer, who remained silent, returned to his bedroom and began to pack his bags.

He had not quite finished, when Hannah ran into his room, tears in her eyes. She went to embrace him, but the DIS agent prevented her. "Please, allow me at least to embrace my friend before he leaves the country!" Hannah urged, distraught. The officer relented, and allowed them to embrace. Hannah began to weep. She spoke to Kerry in English, not wishing their final intimacies to be intelligible to this unsmiling agent of oppression. "I'm so sorry this is happening, Kerry! You are a dear, sweet man, and I will miss you very much!"

Kerry knew that the moment had come, and that if he allowed it to pass, it may not come again.

"Hannah," he said, "I love you."

"Well, I love you too, my dear friend. You're such a good man, and you've been such a wonderful member of our team. We all love you."

"No, Hannah, I don't mean that. I mean, I love you. *I love you.*"

Hannah pulled back slightly, so that she could see his face, while keeping both her hands on his shoulders.

"You love me?"

"I love you. I love you. You're the only woman I've ever loved. I didn't think I could love, but I know it now. I love you."

"Oh, Kerry! Oh, my dear friend! Oh, I am so touched!" She embraced him again, tightly, her right cheek against his, hot with embarrassment and tears. "But didn't you know? Didn't you realise? I'm a lesbian! I mean, I'm not *with* anyone, but I love *women* in that way, not men!" She pulled away again, so that she could look him right in the face. "Oh, Kerry, Kerry, what a dear, good, beautiful man you are! As a friend, how deeply I love you! You are almost all that I would look for in a partner, except... Oh, Kerry, my dear friend, if only you were a woman!"

WEST

the direction of self-knowledge and healing

One: Kerry makes an ill-judged sacrifice

Back home in England, after Christmas, Kerry could think of nothing and no-one else but Hannah. Their sudden and enforced separation, her evident and deep affection for him, and his own unfamiliarity with love, combined to engender in him a sense of utterly helpless yearning for her. He needed to be with her, he needed to speak to her, to hear her sweet voice, to converse with her, but he could not. Oh! The sweetness of that beautiful voice! Oh! The beauty of that sweet, sweet voice!

And – oh my goodness! – it was not only a depth of admiration for her character that he felt, nor a fond remembrance of the sweet sound of her voice that he cherished, but something more physical, more animal than that. He tried to force himself *not* to think of those parts of her which she had not vouchsafed to present to public scrutiny. It was not right, he supposed, to think of such things without her express permission. He meditated, without guilt, on the noble curve of her beautiful forehead, the fineness of her jet black hair, the sparkling brightness of her dark brown eyes, the fullness of her lips and the radiance of her smile. He thought of the delicacy of her strong, but tender, hands and the soft, bronzed, hairless, smooth, curved surfaces of her calves and forearms… But it seemed to him morally unacceptable to imagine the form beneath her clothing, unless she herself had invited him to do so, and she had not. Oh! But how difficult it was *not* to begin to speculate about what lay beneath her always tasteful, always fetching, outfits!

He knew that he was being foolish, that there was no hope in this increasingly obsessive love, that he should be content with friendship – but he could not be. What unspeakable injustice was this, that having at last learnt what it was to fall in love, the object of his love should lay absolutely and irrevocably beyond his reach, because of the senseless accident of his sex and her sexuality? What irony, that now that he had at last felt, and with such power, the force of a love that was common to men, his very manliness, poor and unmanly as it was, should prove the insuperable barrier to that love's consummation!

Unusually for Kerry (well, his entire existence was unusual at that moment) he did not immediately look for work. The legacy from his mother meant there was still no pressing need to find paid employment. He fell into a mild depression. He knew that he should not dwell constantly on his unrequited love, that he should, instead, find something constructive to occupy his time, but he felt unable to do so. Oh! If only his beloved parents were alive to guide him in his melancholy and confusion!

He admitted to Peter, in an email, that he had fallen hopelessly (truly hopelessly!) in love with Hannah, and Peter reacted with clear-sighted, compassionate firmness: Kerry had got to get over it. There was no hope and he should not torture himself by thinking that there ever could be. He needed to throw himself into the struggle for justice in whatever manner lay to hand, and stop thinking about her all the time. Kerry knew he was right, but felt unable to follow his wise counsel. He did not raise the matter with his friend again, for fear of irritating him. Nor did he tell Mario. He feared the response would be one of gentle, and tastelessly vulgar, mockery, and he felt too raw for that.

He and Hannah kept in fairly frequent contact by email, and Hannah's messages were always warm and affectionate, though she did not refer to what had passed between them in that bedroom in Romania. Rather, she behaved as if what had happened had not happened, that those words had not been said.

Then, on one occasion, Kerry, in the agony of his yearning, transgressed the unwritten rule by telling her once more of the strength of his feelings for her, and asking her whether it might not be possible for her to reconsider the form of her affections for him. After all, he asked himself, why should he accept a set of circumstances that was inherently unacceptable? Surely, it must be possible that Hannah was mistaken about her orientation? Surely people could change? Surely the affection – no, she had said herself, the *love* – that she felt for him could overcome this little thing, this scarcely relevant accident of his gender?

She did not reply for a fortnight, and when she did, she was frank. "Kerry," she wrote, "you are, and will remain, a very dear and valued friend to me, but I cannot love you as you love me for the simple fact – as I made clear before – that you are a man, and I am a lesbian – not through choice, but because it is truly who I am, and I am neither ashamed nor proud of it. It is simply me. Were I ever again to have a lover (as I have had on occasions before) she would be a woman. As I said to you the day you left here, you are truly lovable, but you are not a woman, and I, therefore, cannot return your feelings. Please, for the sake of our strong friendship, do not mention this again. For the moment, I ask you to give me some space and not write to me. I will write to you again before too long, but when I do, I ask that you respect my wishes in this matter, and that we proceed as friends."

Kerry, being a deeply honourable man, respected Hannah's wishes to the letter. But how could he respect their spirit? He was on fire with love! It was as if all the turmoil of adolescence, a turmoil which had passed him by while it afflicted all his contemporaries in their teenage years, had suddenly seized upon him. All the years of hormonal madness and heartache were now concentrated into this delayed and overwhelming experience of romantic love. His sharp mind, misled by the unexpected power of unfamiliar emotions, began to work away on Hannah's words, and to shape them into forms they were never meant to take. Had she not said to him in Romania, "If only you were a woman…" Yes, she *had* said that, he remembered it with crystal clarity! And had she not said, that other than this small thing, he was almost everything she could wish for in a partner? And had she not just written, "You are truly lovable, but you are not a woman, and I *therefore* cannot return your feelings…?" The *only* reason that she could not return his love was the absolute accident of his gender, a gender that had never meant anything to him anyway.

It was, perhaps, unfortunate for Kerry that it was at that juncture that the BBC chose to broadcast a compelling documentary about gender reassignment, and that Kerry, having nothing else to do that evening, happened upon it while channel hopping. It told the story of a courageous individual who, having been born male, never felt quite at home in his own body, and having reached adolescence, knew for sure that he was psychologically a woman. Having undergone gender reassignment at a relatively early age, she had then devoted herself to campaigning for transsexual equality, a cause for which she had suffered much misunderstanding and rejection.

This was quite sufficient to inspire Kerry with a sense that such a course of action might not only be possible, but admirable. He recalled the verse from the Song of Songs which he had read at Morning Prayer in the seminary on certain saints' days; "For love, a man will give up everything he has in the world, and think nothing of the loss."

Kerry found Father Patrick and Father Donald Black to be sources of limited comfort in his broken-hearted distress; limited, because both of them, in their different ways, said the same as Peter, that he must do all he could to overcome his hopeless obsession. They both told him that he needed to allow his disappointment to expand his capacity to love. It is certain that they did not intend to fuel the train of thought upon which Kerry had already embarked and which was creaking towards its destination. Neither priest had any idea of what was in their young friend's mind, because they were too discreet to pry without invitation into other people's private thoughts, and Kerry had not divulged all of his to his spiritual counsellors.

Kerry was experiencing extreme difficulties in his prayer. He meditated daily, but it was hard work concentrating, and although he felt surrounded by the love of God, he experienced no enlightenment, no flash of inspiration about how he should proceed. He prayed for guidance, but received none. Once, only once, he felt he had almost heard with his own ears the voice of God. God had said, or seemed to say, "I don't know why you're seeking guidance from me, you've already made your mind up anyway."

Father Donald taught him a prayer much loved by Orthodox Christians, the Jesus Prayer. "Lord Jesus Christ, Son of God," he prayed in silence, as he breathed in slowly. "Have mercy upon me," he prayed as he exhaled. Over and over again, he prayed the same silent prayer. It brought some peace to his breaking heart and his overheated mind, but no miraculous enlightenment.

Something about his interior conflict made Kerry feel uneasy in the company of his friend, Francis Neale, whose quiet certainties, and exemplary spirit of service, seemed to show Kerry's spiritual turmoil to him in an unflattering light. Kerry communicated less and less frequently with Francis. He felt guilty about this, wondering what Francis would think of his intentions. But Francis was busy with his parish work on the Kent coast, so their paths did not often cross.

Nor did he speak of what was in his heart to his old friends from university, Chris and Brett. He felt certain that they would not understand.

Aunty Liza was pleased to learn that Kerry had fallen in love and deeply sympathetic to him in his sufferings. But her rather military, no-nonsense temperament pre-disposed her to expect him to keep a rather stiffer upper lip than he felt was possible for him, and to counsel him rather too quickly to accept that there were plenty more fish in the sea. So he did not reveal his intentions to her either.

Mario's news was uniformly good. He was making swift progress in his language studies in La Esperanza, and Claudia was enjoying her teacher training. He had decided that he, too, wanted to be a primary school teacher and as they got to know each other, they loved each other more and more. Her father had retired, and seemed to have gone straight. Barring second thoughts and problems with Mario's planned application for a resident's visa, they would marry some time late the next year, when Mario would have finished his teacher training and be in a position to find paid work to support his wife. This was of immense importance to her father, even though, given the extent of his own wealth, there was no practical need for it whatever.

The flowering of their love gave Kerry both great joy and great pain. He wished well for his friend, but he wished it for himself too.

The news from Romania was not so good. Peter reported that every assurance made in London by the multinationals and their agents (including the ubiquitous Mr Bloemen) had to be followed up painstakingly on the ground, because the local management of the mine seemed as determined as ever to provide as little comfort to the communities as possible. Between them, Peter and Hannah were trying to fulfil the role that Kerry had been playing, ensuring a flow of communication between the communities and the support groups in London, but with all their other responsibilities, it was impossible. Kerry had met with the groups in London, and felt confident that they would do their best to ensure that the people of San Martin de Porres received the support they needed. He began to feel that his own role was now redundant, that others could offer that support better than he. He had been effective *in situ*, but far from the scene of the unfolding drama, he felt detached and unsupported in his turn by the warm humanity of the people whose struggle he was assisting. Caribe began to seem like another world.

Except that one person in Caribe was all too present, all the time, filling his waking thoughts, walking through his dreams at night. He wished that he could be more like his friend Peter, who expressed his love by his pastoral care and political solidarity for great quantities of people. This was a noble, honourable love. But it was not the love that came most naturally to Kerry, who relied at any one time on very few, but quite intense friendships; and now, at last, he understood, or thought he understood, romantic love. He had more in common with Mario than he had thought.

When, after a few weeks, Hannah wrote to him again, her tone was exactly as before; full of affection, affirmation, joy, kindness and commitment to the cause of justice in Cortesia. She never once referred to the tension that had passed between them, and nor did he. But he rejoiced in her affection for him, and his love for her possessed him utterly. And if, he reasoned, a man could 'give up *everything* he has in the world for love,' surely he could give up this small thing, this irrelevant nothing of his unvalued maleness.

And so it was that, some time after Easter, without consulting anyone, Kerry took a job in Rio de Janeiro, teaching English as a foreign language. There, unseen by any of his intimates, he could seek out a surgeon who could make the changes necessary.

Kerry kept in touch by letter with Aunty Liza and Father Patrick, and by email with his friends in England and Cortesia, but he told them nothing of his plans. He wanted no discussion. He feared that they might attempt to persuade him to abandon the course of action he had chosen, and that they would succeed. For the first time that he could remember, he had found the courage to choose his own path, and he could not risk being deflected from it. He would present his loved ones with a *fait accompli* and, since they loved him, he hoped they would accept it.

He did not write to Francis, and did not hear from him.

He had begun the hormone treatment with its attendant daily feelings of nausea, when he heard, from Father Patrick, that his Aunty Liza had had a stroke, and died. She was his last remaining relative, the last link with his childhood. He mourned for her, and for himself, as he believed that she, of all people, would be most supportive of the decision he had made. She had left him her house in Westhampton in her will. He arranged for the lawyer to pay the inheritance tax from the money that he had saved from the sale of his mother's house some years before, and ensure that someone took care of the place, while Kerry decided what to do with it.

How he missed his dear parents now! How they had loved him, and he them! All of a sudden, he wished he could talk to them about this choice that he was making. Would they understand? Would they be supportive? Would they counsel him against it? Of course they would, he knew that. Would they accept him anyway, whatever choice he made? Of course they would, he knew that too. Would they be ashamed of him? Never openly, but perhaps in their heart of hearts? Oh, how he needed their quiet wisdom, their warm affection, their absolutely unconditional acceptance, their unwavering love! But now he was all alone in the world!

It must be said that the clinic which granted Kerry what he took to be his heart's desire was looked upon with disdain, though Kerry did not realise this, by the better practices in Rio de Janeiro. Kerry felt the need for speed, which is why he chose it. The psychological investigations and preparation, which were *de rigueur* in any establishment that valued its reputation, and which would have revealed beyond doubt that Kerry was not a suitable candidate for gender reassignment, were curtailed inexcusably.

When Kerry began the exercise of living as a woman, he changed jobs to avoid tittle-tattle. Although it saddened him, he deliberately avoided making close friendships with anyone at work, or in the rather respectable local church where he attended Mass; so he had no ties to mourn when he moved on.

Now, the clock was ticking. Kerry had ascertained that, to change his gender legally under English law, and thus obtain a passport proclaiming him to be a woman, he would have to live as one for two years.

He had also learned, with consternation, that men living as women in this seemingly accepting city suffered extreme prejudice from some. Those whose circumstances led them into the world of sex work, so unspeakably alien to Kerry, so unfathomable and incomprehensible, were often objects of murderous attack by gangs of armed, moralising thugs. To remain resolute in his chosen course of action, out of love for a woman of whose future attraction to him he could not be sure, was an act of outstanding courage and extraordinary foolishness.

The next milestone, so to speak, was the breast implants. When the initial pain was over, Kerry accepted them as part of him, though he was getting better now, through hormone treatment and perforce, in remaining conscious that they were part of *her*.

Kerry changed jobs, and lodgings, and church, once more, and it was only then that she felt able to begin making closer connections with people, since they would never have known her in her former form. But she allowed nobody to become too close to her, because she knew she would be leaving this chrysalis of metamorphosis, and once she had left it, she did not intend to return.

Despite her best mental efforts she was, through the fault of the clinic, ill-prepared for the final surgery. When she emerged from the anaesthetic, and acquainted herself for the first time with the latest changes in her body, she felt disoriented. She did not feel, as so many of those undergoing similar alterations have felt, that they had simply become who they knew themselves to be. Kerry had now assumed the outward vestiges of an identity into which she would have to grow through courageous, self-disciplined dedication. And self-discipline was most certainly necessary to face the excruciating pain she felt between her legs, a pain which continued for weeks and which was, for several months, refreshed daily by the necessity of inserting a dilator into her reordered abdomen to prevent the new opening from closing up. This sacrifice, made for love, now felt less like a simple renunciation, and more like a sharing in the crucifixion. Kerry's fervent hope was that the suffering might be simply the precursor of a resurrection to new life.

But at length, after the requisite investigation by the British consulate and the necessary letters from the surgeon, she received the papers that she needed to prove that she was indeed a woman, and her new passport meant that immigration officers across the world would allow her to pass freely in the name of Her Britannic Majesty.

Two: Kerry seeks out the beloved

Meanwhile, Hannah completed her year as a volunteer in Caribe, returned home to Massachusetts and began her studies at Harvard Law School. And yes, of course Kerry would be welcome to visit. She just needed to know the date of arrival and the spare room in her apartment, near the Harvard Square T station, would be made ready.

So it was to Logan International Airport, rather than to London or La Esperanza, that Kerry flew, some two and a half years after his flight to Rio, arriving in an early December downpour and using Hannah's emailed map to find her way, with her two small suitcases, through the T system to Harvard Square and her apartment.

Kerry had dressed as attractively as she knew how to, though she was acutely aware of her ignorance of Hannah's tastes in other women's clothing. She wore skin-tight blue jeans, royal blue woollen leg warmers and matching soft leather ankle boots, a loose fitting pink silk blouse and scarf, an embroidered blue waistcoat, a thick royal blue down jacket and a brightly coloured knitted woollen cap. She wore just a little makeup: lip gloss rather than lipstick, a discreet eye liner, a hint of rouge. She felt quite pretty, but she realised with sudden horror that perhaps Hannah would have preferred something darker or more masculine. Should she have consulted her about the changes? Should she have warned her? Yes, of course, of course, but she had been too scared to do so, too caught up in romantic imagination, too determined to pursue a course of action, for which she had sought too little counsel. And now she must live with the consequences.

She rang the doorbell and waited with pounding heart, her down jacket zipped up against the damp winter cold, obscuring the otherwise obvious changes in her physique. Her nervous smile, as the door opened, met Hannah's broad smile of welcome, which quickly became quizzical, intrigued, amazed – perhaps amused? Hannah's arms, raised ready to embrace her visitor, fell back to her sides. "Kerry!" she said, "You look... different! Gee, I guess you look a little...feminine."

"Do I?" asked Kerry.

"Gee," said Hannah, "you *sound* a little feminine as well! Are you tired?"

"Oh, I can explain," said Kerry, her heart pounding.

"Hey, what am I doing?" said Hannah, smiling broadly again. "I didn't even hug you yet! Come here!"

She grasped Kerry in her arms, embracing her tightly for a few moments; then sprang back, staring at her friend. "My God!" she cried, "You *feel* feminine as well! What's going on?"

"Maybe I should come in?" suggested Kerry. "It's a bit cold out here."

"Yes, yes of course," agreed Hannah, obviously disoriented. Kerry crossed the threshold, a case in either hand, and Hannah shut the door behind her.

"Hey, let me put those in your room," offered Hannah, her smile gone but her sense of hospitality intact. Kerry took off her hat and unzipped her down jacket. Her transformation was obvious now. Hannah spotted it as she turned round from the door of the guest room, and froze.

"What have you done, Kerry?" she asked her.

Kerry swallowed hard. This was not the scene she had rehearsed so often in her imagination. "I had gender reassignment surgery in Rio," she replied.

"Oh," said Hannah. "Oh, I'm sorry, please excuse me. I'm just surprised, that's all. There's no reason you shouldn't have reassignment surgery. It's totally up to you. I'm so sorry, I'll get used to it in a minute. It's just a bit of a surprise, that's all. It's fine, I'm just a bit...a bit freaked out, that's all. Let's go into the kitchen and I'll make some coffee. Would you like a coffee? I think I need one."

Kerry sat down at the kitchen table. "You've got a pretty apartment," she said.

"Yeah, yeah, it's okay, isn't it?" said Hannah, attempting a smile. "I'm glad you like it."

Kerry looked around the kitchen in embarrassed silence.

Hannah said, "Look, I'm sorry about this, Kerry. You are not responsible for my reactions. I really apologise. It's just this is new to me. I haven't met anyone who's had reassignment before now, and it's just new to me, that's all. I'm totally cool with you changing, I have no problem with it, it's just I'll need to take a little time changing my perception from knowing you as a dear male friend to a dear female friend. I just…I mean…Why didn't you tell me?"

"I wanted it to be a surprise."

"Oh, Kerry, you and your British sense of humour! I guess Peter and Mario are in on this too! Give Hannah a bit of a shock!"

"Nobody else knows," said Kerry. "I mean, none of my friends knows. You're the first."

"Me? Oh, gee, that freaks me out a bit more, Kerry. Why didn't you tell anybody? Were you ashamed? There's no need to be ashamed! You have to be who you are! You have to know who you are! You have to be honest about who you are!"

"It's just that I wanted you to be the first to know."

"Me? Why? I mean, you've known Peter and Mario way longer than you've known me!"

"Because I did it for you."

Hannah stared at her in disbelief.

"You did it for me?"

"I told you that I loved you and you told me that you loved me as a dear friend, but you were a lesbian, and you said, 'You are almost all that I would look for in a partner, if only you were a woman!' I remember it word for word the way you said it, because I wanted you to love me!"

225

"So you had gender reassignment surgery because you wanted me to fall in love with you?"

"I did it because I love you, and I thought if I did it, we could be together."

"You had your *own body mutilated* because you thought it would make you more attractive to me?"

"Mutilated? How can you say that? I was a man and now I'm a woman, that's all!"

"That's *all*?"

"Yes, that's *all, all* for you, *all* for love, *all* because I love you! The first thing I have ever done because *I* chose it, *I* wanted it, instead of having someone else make a choice for me, or persuade me into something because I was too weak willed. *I* chose it, *I* did it, because *I love you*."

"Oh my God. Oh my *God*! Oh – my – God! Oh – my – *God*!" Hannah was nearly screaming. "Oh my God! Oh my God oh my God oh my God oh my God! I don't know what to do! Oh my God oh my God oh my God oh my God!" She sat down on the floor and covered her eyes with her arms, resting arms and head on her knees. She began to weep, sobbing as if from the depths of her being, keening with a grief that sounded so deep, and so forlorn, that Kerry herself burst into uncontrollable tears, resting her arms on the table and her head on her arms. Thus it was that they sobbed themselves into silence, a silence which lasted for a good hour and was broken only by the occasional sound of passing traffic in the street below.

At last, Hannah looked up, and spoke.

"Kerry," she said, "I am truly, truly sorry that my words gave you the impression that if you had gender reassignment, we could become partners. That thought never entered my mind, and if I had had the least idea that you had taken that meaning from my words, I would have corrected that false impression straight away. You were, and I hope you will be again, a very dear friend to me. You had – have – a beautiful personality. But you are not a potential partner for me. If you really want to know, I am drawn to masculinity in a woman's looks. Think Sister Alison, not that we're an item, either. You make a convincing woman, because you were always rather delicate. But you're not my kind of woman, not in that way."

Kerry listened in pained silence – excruciating, crucifying pain.

"In any case, there's something I was going to tell you. It was my surprise for you. I recently decided, and this really is recent, that I want to join the Sisters after all. I knew it half way through the last semester here. I don't want to be some fancy lawyer any more. I want to work with those wonderful women in the Sisters of Charity of Jerusalem Massachusetts and serve God wherever She, and the Sisters, care to send me. I'm completing the term paper I'm working on, and then I'm going out West to the Reservation where the Sisters work in Yellowstone State to live with them till next fall, when I'll enter the Novitiate back here in Massachusetts."

Kerry gazed at her beloved, and the tears began to roll once more down her cheeks, delicately stained with eye liner. "I'm sorry," she said. "I'm so sorry."

Hannah stood up and stroked Kerry's hair. "I'm sorry, too," she said. "Look what I made you do to yourself."

"Are you angry with me, Hannah?"

"What right have I to be angry with you, Kerry? I'm not angry with you. But right now I am freaked out – very deeply, deeply freaked out, such that I need other company. I apologise for this, but I need to leave you here and go and stay tonight with the Sisters. I am really sorry. If you can bring yourself to do so, make yourself at home, watch the TV, sleep, eat, drink, take a bubble bath, whatever you like – but I need to be with someone else right now. I'll come back first thing in the morning. I can't say we'll behave as if this hadn't happened, but we'll start over. Is that okay?"

"That's okay," said Kerry.

"Okay," said Hannah. She took a down jacket off the peg behind the kitchen door, put it on, and left.

Kerry drank a cup of coffee, took off her boots, lay down on the bed, and cried herself to sleep.

When Hannah returned in the morning, she found Kerry sitting motionless at the kitchen table, an unfinished letter to Father Patrick on a pad of writing paper in front of her. Kerry was staring vacantly at nothing in particular.

"Kerry?" said Hannah. "Are you okay?"

Kerry turned her head slightly towards Hannah to acknowledge her presence.

"Not yet," she answered. "But I will be."

Hannah took off her down jacket and sat down at the table, hanging her jacket over the back of her chair. "You know, you can get this surgery reversed," she said.

"Yes, I know," said Kerry. "But it's very rare, very difficult, and you never regain all that you had before."

Hannah gazed at her friend for a while in silence. "Will you, though?" she asked.

"Who knows?" replied Kerry.

They sat in silence for a minute or two.

"Would you like a coffee?" asked Hannah.

"Why not?" replied Kerry.

Hannah stood up and began making a pot of coffee.

"Have you read much Thomas Aquinas?" asked Hannah.

"Not a lot," replied Kerry.

"You didn't study him at the seminary?"

"Got chucked out before I got the chance."

"Have you heard of substance and accidence?"

"I think so."

"It's Aristotelian philosophy."

"Oh."

"Aquinas uses it to explain the Real Presence of Christ in the Eucharist. The outward form, the accidence, of the bread and wine remain the same, while the substance, the inner reality of the bread and wine, changes to the Body and Blood of Christ."

"I see."

"Well, the point is, I love – I mean, I'm using the Greek 'phileo' here, friendship love, you know – I love the you beneath the form of you. I love the substance of you, whatever the accidence. I love the Kerry beneath the male or the female

228

form of Kerry. You're my friend, Kerry, whatever you do. Can you accept that?"

"Yes, yes, thank you. I do appreciate that. I'm glad. I'd rather have friendship than nothing, truly I would, it's just I had dreamed of something other."

"I know. I'm sorry." She sat down at the table again.

They sat in silence, while the coffee percolator finished its work. When it stopped churning and hissing, Hannah stood up, poured two cups of coffee, brought them to the table and sat down. She put Kerry's coffee in front of her, and suddenly looked as though a hugely significant thought had struck her. "Or would you prefer tea?" she asked. "That's what you Brits drink, isn't it?"

"It was when I was growing up," replied Kerry. "It was our way of coping with anything. Injury, shock, bereavement, anything. Nice cup of tea. I think it's changing now. But anyway, coffee's fine. Thanks."

They sat in silence again, sipping their coffee.

This time it was Kerry who broke the silence.

"I'll get a flight back to London as soon as I can. Today, if there's a seat available."

"You don't have to. Not on my account."

There was another long silence.

"Really?" asked Kerry.

"Really what?"

"Really, I don't have to go back to London?"

"Not on my account."

"Really?"

"Really, really. Maybe it's better if you don't go. We could spend some time learning to be friends in altered circumstances. As long as it's not going to cause you even more grief, or cause you to build up hopes that are going to be frustrated."

"At the moment, I feel like as long as I live I'll feel disappointed that things couldn't be as I'd hoped. But I accept that things are as they are. It sort of makes it easier that you're going to be a nun. I don't know why it does, it just does."

"Well...good!"

"It would be a shame to leave straight away, when I've never even been to this country before."

"You're right. So stay."

"Okay."

They sat in silence for a few minutes.

"This is going to feel a little weird for a bit," observed Hannah.

"Yes, it is," agreed Kerry.

"Can you cope with weird?"

"I think so. Can you?"

"I'm up for a challenge. Let's go for it."

Kerry laughed.

"Ah, that's it!" exclaimed Hannah. "It's good to see you laughing!"

"Better to laugh than cry," said Kerry.

"You're right," agreed Hannah. She stood up and put her empty coffee cup in the sink. "Look," she said, "I'm going to go down to the school and sort out a few things, and call in on the Sisters and sort out a few other things, and when I get back around noon, I'll have some kind of a plan. Are you okay on your own for a couple of hours?"

"I'll be okay," Kerry assured her.

"Okay," said Hannah. She put her jacket back on. "See you later." She left the apartment.

Kerry began to cry again, but by the time Hannah returned three hours later, Kerry had done all the weeping she was willing to do over this particular matter. She decided that the shedding of any further tears would be a waste of time and energy. Admittedly, she had wasted over two years of her time, and a great deal of her late mother's money, causing herself great physical pain and previously unimaginable grief, but Kerry was at least an admirably practical individual. Better to make the best of what is, rather than yearn for ever for what cannot be. As for the reversal of the surgery, she was unsure. Reassignment surgery was not an experience she would wish to repeat, but on the other hand, she did not feel at home in her new body, or at least, not yet. This would need further thought.

Three: Kerry and Hannah head west

"Here's the plan, then," said Hannah, when she returned. "I'm going to take the next three days to finish my term paper. If you feel you can, you could spend that whole time just looking around Boston. There's plenty to see. You could even get a train out to Salem and visit all the sites connected with the witch trials. We'd see each other each evening. I decided not to stay on at the Law School till the end of the semester. There's no point. It's nearly over anyway, and the term paper was the last thing I had to do. The Sisters are happy enough for me to leave as soon as I've finished it and travel out to Yellowstone State, without any further delay. You could come too, see a whole lot of this country, see the Reservation and meet some of the Native American people I'll be working with, and you could still get back to Boston easily in time for your flight to London, in time for Christmas. How's that sound?"

It sounded good to Kerry, better than loafing around being depressed, whether in Cambridge, Massachusetts, or in London.

The rain had cleared that morning. The afternoon was cold and brilliantly sunny. Kerry took the T into the city and wandered disconsolately on Boston Common, through crooked streets of attractive old houses and down to the harbour, where she sat at a café and drank a blueberry smoothie, as she watched the light fade over the melancholy Atlantic. She brooded continuously over the decision she had made and the absurdity of it. What had he been thinking of? What should she do now? Now she realised with crystal clarity that love could inspire not only great sacrifice but enormous folly. But how to redeem her circumstances now that she had done what she had done?

The next day, she caught a train to Salem. She was impressed. There were houses there that would count as old even if they were in England. She visited the witches' house and the memorial garden for those who had been executed in the persecution. At least her own suffering was not fatal, and it had been occasioned by her own free choice.

On the third day, she rose early and spent the entire day visiting sites connected with the American Revolution, inspired by all the rhetoric and symbolism of liberty, but wondering what the dispossessed Indigenous Peoples and the enslaved Africans had made of it all. She found, along the revolutionary trail, a very simple Catholic chapel, devoid of almost any ornament, occupying a building which had originally been a Congregational church. Here she sat, gazing at the plain altar for a long time in a silence which began in repressed agony and progressed into resigned peacefulness.

They were to travel to Yellowstone State by bus, not because the Sisters could not afford to fly, but as an act of solidarity with the poor, for whom the bus was generally the only means of transport they could afford. It was also out of concern over climate change, of which Kerry was only just beginning to become fully aware. By air, the journey would take a few hours, even with the necessary change at Minneapolis or Denver. By bus, it would take more than two days and two nights, with several changes of vehicle. They would be accompanied by Sister Anne-Marie Phelan, the Vocations Director for the Sisters of Charity of Jerusalem, Massachusetts.

Hannah had completed her term paper, submitted it, and formally left the Law School. Kerry had completed her brief tourist's experience of Boston and Salem. On the fourth full day of her visit, while Hannah packed her bags ready for her long sojourn in the Far West, Kerry wrote her long-overdue letter to Father Patrick, and another to Father Donald, describing everything that had happened and telling them she would be back home by Christmas. She headed to the local library to send the emails she should already have sent to Mario and Peter, explaining what she had done.

Mario must have been at an internet café in La Esperanza at the very same moment, as his response came back only ten minutes or so after Kerry had sent her somewhat agonised explanation.

"No," wrote Mario. "Don't give me that. You're pulling my plonker. This is a wind up, isn't it?"

Kerry replied that it was not, and suggested they shift to Skype. Mario agreed.

"Are you serious?" he replied.

Kerry replied that she was completely serious.

"Gordon Bennett," replied Mario. "You're really serious?"

Kerry, slightly irritated by now, asked whether Mario required medical documentation or photographic evidence.

"Keep your hair on," replied Mario. "I'm in shock, that's all."

Then, before Kerry had replied, "What did you do that for? You tosser." And, as an afterthought, "Speaking of which, can you? I mean, how can you? Or rather, how do you? What's it like?"

Kerry was reassured to see that her friend's pastoral sensitivity had not deserted him.

"I don't know," she replied. "I haven't. I hadn't even thought about it. I did it for love, not for thrills."

"Funny to think of you as a woman, Kerry," wrote Mario. "Are you as f*cking ugly as you were when you were a bloke?"

"That's no way to speak to a woman," replied Kerry. "Anyway, I've never been as ugly as you are, you short, squat, ugly little git."

"That's nice, isn't it? You've got more of a mouth on you now than when you were a bloke. You want to calm down, woman. Anyway, I've got to get home to the missus, or she'll miss us (geddit?). So take it easy. I'm still your mate, even if you have been a total f*cking tosser. I still want you at the wedding. I'll let you know when we've got a date. Take care."

Kerry felt reassured by her old friend's abuse. She had not expected such speedy acceptance.

Acceptance was not what she felt when she met Sister Martina the next morning. Martina came to drive Hannah and Kerry to the bus station, where they would meet Sister Anne-Marie. Hannah was not quite ready when Martina rang the doorbell, and she told Kerry to go on down to the waiting car. She would be down in a few minutes.

Martina, who was a few years older than Kerry, introduced herself as "a friend of Hannah and Hannah's family from way back." She had entered the Congregation straight after university and was now fully professed – in other words, a full member for life. She put Kerry's two small suitcases in the vehicle's trunk and opened the back door for Kerry to take a seat. She sat back down in the driver's seat and twisted around to speak to Kerry. Kerry felt an uneasy atmosphere between them.

"Kerry," said Martina, "Excuse me, but I feel the need to be open and honest with you."

Kerry was not looking forward to whatever was coming next.

"As a Christian and as a Catholic nun," continued Martina, "I love you."

Kerry could sense a "but" coming.

"But as an old friend and a colleague of Hannah, who you have deeply upset," continued Martina, "I have to tell you that you have really, really, *really* pissed – me – off. Maybe I'm old-fashioned, although I'm not that much older than either of you, but when I was coming to consciousness as a feminist, things were more straightforward. As far as I'm concerned, you're play-acting. You're not a woman. You're just a man in anatomical drag. I don't go along with all this gender-reassignment malarkey. You're either a man or a woman. It's a totally essential part of your human identity. You may be gay, straight or bi, but you're either a woman or a man. You don't know what it is to grow up as a girl, to have spent years facing the discrimination girls and women face. You'll never know what it is to have a period or PMS. Men who become women think they can just waltz in on the party and enjoy all the perks, without having gone through the suffering. Women who become men are traitors to the cause. You may look like a woman, or even feel like a woman, but as far as I'm concerned, you're still a guy. And you've caused enormous pain to my friend Hannah, so I'm angry. As far as I'm concerned, you'd do Hannah a favour if you'd just get the hell back to London. This idea of hers of taking you out to Yellowstone State with her is totally crazy. I don't understand why Anne-Marie agrees with her. Anyway, I just thought you ought to know."

"I see," replied Kerry. "Well, thank you for telling me."

She did not feel thankful. It was just a polite form of words. She was British. She had often admired the straightforwardness of American friends and colleagues but now she saw much to be desired in British middle-class hypocrisy. She did not necessarily need to know exactly where she stood with someone, as long as, wherever she was standing – or, as in this case, sitting – people were being nice to her. If she herself thought ill of someone, she was happy to do them the honour of not telling them what she thought either, except with the most diplomatic of circumlocutions.

"Well, now I've cleared the air, we can relate to each other more easily," said Martina.

"Good," said Kerry, thinking that Martina's frankness had certainly not made relating to Martina any easier for her. She was glad that Martina was not travelling with them any further than the bus station, but now she was worried about the reception she might receive from Sister Anne-Marie.

Anne-Marie, however, had had a good three decades more than Martina to develop human sensitivity. Whatever she thought of gender reassignment, or of the impact of Kerry's choices on her young postulant, she greeted Kerry kindly and treated her exactly as she would have treated her had she not spent an evening drying Hannah's hysterical, self-condemnatory, near-despairing tears five days before.

Anne-Marie sat with Kerry on the bus to New York.

"Do you mind if I speak to you about what happened between you and Hannah?" asked Anne-Marie.

Of course Kerry minded. She would rather die than discuss it any more.

"Not at all," she said.

"You know that Hannah told me about it all, don't you?"

"Well, she said she needed to go and talk to the Sisters, so yes, I suppose I realised you would know."

"I know it's been real difficult for you, that Hannah was real upset, and that you've been doubly unhappy because you were disappointed in love, and because you didn't want to hurt the object of your love. I just want to say this to you: whatever you feel now about the choice you made, there's no situation God can't take and use for some good purpose. Whatever you decide to do in the future, God can use the decisions you've already made to do some good for other people and yourself, even if you can't see the way ahead just yet. Never give up hope, even if you have to let go of some particular hope right now. There's no situation God can't redeem somehow. Christ became a human being, was crucified, died and rose from the dead. What situation could be more hopeless than death itself? What liberation greater than liberation from death? Hannah's told me all about the work you did in Cortesia, Kerry. You have great gifts. What's happened recently doesn't change that. You can do great things, with God's help. Don't ever give up hope. I just wanted to tell you that. I hope you don't mind."

Kerry felt deeply moved.

"Thank you," she managed to say, at length.

Anne-Marie simply grasped her hand, and squeezed it for a while before letting go of it. They sat in silence for a few miles.

"If you ever feel the need to talk to anyone," said Anne-Marie, "feel free to talk to me."

"Thank you," said Kerry.

Somewhere in the middle of Pennsylvania, Kerry began to understand, in her own flesh, the sacrifice involved in making the journey out West by bus. She felt desperately cramped and restless. They had been on the road all day, and the whole night lay before them, then another whole day, then another whole night, then half a day more. As for the view, the daylight hours had been filled with motorways and traffic, and now, as Kerry had been told, they were passing through particularly beautiful hill country and it was pitch dark.

It was getting on for midnight when they arrived in Pittsburgh. Kerry had fallen asleep, but she woke up when the bus stopped at the first traffic light. They pulled in to the bus terminal and the bus driver announced that they all had to get out and wait inside the terminal, while the bus was prepared for the onward journey to Chicago.

The terminal was filled with noise and people. Children ran around laughing. Teenagers stood transfixed by video games emitting bleeps and jingles and the sound of gunfire. A large middle-aged man was trying to get some rest lying across four hard plastic chairs.

On the way to the restroom, Kerry was approached by a tall man who asked her quietly, "Hey babe, want some snow?" Kerry had no idea what 'snow' might be in this context, judging that the individual concerned probably had no shamanic powers over the weather, but assumed that if the offer had not been somehow nefarious, it would not have been made in such a manner. "No, thank you," she replied, and hurried on, taking refuge in the women's restroom, which was still an odd experience for her, since such places, under whatever name, had until fairly recently been barred to him by a cultural and psychological gulf: a gulf as absolute as that which divides the living from the dead, places of horror and morbid fascination when he was a young child, and of fear when he was a teenager, fear that he might accidentally wander into one and be discovered, leading to arrest and imprisonment, or unmanning by hysterical Amazons, or jeering contempt from his male comrades. How life had changed!

Just before three in the morning, the bus pulled in to the Cleveland bus terminal, and all passengers were required once more to leave the bus. The inside of the terminal was like a gathering of zombies, people wandering around in a state of semi-consciousness, others attempting rest in a variety of extraordinarily uncomfortable looking positions, while wakeful teenagers rendered all such efforts futile through the continuous operation of the video games provided for the purpose of afflicting the damned: the damned being those who, failing to pursue the American dream with sufficient ruthlessness, efficiency or luck, experienced instead the American nightmare, poverty in the midst of plenty, a level of plenty unattained since the beginning of the world.

For want of anywhere to sit down, Kerry stood with Hannah and Anne-Marie in a collective stupor in the middle of the waiting room. Kerry's eyes closed for a while, until she suddenly became aware of something brushing across her denim-clad buttocks. She started fully awake and looked over her shoulder. A rather unattractive, thin young man with a stubbly face and a baseball cap turned back to front withdrew his hand from her behind, winked at her and whispered, "Nice ass, baby," before wandering away as though without a care in the world. Kerry felt violated. She had never experienced such a thing before her operation, not even at the seminary.

After three quarters of an hour inside the terminal, they were able to re-board the bus. Now, nothing was able to come between Kerry and an exhausted sleep. She slept heavily for nearly three hours, and only woke when the bus driver announced they were stopping for their breakfast break at some anonymous roadside fast-food emporium. The sky was lightening, but stars were still visible in the clear sky over the lights in the vast parking lot.

Kerry chose a stack of pancakes with blueberries for her breakfast. She had never come across such a thing before – not for breakfast. As a man, she had never put on weight easily, and assumed she would not put it on easily as a woman either. She did not only assume so. She hoped so. She noted that she hoped so, and was interested in the fact. Why did she hope so? It was, she assumed, the kind of thing that many women hoped, within the context of a patriarchal society which had a tendency to objectify women. But she had never even thought about her figure before. Now she wanted to be pretty. Why? Was she beginning to think like a woman? And if so, was she internalising an oppressive false consciousness imposed on her by a domineering and sexist society? Was the very fact that she was observing her own thoughts in this way evidence that she really was still a man inside, and that only the outward form of her body had changed? After all, she had not really considered herself a lesbian for continuing to love Hannah after her gender reassignment. She had lost such maleness as she had had, without truly becoming female. She had considered herself to be, essentially, without gender. Whether male or female, Kerry was who Kerry was, and Kerry loved Hannah. Gender was irrelevant; its only function was as a bridge or a barrier to Hannah's love. Except, of course, that now she realised that it never could be a bridge. But she had taken on certain forms of behaviour that she had assumed were expected of women; certain forms of clothing, a certain gait, even a modest and judicious use of makeup. Did behaving as if you were a woman have the effect, at length, of turning you into one? And if so, was the woman you turned into some unchanging biological essence, or a social and cultural construct, the form of which depended entirely on the time and place in which you lived? In which case, what kind of modern western woman was she likely to become? How much control did she exercise over such a transition?

She wished Peter were here. He would be able to guide her in such matters. She could ask Hannah and Anne-Marie too, but she felt too awkward to do so. Anyway, it was much too early in the morning and she was scarcely capable of rational thought. She needed more coffee. Between the three of them, they consumed an enormous and unhealthy quantity of the hot, black liquid, succeeding in shocking themselves into waking consciousness to the point that Kerry began to tremble.

The sun rose behind them on the highway to Chicago, and Kerry saw around her an unending flatness: a flatness that seemed flatter and more extensive than anything she had ever seen before, perhaps because, unlike the English Midlands or the Fens, she did not know where the flatness ended. The land was brown and dull, the soil bare, the grass dead, the trees few, the fields regular and square, the roads straight, crossing each other at right angles at regular intervals, and Kerry wished they were travelling in summer, yearning for greenness and variety.

Kerry overheard the people behind her talking about the weather. They were amazed, indeed, alarmed, that it was December and still no snow. Little rain, either. They worried about the next year's growing season and how crazy the climate was becoming. They discussed the difficulties their children were having running the farms that they had run before them. It was hard enough to make a living with the banks and seed companies always on their heels, and the weather was making it a whole lot worse. Who'd be a farmer these days? It was no way to get rich. Yet, if nobody did it, all the bankers and the seed company executives would starve to death.

Kerry could see the sun sparkling on the lake beyond the skyscrapers of downtown Chicago as they drove into the city centre. Another large bus terminal, more crowds, a bottle of water, and another bus – this time for Minneapolis.

Hannah, Anne-Marie and Kerry swapped seats at every stop now, to ensure that none of them grew lonely. Although, there was not much chance of that for Kerry, as whoever sat next to her, when the seat was unoccupied, chatted freely to her. She seemed to attract people who needed to share their life stories with her.

Towards the end of another long and wearisome night, the bus pulled in to a diner in some small town in rural West Dakota.

Kerry, Hannah and Anne-Marie said little over breakfast. They were all utterly exhausted. They each guzzled coffee, but with diminished effect. This weariness would only be overcome by rest.

Emerging from the diner, Kerry smelt the air. It was bitter cold, and fresh, with some subtle, clean scent that she did not recognise. As the bus pulled out of town, the sun rose behind them, setting the surrounding land aglow. The high plains rolled away on three sides of them, undulating like an ocean of dry yellow grass with patches of a pale silver-grey plant which Anne-Marie, sitting in the seat behind her, told her was sagebrush. On the fourth side, to their south, great bluffs rose up, topped by sandstone cliffs, with here and there, between the highway and the bluffs, a sandstone formation carved into weird shapes by the wind. If Kerry ignored the highway, with its attendant fencing and lines of telegraph poles, there was no evidence of human existence in any direction. The early morning sunlight picked out every blade of grass and every strand of sage, throwing sharp shadows north-westwards. Not far from the road, towards the north, a group of antelope ran across the grass and down a gully, out of sight.

Unlike the flat land further east, Kerry found these Great Plains infinitely fascinating. She felt she could watch them for ever: the undulations in the land, the play of light over the winter-yellowed grasses, the gullies and bluffs, the ranges of dry hills covered with sparse pine woods, once in a while, a river running through a cottonwood-filled valley; and everywhere, the sense of unending space, but space without boredom or intimidation, a space full of distinctive landmarks, of intimate differences, of particular places within the greater space, under the clear, blue, enormous, overarching sky. Having never seen such country, she loved it at first sight, with a deep, awe-struck, adoring love. She felt expanded by it, inspired to the point of elation, overwhelmed with a beauty that combined delicacy with grandeur. And this was winter! What, she wondered, if she were to stay to see the spring?

Sister Frances was waiting for them at the bus depot at Cottonwood Creek. She was a discreet and diplomatic woman and had been fully briefed, so there were no indelicacies. She explained that she had arranged for Kerry, after one night at the convent, to stay with a very lovely local lady, Vera Shoots Straight, one of the elders, who she was sure Kerry would find very hospitable and very interesting.

At the edge of the small town of Cottonwood Creek, the blacktop road gave out, and the dirt road to the Reservation began. As Sister Frances drove the Sisters' van, great clouds of red dust billowed out beside and behind them. The sky began to cloud over from the West. By the time they arrived in the little town of Dusty, at the eastern edge of the Reservation, the light was beginning to fade, the sky was filled with low grey clouds, and it began to snow.

Four: Kerry meets Vera Shoots Straight

Vera Shoots Straight's house was painted orange. It lay off the blacktop road running north along the river from Dusty to the edge of the Reservation. A rutted track, still visible beneath the light snow of the night before, turned off the road as it approached the top of a small incline, and ran downhill and around the back of a hillock surmounted by pine trees. The house lay between the hillock and the river, the course of which was marked by willow thickets and large cottonwoods. Like all the other houses Kerry had seen so far, it was single storey. There being so much space in Yellowstone State, there was clearly little need for an upstairs.

To the right of the house were three large old vehicles in varying states of decay: a green, rusting pickup truck with no glass in its windows, and two cars, one of which lacked a passenger door and the other a wheel. All the tyres were flat.

Sister Jackie parked the car in front of the house and led Kerry up the three wooden steps to the front door, which she knocked on once, before entering without waiting for a reply. They entered a large, warm, brightly lit room that looked as if it served as kitchen, dining room and sitting room combined. On one wall hung a vibrantly coloured blanket, on another, a quilt decorated with a star design, and on another, a three dimensional picture of the Sacred Heart, along with numerous photographs of people Kerry took to be family members.

A short and slightly plump Native American woman with a round, wrinkled face and thin grey hair gathered into a loose bun behind her head was struggling to her feet from a chair by a table near the door. She wore a loose, calf-length, pale blue cotton dress and a dark blue woollen cardigan.

Surrounding the table, and filling the floor of the rest of the large room, except for spaces by the stove and fridge, and aisles leading to the doors, were cardboard boxes, piled up in twos and threes (and a few fours by the walls).

"There's no need to get up, Vera," said Sister Jackie.

"Oh, I like to greet my guests properly," replied Vera. "But my legs are a bit bad today."

"Why don't you sit down again, then?" suggested Jackie.

"I guess I'll sit down, then," agreed Vera, and sat back down again. "You guys better get yourselves some coffee. It's there on the stove."

Jackie fetched two blue enamel mugs from the top of the refrigerator and filled them with hot coffee from a pot on the cast iron wood stove, handing one to Kerry and taking a seat with Vera at the table. Kerry remained standing by the front door. Vera looked her up and down.

"I guess you're Kerry, then?" said Vera.

"Yes," said Kerry.

"You're from England?"

"Yes, that's right."

"Oh." She paused. "That's way over there, isn't it?" Vera indicated vaguely eastwards, with her lips.

"Yes, I suppose so."

"My Ernie was stationed there in the war."

"Oh, do you know where?"

"Oh, someplace over there. He went to France."

"On D Day?"

"I guess so. You better sit down. Take that box off the other chair, there," said Vera, pointing with her lips to the third chair at the table. "I was going to sort through some beads in there. I'm making moccasins for my grandson's give-away."

Kerry moved the box from the chair and put it on top of the box on the floor next to the chair. In the box were glass jars of brightly coloured beads. She sat down.

"What lovely colours!" observed Kerry.

"I usually use blues and reds," said Vera.

"Vera does beautiful beadwork," said Jackie. "May I show Kerry some of what you've made?" she asked Vera.

"Go ahead," replied Vera. "The things I've finished are in that box by my bed."

Jackie made her way, with some difficulty, into the bedroom that opened off the main room, just behind where Vera was sitting.

"There are quite a lot of boxes here by the bed," she called. "Which one is it?"

"That one box," explained Vera. "That one by the bed."

"That's what I'm saying," replied Jackie. "There are quite a lot of boxes by the bed."

"Oh. I guess it's a white box. By the top of the bed."

There were rustling sounds as Jackie opened various white boxes until she found the one she was looking for. She carried it in to the main room and put it on the table. Opening it again, she lifted out half a dozen belt buckles, a dozen pairs of long earrings, two pendants and two pairs of moccasins, one fully beaded and the other decorated with thick lines of beads on a white buckskin base. She spread them out on the table. They were all adorned with intricate geometric designs. The colours glowed like light through stained glass. Kerry was spellbound. "These are beautiful!" she exclaimed. "May I touch them?"

"Go ahead," said Vera. Kerry picked up the fully beaded moccasins and felt the surface of the beads and the thickness of the hide. The hide was soft and supple and smelt of smoke.

"How long does it take to make a pair of moccasins like these?" asked Kerry.

"Oh, quite a while," replied Vera. "I been working on these things for a couple years now. Still got some more to do. I want to make a jacket, too."

"When's your grandson coming home?" asked Jackie.

"In the summer, I guess," replied Vera. "I'm worried about him, out there. I pray for him all the time."

"Where is your grandson?" asked Kerry.

245

"In the service," answered Vera. "He finishes in the summer. When he comes back, we'll have a giveaway for him at the Dusty Powwow."

"Powwow?" queried Kerry.

"Dancing," said Vera. "Everyone gets together and there's all kinds of dances; traditional, fancy dance, grass dance, jingle dance."

"Powwows are wonderful occasions," said Jackie. "The dancers wear such beautiful costumes, and people come from all over to sit round and watch the dancing and visit with each other."

"What's a giveaway?" asked Kerry.

"That's where we give everyone gifts as a way of thanking Creator for something, like my grandson coming back home safe from the war, or if someone's died we have a giveaway in memory of 'em."

"The family of the person in whose name the giveaway is done give blankets, beadwork, clothing and groceries to other families," added Jackie. "People are very generous here."

"That's why there's all these boxes," said Vera. "I got beads and buckskin and thread and canned goods and shirts and cloth all over. I still need to make some ribbon shirts. I got yellow ribbon for blue shirts and pink for the red ones. I want to make a star quilt too."

Kerry continued examining the beadwork.

"Do you sew?" asked Vera.

"No," said Kerry. "I wish I knew how."

"I'll show you," said Vera. "If you like it, you can help me decorate a ribbon shirt. I can teach you beadwork too, if you want."

"I'd love that!" said Kerry.

"How long are you staying?" asked Vera.

"Oh," said Kerry, disappointed. "Less than a fortnight. That's not long enough, is it?"

"Four nights?" queried Vera. "We can't do much with that. I thought you were staying nearly two weeks."

"Yes, that's right, nearly two weeks," said Kerry.

"Well, we'll see what we can do," said Vera. "You can sleep in that room over there," she said, pointing with her lips to the other side of the main room. Maybe put your bags in there now."

"Thank you," said Kerry. She picked up her bags from where she had left them by the front door and carried them into the bedroom. It was very small, and nearly filled by the single bed, which was covered with a star quilt in shades of yellow and orange. The window looked out to the front of the house, towards the pine-covered hillock. She stood and gazed at it for a while, then turned and went back into the main room.

"You know," Vera was saying. "My sister Rose's husband's ex-wife Thelma's grandson. *That* Richard."

"Oh, I remember," said Jackie; but Kerry thought she looked as though she did not.

"Anyway," continued Vera, "Richard's gonna marry Verlene this summer."

"Verlene?"

"You know."

"Have I met her?"

"My brother-in-law, Freddy, his brother's first wife Arlene's granddaughter. You know."

"Freddy was Ernie's brother?"

"No. My sister Clarice's second husband. You met him two years ago at the Oil Bluffs Powwow. Died last October. *That* Freddy."

"Oh, yes," said Jackie, clearly none the wiser.

"Well, that's the big surprise," said Vera. "I thought Verlene was going with Eddy."

Jackie looked blank.

"You know. Eddy. My cousin Georgia's oldest daughter Erica's son. Lives over at Lonely Woman Creek."

"I don't think I've met him," said Jackie, boldly.

"You have," said Vera, firmly. "Last summer at the Dusty Powwow. I introduced you."

"Oh," said Jackie, meekly.

"Well, we better eat," said Vera. "It's about noon, ain't it? There's some deer stew in the refrigerator and a bit of potato salad and some corn. Can you fix that for us, Sister Jackie?"

"Sure," said Jackie. "Then I'd better be on my way. Kerry, will you be okay here today with Vera? Tomorrow, we can come by and pick you up and start showing you around."

"That's fine," said Kerry. "There'll be plenty to do here."

"It's just that Vera's place is a bit isolated if you don't have a vehicle."

"I have a vehicle!" exclaimed Vera. "I got three out there!"

"But those are all broken down, Vera," said Jackie.

"They just need a bit of air in the tyres," said Vera. "Maybe the pickup needs a new battery."

"And glass in its windows," added Jackie.

"At least you can see out of it," said Vera.

"I don't think any of them would work any more," said Jackie.

"They'd work!" asserted Vera. "They all worked fine when I last drove 'em."

"That was quite a time ago, though, wasn't it, Vera?"

"Only ten or twenty years or so. Maybe thirty, with the pickup."

"Well, at the moment, I don't think Kerry could drive any of them into town."

"Maybe I'll get Will or someone to bring a pump next time he comes so they can sort out those tyres."

"Okay, Vera," said Jackie. "Well, I'll get the meal together."

Kerry had never eaten deer meat before. It was very tender and tasted unlike any other meat she had eaten. Vera had stewed it with onions and dried wild turnips. "Not much fat in this stew," said Vera. "There ought to be a nice layer of fat on top of it, but white people don't like fat, do you?"

"I expect some do," said Kerry.

"Well, when I used to serve the priests and sisters stew in the old days, they always seemed to pick the fat off the top and put it to one side. So I started making white people's deer stew, without much fat. Doesn't taste so good to me."

"It's very nice," said Kerry. "Thank you."

"What kind of food do you guys eat over there?" asked Vera.

"Oh, all sorts of stuff," said Kerry. "I suppose the traditional English foods are roast meat with roast potatoes and boiled vegetables and gravy, and fish and chips, and sausages and mash."

"I like the sound of the roast meat," said Vera. "I like to eat roast buffalo when I can. Makes me think of the old days."

"But you weren't around in those old days, Vera," said Jackie.

"I can still think of 'em if I like," said Vera.

"Are there still buffalo around?" asked Kerry.

"There are now," said Vera. "The tribe's got a small herd that lives up in the hills over beyond Prairie Dog Flats. They only take a couple of animals a year, but when they do, us elders get some meat."

When they had finished the meal and cleared away the dishes, Jackie left them. Vera said she was going to have a rest, and went to lie down on her bed. Kerry went and lay on the bed in her room and began to read the book she had brought with her on Transsexuality and Queer Theory, hoping for some clarity of thought about how she should regard herself in the light of the change she had had inflicted on her body, indeed, whether she really wished to persist in the struggle to be a 'she' at all, but after a few pages, she decided she would rather think about something entirely different. So she continued reading Louis de Berniere's *The Troublesome Offspring of Cardinal Guzman*. She had read it before, but she loved de Berniere's version of magical realism, and never tired of re-reading his Latin American trilogy. In fact, she admitted to herself uneasily, she much preferred it to the work of the founder of the genre, Gabriel Garcia Marquez, the Colombian whose famous *One Hundred Years of Solitude*

Kerry considered would have been much better if it had been twenty-five years shorter.

Even de Berniere's unsurpassed ability to evoke a magical parallel world, however, was insufficient to prevent Kerry's thoughts drifting back to the events of a week ago, and to mournful reflection on the futility of what he had done to himself, or what she had done to herself. She was not at home in her own body, and the sacrifice he had made for love had all been for nothing. She put the book aside, lay on her back on the bed and tried to pray. "Lord Jesus Christ, Son of God," she prayed, "have mercy upon me; Lord Jesus Christ, Son of God, have mercy upon me; Lord Jesus Christ, Son of God, have mercy upon me."

No words formed in her mind in response to her repeated prayer, but as she repeated it, she was overcome by a feeling of absolute acceptance, uncritical love, infinite kindness, total affirmation. She felt immersed in a love so enormous that there was no end to it, no edge to it, no top or bottom to it. She felt like a tiny sponge floating in a shoreless ocean of love. She felt completely saturated with a divine love that made her feel like laughing out loud in delight. Usually strong emotions made Kerry weep, but this had so little in common with sadness that she felt elated, exhilarated, ecstatic. She did not care about the future, whether she ended up male or female or something in between. Even if she could never attain the love she had sought from Hannah, she felt a serene certainty that, whatever her future held, it would be happy. She lost track of time. She had no idea how long she lay on the bed, her heart filled with this sudden and inexplicable joy.

Suddenly, there was an extraordinarily loud bang. Kerry leapt to her feet and ran into the main room. A bitter cold draught blew in from the open front door. Vera was leaning against the doorpost, silhouetted against the darkening sky outside as the sunset faded behind the pine trees on the hill. "Hit it!" she exclaimed. She lowered her rifle, turned rather awkwardly and leant it once more against the wall to the right of the door, which she shut. "It's pretty cold out there," she observed.

"What was out there?" asked Kerry in alarm.

"Deer," said Vera. "Young one. I'll call Will now and get him to come on down and butcher it." Then she added, "You don't know how to butcher deer, do you?"

"No, I'm afraid not," replied Kerry. "Sorry."

"Thought not. I guess you guys don't hunt much in England?"

"Some people hunt foxes, or they used to until a few years ago."

"Foxes? I wouldn't want to eat fox meat."

"Oh, they didn't eat them," explained Kerry. "Just killed them."

Vera looked confused. "They don't hunt things they eat, but they hunt things they don't eat?" she asked.

"Yes," confirmed Kerry.

"White people do some real strange things," observed Vera.

She picked up the phone mounted on the wall above where she leant her gun, and keyed in a number. She waited. "Will? That you?...Yeah, I shot a deer. Can you come right now and butcher it for me?...Oh. Okay. How long you gonna be?...Oh, alright, then." She hung up.

"He'll be a little while," she said. "Just closing up the store. Then he'll come." Then she said, "Can you get me my stick? I left it over there by the table." Kerry saw a walking stick leaning in the corner of the room, right by the table. She navigated the aisle between the boxes between the front door and the table, and brought it to her.

"Right now, we're going to the stove," said Vera, and began making her way slowly and painfully to the stove, leaning heavily on her stick. Kerry followed her. Vera lit the gas and put a small cast iron skillet on the heat. "See that brown paper bag up on the refrigerator?" asked Vera. "Get me that, please." Kerry reached the brown bag down from the top of the refrigerator and handed it to Vera. Vera put her hand in to the bag and drew out a handful of what looked like dry, dark green granules, which she dropped into the skillet. After a few moments, fragrant smoke began to rise up from the granules as they began to smoulder. Vera extended her hand over the pan and wafted the smoke into her face and over her body. "Cedar," she said. "We need to pray to Creator, say thank you for the deer, ask forgiveness for killing it, ask the deer to forgive us and ask Creator to bless the deer's spirit. I'm gonna pray in my language. You bless yourself with the smoke, like you saw me do. We call that 'smudging'." Vera began to pray quietly, her eyes closed, her hand on her heart. Her words sounded like a gentle breeze riffling the leaves of the trees on a warm day in spring. Kerry listened as she wafted smoke from the cedar in the skillet over her face and body, thinking of the deer lying dead outside and asking forgiveness for the taking of a life and gratitude for the fact that Vera would have plenty to eat.

"That should do it," said Vera after a while. "We better sit down and wait for Will, now. I hope it won't be too dark for him when he gets here. More or less dark already. I'll put some water on for tea."

Five: Kerry gets acquainted with Will and Whispering River

About twenty minutes later, there was a sharp knock on the door, and Will entered the house. He looked around thirty. Despite the cold, he was dressed only in jeans and a t-shirt, with a thickly lined red and black checked cloth jacket that hung open. He was around six feet tall, with fine, jet black hair that fell to his shoulders and curled under slightly at the ends. The colour of his skin, like that of Vera's, was not the copper that Kerry had expected but paler than that, closer to gold than copper. Will had a longer face than Vera's, with high cheek bones, very dark brown eyes, whose size was magnified by his spectacles, and very full lips. He was clean-shaven, or, rather, he looked as if he had never had to shave. His face was smooth and almost completely hairless. Despite the masculinity of his figure – the height, the broad shoulders and narrow hips – his smooth skin and long hair gave him an air of femininity that Kerry found arrestingly beautiful. He reminded her of Hannah.

"Hi, Grandma," he said to Vera, and then turned his attention to Kerry. "Hello," he said, smiling radiantly. His teeth were perfectly regular and brilliantly white. He held out his hand and Kerry stood up and shook it. He had a firm grip and held her gaze as she looked at him.

"I'm Will," he said. "Short for Wilhelm. Wilhelm Many Paint Horses."

"I'm Kerry," she said. "Kerry Ahern."

"You're not from round here?" asked Will.

"No," said Vera. "She's from way over there, in England."

"England?" queried Will.

"Yes," said Kerry. "I'm a friend of one of the Sisters. Just visiting."

"Oh," said Will. "Well, welcome to the Rez."

"Thank you," said Kerry.

"Do you want to help me butcher that deer?" asked Will.

"Oh. I'm not sure," replied Kerry. "I'm not very good with blood."

"Well, come and keep me company while I do it, then," said Will.

"Alright," said Kerry.

"Better put your jacket on," said Vera. "It's cold out there."

Kerry fetched her down jacket from the bedroom.

As Will left the house, he pushed a switch by the front door and the snowy ground in front of the house was illuminated for thirty feet or more by the yard light. Will led Kerry out of the house, away to just beyond the patch of light, where the deer lay where it had fallen, killed by a single expert shot to the heart, a small patch of frozen blood darkening the snow on one side of it.

"Okay," said Will. "We're going to have to drag it a bit to bring it into the light. Can you grab her back legs? She'll feel pretty heavy if you've never dragged a dead deer before."

"Not that I remember," said Kerry.

The deer did feel heavy. Kerry felt uncomfortable, handling a dead animal. But she had never felt cruel eating meat, and she thought that it was unlikely that any of the animals she had eaten in her life had had such a natural life, and a quick and humane death, as this deer.

"Okay," said Will. "I'm going to get my knife from the pickup. It's real sharp, so stay well clear while I use it, it'd have your fingers off as soon as look at you." He walked over to his truck and returned with a large knife. With a few expert cuts, he had loosened the deer's skin, which he then drew off the carcass like a pullover. Kerry felt mildly nauseous.

254

"If you don't feel good, go ahead and go back in," said Will.

"No, I'm okay," said Kerry. "I've been in butchers' shops before. I've just never seen a whole animal being cut up."

"The important thing is to show the animal respect," said Will. "It's given up its life so we can eat; its death gives us life. That's why we have to give thanks to its spirit and ask its forgiveness."

Will made a long cut down the length of the deer's belly and began cutting out the internal organs. Kerry felt distinctly queasy, but did not wish to admit defeat. She did not like being around spilt blood but she found that she did enjoy being around Will.

Will pulled out a large, bloody, rubbery-looking organ and held it up to Kerry. "This is the deer's liver," he said. "Now, don't be upset, but it's important to us to show the animal respect by eating a bit of the raw liver." He cut a small piece from the liver, held it aloft for a while, and put it in his mouth, chewing carefully for a short while and swallowing. "Okay," he said. "I'm going to be as quick as I can now because it's getting colder. Supposed to fall to about zero tonight. That's zero Fahrenheit, so that's a bit chillier than zero centigrade. You could go and ask Grandma Vera for her big plastic coolers so we can load up the joints and offal."

Kerry went back to the house and returned with two large plastic containers, which Will began to fill with the constituent parts of the butchered carcass, while Kerry returned to the house and came back with two more.

"So Vera's your Grandma?" asked Kerry.

"Well, we call her Grandma, but I guess you wouldn't in your way," said Will. We're related on my mother's side, and she's two generations above me, so she's Grandma."

"Oh, I see," said Kerry.

"Our mom's mom was Vera's mom's sister's daughter."

"I see," said Kerry.

Will laughed. "I bet you don't," he said. "Ask Vera about her relatives and you'll end up with a real bad headache. She's related to practically everyone on the Rez, and she can explain exactly how everyone is related to everyone else, back at least four generations."

Kerry felt suddenly lonely. "I haven't got any relations any more," she said.

"I bet you do," replied Will. "It's just that white people forget who they're related to. With us, all our mom's sisters are our moms, all our mom's brothers are our dads, our dad's brothers and sisters are our aunts and uncles, we call all our cousins brothers and sisters, and anyone else vaguely related to us is a cousin."

"Do you have big families?" asked Kerry.

"Not in the sense of people having lots of children. Traditionally, we only had as many children as the land could provide for. But in another sense, we're all one enormous family covering the whole Rez."

"How many of you live on the Reservation?"

"Probably around three thousand. Then there's another couple thousand tribal members scattered all over the West because there's so little work out here."

"And you're related to all of them?"

"I guess so, but to some more closely than others. I certainly don't know everyone. But I bet Vera does. Don't ask her. She might tell you. Then she'll expect you to remember it."

Will stood up. "That's it," he said. "We better find out what Vera wants done with all this meat. Then I better put the head and the spine and the hoofs down in the willows by the river. I guess Grandma'll let me keep the hide."

Kerry followed him into the house.

"Take some down to old Vernon," said Vera. "Give the heart to Eddy. He likes that. You can put some cuts in my freezer and keep a couple for yourself. Then give some to old man Joe and some to Flora. That'll be about it, I think."

"Okay, Grandma," said Will. He went outside, put three coolers in the back of his pickup and brought the remaining one inside, washing and bagging the meat and filling Vera's freezer with it. Then he went out and disposed of the remains of the carcass. When he had finished, he came back in and

256

said, "I'll get going, now, Grandma," but Vera said, "You better stay and eat with us. The meat'll be okay in the pickup for now." So he stayed and prepared supper under instructions from Vera, who sat at the table all the while, and then stayed on longer to watch Kerry have her first sewing lesson under Vera's expert and patient tuition. It was gone nine when he left. "Come and see the store tomorrow," he said. "The Sisters'll know where it is. You might like it."

Sister Jackie came by in the morning to take Kerry down to the Sisters' house.

"Would you like to take a look in the church first?" she asked.

Kerry was not that interested.

"Yes, I'd love to," she said.

Jackie brought the car to a halt in front of the church building – a small, white weatherboard building with a short spire-topped square tower on the west end, facing the road. Colourful geometric designs were painted on the double doors and to both sides of them. The porch was warm and the air smelt of cedar smoke. Jackie led the way through another set of double doors into the church itself.

Kerry caught her breath. Coloured light filtered through six large stained glass windows, one above the altar at the far end, one above the porch behind them, and two in each of the longer walls. Each was decorated with an abstract design in variations of one colour. To the East, behind the altar, the window was red; to the South, both were in shades of yellow; to the West, above the porch, the window was in shades of dark blue, fading to blue violet; and to the North, the clear glass of both windows was blindingly white, but etched to look like falling snowflakes. Every inch of wall space was painted with what looked like scenes from the life of Christ, but in a Native North American idiom. To the right of the altar, some radiant spirit-being appeared before a young Native woman dressed in beaded buckskin; to the right of that, she had just given birth in a lone tipi, accompanied by, Kerry supposed, her husband, and visited by hunters and by three

257

medicine men, clearly from some other people, as they were dressed strikingly differently from the woman and her husband and the hunters. Around the walls were scenes showing a Plains Indian Christ teaching and healing, eating the last supper, in another, larger tipi, being arrested by white soldiers, and tried before a white judge, and being crucified on a cottonwood trunk. Immediately to the left of the altar, this Christ was being laid to rest on a burial platform made of wood and hide; and behind the altar, he was rising to life from the platform, stretching out his arms in an embrace directed outwards to everyone in the building and at the same time upwards in an act of surrender to some unseen force which was drawing him into itself.

"These were all painted by young Native artists from this community," said Jackie. "It was a beautiful process. They studied the Gospels with us, talked to the elders, and then planned and painted these scenes. We never told them what they ought to paint. It was all their own concept, and they all worked together on it."

"How many of them?" asked Kerry.

"Four," replied Jackie. "There was Herman Red Buffalo, Ernest Tall Woman, Justine McCafferty and Mariella Big Crow."

"It's beautiful," said Kerry.

"Isn't it?" agreed Jackie. "This wouldn't have happened in the early days of this mission," she went on. "In the beginning, the missionaries thought they had the whole truth and nothing but the truth, so help them God. It was only really in the sixties that they started actually listening to Native American tradition and realising that they had much to learn from it. That's when the clergy started going to the elders to learn from them, to share in their ceremonies and find out how to see our teachings from a Native perspective. It's funny, though; as soon as we started trying to show real respect for Native traditions, in moved the Pentecostals to tell everyone they were going to hell unless they saw things their way. It's pretty frustrating."

"What do people on the Rez think of it all?" asked Kerry.

"Well, I think most of them take the view that God is God and prayer is prayer and all prayer is good. So they're happy to attend traditional ceremonies, come to Mass once in a while, go to Native American Church gatherings, which are kind of syncretic and involve the use of peyote, and attend Pentecostal prayer meetings as well. We share with them the Gospel to the best of our understanding, and pray with them, and it's really up to them to decide what to do with it all."

"Have any of the people here joined the Sisters or trained to be priests?"

"Never. I think the Church structures are so alien, so Eurocentric, it really inhibits people from taking leadership roles in what is essentially a foreign institution. It's a real shame. I just wish the Church could see it, and change. The main thing is celibacy. I mean, it's fine by me. I feel called to it. But to almost everyone round here, even though they seem to like us as people and they certainly show us respect and kindness, celibacy is just incomprehensibly weird. Traditionally, they were very accepting of diversity, people being what we might call gay, lesbian or transgendered, but they never had any tradition of celibacy. It's really crazy to impose it on them as a condition of ordained ministry, in my view. Other Churches, the Episcopalians and United Church of Christ, do have Native ministers precisely because they can be married. Those Churches don't have a presence on this Reservation but they do back in the Dakotas. It makes them stronger to have a Native clergy."

"Is there a priest living here?" asked Kerry.

"No," replied Jackie. "There's a priest's house here, so he can stay there when he comes, but nowadays there's only one priest for the whole Reservation and he lives over at Red Willow Creek because it's bigger than here and more in the middle of the Rez. So he'll celebrate Mass here and down at Chokecherry Butte one Sunday, and over at Red Willow Creek and Antelope Flats the next. Father Karl, his name is. He's a nice guy but he's getting on a bit now, not too much energy. But kind, a very kind and gentle man. The people round here really love him. But who'll come after him? There's nobody joining that religious order, and the Yellowstone State Diocese doesn't have enough priests any more either. I worry it'll all fall apart without a priest on the Rez. It shouldn't be like that. Things shouldn't be so dependent on one key man, and the Church is crazy to have allowed things to develop the way they have. But then, given that that's the way things are, the Church has to make the changes needed to make sure that there are enough clergy – and that has to mean ordaining married men, and women too. We can't go on the way we're going."

"What about all the stuff about abuse?" asked Kerry.

"Well, thank God, we seem to have escaped most of that here," replied Jackie. "There was never a residential school here, only a day school. It seems there was probably some physical abuse in the early days, you know, beating kids for doing wrong like they did in European schools, which was total anathema to Native people, who never, ever hit their kids for any reason. But there haven't been any allegations of sexual abuse on this Reservation. I don't know. It's hard to think that such things might have happened, but it's probably wishful thinking to believe they never did, either. The combination of power and repressed sexuality is pretty toxic."

They fell silent and gazed for a while at the extraordinary art work. The cedar-fragrant quietness was so deep that it felt as if it were alive, a real presence in its own right, made up of the prayers of generations of Native Americans and Catholic missionaries. At first, perhaps, they had been suspicious of each other's praying and then they had found ways to appreciate the other so that they could construct ways to the spirit world drawing on the wisdom of both traditions. Kerry was sorry to leave.

Dusty was a border town. It lay half on, half off the Whispering River Reservation. The river formed the eastern boundary of the Reservation and a few dozen houses lay on the west side of it, clustered near the bridge carrying the road from the city of Oil Bluffs, about a hundred miles to the west of Dusty, to the West Dakota border a few miles to the east. The Catholic Mission of St Henry was on the Reservation side of the river, with the priest's house and the Sisters' house nearby. But the construction of the mission church towards the end of the nineteenth century had encouraged the settlement of some German Catholic families in the area, and a small town had grown up to service the growing community of ranchers and farmers. It consisted of one street, running west to east from the river, along which were a few houses, a gas station, a Pentecostal church, two bars, Schultz's diner, Wittwer's hardware and ranch supply store, Rohrbach's grocery store and, at the far eastern end of town, the Eastern Yellowstone State Wholefood Store and Eco-Activism Center. Beneath this store's sign, written in smaller, black letters, were the words 'Proprietors: an Injun and a Forr'ner.' Beneath this declaration, on the wall beside the front door, a large target was painted, marked by several bullet-holes. It was here that Sister Frances parked the car later that morning when she drove Kerry and Hannah up town. "You two go visit with Will while I go and get groceries," she suggested.

The door tinkled when they opened it, and Will turned round from the shelf he was filling. His face lit up. "Kerry!" he said. "You came!"

Kerry smiled at him. "Of course!" she said.

"And who's your friend?" he asked.

"I'm Hannah," said Hannah. "I've come to work with the Sisters for a few months."

"Oh, well, you're welcome," said Will. He stepped forward and shook her hand warmly.

Country music was playing on the radio in the background, but a song came to an end and a male voice announced, "You're listening to K-R-E-Z, Krayzee Radio, the Voice of the Rez," and there was a brief burst of drumming and chanting before the voice announced, "And here's another in our special series of songs about broken-hearted lovers driving eighteen wheeler trucks across country for no good reason," and another country song began.

"How do you like the store?" asked Will.

"What do you sell?" asked Hannah.

"Not enough," replied Will. "But what we're trying to sell is cheap food with low sugar and salt content, organically produced fruit and vegetables and anything else we can think of to help people eat more healthily. There's big problems with diabetes on the Rez and people usually can't afford good quality food, or they're not familiar with this kind of food, so we started this store to try to address that."

"And is it working?" asked Hannah.

"Too early to say," said Will. "We make a big loss because we need to keep prices lower than the cheap, unhealthy alternatives, so we're relying on grants from foundations to subsidise it all. If enough people start buying, we can lower prices and eventually break even."

"Who are the 'we'?" asked Kerry.

"Oh, a friend of mine from Ontario in Canada," replied Will. "He and I had the idea while we were discussing Native diet and health problems a couple of years ago. We own it jointly but I run it because he's only down here once a year. He's a sleeping partner, I guess. Lives over in Toronto. We hardly ever get to see each other any more."

"Hence the sign over the door?" asked Hannah.

"Yeah," replied Will. He laughed. "When we started this place, some dumb rancher came in and told me as far as he was concerned 'whole food' was a whole lot of bull and that I was a Communist – as if it wasn't enough being an 'Injun'. He said I'd better close up or he'd run me out of town. I told him he was welcome to try, but that I had a pretty good all-round record in the marines and that he'd better catch me by surprise because my reflexes are pretty sharp. That took the wind out of his sails a bit. He shot the place up just the once and grew bored of it, so I painted the target around the bullet holes and added the bit about the proprietors. Thought the 'forr'ner' would help aggravate him a bit more – I guess it'd be hard for him to know which to hate more, the 'injun' or the 'forr'ner'. Anyway, the guy kind of flipped anyway, and took off to join one of those survivalist communities up in the mountains. He claimed the Republican Party had finally been taken over by the Communists, and that we all had to prepare to defend ourselves. I told him he was behind the times, that we're all supposed to be afraid of Islamists now, but he said he didn't know what I was talking about."

"What's with the Eco-activism bit?" asked Hannah.

"Well, that started with the debate about coal concessions right around when we opened this place," replied Will. "There are coal strip mines to the south of the Rez and there's a whole bunch of coal underneath the Rez as well, and the coal company wanted to get its hands on it. They had to get the consent of the tribe, and a bunch of us were saying we didn't want our land dug up for anything, that Mother Earth is sacred and we don't want anybody digging up her insides. We tried to persuade the whole tribe to vote against the mining – hence the Eco-activism. But we lost. Even the elders were mostly in favour of the mining, in the end. They said, we don't like the thought of the earth being dug up either, but there's hardly any work for the young people here any more, and we haven't hunted buffalo for a hundred years and more, and the land's no good for farming, and we've tried running a casino but there's no big cities anywhere around, so the casino went bust. So, what else are we gonna do? And we didn't really have an answer to that, because we didn't know. So it was about a 60/40 split in favour of the mining in the end, and before long they'll start stripping the southern edge of the Rez. Makes me sad. But at least we had a proper process. We all got to look at the way the company operates off-Rez, and they're pretty careful about reclamation, because they have to be, because of state and federal law. Maybe when they're done with mining, the land will look natural again. But it won't look like what it did before. They never get the contours just the same as what went before, and the small creeks are gone, and the sand rocks, and they never seem to get the sagebrush growing properly again either. And then there's the water pollution that goes on for years after the mining stops, and then the whole impact of burning the stuff, which is the craziest thing of all, now we know about climate change."

"What's the company?" asked Hannah.

"Well, they're owned by a bunch of forr'ners too," said Will. "Brits, in fact. The company's called Whispering River Coal, but it's owned by some massive company run from London, called Anglo Australian."

"Oh, gee," said Hannah. "Kerry and I know all about that bunch." And they began to recount the story of their work in Cortesia.

"You guys were in Cortesia!" exclaimed Will. "When?"

They told him, and he looked relieved. "I was there too, for a while," he said. "But it was a good few years ago now." He paused, and looked troubled. He was on the point of speaking again, when the door opened and Sister Frances came in.

"Hi, there, girls! Hi, there, Will!" she called cheerily. "We better be on our way now, girls. We got a lot to see."

"How about if we meet up for supper?" asked Will. "We could go to the diner."

"Well, we Sisters have some stuff we need to do this evening," replied Sister Frances, "but maybe Kerry could join you? Kerry?"

"Oh, yes," said Kerry. "I'd like to."

"Well, we can drop you off here later on," said Frances, "And I guess Will can get you back to Vera's tonight."

"Sure," said Will.

Sister Frances drove them down the river road south to Chokecherry Butte, where they visited one of the elders and a young family struggling bravely to overcome parental alcohol addiction. It was clear that nobody in Chokecherry Butte had much money. Some, apparently, had high hopes for the coal mine. The mine would be constructed to the South West of the village, and there was hope that there would be well paid work for local people. Kerry and Hannah wondered whether the local people would simply experience the dust and blasting, while the paid jobs went to outsiders. But they said nothing, for fear of causing discord when the tribe had already made its decision on the matter.

They drove through the pine-clad hills north westwards to Red Willow Creek, where Sister Frances showed them the tribal offices, the office of the Bureau of Indian Affairs, the elementary and high schools, the tribal college, the medical centre and the church. Father Karl was kind and welcoming and spoke to them about how much he loved going out into the hills on his day off, to pray and contemplate the beauty of the land. He spoke of the people's richness of spirit and poverty of means; the damage done by forcing people to abandon their culture and way of life; the problems which had been caused by alcoholism; the positive role played by traditional Native spirituality in combating addictions and the divisions caused over the question of coal mining. He seemed to have an immense compassion and a great respect for the local people, but unlike Peter Steel, he did not seem to burn with passion to see justice prevail. Perhaps it was because he was older, or because the issues were more complicated, or because the Catholic Church was now of such marginal importance on the Reservation, or because he had never read Marx or the writings of Latin American liberation theologians. He was much more like Kerry than Peter was, but he left Kerry missing her old friend, whose very difference from her had challenged her to look beyond the horizons to which she had become accustomed.

Six: Kerry passes a pleasant evening but is disturbed by two developments

It was getting dark when they returned to Dusty and dropped Kerry off at the Wholefood Store. The radio was playing flute music when she walked in. It sounded vaguely melancholy, but Kerry found it beautiful. Will smiled broadly when he saw her. "Hey, there, Kerry!" he greeted her. "How was your day?"

"Lovely, thank you," replied Kerry.

"I like that word," said Will. "It's so English."

"Am I the first English person you've met?" asked Kerry.

"No," replied Will. "I've met loads of 'em."

"What, here?" asked Kerry, in surprise.

"Yes," replied Will. "A few years back, some of us involved in the North American Aboriginal Ecological Coalition started running workshops for the non-Native people who were coming to help us in various struggles over Indigenous rights and the environment. We'd get young people from the East Coast and California and different countries in Europe coming to the Plains and up into Canada wanting to help us Native People with campaigns against logging and oil and gas and mining, and they were mostly really good people, but they didn't have a clue about how to behave in Indigenous communities. A lot of 'em got really freaked out with the way we do things. Especially the English, the Germans and the Swiss. Jiminy-criminy! No disrespect, but most of them were so uptight you could have tapped the tension and run an engine off of 'em. Everything had to be all planned in advance, with them. Couldn't cope with changes of plan. So we started running residential workshops called 'Planning for spontaneity'. They were great. We kicked off by having the workshop begin a day later than advertised, and seeing how angry and freaked out everybody got; then, how angry and freaked out they got when we told them we'd done it deliberately, as a test.

"There was this one guy, from England, really good guy, very kind, but he really couldn't hack the way people behave here. He had to plan in advance when he was going to blow his own nose. The first day he was here, after a while I asked him if he was hungry. You know what he did? Looked at his watch! He had to check whether it was time to be hungry or not. Luckily, it was about 12.30, so he was allowed to be hungry. Which was good, because I was hungry and I wanted lunch. But, you see, I wanted lunch because I was hungry, whereas he wanted lunch because it was lunchtime. A couple days later, there was a forest fire burning up the pine woods on the hills west of town, and we had to move old Byron and Monica out of their house, because it looked like it was gonna burn. So I ran into the house where this English guy was staying, and he's in there in the main room ironing his clothes, and I said, 'Come quickly, we've got to help Byron and Monica move their stuff out of their house, it's all going to burn up in the forest fire.' And he said, 'Well, I can't come now, I'm doing my ironing,' and I just looked at him, because I really couldn't believe my ears. But I thought, well, the poor guy's English, he probably can't help it, and I turned 'round and left. It took him a full two minutes to work out that maybe a forest fire, which wasn't planned, takes precedence over his ironing, and then he runs out after me and ends up doing most of the work. But he told me how it took him two minutes to figure out that he needed to be spontaneous for a change. It was him who inspired us to start the workshops."

"What happened to him?" asked Kerry.

"Oh, he went back to London. I think he runs some anti-mining group now. I'm sure he'd have helped us out with fighting the coal plan here, if we'd have needed it. But the people made their decision, and it wasn't for those of us who lost to try to stop them."

"I don't think I'm quite that uptight," said Kerry.

"No," agreed Will. "You're not. You're just lovely."

The light-hearted affirmation made Kerry's heart flutter. She felt surprised and mildly disturbed by this, not knowing what it might signify, but she put it out of her mind.

"Well, shall we close up and go eat at the diner?" asked Will.

"Lovely," said Kerry.

"Now, don't start that all over again," said Will.

"Sorry," said Kerry.

"That's another one," said Will. "I never knew anyone like English people for saying sorry."

"Perhaps we've got a lot to be sorry about?" suggested Kerry.

"Well, invading half the planet would be one good reason for saying sorry."

"Don't exaggerate. At most it was a quarter."

"Oh, okay."

"And what about the Americans?"

"Yeah, well, that's the reason I left the service." He paused. "Hey, let's sit down for a while. I'm going to close the store and then we'll have some tea and talk a while before we go to the diner. There are certain conversations I prefer not to be overheard round here. People can get a bit upset if they hear you badmouthing the US armed forces. I don't want to cause an ugly scene."

Will stood up, locked the front door of the store, pulled the blind down over the front window and turned out the light in the front portion of the store. He went into the office and brought out two chairs. Then he put some water on to heat on the gas ring in the office.

While Will was busy with these things, Kerry listened to the radio. The flute music had ceased and been succeeded by some drumming and chanting. When the drumming abruptly ended, the announcer said, "You're listening to K-R-E-Z, Krayzee Radio, the Voice of the Rez, and this hour of traditional music is brought to you by Tribal Gas, Autoparts and Autobody Repair. When your motorised war pony won't go any further, let Tribal repair *your* autobody. Well, now, you've just heard a couple pieces from our friends at the Drums of Chokecherry Butte, and now we're going to range a bit further afield and hear from some of our Lakota friends over the border in West Dakota. Remember, we can broadcast your own music too if you just send us a CD or email us a link to your uploaded recordings. Krayzee Radio is *your* radio and we want to showcase *your* skills, so keep that traditional music coming. So now, we have a grassdance song for you, from our neighbours in West Dakota." The drumming began again, and Will brought in two mugs of black tea.

"I guess you probably take cream in tea, do you?" he asked.

"Well, milk," replied Kerry.

"Yeah, that's what I meant," said Will. "I'm afraid I don't have any. We usually drink it without."

"Well, that's okay," said Kerry. "I'll drink it your way."

They sipped the hot tea.

"Interesting radio station," said Kerry.

"D'you like it?" asked Will.

"Yes," replied Kerry, "though I'd like to understand the music better. I'm unfamiliar with it."

"It's another project I've been involved in," said Will. "When I was still working as an accountant up in Oil Bluffs…"

"You were an accountant?" asked Kerry, in surprise.

"Yes," said Will. "Is that okay?"

"Yes…yes, of course", said Kerry.

"You just didn't associate being Native American with being an accountant?"

"Well…no. Sorry, stereotyping, I suppose."

"We'll deal with that later. Anyway, it suddenly struck me that here we've got this beautiful culture with a language and a musical tradition, but you never hear it on the airwaves, so I thought, we need a radio station for the Rez. So I talked to some of the elders and a couple friends of mine, and I put some of my own money into it, and we managed to get a start-up grant from some Foundation on the East Coast, and we started up a radio station. It's only a few days a week, but it's really good now. We broadcast country music because people like it, but we also broadcast traditional music, we have an hour a day in our language, so the elders feel good and the kids can begin to feel the language is cool again, so they might want to learn it, and we have discussions about all sorts of issues affecting the Rez or Indigenous People in general. During all the discussions about the mining, we made sure we had both sides of the story aired. It's a shame you and Hannah weren't here then, you could have spoken about the way Anglo Australian behaves in Cortesia. Still, it's all polluted water under a blast-damaged bridge now."

"You were going to tell me about leaving the armed forces," said Kerry.

"Oh, yes," said Will. "Yeah, well, like so many of our people, I joined up, partly because it gives us opportunities we'd never have otherwise, partly because of our own warrior tradition, partly because of patriotism."

"But I thought the US invaded your people and took your land," said Kerry. "How can you be patriotic?"

"Well, the Americans took up where the Brits left off," said Will. "But the point is, now we're part of the USA. Nobody among our people seriously thinks we could go it alone. Wouldn't want to, anyway. We may be members of our own People first, and Native Americans second, but we're also Americans. That's just the way it is. And lots of Native Americans serve in the US armed forces."

"I see."

"Well, anyway, I joined the marines, and I'm not sorry I did it. There are some real brave, good people in the marines, in the service in general. But I was disgusted with what the Government got us to do. After a couple years, I was sent as part of a special forces contingent to Cortesia."

"Ah! That's what you were doing there!"

"Not for long, thank God. We were there to assist the Cortesian armed forces in 'special operations'. We were supposed to help them track down and neutralise dangerous communist insurgents who were threatening farming and indigenous communities in the mountains. 'Neutralise' means kill or capture. I thought I was serving my country and defending liberty. When I saw what was going on, I was so disgusted, I applied for a transfer to other operations, and after that, once my term ran out, I never enlisted again."

"What was going on, then?"

"The 'insurgents' the Cortesians wanted eliminated weren't threatening farmers and indigenous people, they *were* farmers and indigenous people. They looked much the same as me. So did most of the regular Cortesian soldiers who were made to hunt them down. But their officers, and ours, were white. It was like the high and mighty colonists were paying the Indigenous people to kill each other off for them, and the reason wasn't freedom or democracy. It was because the small farmers and indigenous communities were in the way of rich Cortesian families and US oil and mining companies getting their hands on land and minerals. And some of the techniques the Cortesian soldiers used were just completely brutal. In rural communities, where they reckoned people sympathised with the guerrillas, they'd just move in, pick a few people at random and torture them to death in front of the whole village, children included, just to terrorise them into submission. I only saw that happen once, but I am totally sure it happened more often than that because of what other people told me. It made me so angry I demanded my superior stop it, but he said he couldn't, it would break the conditions of our bilateral military aid agreement. Then, after a bit more digging, I found out that the Cortesians were only doing what they had been deliberately taught to do by the CIA. If I hadn't had such a good record, I probably wouldn't have been allowed to transfer to other operations, but if they hadn't allowed me, for sure I'd have ended up being court-martialled for insubordination. It made me sick. It made me so sick, I didn't just leave the service, I decided violence of any sort could never be the way forward in any struggle or for any cause. I wanted to be a warrior in some other way. That's why I got into all these struggles for our culture and for the Earth."

Kerry looked at Will with admiration. "You remind me of my friend Peter," she said. "In his own way, he's a warrior like that, too. I think that's really good."

"It's difficult for a lot of folks round here to understand it," said Will. "Round here, everyone has such respect for the armed forces that they don't usually ask whether the Government's using the armed forces in a good way or a bad way. Despite most of the white folks round here being Christians of one sort or another, nobody ever asks how killing people goes along with the non-violence that Jesus clearly preached. So I try to get on with the struggle for our land and culture without talking about the military."

"It's different in England," said Kerry. "We don't have that culture of great respect for the military, though some politicians are trying to encourage it now. I feel sorry for our soldiers – sent away to risk their lives to make politicians feel important or defend oil company profits." She realised she had expressed a firm opinion about something important, and was surprised at herself. "Oh, I don't normally say things like that," she said. "I must have learnt more from my friend Peter than I thought I had."

"Sounds like I'd get along fine with your friend Peter," said Will. "What kind of a friend is he?"

"Oh, a really good friend," said Kerry, then realised the implication of Will's question. "But not like that! No, I'm not like that!"

"Not like what?" asked Will, laughing.

Kerry realised that she was about to say that she would not be romantically involved with another man, but stopped herself, remembering herself as a woman. She blushed.

"He's a Catholic priest!" she explained.

"Oh!" said Will.

"Anyway," added Kerry, "I never fancied him."

Will laughed. "Well," he said, "let's go get some supper now."

They closed up the store and drove the short distance down the main street to Schultz's Diner. The diner was in a long grey trailer house parked on the north side of the street. Several pick-up trucks were parked in front of it, and Will pulled in beside them.

"This trailer was dragged here about twenty years ago when it was condemned in Oil Bluffs as unfit for human habitation," said Will. "But it works okay as a diner. Old man Schultz and his sons have been cooking in it for all those years and nobody got sick yet."

They climbed up the front steps and entered the warm trailer. The light inside was dim, and country music played in the background. Will chose a table at the far end of the diner and sat facing the entrance. "I like to sit here," he explained. "I can see who all's coming and going."

Old man Schultz's wife Marlene approached them with a note pad. "Hi, Will," she said. "How're you doing?"

"Good," replied Will. "This is my friend Kerry."

"Nice to meet you, Kerry," said Marlene, smiling.

"Hello," said Kerry.

"She's from England," said Will.

"England? Oh, my!" replied Marlene. "You're a ways from home!"

"Yes," said Kerry. "I'm visiting friends out here."

"Well, you have a good time," advised Marlene. "Now, what can I get you guys?"

There was not an extensive choice. Will ordered hot beef with mashed potato and gravy, followed by cherry pie a la mode, which apparently meant that it was served with ice cream. Kerry ordered hamburger with fries and salad, followed by blueberry pie a la mode.

"I brought one of my European colleagues in here once," said Will. "He was a vegetarian. He looked all through the menu and asked Marlene what she would advise for a vegetarian. She said, 'Oh, my, I think I'd advise they get out of Yellowstone State or they'll probably starve to death!' I think they made him a cheese omelette. That was the closest they could get to it. They were all freaked out to meet someone who didn't eat meat."

"That must have been embarrassing," said Kerry.

"It's lucky it wasn't worse," said Will. "I read a report in the West Dakota Gazette one time, and it was describing the escape of a dangerous convict from the state penitentiary. Half way through it said, 'the escapee, a self-confessed vegetarian...' I can't remember what it said after that. I just remember that phrase. It was like the fact that he was not only a *vegetarian,* but had the bold-faced effrontery to *admit* to it, just showed the kind of sick, deranged criminal they were dealing with here – a kind of warning to people to stay well clear and let armed police deal with the freak."

"I like vegetarian food," said Kerry. "I should probably be a vegetarian, because I don't like the idea of killing animals."

"Oh, it must have been difficult for you yesterday, butchering that deer. You didn't have to, you know."

"I know. It's okay. That was different. Anyway, I'm a hypocrite because I do eat meat."

"It's kind of difficult not to out here," said Will. "The land isn't very fertile and the climate's pretty dry, so it'd be difficult to grow enough vegetables to eat well. We have to get most of our vegetables trucked in from hundreds of miles away, and that jacks the price up. I hope, if the store takes off, we could start some hydroponic gardening projects on the Rez and get people growing stuff. But our recent tradition is totally a hunting tradition, not a farming tradition, so it feels kind of weird doing stuff like that. It's pretty much the same with the white folks round here, too. They came here mostly as ranchers, grain farmers or traders, so there's no tradition of growing vegetables."

Marlene brought their meals. "Enjoy," she said. Kerry was glad that Peter was not there to hear it. He would have complained that 'enjoy' is a transitive verb and therefore needs a direct object. Kerry surmised that Marlene would not have understood what on earth he was talking about.

"One of the things I worry about the coal," said Will, "is people moving in from all over the country for any jobs that are going. The tribe insisted on a quota of local jobs at the mine, but there's going to be jobs that folks round here don't have the qualifications for. If we get a whole bunch of new white folks coming in, how's that going to alter the atmosphere round here? I mean, us and the white folks in Dusty have had several generations to get used to each other. Most of us get on fine. There's only one or two white folks who are openly racist, though I suspect there's a whole bunch more who are nice to our face and racist behind our back, but what are the new ones going to be like?

"Then, there's attitudes to land. We get white folks come and live here for a year or two – maybe they get work in the school or something – and then they say it's time to move on, as though there's some natural phenomenon that prevents them staying in a place for more than a couple years. Sometimes, I ask them, 'Why is it time to move on?' And they look at me funny, as though it was a dumb question, and they say, 'Oh, I guess it's just time to move on,' which doesn't get me anywhere nearer understanding it. I think, well, our people used to move on all the time, but we moved on within an area that we regarded as the part of Mother Earth that we belonged to, so we were moving around but not moving out. We had a deep sense of connectedness to a whole great area. We'd keep coming back to the same places over a cycle of seasonal migration. Even though so much of our land has been stolen, at least we can say we belong to the Rez. I wouldn't want to go and live someplace else. I belong here. Our people who go and get work on the west coast, or down in Denver or in the South West, they always think of here as home, and they come back when they can. They don't drift about like tumbleweed. They belong here. But these white folks, who don't seem to have any place to call home, they're not going to care about what the mining does to the land because they don't identify with the land. I worry about that."

"Do you think all white people are like that?" asked Kerry.

"Demonstrably not," replied Will. "The white folks who've lived here for a few generations feel like they belong here too. Not as much as us or as deeply as us, but they love the place and belong here. I think white folks on the East Coast feel like they belong there too. I guess a lot of Europeans feel that way about where you guys live, don't you?"

"I suppose so," said Kerry.

"The thing is, though," said Will, "even white folks who feel like they belong in a place often take a utilitarian attitude to land. The land isn't Mother Earth, it's an 'it' that's there to be used as long as you can make a profit out of it. I can't imagine coal strip-mining ever developing naturally in Native American society. We just wouldn't do that kind of thing. The tribe's accepted it because people could see no alternative way of making a living. It kind of violates our spirit, and we're forced into acquiescing in it for lack of land and cash."

Will was still speaking and looking at her intently, when Kerry heard the diner door open behind her, and a buzz of conversation as a group of people came into the trailer. There was a scraping of chairs as people seated themselves, and Kerry's ears habituated themselves to a higher background noise level as conversation blended with country music.

Will began to talk about the health impacts of burning coal: the release of mercury into the atmosphere, the danger of respiratory diseases, the cocktail of toxins in the ash left after combustion and the difficulties of safe disposal of it. Kerry listened with concentration and concern, but her attention began to wander as she caught snatches of conversation from the tables behind her. It was not the subject matter that caught her attention; it was the accent. It was one voice, strident, somewhat aggressive. It was a voice which, from time to time, rose up above the other voices; an unmistakably South African voice. She looked over her shoulder and caught the eye of Mr Pik Bloemen, three tables away, near the door. Hurriedly, she turned back to face Will.

"Is something the matter?" he asked.

"Do you know a man called Pik Bloemen?" asked Kerry.

"I've heard of him," said Will. "He was the guy who used to sign most of the letters to tribal members, telling us how wonderful the mine's going to be. He's Anglo-Australian's VP for PR or something like that, ain't he? I never met him."

"Well, he's sitting by the door."

Will looked towards the exit.

"Talking with a South African accent," added Kerry.

Will listened for a while, looking in Pik Bloemen's direction, while trying to avoid obviously staring. "Ah," he said after a while. "So that's the face of the enemy. You met him in Cortesia?"

"Yes," said Kerry, uneasily.

"Will he recognise you?" asked Will.

"I don't know," replied Kerry. "I hope not. I…er…I had shorter hair then. Maybe he'll have forgotten. I mean, we hardly had much to do with each other. But I can't say we got on well."

"No, I guess not. Well, maybe he'll have gone by the time we've finished our pie."

Marlene, busier now, took a while to bring them their pie a la mode, and Kerry took as long as possible to eat hers. By the time they had both finished eating, Pik Bloemen and his group had left. Kerry was spared the danger of possible recognition and difficult questions. She did not want anyone, other than Hannah and the Sisters, to know her recent history yet.

Will drove Kerry straight back to Vera's house. "Say hi to Grandma for me," he said. "I won't come in right now. Better be getting home. D'you wanna come to supper at our house tomorrow?"

To her surprise, Kerry's heart leapt within her, and for two reasons. "Oh, I'd like that!" she said, conscious that she very much enjoyed Will's company. But "our house"? Who lived with Will? And why did it matter to her? She was in love with Hannah – hopeless as that was. What did it matter who Will lived with? Obsessed though she still was with Hannah, was her heart somehow divided? Was she responding romantically to a man? The day before, she had been wondering whether she was really a woman, or a man in female form. Was she now truly becoming female inside? If she were still a man, was she gay? Or was she responding to Will's femininity rather than his maleness? In which case, given the female form of her body, was she, in fact, a lesbian? If she were, did it matter? This was most confusing. Just as well Will was already spoken for. It was enough trouble dealing with the shattering experience of her disappointed love for Hannah, without falling for someone else on the rebound. Truly, if she had known how desperately painful romantic love would turn out to be, she would have torn it out by the roots when she first realised it was growing, unbidden, in her inexperienced heart.

Seven: Kerry passes another pleasant evening, ending with a nice surprise

Hannah came by with Sister Jackie in the morning. Kerry was having another sewing lesson with Vera. Vera was introduced to Hannah, and immediately welcomed her by inviting her to fetch things for her and make the coffee for the others. Vera commented favourably on the way the Sisters visited people. She said that in the old days, the priests and Sisters used to visit people a lot, but for a while they stopped, because they were too busy running programmes at the Mission. But when they realised hardly anyone was coming to the programmes they were running, they started getting out and about and visiting again. Vera approved. She was especially insistent that it was most important for priests and Sisters to eat with people. She took a very dim view of those who, for whatever reason, declined the offer of food.

So, when she offered lunch at about noon, it was not possible for the visitors to decline it. Hannah was given the honour of preparing it, under detailed instruction from Vera, who remained at the table, since her legs were causing her great pain.

After lunch, Hannah had a private word with Kerry in her room, while Vera chatted with Jackie. "I feel bad that I'm neglecting you," said Hannah. "I didn't realise there'd be so much to do in the first week."

"Don't worry," said Kerry. "I'm fine. Vera's good company, and Will's invited me to supper this evening. I've got plenty to do."

"I've been asked to go and spend a few days over at Antelope Flats," said Hannah. "How would you feel if I abandon you like that?"

Kerry did not know quite what she felt about that, or about anything.

"That's okay," she said. "You have to do what you have to do. We can spend some time together again when you get back."

"I don't want there to be any awkwardness between us," said Hannah. "Though, I guess it's inevitable there will be for a while."

"I think you're right," said Kerry. "But it'll pass. We'll get over it." She paused. "I really appreciate you inviting me to come out west with you. You could have let me get on that first flight back to London."

"I feel responsible for what you did to yourself."

"Well, don't. I have free will. I chose to do what I did. It was ridiculous. But there we are, I did it. Now I have to work out quite what to make of it all."

"But your feelings for me..."

"Are my responsibility. You did nothing deliberate to encourage them, and if I had had the sense to talk to you about them earlier, we might have avoided all this. But I'll survive."

Hannah still looked painfully concerned.

"Don't worry," said Kerry. "I plan to enjoy the cross-cultural experience of two weeks on the Rez, and then I'll be off back to England to think about what the future holds. We're supposed to trust God, aren't we? Well, I think I do. I think things will be alright. I just don't know what form they'll take yet, that's all. Now, you go and enjoy Antelope Flats."

After Hannah and Jackie had left, and Vera had gone for her afternoon rest, Kerry spent a few minutes weeping gently, before once again lying down and praying the Jesus prayer. Once again, a feeling of peacefulness and calm came over her, and then joy, a reckless joy that she felt entirely unable to explain or understand. At one level, she felt that there was nothing in her life to warrant anything other than the most profound despair. Yet, she felt a joy borne of a conviction that all would be well, in some inexplicable and unimaginable manner; that all wrongs would be righted, all sins forgiven; that there was no foolishness that she had committed that could not somehow be worked into a brighter and more delightful pattern of life.

She returned to the table and had finished sewing the ribbon on both sleeves of the red ribbon shirt that Vera had started her on, before Vera woke up from her nap.

"You're gonna meet Billie tonight, then," said Vera.

"Who's Billie?" asked Kerry.

"Will's sister," replied Vera. "They're Wilhelm and Wilhelmina, but they've always been called Will and Billie."

"Is she coming to supper with Will too, then?" asked Kerry.

"She lives there with him," said Vera. "Billie and her daughter, Missy, went back and lived with their mom and dad when Billie's husband took off, and then Will came back when he came out of the service. Now their mom and dad have passed away it's just Will, Billie and Missy. Missy's six years old now."

"Isn't Will married, then?" asked Kerry.

"No. I keep telling him he needs to find someone. First, he was in the marines, then he's been running around all over the place trying to run that radio and that store and stop the mines and all that. Never got time to find himself a good woman. I told him he ought to get together with that Darlene Black Wolf from over at Chokecherry Butte. Her boyfriend left her two years ago. Nice girl. Needs a good man like Will. He says he needs someone who cares about the same things as he does. I say you can't be too picky, or you'll end up a lonely old man."

Kerry wondered whether the fact that Vera's revelation brought her a sense of delighted comfort was the result of desperation, treachery or folly. She knew, with no possibility for doubt, that however deep her feelings for Hannah, they would lead her nowhere. Her innate wisdom was beginning to assert itself. But the realisation that she had wanted Will to be single both shocked and intrigued her. She had no right to feel any animosity towards Darlene Black Wolf, but she did not wish Will to take any interest in her. At the same time, she was well aware that her own feelings were in a state of such fragility and confusion, that she could not trust herself to make sensible judgements about what was good either for herself or for anyone else. She would do nothing at all to pursue her half-formed and confused feelings of attraction to Will. They might be a self-deception born of bitter disappointment and painful hurt. She simply noted them.

Will called for her around six o'clock. Krayzee Radio was playing in his truck. The announcer said the music was hand-game songs.

"What are hand-games?" asked Kerry.

"Kind of betting games," replied Will. "Teams compete to guess who's holding a painted bone. There's all kinds of bluffing and subterfuge and second-guessing, and while the teams are playing, a drum group'll be drumming and singing. Kind of light-hearted stuff. My uncle Ben goes all over the state playing at hand-games. People can win big money and the drum groups get paid well too."

They drove back towards the Mission, but passed beyond it, over the crossroads with the main Oil Bluffs to West Dakota highway, and after a few miles, Will turned off the blacktop road to the left, towards the river, down a narrow dirt road patchily covered in snow. Beyond a clump of bushes, the track veered to the right and Will stopped the pickup in front of a yellow-painted wooden house, lit by a yard light on the front porch. Behind it were some cottonwoods, and beyond them, Whispering River. Kerry stepped out of the truck. A light, cold breeze blew, and large wind chimes on the front porch blew against each other, producing a gentle, wistful music. On the front door was a framed poster. It said, "Don't walk in front of me; I may not follow. Don't walk behind me; I may not lead. Just walk beside me, and be my friend." They entered the house.

Inside was a large room, warm and well-lit, a roaring wood fire in a clear-fronted wood stove on the right-hand side, soft chairs in the front of the room, a table and dining chairs in the middle and a kitchen area at the back, by the back door. The room smelt vaguely of wood smoke mixed with cedar smoke, but overlaid with cooking smells – onion, garlic, tomato, maybe basil. A young girl was drawing with crayons at the table and a tall woman, with flowing black hair, was standing over the sink, her back to them. The girl looked up and the woman looked 'round when Will and Kerry came in. The woman smiled. "Hi there, Kerry!" she said, dried her hands and came towards Kerry to shake her hand. "I'm Billie, Will's sister." She was strikingly beautiful, a fully feminine version of her brother, as tall and strong as him.

The girl looked shy. Kerry, after greeting Billie, smiled at the girl and said, "Hello, I'm Kerry. Are you Missy?"

"Yes," said Missy, and resumed her drawing.

"Say hi, then, Missy," said Will.

"Hi," said Missy.

"She'll get used to you in a minute," said Billie. "Do you eat lasagne?"

"I do," said Kerry. "Is that traditional?"

"It is in Italy," said Will. "But we like it. And I think you've probably had plenty of traditional food at Vera's."

"Did you eat any fry bread yet?" asked Billie.

"I don't think so," replied Kerry. "What is it?"

"It's deep fried dough," replied Billie. "Kind of like savoury doughnuts. We eat it with meat or soup or fruit pudding. Makes you fat if you eat too much, though."

"It sounds nice."

"Well, we can eat that next time you come."

They all sat down with Missy at the table and conversed for a while about food, which led them on to cultural change and language. Will and Billie had grown up speaking only English. Their parents understood their own language but did not speak it. Their grandparents had spoken little else, finding some difficulty with English. Now, Will was learning the language and making good progress with it. Billie wanted to learn but found the task more difficult. They moved on to accent and idiom in Whispering River Reservation English. Kerry learnt that when a woman was joking, she would often say, "Eeyyyy!" at the end of the sentence, with a gently rising inflection from beginning to end; and a woman from Antelope Flats would elongate the sound, and finish it with a sharp and sudden rising inflection that women from Dusty and Chokecherry Butte found highly amusing. Kerry tried this a few times, causing uncontrollable hilarity and enabling Missy to lose her shyness completely. Before the food was ready, Missy was showing Kerry all her drawings and explaining why she liked green and pink better than other colours. She also tried mimicking Kerry's English accent, with variable success.

After a while, Billie cleared the table, Will set it with plates and silverware and Billie placed a large dish of salad on it. Then she drew the lasagne out of the oven and placed it on the table. They all sat down, Will and Billie at each end of the table, Missy and Kerry opposite each other on the long sides. Will and Billie reached out and took the hands of Missy and Kerry, and fell silent for a while. Kerry looked up. Everyone's eyes were shut. She shut her eyes. Then Will said, "Creator, we thank you for this food. We thank you for our Mother Earth who looks after us and provides us with all that we need. We thank you for the animals and plants that have given themselves up for us, so that we can eat. We thank you for all who have worked to bring this food to our table, especially Billie, who has worked hard to make this meal for us. We thank you for our new friend Kerry, for bringing her safely to visit us here in our land. We thank you for life. Aho!"

"Aho!" replied Billie and Missy.

They let go of each other's hands and Billie said, "Enjoy the meal!"

Kerry did not recall ever enjoying a meal quite so much – not primarily because of the food, tasty as it was, but because of the company, and the atmosphere of simple delight and uncomplicated kindness. She was sorry it had to come to an end.

About ten o'clock, Missy could not stay awake any longer, and Billie excused herself and said she would help her daughter prepare for bed. Will said he would run Kerry back to Vera's house.

"When do you have to go back to England?" he asked Kerry, as they came to a halt in front of Vera's house, fifteen minutes later.

"I'm booked to fly out at the end of next week," replied Kerry.

"Oh," said Will. "That soon, huh? I guess you have to get back to work?"

"Well, no," said Kerry. "That's when my flight's booked, that's all."

"You never even told me what work you do," said Will.

"It's not that exciting," said Kerry. "I'm a translator and I teach English as a foreign language."

"That's exciting!" said Will. "When do you have to start back at work, then?"

"I haven't got anything set up back in England yet," answered Kerry. "I've been working in Brazil the last two and a half years, but I'm not going back there."

"Stay, then," said Will.

Kerry felt flustered. "I can't," she said. "I'm only here on a tourist visa. I don't have the right to stay in the US."

"How long's your visa for?" asked Will.

"Six months," said Kerry.

"Stay six months, then," said Will.

"But...I can't stay all that time at Vera's house! She's only expecting me to stay two weeks!"

"Come and stay with us. There's plenty of room."

"I...oh...I...that's really kind. Thank you. I...I'll think about that. It's just...It's just..."

Will turned and looked at her. Then, very slowly and gently, he brought his lips to hers and kissed her. Startled, she let him do so, but without response. He drew his lips away. She looked at him, saying nothing. He gazed at her for a while in silence. Then he kissed her again, at greater length this time, and with great tenderness. Kerry felt every muscle

285

within her relax. She felt a flood of elation sweep across her. She began to weep. Will pulled away from her, suddenly concerned.

"Oh, I'm sorry, I didn't mean to upset you!"

"You didn't," said Kerry. "The very opposite, the absolute opposite. Oh! Oh...I think I'd better go in now. Will I see you tomorrow?"

"Shall I come by about the same time as today?"

"Yes, yes, anytime. Anytime, day or night. Six will do fine. Bye!"

She jumped out of the cab, awash with feelings of unutterable delight, appalling foreboding, joy, guilt, fear, confusion, and gratitude. She realised that she did not care whether she was male or female, gay or straight, a gay man in a woman's body or a lesbian responding to a man's femininity. The fact was, she had been lacerated by unrequited love and now, in the midst of her agony, a beautiful and deeply admirable human being had shown her love, and it felt, to Kerry, like healing balm poured into the painful wounds of her aching heart.

Eight: Kerry learns to kiss

"You're doing real good," observed Vera as she sat with Kerry, sewing ribbon shirts. "You do careful work. Looks neat."

"Thank you," said Kerry.

"You ain't married yet, are you?"

"No."

"Any kids?"

"No."

"You should get married, have some kids."

Kerry continued sewing, in silence.

"I think Will likes you," said Vera.

Kerry pricked her finger and drew blood. Vera saw, and chuckled.

"I think you like him too, don't you?" She smiled. Kerry remained silent. "You could give him that ribbon shirt you're making."

Kerry looked up. "But it's for your grandson's giveaway," she said.

"There's plenty for that," said Vera. "It'd be nice to give Will that shirt. He'd look good in it."

"But this is expensive!" said Kerry. "If I'm going to do that, at least let me pay you for it."

Vera looked at her rather disdainfully. "You're talking like a white person," she said. "Here am I, trying to help you behave like an Indian, and you start talking about paying me for something I'm giving you. It'll make me real mad if you go on doing that."

"Sorry," said Kerry.

"That's alright. You're learning."

They sewed in silence for a while.

"Your mom still alive?" asked Vera.

"No, she died a few years ago," replied Kerry, sadly.

"Oh," said Vera. "I better be your mom, then. You make a good daughter."

Kerry looked up again, startled. Vera was looking down at her sewing, concentrating. She had just said it in a matter of fact manner, as though adopting an adult daughter was the easiest and most natural thing in the world. Kerry did not know how to take what Vera had said. She decided to make light of it.

"I'm not sure how good a daughter I would be," she said. "You might get fed up with me pretty quickly."

"I won't," said Vera emphatically. "I got lots of daughters. I had all my own ones with my Ernie, and then I took on a whole bunch more, people who lost their own mothers or were far from home. Sister Jackie's my daughter too. Her mom lives way back east, so she don't get to see her much. So while she's out here, I'm her mom."

Kerry felt touched. "Well, I'm glad and honoured to be your daughter," she said. "Thank you."

"Thing is," said Vera, not looking up. "Now you're my daughter, you're gonna have to remember who all you're related to on the Rez." She looked up at Kerry and chuckled. "You want me to start now? We might get done by the time Will comes for you this evening."

They both laughed.

"It's okay," said Vera. "We'll do it a little bit at a time. Then you'll remember. Just like Sister Jackie." She laughed quietly, her shoulders heaving so that she had to stop sewing for a while.

"Trouble is with you white people," she said after a while, "you think you're all alone in the world, then you behave like you got no relatives. But we're all related – all us Indians, all you white people, black people, all them Muslim people, and all the animals and plants and rocks, water, air – we're all

288

related. Just need to keep that in mind, then you won't go wrong."

In the afternoon, they laid aside the ribbon shirts and Vera began to teach Kerry how to do beadwork. She made progress, but slowly. By four o'clock, she was unable to concentrate.

"You better take a break," said Vera. "Your mind's already gone out for the evening. Better get yourself ready for him."

Kerry looked up at Vera, embarrassed. "You're right," she said. "You always know what I'm thinking!"

"You got it written all over you," said Vera, and chuckled. "That Darlene Black Wolf's gonna be upset."

"Oh dear," said Kerry. "I don't want to upset anyone!"

"She'll get over it," said Vera. "Will never wanted to go with her anyway."

Will arrived at six o'clock. "Where are we going?" asked Kerry, as she climbed into the truck. Will kissed her gently, and she kissed him back.

"How about the diner?" suggested Will. "Then we could hit the town. We could drive up and down the main street, or go visiting, or drink tea in the back of the store, or even go drink it at home. Pretty amazing night life here in Dusty. Could even rent a video and go watch it at home."

"Let's do that!" said Kerry. "The diner, followed by the video."

"Good!" said Will, put the truck in gear and pulled away.

Pik Bloemen was in the diner again. This time, they walked right into him as they were going in. Kerry found herself looking right at his face as he turned from the counter after paying his bill.

She couldn't stop herself. "Hello, Mr Bloemen," she said.

Pik Bloemen looked startled.

"Do I know you?" he asked.

"Oh, well, I think maybe we met once," said Kerry, deeply regretting having spoken.

"You're not from round here," said Pik Bloemen.

"No," agreed Kerry.

"You're not one of those European activists I met at our operations in New Mexico?"

"No, no. Perhaps I'm mistaken. Perhaps we haven't met."

"But you knew my name."

"Ah, yes."

"Hang on. Have you got a brother?"

"A brother?"

"Yes! Yes, that's it! I got to know your brother in Cortesia! Yes. Not always an easy relationship, I have to say. What was his name now? Kerry! That was it! Kerry Ahern!"

Now it was Will who was looking startled.

"So, you met me with your brother? You'd have thought I would remember. You both look so similar."

"I think it's just that he told me so much about you. He must have shown me photos with you in. That's how I recognised you."

"Very flattering, I'm sure. And what brings you to these parts? I trust you are not following in your brother's footsteps? I trust we can enjoy a harmonious relationship?"

"Oh, I'm just on holiday," said Kerry.

"What a coincidence," said Pik Bloemen. "Well, you may wish to take a guided tour of our state of the art opencast coal mines to the south of here. The tribe was convinced by seeing the facts for themselves. I am afraid your brother was sadly misled by that misguided padre and his communist friends." He looked at her intently. "Anyway," he said, "I must go. I am at work." He forced a smile and held out his hand to Kerry. "And what is your name?" he said.

"Kerry," said Kerry, shaking Pik Bloemen's hand.

Pik Bloemen looked perplexed.

"Is that not rather confusing?" he asked. "Was it not difficult for your family and friends? Was it not irresponsible of your parents to give you and your brother the same name?"

"Oh, they liked the name so much, they saw no reason not to use it as much as possible," said Kerry.

"Most peculiar," said Pik Bloemen, and left.

"What was all that about?" asked Will, deeply intrigued. "You didn't tell me you were in Cortesia with your brother. I didn't know you had a brother."

"I haven't," said Kerry. She felt flustered, nervous, vulnerable. She feared for her new-found love. If Will were to know... What would he think? What would he do?

They sat down at the table at the far end of the diner.

"I told you I had shorter hair then," she said. "And I always wore trousers. And I hardly spent any time with the man."

"But how could he think you were a man?" asked Will. "You're so womanly!"

"Some people can be pretty stupid," said Kerry.

"He must be real dumb," said Will. "But why didn't you set him straight?"

"Because I didn't want him to know that I was the one who worked so hard against him in Cortesia," replied Kerry.

"Then why did you speak to him at all?" asked Will.

"Some people can be pretty stupid," replied Kerry.

Will laughed. "I like you," he said.

Will rented *Thunderheart* from the grocery store, because Kerry said she hadn't seen it and Will said that watching it would be a good way of beginning to understand Native American struggles against mining companies.

There was a note on the table when they arrived at Will and Billie's house. "I took Missy over to her friend at Red Willow Creek. Laterz, Billie xox."

Will swallowed hard.

"I'll make some tea," he said. He put some water on to boil. He looked preoccupied.

"Is something the matter?" asked Kerry, already nervous because of the confusion around her conversation with Pik Bloemen.

"No," said Will. He stood over the stove, waiting for the water to boil.

"Yes," he said, turning to her. He stepped towards her. "Oh," he said. "Oh, I want to kiss you. I mean, really kiss you.

Billie and Missy aren't here. Oh!" He embraced Kerry powerfully and kissed her forcefully on the lips. She allowed him to do so, accepting his gesture of passion without responding in kind. He released her. "I'm sorry," he said. "I need to control myself!" He turned back to the stove. The water boiled. Kerry watched him. He took two plastic mugs from the cupboard by the stove, put a tagged teabag in each and poured on the boiling water.

Kerry stepped towards him and touched his back. This was it. She did not care if she were male, female, gay or straight. "I enjoy your kisses," she said. "Nobody's ever kissed me before. Not like that."

Will looked straight into her eyes. He put his arms around her and kissed her again. This time she did respond, and their kiss lasted for at least a minute. Kerry noticed this, by virtue of the fact that she was facing the kitchen clock.

Then, Kerry felt as if fire had ignited inside her. She noted the sudden and unceremonious departure of any sense of either embarrassment or propriety, and kissed Will again, fiercely, as if she wanted to eat his tongue or disappear entirely into his mouth. She noted, briefly, like a passing distraction in meditative prayer, the fact so shocking to her English sensibilities, that she was interfering with the brewing of tea. Suddenly, the tea had become a matter of unimportance. There was one thing only that she wanted, and she wanted it now. Will sighed deeply as he kissed her, and reached behind him to replace the teaspoon which he was still clutching on the counter, and in an act of flagrant and remarkable dissipation they abandoned the teabags steeping in the scalding water and by mutual unspoken consent, shuffled, kissing, to the sofa. Kerry sank upon it invitingly, and Will laid the whole length of his tall body over her and began to kiss her with such force that she feared for the lumpy springs, which groaned and pinged under the weight of their passion.

Will laid his hands on her shoulders; then brought his left hand to rest, gently, on her shapely, sensitive but artificial breast. And it was then that she recalled herself, and the nature of reality. She felt the power of Will's hand through her clothing; an ecstatic thrill in her loins; and an urgent need to confess. She caught hold of Will's shoulders and pushed him apart from her, so that she could speak. He tensed. "I'm sorry," he said. "I'm getting carried away. Forgive me."

"No, no, it's not that," said Kerry. She looked wide-eyed and fearful into his beautiful, compassionate face. He gazed at her quizzically. "It's just...," she said. "I...I'm not quite what I seem." He continued gazing at her, waiting.

Her heart was thumping now. She was afraid. He was powerfully built, strong, he could do her a lot of damage if he became angry.

"I...I used to be a man," she said.

Will's quizzical expression changed to one of compassionate understanding. He smiled. "I told you," he said, "I used to be an accountant. People get over these things." He kissed her again, more tenderly this time, then pulled back again, gazing into her face. "I don't care," he said. "You're beautiful and I love you. I think I probably wouldn't even care if you were still a man. You're just beautiful." He kissed her again, and she began to weep with relief and gratitude. He kissed her tears. He kissed her forehead, lips, cheeks, eyes, neck, and again and again her lips, and their passion was becoming fierce and overwhelming again and Will's right hand was working its way up inside Kerry's t-shirt, when the back door opened and Missy called out, "Hi, Will, look what I got at the party!" and Will leapt from the sofa and Kerry ran into the bathroom to rearrange her ruffled clothing.

Billie was just behind Missy.

"Did we disturb something?" Billie asked.

"We were about to watch a video," said Will.

Billie laughed.

"Eeyyyy!" she exclaimed. "When were you going to do that?"

"Well, we had a few things to do first."

Billie laughed again. "Do you want us to go out again?"

"Why did Kerry run away?" asked Missy.

"She's only gone to the bathroom," said Will. "She'll be back soon."

They heard the toilet flush.

"I'd better tell you," said Will, "so she won't be worried the whole time. She used to be a man."

"Oh," said Billie.

"Did you used to be a man, mommy?" asked Missy.

"No, I was always a woman, and before that a girl," replied Billie.

"Were you ever a woman, Will?" asked Missy.

"No, I was a boy and then I became a man," said Will.

"Oh," said Missy. "Look, I got this bag of candy at the party!" She held it up for Will to see.

"That's nice," he said.

Kerry emerged from the bathroom.

"Why did you stop being a man?" asked Missy.

Kerry blushed so deeply, she felt she was going to auto-combust. "Will!" she began, shocked and perplexed, "you shouldn't have..."

"It's better to get it over with," said Billie. "It doesn't matter to us."

"Didn't you like being a man?" asked Missy.

"I didn't mind being a man," replied Kerry, deciding that it was really more sensible to be as straightforward about the matter as her Native American hosts, "until I fell in love with a lesbian."

"Oh," said Missy.

"Didn't it work out?" asked Billie.

"She was a bit surprised when I changed," said Kerry.

"Kind of freaked her out, huh?" asked Billie.

"Yes, very deeply. Anyway, she decided to become a nun."

"Oh," said Billie. "Because of that?"

"No," said Kerry. "While I was making the change."

"Oh," said Billie. "Kind of frustrating."

"Yes," said Kerry.

"So, do you regret it?" asked Billie.

"Not now," replied Kerry.

"You didn't look like you were regretting it when we came in," said Billie.

Kerry blushed again. "No. No, I wasn't regretting it at all," she said.

Will and Billie laughed. Billie put her arms round Kerry and kissed her on the cheek, sufficient to cause Kerry a definite flutter of the heart. "Well, you're welcome here, and you're good for my bro," said Billie. She disengaged herself and went over to the stove. "Hey, there's tea here!" she said. She felt the mugs. "It's nearly cold and looks like the tar sands." She looked back at Will and Kerry. "How could you do that? You've both got a warped sense of priorities. You disappoint me."

Will dropped Kerry off at Vera's some time after ten.

"Did you have a nice time?" asked Vera.

"Yes, thank you," replied Kerry.

Vera looked at her. "Your face is shining," she said. "Did he kiss you?"

Kerry blushed. "Yes," she said.

Vera laughed. "You're good for each other. You better stay here on the Rez."

"I don't think the US immigration authorities would let me," said Kerry.

"What's it got to do with them?" asked Vera. "This is Indian country. Ought to be up to us who we let stay here, not them."

"I'm not sure they'd see it that way," said Kerry.

"Don't make no sense to me," said Vera. "White people are crazy."

"Even me?" asked Kerry.

"You're good crazy. Immigration department's bad crazy."

"Well, this crazy white person's going to bed now," said Kerry.

"Good night, then," said Vera. "Sweet dreams."

Nine: Kerry sees the Spirit

Will arrived before it got dark. Kerry was not ready. She was still trying to get the hang of stitching moccasin soles on to the uppers. It was much more difficult than sewing ribbon shirts, because the hide was so thick.

"Will you come with me to see Grandpa?" asked Will.

"Yes, I'd love to," replied Kerry.

"I want to ask him if he'll put on a sweat ceremony for me tomorrow."

"You want to be careful with those sweats," said Vera. "Too much of it and you'll get sick."

"I haven't sweat for weeks, Grandma," said Will. "I need to give thanks and pray for guidance."

"It ain't good in this cold weather," said Vera.

"It's not that cold yet," said Will.

"Old man Jimmy makes the sweatlodge too hot," said Vera. "That ain't good when it's so cold out."

"It'll be okay, Grandma," said Will. "Don't worry about us."

"Well, tell old man Jimmy I said hi," said Vera.

Old man Jimmy lived in a green house about a mile further down the river road from Vera, on the other side. It nestled against a small hill. Will pulled off the road and drove the truck up to the house. The sun was going down behind the hill.

"Is Jimmy your actual grandfather?" asked Kerry.

"Yes, he is," replied Will. "He's my mom's dad."

"What's a sweat?" asked Kerry.

"I'll show you when we get there. It's a ceremony. It purifies and strengthens people, and we pray in the sweatlodge for all sorts of things, for our families, for problems we have, all sorts of stuff. One problem is, and I feel badly about this, I can't invite you to come in to the sweatlodge. The elders decided a few years back, that for the time being, we can't have non-Native people in the sweat. It's because many of our elders, especially Grandpa Jimmy, welcomed white folks into ceremonies, and they didn't treat them with respect. Some didn't behave well at the time, but it was more a question of people going away after one or two sweats and carrying on like they had some intimate knowledge of Native spirituality. White folks started putting on sweats all over the place and charging money for other white folks to attend them, and then saying they had studied under Grandpa Jimmy or whoever, as if the elders had given them permission to run ceremonies and even to charge money for them. That's such an abuse! The elders even got sick of people writing about the ceremonies, too. Most of the elders took the view that Creator gave these ceremonies to our people, and that other people needed to relate to Creator in the ways Creator had shown *them*. Grandpa Jimmy didn't go along with that. He reckoned, if someone had a good heart, whoever they were, they should be welcome in our ceremonies, especially if they were living among us or working to help us. But he went along with the decision to close the ceremonies for a while, because of all the abuse that had happened.

"There is another good reason for you not coming in the sweat, though. It can get real hot in there, and I don't know what impact that would have on those implants."

Kerry felt embarrassed. She had not thought about the effects of heat on breast implants before. She had no idea what the impact might be.

They climbed out of the truck and went into the house.

The main room smelt of cedar and woodsmoke. A pot of stew was bubbling on the wood stove to the left. There were windows on three sides of the room. One was right by the wood stove, one by the door and one opposite the door.

Underneath the one opposite the door was a table, with three plastic chairs. On the table was a newspaper and a small portable radio, playing K-R-E-Z. Underneath the window by the door was a battered-looking armchair, the stuffing leaking from tears on both arms. The only adornment on the walls was a picture of the high school basketball team, cut out from a newspaper, with a list of fixtures beneath it.

"Grandpa!" Will called out.

They heard the toilet flush. After a few moments, a thin, elderly man, with a deeply lined face and short grey hair, emerged from the corridor and came into the room.

"Grandson!" he said, smiling at Will. He turned to Kerry, smiled at her and offered his hand, which she shook. "Welcome!" he said. "Sit down," he suggested, indicating the three plastic chairs. "I make tea." He spoke softly and hesitantly, with an accent similar to Vera's, but much stronger. He filled a pot with water and set it on the woodstove, then joined Will and Kerry at the table. "What's cookin'?" he asked Will.

Will took a packet of tobacco out of his jacket pocket and laid it on the table.

"Would you run a sweat for me tomorrow, Grandpa?"

Jimmy looked steadily at his grandson. "What's on your mind?" he asked.

Will began to speak to his grandfather in their own language. Will sounded as hesitant as Jimmy did in English. Once, he mentioned Kerry's name, and Jimmy briefly looked at her, smiling kindly. After a few minutes, Will fell silent, and Jimmy continued to look at him. Then he took the tobacco and put it in his own pocket. "Aho," said Will. Jimmy nodded once, and stood up from the table. He went to the stove, where the water was coming to the boil, and made three mugs of tea. He brought them to the table, put them in front of his guests, and sat down again. He looked at Kerry, smiled, and continued looking at her, observing her, for what seemed to Kerry like a very long time. But Kerry did not feel uneasy, or offended, as she might have done under other circumstances. She felt entirely secure. But she also felt as though the old man was looking right inside her, observing her, understanding her, rather in the manner in which she had always felt observed, understood and accepted by God himself.

"England, huh?" said Jimmy at length. "Way over there. Long way."

"Yes," said Kerry.

"Different there," said Jimmy.

"Yes," said Kerry.

"Crazy people," said Jimmy, cracking up into laughter.

"I suppose so," said Kerry, a little at a loss.

"Crazy here, too," said Jimmy, and laughed again. "That guy," he said, pointing at Will with his lips. "Crazy. He got crazy grandpa, too!"

"At least he admits it," said Will. "If I'm crazy, I get it from him!"

"Come take a look at the sweatlodge," said Jimmy. He stood up from the table and they followed him outside. The last of the sunlight was fading behind the hills. Jimmy led them through the snow past a great clump of bushes. "Chokecherries," said Will. Between the bushes and the hillside was a low hemispherical structure about two metres wide, covered in blankets, one of them folded back to make an entrance way on the eastern side. A few yards east of the lodge was a fire pit, to one side of the fire pit a large pile of rocks and to the other side an equally large pile of rock fragments. Old chairs stood around the pit.

"We make a fire," said Jimmy. "Heat the rocks. Then, we put the rocks in the lodge, put water on them, make steam. We pray in there."

"The water vapour purifies us and the heat teaches us patience and willingness to suffer if we need to," added Will. "I never pray more strongly than in the sweatlodge."

Kerry asked, "May I look inside?"

"Go ahead," said Jimmy.

Carefully, Kerry stooped to look into the lodge, which smelt of cedar and sage. She saw a round pit, about a foot deep, in the middle, and space for the participants to sit round it, the earth floor covered with pieces of carpet. She felt the same kind of respect that she felt when entering a church, or that she had felt on the few occasions that she had visited mosques or temples. She stepped back from the doorway and stood upright, inclining her head briefly as she might have done to acknowledge the altar in a Catholic church. She turned round and saw Jimmy observing her again. He smiled.

Jimmy spoke to Will in their own language, and Will made a brief reply. Then Jimmy spoke for some while, as the last of the light faded and a bitter chill began to descend. Jimmy said, "Better go indoors. It's cold." He led the way inside and shut the door. Kerry was glad of the heat from the woodstove. Jimmy spoke for a while longer with Will, then said to Kerry, "See you in the morning," and smiled at her again. Will led the way to the truck, and they drove the mile back to Vera's house.

"Grandpa likes you," said Will, as they pulled on to the road.

"Oh, good," said Kerry. "I felt as if he was reading me like a book."

"He said you have a good heart, that you showed respect for our ways and our language."

"Oh, I'm glad," said Kerry. "Does he have difficulty with English?"

"He understands it perfectly," replied Will, "but he doesn't like speaking it, so he avoids it as much as he can. In our language, he's as eloquent as Shakespeare. He says he can't express himself fully in English."

"Is everything okay, about the sweat?"

"Yes. I asked him to run the sweat in thanksgiving for bringing you into my life and asking for guidance in our relationship. I told him there may be problems about us being together, because of you being English and not having the right to live here."

"Goodness!" exclaimed Kerry, nervously. "This sounds a bit serious. We've only known each other a few days! I'm still getting over Hannah! You're speaking as though we're planning to stay together always."

"Aren't we?" asked Will.

"Oh, goodness, I don't know....I hadn't thought about that. It's all a bit sudden!"

"Sorry," said Will. "I didn't mean to shock you."

"No, no, that's fine," said Kerry. "This is all a bit new to me. I don't know what to think."

They fell silent until Will pulled up outside Vera's house.

"Did you tell him about...you know, about...?" asked Kerry.

"I didn't need to," replied Will. "He could see. He asked me whether I knew you were two-spirited. I said yes, I knew. He said, it's like in the old days, when some boys knew themselves to be girls, and they had a ceremony to make it publicly known that now the boy would live as a girl, and be treated as such."

"So he's okay with it?"

"Yes."

"Okay. What time should I be ready tomorrow?"

"Dawn. It'll be real cold, so make sure you bring lots of warm clothing. You can sit in the house while we pray, but when we've finished, you can come and sit with us round the fire until we're ready to go indoors. Is that okay?"

"Anything you say is okay, as far as I'm concerned."

Kerry greeted Vera then went and lay on her bed. What on earth was she doing? She had behaved with utter stupidity over Hannah, and now, still in the early stages of recovery from that romantic catastrophe, she was getting involved with someone else, and a man at that. But oh! Such a man! Physically, it was his femininity that attracted her more than his masculinity – his smooth skin and long hair more than his strong muscles and male genitalia. But how she loved the confident, gentle masculinity of his character! She felt safe with him. She believed she could trust his judgement, look to him for guidance, as she had done with Peter, that he would protect her and keep her safe. She had no idea whether the nature of the love she had begun to feel for him was typical of the love that a woman feels for a man or not, and she did not care. Here were two human beings who loved one another, and she was one of them.

In the morning, long before dawn, Kerry was woken by a loud knocking on the front door. She got out of bed and had reached the door of her room when Grandpa Jimmy came into the house.

"Time to go now," he said. "Wear something real warm. Bring other clothes too – shorts, t-shirt, sweater, towel. I'll be outside." He closed the front door behind him.

Kerry felt disorientated. She was still half asleep. She went to the bathroom and washed her hands and face. She dressed in her warmest clothes, put on her boots and down jacket, and rolled a pair of shorts, a sweat shirt and a t-shirt in a towel, and hurried outside, through the bitter cold, to Jimmy's waiting truck.

"I thought Will would pick me up," said Kerry.

"He's coming," said Jimmy. He put the truck in gear and they moved off. They drove in silence.

Jimmy turned off the road into the driveway leading to his house and parked right by the back door. He got out and went into the house. Kerry followed.

On the table was a pot of hot coffee, a blue enamel mug and a plate of doughnuts. "Better eat some breakfast," said Jimmy. "I'll be back soon." He went out again, and Kerry took off her jacket and sat at the table, nibbling a doughnut and drinking a mug of scalding hot coffee. As soon as she had finished, Jimmy came back in. "Come now," he said, leading the way out of the back door and round behind the chokecherry bushes. A great fire was burning brightly in the fire pit. Beneath large pieces of pine and cottonwood, Kerry could see a pyramid of rocks, some of them already glowing red in the heat.

"Take a seat," said Jimmy, and Kerry sat down in one of the decaying chairs near the fire. She could feel the heat of the fire on her face and chest, the cold of the night on her back.

Jimmy tended the fire with a pitch fork, piling burning logs on to the rocks whenever a log burnt through and fell away from the pile. His face glowed.

Across the river, the sky began to grow light, and the Morning Star shone clearly as it caught the rays of the still invisible sun.

Kerry heard a vehicle approaching. It came to a halt on the other side of the chokecherries, and after a few moments, Will, Billie and Missy walked around the bushes. They greeted each other rather sleepily. Billie and Missy sat down by the fire, while Will took the pitchfork from his grandfather and began to tend the fire. Jimmy sat down. Missy yawned. They all sat in silence, watching the fire and leaning into its heat.

After another quarter of an hour or so, Kerry heard another vehicle approaching. It came to a halt the other side of the bushes and she heard the door slam. "That'll be uncle Eddy," said Will. A few minutes later, a tall, elderly, barrel chested man appeared around the bushes and called a greeting. Coming up to the fire, he took a seat and began to tease everyone for their sleepiness.

"Ho-ly!" he said. "You all look like you're still dreaming! Or did someone steal your tongues? You're all sat here like you're already dead!"

"It's cold!" complained Missy.

"It'll get hot pretty darn soon!" promised Eddy. "Then you'll be saying it's too hot."

"Missy ain't coming in the sweat," said Billie. "She and Kerry can sit in the house."

"Well, pretty darn warm in there, too," said Eddy. "I just went in there for a pee. Pretty darn warm."

"How come you didn't go behind the bushes?" asked Will.

"It's dangerous peeing outdoors in this weather," replied Eddy. "Your pee can freeze up and then you're stuck there with a big old icicle coming out of your you know what. Have to wait till spring before you can move off the spot."

"Don't lie!" said Billie.

303

"I ain't lying! I've seen it with my own ears!"

Missy laughed. "You can't see with your ears, uncle!"

"Can too," replied Eddy.

Eddy turned to Kerry. "So, you're Kerry, from England?"

"That's right," said Kerry.

"And you ain't coming in the sweat with us?"

"No," said Kerry.

"Then you can let us out if we get stuck in there."

"How would you get stuck in there, uncle?" asked Missy.

"Frozen," said Eddy. "Didn't I tell you about that one time I got frozen in to a sweat down at Chokecherry Butte? Mind you, it was a lot colder than today. Vera told us it was too cold to sweat but we didn't listen, me and old man Jimmy. Went over to Chokecherry Butte to old man Butch's place, and it was about thirty below – ho-ly, it was cold! And old Butch put so much water on them rocks in there, we were just waiting to get out of there, it was so darn hot, but when it was time to open up, the door flap had frozen shut! Too much steam in there – it soaked all the blankets and then the ones on the outside froze up in the cold. We had to scrabble at that door flap like a bunch of gophers digging."

"Tchaaa!" scolded Jimmy. "He tells that story every time."

The fire had nearly burned down by now, and the rocks were glowing red in the dawn light.

"I guess it's time for you and Missy to go indoors," Will said to Kerry. "Will you be okay?"

"Of course she will," said Missy. "I'll take care of her."

Kerry and Missy walked around the bushes and back to the house. Despite the fire, Kerry felt chilled to the bone. She shivered as they walked up the steps to the back door.

"You'd better have some more coffee," said Missy. "You look cold."

"That's a good idea," said Kerry. "I think I will."

Indoors, Kerry heated up the remaining coffee in a saucepan on the wood stove, and Missy sat in the old armchair and fell asleep in the comforting warmth of the room. Kerry drank her coffee at the table looking through the window at the lightening sky. The sun rose over the hills beyond the river, filling the room with its brilliance. Kerry finished her coffee and settled herself to pray, keeping in mind her friends praying in the lodge. Although she wished she could be with them, she did not feel excluded. She could understand why she could not undergo that experience with them, why they could not invite her to share it with them. She prayed for them, as she knew they were praying for her, and she felt united with them in that loving intention of the heart.

She lost track of time. She was not wearing her watch, and there was no clock in the room. From the position of the sun, she guessed that something over an hour had passed when Will came in, wearing only his shorts, his shoes and a towel draped over his shoulders. Kerry leapt up from the table. "You'll die of cold!" she said. "Why aren't you dressed warmly?"

"We just now got done in there," said Will. "I came straight on over to say you can come and sit by the fire with us. Jimmy wants to pray with you, too. He dreamt about you last night."

"What did he dream?" asked Kerry.

"He'd better tell you that," said Will. "Come now. I'm gonna dry off and get my clothes on again." He woke Missy. "Missy, you gonna come over there with us?"

"No, I'm sleepy," said Missy. "I'm gonna stay here."

Will and Kerry hurried over to the fire, which had been fed with fresh logs although all but one of the rocks had been removed. Billie, already fully clothed, was just zipping up her jacket. She sat down close to the fire. Eddy was sitting by the fire in his shorts, looking as red as a cooked lobster. "Phew," he said, "That was a hot one!" He began drying his feet with his towel. "Should've brought my nail clippers," he said. "Best time to cut your toenails is after a good sweat. Softens them up." Will nipped behind the sweatlodge to take off his wet shorts, dried himself and dressed as quickly as he could. He returned, shivering, to the fire.

"Where's Grandpa Jimmy?" asked Kerry.

"In here," answered Jimmy, from just inside the sweatlodge. He looked out at Kerry. "You better put your shorts on and come in here," he said.

"I left them in the house," replied Kerry.

"Go put 'em on," instructed Jimmy.

Kerry was not eager to change into shorts and a t-shirt in weather that was so far below freezing, but she did not wish to be rude. She hurried indoors, where Missy was still sleeping, and changed into the shorts and t-shirt that she had brought with her. Wrapping herself in her down jacket, she hurried back through the bitter cold to the fire. "You can come and sit in here now," said Jimmy. "Leave your jacket on the chair."

Kerry took off her jacket and stooped to enter the sweatlodge. Despite the open door flap, it was still intensely hot inside, as the rocks were still throwing off their heat. The air smelt of damp earth and steam and musty blankets and fresh cedar smoke. Jimmy was sitting cross-legged to the left of the door and indicated that Kerry should sit to its right. She folded her legs under her and to the right, and sat with her weight on her left arm.

"Bring that last rock, now," called Jimmy, and Will brought the rock from the fire, placing it with the pitchfork on top of the other rocks in the pit. It glowed red, and Kerry felt an intense blast of heat against her face and her bare legs. She hoped the heat would not damage her implants.

"It'll be alright," said Jimmy. "Won't take long. No steam."

He called out some instruction in his own language, and Will closed the door flap from outside. The lodge was pitch dark apart from the dull red glow of the new rock.

"I had a dream last night," said Jimmy. "Creator showed me things. You don't feel right yet. You don't feel at home in your new body. Spirits don't know you as woman. Spirits still think you're a man. So we'll pray now, so spirits know you as woman. Then you'll feel peaceful, feel okay."

Kerry remained silent, listening.

"I'll bless you with cedar, then I'll pray in our language, then you'll feel better," said Jimmy.

Jimmy threw dried cedar on to the fresh rock, and Kerry could see the smoke rise against the fading red glow. She felt Jimmy fanning the smoke over her, though she could not see with what. Then he began to pray quietly in his own language, his words sounding like the whispering of a fast-flowing stream over rocks. Kerry shut her eyes, then opened them into total blackness. The red glow of the rock had faded, and she could see absolutely nothing.

Then, all of a sudden, the dark lodge was filled with light, and she saw in front of her the smiling face of an immeasurably old Native American man, gazing into her face. His eyes were full of compassion. He looked away to his left, and Kerry turned her eyes to where he was looking. She was unnerved to see a small boy playing in a garden. The boy was Kerry himself. But as the child played, he grew and aged, and as he aged, he became a woman. Then, the woman was no longer in the garden, but in the sweatlodge, sitting opposite Kerry, though she *was* Kerry. Kerry looked away from this figure which was herself, and there was the elder, gazing at her, smiling. She shut her eyes, and heard the soft voice of Grandpa Jimmy praying. Then the words ceased, and she opened her eyes, and saw only blackness in front of her. Jimmy called out, and the door flap was opened from outside. Bitter cold air flowed into the lodge, and Kerry shivered. She looked over at Jimmy, who was smiling serenely. "You can go out now," he said. She thanked him, and crawled out of the lodge.

Will helped her up and handed her jacket. "Do you feel any different?" he asked.

"I don't know," she answered. "How am I meant to feel?"

"Like a woman who knows she's a woman, and knows that she's accepted as a woman by the Creator and the whole spirit world. But I don't know how that feels."

Kerry thought for a moment. "I feel peaceful," she said.

"That sounds good," said Will.

Kerry thought for a while.

"I don't seem to feel anxious any more," she said.

"Good," said Will.

"How long was I in there?" asked Kerry.

"Oh, about two or three minutes, I guess," replied Will. "Not long."

"It seemed like ages."

"I always lose all track of time in there. Time's different in there."

Jimmy emerged from the sweatlodge. He stood in silence for a while, facing the sun. Then he turned to the south, standing silently again.

"Grandpa's greeting the Four Directions," whispered Will. "Powerful spirits live at each point, and each direction has a different significance in our way."

Jimmy turned to the West, and after a while, to the North; then once more towards the East. Then he looked at Kerry. "Time to get dressed now, then time to eat," he said. He led the way to the house, where Billie and Missy and Eddy were waiting. Jimmy went to his room to change, and Kerry to the bathroom. As she dressed, she felt oddly different. She no longer felt as if she existed inside a body that was not quite hers. She felt that her body and her sense of self belonged together. She felt devoid of regrets.

Jimmy climbed in to Eddy's truck and Kerry into Will's with Billie and Missy. "What happens now?" she asked.

"We're going to eat at our house," said Billie. "Uncle Eddy's going to go and get Vera and they'll come up too."

Vera was surprised to learn that her newest daughter might have been a son. "Oh, like in the old days," she said. "Then, they used to have a ceremony for a boy who wanted to be a girl or a girl who wanted to be a boy. The missionaries didn't like that, so they stopped it. But you make a real good woman," she said. "You do neat work. You got a kind heart. Maybe good idea not to tell Darlene Black Wolf yet, though."

"I never wanted to go with Darlene Black Wolf, Grandma!" protested Will. "It was all in her imagination!"

"Pretty powerful thing, imagination," said Vera.

They ate deer meat stew with fry bread, then more fry bread with pudding made from dried chokecherries. Eddy and

Jimmy left with Vera when they had eaten, and the others all fell asleep in the warmth of the room as the sky clouded over and it began to snow again.

Ten: Kerry and Hannah confront the company

Hannah told Kerry she was not entirely sure what she thought about her getting together with Will. Despite the horror of being responsible for such suffering on the part of her friend, she admitted there was something rather flattering about being the object of such devotion. What did it say about her worth as an object of devotion, that her aspiring lover's affections could so quickly be redirected to another? She confessed to feeling somehow disappointed. At the same time, she felt relief that her friend was distracted from thinking about her all the time. But she was worried that Kerry was simply suffering from the rebound, and making choices which were unwise and unhelpful.

"Do you really intend to stay longer so you can spend time with Will?" she asked.

"Yes," said Kerry. "I know this has developed much too quickly to be sensible, but that's all the more reason to spend time with him to see whether this is a passing fancy or a genuine love."

"And you're moving in with Will?"

"Yes, I don't feel I can stay for weeks and weeks at Vera's. It would be unfair to her."

"Jackie says Vera loves having people to stay."

"Well, she seems to approve of me and Will being together, and I can still visit her lots."

"Don't go and get hurt again, Kerry. I don't want to hurt your feelings any more than I have already, but I do sometimes question your judgement."

"I'm too easily led, aren't I?"

"Yes. But the people leading you often don't even know they're doing it, because they assume you're as sure of yourself as they are."

"I've never been sure of myself. Most of my life I haven't really known what I thought about anything. I've let people I admired tell me what to think or what to do. The first thing I really chose to do of my own free will was the gender reassignment, and in my case, it was a stupid thing to do. But this being with Will is the second thing I am choosing of my own free will, and it's redeeming the first decision." She thought for a while. "The thing is, loving you was going to go nowhere. Then, along came Will. He loves me. That's what made me love him. But the more I think about it, the more I love him. Including his physical beauty, which is feminine and masculine at the same time. I am captivated by that."

"Well, please don't get hurt again. I couldn't bear that. I'd feel responsible."

"I've told you before that you're not responsible for my feelings. I am."

The time for Kerry's flight back to Boston and on to London passed, and Kerry stayed. She wrote again to Father Patrick and Father Donald, telling them that she would not be home for Christmas, explaining that she had found love again, and asking their forgiveness.

She checked her email again. Peter had written to her some days before, in response to her big news. He confessed to being shocked. Shocked did not mean disapproving. But he was very surprised, and somewhat disoriented. He would need time to come to terms with it, he wrote. Meanwhile, the struggle in Caribe continued. Every concession the company made on paper had to be rung out of them in practice by continued complaints and international campaigns and threats of lawsuits. It was like walking through treacle. But they were making progress. A complaint had been brought against both mining companies to the UK National Contact Point of the Organisation for Economic Co-operation and Development. It was an utterly toothless organisation, but the existence of the complaint had embarrassed the companies and driven them to more concessions. It looked as though the promised new village for the people of San Martin de Porres really was going to be built at last.

Kerry wrote back to send good wishes to the San Martin Relocation Committee, and to apologise for Peter's discomfiture. Although, she realised after sending the email, that it was not for her to apologise for what Peter felt, and Peter would not expect such an apology.

Mario had also written, asking Kerry whether she was 'getting any' yet, and if so, what it was like. She answered that it was none of his business.

At Midnight Mass, Kerry sat between Will and Grandpa Jimmy at the back of the church, where Jimmy always sat, without fail, every Sunday and holy day. Grandpa Jimmy was wearing new jeans and a red jacket advertising the high school basketball team. In his hands, he held his Whispering River Indian Tribe baseball hat, which he had taken off his head out of respect for the church. Vera sat at the front with Billie and Missy. The church was packed with tribal members and the local whites. Father Karl preached about the humility of the God who chose to be born a helpless baby, a homeless outcast among an oppressed and divided people.

Kerry thought that God's humility was beautifully manifested in the lives of both Father Karl himself and Grandpa Jimmy. She wondered whether God was more like Father Karl, or Grandpa Jimmy, or Vera, or Peter, or Bill Cowley, and decided that since each of them was apparently made in the image of God, there must be something about each of them that reflected that Reality that was beyond thought. But by that argument, there must be something in God that was reminiscent of herself, or Pik Bloemen, or Tony Conwell. She did not know what to make of that, and decided that theology was not her strong point, and that, maybe, the most important thing was to remember that whatever else God was, or is, first and foremost God is love.

She wondered for a while what Christmas would be like if she were not a believer, but she found it impossible to evaluate, as she could not imagine her own existence if she were not a believer. How odd, she thought, that some of the more fashionable apologists for atheism attacked religion on the grounds that it was a false explanation of the origin of the universe. Kerry had not practiced her religion because she thought that the notion of God explained the existence of the universe. It was just that God had always seemed so real to her – as a kind of backdrop to everything else, as well as a loving presence within and around everything else – that it had never occurred to her to question God's existence. She did not really care about how the universe came to be. It simply was. So was God. God was the reality through which she approached all other realities. God was not a logical explanation of how the universe came to be. She wondered whether those who made a living by attacking religious aunt sallies of their own creation might benefit from a visit to the Rez, where nobody would want to argue with them, just feed them fry bread and chokecherry pudding and be kind to them, until they calmed down a little.

After Christmas, Kerry began to help Will full time at the store. Word was beginning to get around, and custom was gradually increasing. Not that it was yet sufficient to make assistance necessary, but since they enjoyed each other's company so much, it seemed reasonable to work together.

Will also persuaded both Kerry and Hannah to go on K-R-E-Z radio to speak about what they had seen of Anglo Australian plc in Cortesia. They spoke about the demolition of San Martin de Porres, the contempt shown for the local people by the municipal authorities, the crocodile tears shed by both Anglo Australian and North Atlantic Mining over an action of the planning of which they must both have been aware when they chose to buy the mine, and the feigned regret for a low-level atrocity, about which they cared only as much as public protest compelled them to care. Kerry and Hannah spoke as eye-witnesses. Nobody could accuse them of speaking about matters of which they had no direct experience. When Walter Not Afraid, the interviewer, spoke of his good impressions of the Anglo Australian-owned mines he had seen south of the Rez, they did not contradict him. They could not gainsay his experience. But when Hannah asked him why he thought the company's operations were so exemplary here in Yellowstone State, he answered by saying that the regulatory environment was strict, strict laws being strictly enforced, and largely at the insistence of the Tribe itself, even though the existing mines were off the Reservation.

"Exactly," said Hannah. "It's not the good will of the company, it's the fact they're forced to behave in a certain way by laws passed at public insistence, and enforced because of public vigilance. You can't trust the company to police itself. How could you? Any company exists primarily to make as much money as it can. It's legally obliged to make as much money as it can for its shareholders. That's the problem with the whole system. Profits for shareholders take precedence over every other consideration. Other matters only get taken into account to the extent that the public forces a company to take them into account, either through law enforcement, legal action or threatening damage to reputation through publicising the company's infringements of good practice."

Of course, K-R-E-Z gave air time to the company as well; but Pik Bloemen was out of the country, and the local spokesperson lacked eloquence and had no experience of the company's Cortesian operations, so he was unable to answer the specific points made by Kerry and Hannah. All he could do, was draw attention to the company's US operations, and to its promises of jobs for local people. Kerry and Hannah pointed out that few local people had been offered jobs at the Valle Negro mine and that, on the contrary, many local farmers had lost their livelihoods as a direct result of mine expansion.

The broadcast stirred up a hornet's nest. A lot of tribal members who had voted in favour of the mine were having second thoughts. How could they trust the company's promises if this was the way it behaved towards Indigenous people and people of African descent in Cortesia? It wasn't even as if the company were American; it was a foreign company, so in its eyes, the people on the Rez must be just another bunch of foreigners. Angry tribal members demanded a special meeting of the Tribal Council and extracted a promise that the Council would revisit the agreement with the company, to ensure that all the promises about pollution limitation, waste disposal and local jobs would be improved, and kept.

It was no surprise that, within three weeks, Pik Bloemen was back in town. The VP for CPR was needed to calm the troubled waters. But he was not the calmest of men, and he was rattled. He insisted on air time on K-R-E-Z equal to that given to the interview with Kerry and Hannah, despite the fact that the company had already been given equal time. He insisted that it should be broadcast at peak listening time in the evening, and that Kerry and Hannah should not be given the opportunity to contradict him. He hinted to the radio's trustees, and to Walt himself, that anything less than what he demanded would lead to legal action against the radio station, which would inevitably lead to closure at best, and ruinous legal fees at worst. Furthermore – and this showed Mr Bloemen's complete failure to understand the local culture – the fact that he had insisted on these conditions, and hinted at legal action, was not to be made known to anyone other than the trustees and the interviewer.

By the next day, of course, it was common knowledge across the Rez, and nobody could say who had let the cat out of the bag. Pik Bloemen was intelligent enough to realise that if he took legal action against the trustees or the wildly popular Walt Not Afraid now, he would lose all credibility and do the company far worse damage than it had already suffered. So he decided to show his magnanimity by limiting himself to refuting the wild allegations of the company's detractors.

Walter Not Afraid, however, impressed by what he had seen of Kerry and Hannah, had done his homework, spoken at length in private with the two women and read a number of articles and documents which they had sent him. Pik Bloemen did not like the drift of Walter's questions, and allowed his irascibility to get the better of him. He switched from repeating the same platitudes about the company's corporate social responsibility policies, to making personal attacks on the company's critics.

"Who the hell are these people anyway?" he suddenly demanded, not realising the offence he would cause by using a cuss word on air. Walt decided not to edit it out before broadcast, as he had not been asked to do so. "I'll tell you who they are," offered Mr Bloemen, his accent becoming ever more South African as he lost his cool. "They are outsiders. Miss Ferraro is from the Atlantic Coast and has been out here in the West for only a month or so. Miss Ahern is from another continent altogether – and not only that, she is from Britain, which, may I remind you, was the colonial power in these parts."

"Actually the Brits never ruled this part of North America," Walt corrected him. "Yellowstone State was part of the Louisiana Purchase, bought by the US Government from the French, who thought they owned it, not that they ever asked us about it."

"Well," responded Pik Bloemen, somewhat disconcerted, "I think my point is clear. They are not from around here and cannot be said to have the interests of local people at heart."

"I can't help noticing that you are not from around here either, Pik," said Walt. "Your accent betrays you, if I may quote from the Bible."

"But our company is very much from around here, because the company is none other than our officials and our workforce, and the overwhelming majority of our workers around here come from the United States of America."

"But not necessarily from Yellowstone State," suggested Walt.

"Around fifty per cent of the workforce is from this state," asserted Pik Bloemen.

"But not from the Reservation," added Walt.

"Not yet," agreed Pik Bloemen, "but that's why we have signed an agreement with the Tribe about preferential hiring of tribal members in operations on the Reservation. You can rest assured that the majority of the workforce in our planned operations on this Reservation will be enrolled members of this Tribe."

"Well, I guess that's good news," agreed Walt. "What about shareholders, then, Pik? I guess, in a way, the company's first legal responsibility is to its shareholders, isn't it?"

"Legally speaking, yes," agreed Pik Bloemen. "But those shareholders care about what we call the company's licence to operate, which means it is an integral part of our operating plan to be good corporate citizens and respect the wishes of all our stakeholders."

"Jeez, that sounds intriguing," said Walt. "What's a stakeholder? A guy at a barbecue?"

Pik Bloemen forced a laugh. "No, no, this is the terminology we use to talk about all of those who have an interest in our operations – shareholders, lenders, workers, local residents, even concerned citizens who may be worried about our operations because of reading the misleading information that certain radicals like to put out about us."

"Radicals, huh? Like…?"

"Well, I am sorry to say this, but people like Miss Ferraro and Miss Ahern. I have to say that our operations in Cortesia, which are bringing jobs and prosperity to an area that desperately needs them, are being hampered by the wilful opposition of some in the Catholic Church, who have allowed themselves to be taken in by Communists. I count Miss Ferraro as one of these. And then the Ahern family seem to have declared some kind of vendetta against our company, and even a personal campaign of vengefulness against my own person. How else to explain the fact that in Cortesia Miss Ahern's brother spent several months stirring up opposition to our mine, and when I come to Yellowstone State to help take forward the next stage of our operations here – which will be of so much benefit to this Tribe and this whole area – I find

Miss Ahern herself engaged in the same kind of misguided and ill-informed opposition to our company."

"Well, thanks for being so open with us, Pik," said Walter. "I guess we're running out of time now, but it's been good to hear the company's point of view on this matter."

"I wanted to set the record straight."

"Well, I guess you've been real clear and I think that will help our listeners. Thank you."

"The pleasure's been mine," said Mr Bloemen.

Good, thought Walter. He starts with a cuss word and finishes with a personal attack. That'll turn a whole bunch more people against him. Not that he'll realise that until it's too late.

After the news headlines, the hour of Indigenous language programming began. Four elders were discussing the interview with Pik Bloemen. Not that Pik Bloemen would know, since neither he, nor any of the company's employees, understood the language. Three of the elders had voted in favour of the mining. They were all now having second thoughts. They did not like Mr Bloemen's language, his aggressive demeanour or his personal attacks. They did not yet know Kerry or Hannah but they thought they had sounded pretty convincing when they spoke on the radio a couple of weeks back, and it was a shame to hear this aggressive man from the company attacking them in so personal a way. The elders differed in their views of the Catholic Church, but none of them had cause to complain about the Sisters who were now working on the Rez and they were sad to hear one of them being badmouthed as a Communist. They were not entirely sure what was meant by the term in this context, but Pik Bloemen had clearly meant it as an insult, and it therefore could not be in any way appropriate for the Sisters.

That, at least, was the gist of their conversation, as much as Will could understand, and as he translated it for all those gathered at the Sisters' house to listen to the broadcast.

"After this, I think people will be much more critical of the company, and make sure the Tribal Council enforces real strict regulations, even if it's too late to cancel the contract now," he said. "This is a step forward."

A few days after the interview, Pik Bloemen was asked to come back on to the radio to receive an award from Walter Not Afraid on behalf, Walt said, of a number of listeners who had phoned in and asked Walt to bestow on him an Indian name. Walt pronounced it carefully in the tribe's language, helped Pik Bloemen to pronounce it correctly and explained that it meant 'Walking Eagle'.

Pik Bloemen was suitably impressed, explaining that he felt it a great honour, not only for himself, but for the company, for him to be given such a strong name, which he took to imply both spiritual vision and earthy practicality.

Most of those who were listening at home were doubled up with laughter. Kerry asked Will to explain. "Calling someone 'Walking Eagle' is a real insult, reserved for pompous white people," he said. "It means the man's so full of shit he can't fly."

Eleven: Kerry and Will prepare to go north

Towards the end of January, Will heard from the Aboriginal Ecological Coalition about a logging road blockade near Deep Lake, up in the northern Canadian province of Athabasca. Cree elders and their supporters had blocked a road to stop an area of their traditional territory being clear-cut to make way for uranium mining. The uranium would feed a nuclear power station which was to be constructed to provide energy for tar sands extraction. The mining of the tar sands in the western part of Athabasca had already led to the loss of forest cover over an area the size of England, but now the plan was to extend the mining eastwards, possibly doubling the amount of forest loss. Supplies of natural gas from the Arctic would be insufficient to power the extraction, hence the move towards nuclear power, using the plentiful uranium in the eastern half of the province.

Will was uncharacteristically depressed by the news, not only because of the ecological destruction being planned but because although he wanted desperately to help the Cree elders in their bid to stop this threat, he believed that if he left the store now, in its infancy, the project would fail and the business collapse. He knew that others would be travelling to support the Cree Defenders of Mother Earth and that at present there was nobody to take his place at the store in Dusty. It was clear that he was needed more in his own community than in the North; but he felt ill at ease about it.

About the same time, Kerry received a letter from Father Patrick – a long letter, written in neat copper-plate handwriting. It was just as Kerry might have expected, had she thought long enough about it. There was not a word of condemnation of her choices, just good will and kindness and words of encouragement. Father Patrick admitted to not understanding Kerry's choice of gender reassignment, though he believed that when in love people did sometimes make choices that, under other circumstances, they might hesitate to make. He even went as far as saying that he wondered whether it was a wise choice. But he believed that every set of circumstances, however difficult, was redeemable. He regretted the grief that Kerry had experienced through being disappointed in her first love, and rejoiced with her in her joy over her new relationship. He counselled caution, as he worried that she may have embraced the second romance simply in reaction to the frustration of her earlier hopes, but he also said that, after much consideration, he had concluded that it was possible that in his great wisdom God may be using this new love as a way of redeeming what might at first have been an unwise choice. He referred to the Church's disapproval of gender reassignment, of which he knew Kerry was aware, but expressed his own view that sometimes God used precisely our mistakes and weaknesses to do some great new work in us, and that the joyful acceptance of the difficult consequences of some unfortunate choice may be the path to the redemption of it. He wished her great happiness while in America, expressed the fervent hope of seeing her again before too long, and urged her to write to him again as soon as she could.

Kerry carefully folded Father Patrick's letter, held it close to her heart, and kept it in the bag she carried with her everywhere. She wrote a short reply after another week or so, full of gratitude for his understanding and encouragement, and promising to write with more news at a later date.

She also heard again, by email, from Peter. He was getting used to the thought of his friend's change of gender and had talked about it at great length with Mario, whose main preoccupation was with the erotic possibilities of their former colleague's altered plumbing. Faced with the incorrigible insensitivity and tastelessness of their short, squat mutual friend, Peter had felt an overwhelming sense of protectiveness and affection for his transsexual protégée, and had determined to make whatever mental effort necessary to ensure that he could offer her his wholly non-judgemental solidarity. Kerry felt an enormous sense of relief at her mentor's acceptance of her strange and ill-considered choice.

Will's spirits lifted when his old friend Milton Eastwood came to call. Will and Milton had been in the marines together, and of all Will's white friends, none was as close as Milton.

"Hey, buddy, how're you doin'?" called Milton cheerily, as he came into the store one day in mid-February.

"Milt!" replied Will with evident delight. "What brings you here, you old fart?"

"The desire to see you, my old friend," replied Milton. "It's too many months since we last met, I was down at Oil Bluffs, anyway, and I've got a business venture to discuss with you."

"Well, take a seat, old horse, and let me get you a coffee."

"I'll make it," said Kerry, looking out of the back room door.

"Hey! Who's this?" asked Milton.

"Kerry," answered Will; and Kerry came and shook Milton's hand.

"Jiminy criminy!" exclaimed Milton. "Well, darn it, am I honoured to meet you! Will always did attract the most beautiful of women! What a lucky man!"

Kerry blushed. "Thank you," she said.

"You're still as sensitive and diplomatic as a brick in the face," observed Will.

"I just say it as I see it," replied Milton. "I don't hold with political correctness. Apologies if I've caused any offence, Kerry."

"None taken," said Kerry. "You're very flattering."

"Are you from England?" asked Milton.

"Yes," replied Kerry.

"I love your accent," said Milton.

"Thanks," said Kerry.

Milton suddenly looked troubled. "Hey, I'm sorry! I'm kind of assuming you two are... you know..."

"We are," confirmed Will, taking Kerry's hand and kissing it. Kerry smiled, blushed, and went into the back room to make the coffee.

"Oh, wow, she's...I'm really glad you've found a good woman at last," said Milton quietly. "You deserve it, you old son of a gun."

Will, in a similarly quiet voice, briefly explained, in order to avoid worse embarrassment later, the relevant aspect of Kerry's personal history. Milton looked thunderstruck.

"You mean...?" he asked.

"I do mean," confirmed Will.

"But has she still...?"

"No. They took all that out."

Milton looked relieved. "Oh, good, so she really is a woman now?"

"She can't have children, but externally, yes, she is."

"So, she's not like those women we hooked up with that time on R&R in Thailand?"

"You mean that one time?"

"Yeah."

"No."

"That was kind of a surprise."

"A bit of a shock, really."

"You could say that."

"Maybe we shouldn't have been so forward in any case. Served us right."

"It gets kind o' difficult when you're so long at sea, though, don't it?" The memory clearly pained Milton. He fell silent, gazing into space for a while. "Yeah," he concluded, "some things are best not meditated on too much."

Kerry brought two cups of coffee out from the back room.

"This guy," said Milton, indicating Will and resuming his normal volume of speech, which struck Kerry as rather louder than necessary, "saved my life."

"He always goes on about this," complained Will.

"Well, you did, buddy! I wouldn't be here if it weren't for you!"

"I only did what you'd have done for me."

"He dragged me out of a tight spot when I was wounded and had lost my weapon and we were both under fire," Milton explained to Kerry. "That's the kind of guy he is. You picked a good one."

"You never told me that, Will," said Kerry.

"What is there to tell?" said Will. "Anyone would have done the same for a friend. Anyway, he's told you now. Now, tell us about this business idea, Milt."

"Beans!" replied Milton. "You want to get people to eat healthily. I've been thinking of starting a canning business. I'm sick and tired of working for other people, Donna and I want to start up on our own, and for whatever reason, we came up with the idea of canning. Well, why not can beans and pulses and all that stuff and supply the health food market? It's up and coming now. We can catch the wave as it crests. Would you stock our produce?"

"Well, of course I would, but are you really sure there's enough of a market for it in Yellowstone State?"

"There will be, but in any case we'll look to distributing in the Dakotas and points south too."

"Well, if you're up for it, I'll do my best to move the stuff," offered Will.

In early March, Kerry heard from Father Donald. Before replying to Kerry's letters, he had done some reading about gender identity and reassignment. He wrote with great kindness and humour, encouraging her to accept with joy the consequences of her decision, even though, by her own admission, that decision had not been well thought through. Who knew what great and beautiful possibilities were to be unleashed by Kerry's altered circumstances? And nothing, in his view, limited the divine sense of humour, either. If Kerry were able to find the strength to laugh at her choice and its consequences, she would be well on the way to wisdom.

By April, Will was becoming restless. He felt a strong need to get to the front line, in the woods of eastern Athabasca, defending Mother Earth against uranium mining and tar sands extraction. Business in the whole food store was picking up, and he believed that if the right person could take charge while he and Kerry were gone, the enterprise would survive his absence for a few weeks. After some discussion, Billie agreed to leave her job as a dental nurse over at Red Willow Creek so she could start work at the store and learn how to take charge of it if Will did decide to go up north. Will could trust her completely.

In early May, the AEC sent out an urgent action request. The Defenders of Mother Earth had so far managed to prevent clearing of the forest in the area scheduled for uranium mining, and the police had been stopped from undertaking a forced eviction through legal challenges. But the mine's opponents had nearly exhausted their judicial options now, and if the next decision, which was expected in a few weeks' time, went against them, the authorities would make an attempt to clear the blockade by force. Supporters were urged to make for several different gathering points, and then converge on the blockade to make the authorities' task more difficult. If the blockade could remain firm, extra time would be won for all the other parts of the campaign – the legal challenges, the letter-writing campaigns, the newspaper articles, the cyber actions, the demonstrations outside Parliament in Ottawa, the academic publications, the international awareness-raising – to bear some fruit. And if the authorities did break up the blockade by force, they may well score a public relations own goal, to the benefit of the Defenders of Mother Earth.

The time had come.

It was then that Will's trusty truck broke down, and neither Will himself, nor the mechanics at Dusty or Red Willow Creek, could fix it. Will feared it may be terminal.

It was no good taking Billie's little car. It would never cope with the tracks in the Athabasca forests and it would leave Billie without transport in Dusty.

It was fortunate indeed, then, that Milton arrived with his first consignment of canned beans and pulses the day after the breakdown. Will did not like to call in favours, but since Milton was so insistent, so often, that he owed Will his life, maybe a ride across the border would not be too much to ask.

Kerry examined the cans which they unloaded from two dozen boxes and began stacking on the shelves in the store and in the back room. Each one bore the title 'Eastwood beans and pulses' and a drawing of a craggy-faced individual, clearly intended to be Dirty Harry, with a cloud coming out of his mouth containing the words "I'm gonna blow your ass clean off."

"Isn't this breach of copyright?" asked Kerry.

"Why should it be?" asked Milton. "Eastwood's my name and Donna's. And who's to say that's a picture of Dirty Harry? It could be anybody. Anyway, I'm sure Clint would approve."

"Are you related?" asked Kerry.

"I wish," replied Milton.

"How do you expect to popularise beans and pulses when you put a cartoon like that on the can?" asked Will. "People know beans make you fart anyway. There's no need to emphasize the point."

"That's assuming people don't enjoy a good fart," countered Milton.

"Well, most people don't," replied Will. "At least, not if it's anybody else's. And I don't see how you can possibly enjoy yours. I guess they've stripped all the lining out of your nostrils and destroyed your sense of smell."

"You just don't know what's good for you," said Milton. "If people didn't fart, their heads would blow off. That's a scientific fact."

"Well, then, maybe you should explain that on the can. But you'll need to quote the actual studies that establish that fact."

Milton was silent for a few seconds and looked as if he was concentrating very hard. He then lifted one leg slightly and broke wind loudly. "There!" he said with satisfaction.

"Did my head blow off? No! So I think we've established that fact beyond reasonable doubt."

"*Post hoc* is not the same as *propter hoc*," Kerry pointed out.

"That sounds foreign to me," said Milton.

"It's Latin," explained Kerry. "It means that the fact that something comes after something else, doesn't mean it happens because of it. Just because your head hasn't blown off, it doesn't mean that the reason it's still on your shoulders is that you farted."

"Intelligent as well as beautiful," said Milton. "Well, okay, we'll abandon that line of argument and just say that sometimes people like to laugh. You can sell things through humour."

"We'll see, won't we?" said Will. "Am I paying for these or taking them on sale or return?"

"Just for you, sale or return. You did save my life, after all."

"Ah, yes. Now, I was going to ask you a favour."

"Go ahead, punk. Make my day."

Will explained his predicament. "I'm not asking you to take us all the way to the north woods," he said. "Just to the gathering point over the border."

"And you want to leave when?" asked Milton.

"Tomorrow, if possible," said Will.

"And this protest you're going to, it isn't anti-American or anything, is it? You know I don't wholly share your outlook on these things, my friend."

"It's anti the destruction of the Earth for quick profit; anti the destruction of God's good creation, which God made human beings the stewards of; anti the big corporations that undermine American democracy; anti…."

"Okay, buddy, that'll do. I'm happy to help if it's about protecting nature. I love this country, I love this continent, and I don't want the place ruined any more than you do. I just get ticked off by those folks who blame everything on America, as though we're the root of all evil."

327

"Well, in this case, the big enemies are the Canadian government and a British mining company called North Atlantic."

"Oh, my goodness!" exclaimed Kerry. "Them again! That'll be fun!"

"Hey, if the protest is about a bunch of foreigners, I'm your man!" said Milton. "God bless America!"

"Careful, now, Milton," counselled Kerry. "We're not all Americans in here."

"And some of us are a lot more American than others," said Will, pointedly. "Like, those of us who were here before you white guys got here."

Milton stuck his tongue out at Will and crossed his eyes.

"Well, let me consult my boss and see if it's okay to stay away a few extra days," said Milton. He took out his cell phone and called his wife. He walked up to the far end of the store for privacy, and spent some time talking with her. Kerry overheard numerous touching endearments, and conversations which were obviously with children. After ten minutes or so, Milton ended his call, and announced that he had the permission not only of his wife, but of both his daughters, to stay away long enough to do this favour for the man who saved his life.

They decided it was too late to start out that day, as the journey would take a good twelve hours, and the border crossing they would use was closed at night. So, Milton would stay over at the Many Paint Horses' house and they would leave in the morning.

But there was another matter to be taken into consideration before leaving. Kerry would not be allowed into Canada unless she had a ticket home to England. Should they buy one from the USA and have the added problem of getting her back across the border again before flying, or buy one from Canada? In the end, they decided they had better book a ticket back from Canada, and booked one online that very afternoon for a flight, just under a month later, in early June.

That, of course, meant that there were goodbyes to be said – to Hannah and the Sisters, to Grandpa Jimmy, Uncle Eddy and especially to Vera, Kerry's mother.

As soon as they closed up the store, Will and Kerry went visiting. Jimmy and Eddy were happy enough to offer the assurance of their prayers and to look forward to their return in glory, Will's from Canada and Kerry's, even if somewhat delayed, from across the ocean. But Vera was distraught. She wept freely. "Don't go up there," she pleaded. "I got a bad feeling about this. You're gonna get hurt, Will. I can just see it. Don't go up there. And you, Kerry, don't go! You're my daughter! Maybe I'll never see you again!"

They did their best to reassure her. "It'll be okay, Grandma," Will told her. "Nothing's going to happen to me! I went all over the world in the service and I always came back in one piece. I'll be okay!"

"No, I got a bad feeling about this one," Vera repeated, blowing her nose with one little handkerchief and dabbing her tears with another. "Don't go, Will. Please don't go. And you, Kerry, I know you got to go way over there, but you got to come back! When will you come back? You're my daughter! I got a bad feeling about this!"

They could not soothe her. She was still weeping when they left. So, Kerry was already emotionally ragged when they went to say goodbye to Hannah. It was awkward. By the time Kerry came back, Hannah would most likely be back on the East Coast, in the novitiate at Jerusalem, Massachusetts. Who knew when they might meet again? Hannah still felt guilty and conflicted about what Kerry had done, and Kerry felt embarrassed and disloyal, having made such an ill-considered choice for love of Hannah and then transferred her affections so quickly to another. There was little they could say to each other, so they held each other in their arms for a long time, and said nothing.

NORTH

the direction of old age, wisdom and death

One: Kerry and Will reach Kropotkin

Kerry, Will and Milton were on the road by eight in the morning, heading along the dirt road to Cottonwood Creek. From there, paved roads took them the next three hundred miles north to Canada.

They reached the small border crossing late in the afternoon, passing US border control with its stars and stripes flapping in the breeze, and pulling in a few yards beyond it to the Canadian customs and immigration control post surmounted by its maple leaf flag. Kerry had to leave the vehicle and assure the officer on duty that she had the capacity to support herself during her stay in Canada, and a valid ticket back to her country of residence.

All was well. They were able to continue. A large sign welcomed them to Canada, and to the Province of Assiniboia. They pulled in to a small roadside diner and ate an early supper.

"Now," said Milton, as they headed north. "What's this place we're going to?"

"It's one of the places that the Aboriginal Ecological Coalition wants supporters to gather at before going on up to the road blockade," said Will. "Interesting place, founded by a bunch of British anarchists at the end of the eighteen hundreds."

"Oh, Jeez," sighed Milton, raising his eyes. "British anarchists? Why do I do these things for you?"

"Because I saved your life," replied Will, smugly.

"Asshole," answered Milton. "Anyway, what's this damn place called? I got to keep an eye out for road signs."

"It's called Kropotkin," answered Will. "It's named after a writer."

"Sounds like a damn Communist to me," said Milton. "Russian, was he?"

"Yes," answered Will. "But he lived in England for a while."

"This isn't an ambush, now, is it?"

"No," Will assured him. "We're defending our hemisphere against foreign capital."

"Daah, blow it out your ass," said Milton.

Milton pulled into Kropotkin shortly after eight o'clock that evening, and immediately got lost in the deliberately complicated and chaotic pattern of streets with their whimsical and unpredictable names. He knew they were making for the community hall, but was at a loss to know how to find it.

"How the hell are you supposed to find your way around this place?" he demanded, as he realised that they had returned to the same road on which they had entered the settlement. "There's no rhyme or reason to it."

"It reminds me of England," said Kerry.

"Well, it's pissing me off," said Milton. "Thank Goodness we had a War of Independence!"

"How about we follow those hand-written signs pointing to the community hall?" suggested Will.

"Where?" demanded Milton, crossly.

Will pointed with his lips.

"I can't see where you're pointing when you do that!" said Milton, with great irritation. "Can't you use your damn finger?"

"There!" said Will, pointing with his whole arm to a small sign on the opposite side of the street. "And there!" he indicated, pointing to another, a little distance down the street.

Milton wrenched the steering wheel round and spun the truck's tyres as he changed direction back towards the centre of the village.

"Well, how the hell are you supposed to see little bitty signs like that?" he said. "Especially when you're dog tired from driving all day."

"Thanks for driving us here, Milton," said Kerry.

"You're welcome," said Milton. "Sorry I'm a little on edge. Just a bit pooped out, that's all."

"You're very kind to help us like this," said Kerry.

"He owes me it," said Will. "I saved his life."

"I'll damn well *take* yours if you carry on like that," said Milton.

They found the community hall, got out of the truck and went in. A tall, broad-shouldered man in faded jeans, walking boots, a checked shirt and red braces was standing just inside the door. He welcomed them with a smile.

"Hello, there," he said. "I'm Eric Smith and I'm co-ordinating things here on behalf of our community." He took the new arrivals' details and checked them against his list. "You guys came a long way today, eh?" he observed.

"Too damn right," agreed Milton.

"Oh, it looks like I don't have you all down here in my list," said Eric, rather apologetically. "I have Will and Kerry but I don't have you, Milton."

"That's because he didn't know he was coming," said Will. "My truck broke down so we needed a ride."

"But you'll vouch for him, eh?" inquired Eric.

"For sure," agreed Will. "We've known each other for years."

"Okay, then," said Eric, and amended his list. "Now, I'm afraid the guest house is full up and we've already got people staying with all the families who have offered accommodation. We've had more people turn up than we were expecting. There may be a spare room or two at the guest house over at Nottard, a few kilometres north of here, but I guess you've had enough travelling for today, eh? So, I'll see if I can find anything else for you here first, eh? We're

332

not expecting anyone else to arrive now. If you'll excuse me, I'm going to go and speak to a few folks to see if any more beds are available anywhere. If you can wait here, I'll be back as soon as I can. Did you guys eat yet?"

"Yeah, we ate," confirmed Will.

"Well, there's plenty of coffee over in the corner, there," said Eric, "so help yourselves. I'll be right back."

Eric left the hall, and the three travellers sat down wearily on some of the folding chairs set out around the edges of the hall. After a few light-hearted remarks, they sat in exhausted silence.

Suddenly the hall door flew open and a generously built Native woman burst in. She was a little over five feet tall, with a broad, open face and large, dark eyes, and she wore a tie-dyed caftan in shades of blue and turquoise. Her thick black hair fell to her waist. She looked as though she was in her forties.

"Jeez, that guy pisses me off!" she exclaimed.

The intended beneficiaries of her observation followed her immediately into the hall; a white man with lengthy, thinning grey hair, a florescent grey moustache and a stomach that suggested he had reached his late forties, clad in a similar manner to Eric Smith; and a tall, willowy white woman with long, fair hair, wearing a floaty, tie-dyed green silk skirt and a blue and green t-shirt bearing a picture of the planet Earth and, printed around the picture, the words 'Mother Earth Healing Association'.

"What an asshole!" added the Native woman, seating herself on one of the chairs near the door. It was only then that she noticed the other occupants of the community hall. She stood up again.

"Oh, Jeez, I'm sorry!" she said. "I didn't see you guys over there! That wasn't a very nice introduction, was it? I apologise."

"Don't you worry about it," said Will, standing to greet her. "I'm Will Many Paint Horses from the Whispering River

Reservation in Yellowstone State, and these are my good friends Kerry Ahern and Milt Eastwood."

"And I'm Elaine Macdonald from Mother Earth Healing Association in Strathcona, and these are my good friends Larry Randall and Crystal Macintyre."

They all greeted one another with smiles and handshakes.

"I've seen your name in AEC reports, Elaine," said Will.

"And I've seen yours, too, Will," said Elaine. "You've been putting up quite a fight down there."

"We did our best," said Will.

They all drew chairs up and sat down together.

"Who's pissed you off?" asked Will.

"Oh, sorry about that," said Elaine. "Some guy who's been visiting here today. I didn't catch his name. Some Brit. He's an academic or a journalist or something. Jeez, the guy's arrogant! He came by here on a kind of anti-religious pilgrimage, to pay tribute to the community of Kropotkin, because it was founded on atheism and is still keeping the faith after more than a century. He said he was here to learn, but I don't know what he expected to learn when he wouldn't listen. Nobody was expecting him, and everyone was pretty busy getting ready for the gathering, but he still expected everyone to sit and talk to him about what their atheism means to them, and you could see people thinking, who the hell is this guy?

"The way he seemed to want to push his views down everyone else's throat is so totally alien to the whole spirit of this place! I mean, I've been here quite a few times now, and the people here know about my Native spirituality and they've always shown respect for it. And I respect their views and the fact they're uncomfortable with ceremonies and with talk about the Grandfathers and Grandmothers or about Creator, so we avoid talking about the stuff that the others are uncomfortable with and get on with whatever it is we're getting together to do, which, right now, is trying to stop the destruction of Athabasca for tar sands and uranium mining.

"This guy didn't seem at all interested in any of that, just wanted to talk about the evils of religion. I told him, look,

Native people are more aware than anyone of what religious bigotry can do, what with having Catholicism rammed down our throats for years in disrespect for our own traditions, but that doesn't mean all religion's false. I mean, I'm a recovering Catholic myself, but even I wouldn't say all Catholics are wrong, because some of our greatest allies are Catholics. And they act out of their understanding of their faith and I respect that even if I don't share that same understanding. Larry here's an atheist, but he respects my views, don't you Larry?"

"I guess," said Larry. "Most of the time." He smiled to himself.

"I told this guy, look, I'm not an atheist. That's a European concept. I'm a Native person, I'm Cree, and we look at things a different way, and our understanding of Creator and the spirit world is right at the heart of that, and then he goes off on one about how he has great respect for our people, after what we've suffered from the Church, but what's needed now is a great atheist missionary movement to bring modern knowledge to all the Indigenous Peoples of the world, who are still under the illusion that they need to believe in a Creator to explain the existence of the universe. And I said, Jeez, after the Catholic missionaries, and the Anglican missionaries, and then the Pentecostal missionaries, and now even the Bahai missionaries, the last thing Native people need is another set of missionaries!

"The guy's so damn white! I mean, excuse me, my dear white friends, but this is what white people have been doing to us from the beginning. White people think they've got all the knowledge and they have to come and dump it on us ignorant savages. At least the Catholics have learnt a bit of humility at last, at least, the ones I know have. I'm not so sure about the Pope. But this guy, whatever his name is – Jeez!"

"Is he still around?" asked Will.

"No, he just left," replied Elaine.

"Just as well," said Milton. "I'd have rammed his head up his ass and made him walk around like a pretzel."

Elaine laughed. "Tempting as that may be, this whole gathering and this whole community are committed to non-violence," she said, "so ramming people's heads up their asses is a no-no."

"I'd have done it lovingly," said Milton.

"Interestingly, it wasn't clear to me what the guy thinks about violence or war," said Elaine. "He was talking about religious violence and religious wars, but he didn't say anything about wars for oil or wars for minerals or anything. He talked about crusades and Islamist violence and wars over religious differences, but he didn't say anything about wars where everyone involved is the same religion or wars between officially atheist states or wars where people see themselves as fighting for their dignity against people who disrespect them. Or he may have done, but I didn't hear him. Maybe he's written about all that, being an academic or a journalist or whatever."

"What did you think of him, Larry?" asked Kerry.

"Oh," said Larry, reflectively, "yeah, I thought he was a bit of an asshole."

"Well, that's enough of that, now," said Elaine. "We actually came in here looking for Eric. Is he around?"

"He went out looking for a place for us to stay tonight," said Kerry.

"You guys don't have accommodation?" asked Elaine.

"Not yet," said Will.

"It's a shame there's not room in our camper," said Crystal.

"Well, we could maybe make room for one of them, if there's nowhere else for them to go," said Elaine. "Larry, you wouldn't mind giving up your bed for Kerry and sleeping in here in the hall, would you?"

Larry looked a little surprised. "Oh, no, sure, that would be fine," he said. "My sleeping bag's pretty warm."

Eric returned, greeted Elaine and turned to the new arrivals.

"I'm sorry about this, guys," he said, "but I can't find anywhere where you could easily go tonight. Would you mind sleeping on the floor here in the hall? It's pretty warm, there's a bathroom, there's food and drink and I can get you some foam mattresses to put your sleeping bags on, eh?"

"Sounds good to me," said Will.

"Yeah, I could sleep on my feet right now," said Milton.

"Well, no-one's going to need to come in here till about nine in the morning," said Eric, "and I can bring you some cooked breakfast in here about eight, if that's okay."

"The invitation to Kerry's still open, if you want a bit more comfort," said Elaine.

Kerry looked at Will. She wanted to be with him, but did not want to appear ungracious.

"You go," said Will. "You'll be more comfortable there, and you can get to know Elaine and Crystal."

"Are you sure this is okay, Larry?" asked Kerry.

"Oh, sure," said Larry.

So Larry fetched his gear from Elaine's camper, while Elaine spoke about some organisational issue with Eric, and then Kerry went to stay with Crystal and Elaine.

This did not, however, mean that Kerry got any more rest than she would have got at the community hall. She sat up with Elaine and Crystal well into the night, talking. Elaine had a way of eliciting information about people without in any sense appearing to pry into their affairs. So before too long, and after only one cup of cocoa, Kerry had explained her recent history to her new friends.

"So you had a sex change because you fell in love with a lesbian, but you didn't think to check with her beforehand?" asked Elaine.

"Yes," said Kerry, rather sheepishly.

"And you had no idea what kind of woman she might find attractive?"

"No."

Elaine began to laugh. "Don't you think that was a bit unwise?"

"Yes, I suppose it was."

Elaine was now shaking with laughter and had to dab her eyes with her handkerchief as the tears of mirth began to flow.

"Elaine!" said Crystal, reproachfully. "Don't laugh at Kerry! It's not very nice, is it?"

"Oh, I'm sorry, Kerry," said Elaine, still smiling broadly. "I don't mean to laugh at you – but it *is* rather funny, don't you think?" She started giggling again.

"I suppose it could be seen that way," said Kerry. "I can't say it had struck me that way before now. It's been a little difficult to cope with it, to be honest – though Will's Grandpa Jimmy helped a lot, and so did Vera."

Elaine continued giggling and wiping tears from her eyes. Crystal looked embarrassed. "Well, how's it strike you now?" inquired Elaine, and Kerry pondered the matter for a moment, and she too began to laugh.

"I suppose there is a funny side to it," she said.

"It's better to laugh than cry," declared Elaine.

"Well, you're doing both!" said Crystal. This made Elaine laugh all the more. It was Elaine's laughter, more than any reappraisal of her ill-considered life-choice, that set Kerry laughing, and then Crystal joined in too, until they could not speak for a while, because when any of them began to say anything at all, however far removed from the matter that had started the amusement, they all fell into helpless giggling, so they gave up the attempt to speak until the mood should pass.

It did pass after a while, and Crystal brewed up more cocoa.

"Anyway," said Elaine, when she was able to control herself again, "you found yourself a real good man, didn't you?"

"I did," said Kerry.

"So you don't regret your choice?"

"Not now, no. For a long while I couldn't think of myself as a woman and I felt ill at ease in my new body, but with Jimmy's prayers and Vera's teaching and especially with Will's love, I do feel I have become a woman, and I'm happier than I've ever been before."

"Has anyone rejected you because of your history?" asked Crystal.

"Only one so far," replied Kerry. "My good friends love me anyway, whatever I do. My family are all dead. People that I meet for the first time don't seem to suspect I was ever male – I suppose because I was fairly delicately built for a man. I suppose there must be plenty of people who would be pretty anti, if they only knew what I used to be. I wouldn't know how to deal with violent prejudice. I hope I'll be mentally strong enough to cope with it if I ever have to. So far, the worst I've had was a lecture from a young nun, a friend of Hannah's, who seemed to base her rejection of my feminine identity on a particular form of feminism rather than on her Catholic or Christian faith."

"You mean, you haven't been kicked out of the Church for having surgery?" Crystal asked.

"Well, maybe I'm technically excommunicated," said Kerry. "I know the official Church strongly disapproves of what I've done. But, I confess, I never looked at the official teaching in detail because by the time I remembered that the Church had a view on it, I had already made up my mind I was going to do it. My actual experience of the Catholic clergy that I know, those who know what I've done, is that they accept me. They don't necessarily think it was the right thing to do, but they don't seem to condemn me for it. Maybe, if they think it was a sin, they think the most appropriate penance is to live well as a woman. That's the penance I'd give me, if I'd become a priest."

"Are you still Catholic?" asked Elaine.

"Well, *I* think I am," replied Kerry. "I don't know if the Pope would agree with me, but that's the part of the Christian tradition that I grew up in and that I identify with, and the more Catholics I meet, the more I think there's a great deal of goodness and beauty in the Catholic Church, despite all the bad things that are there as well. And I'm definitely Christian. God the Father, Jesus Christ, the Holy Spirit – they're so real to me. I couldn't *not* be a Christian. For all the sins of Christianity, life wouldn't make any sense to me without it."

"Well, you'd better stick with it, then," said Elaine. "You've clearly had a different experience of it than I did. I mean, I'm happy to work with Catholics, Christians in general, anyone in fact, if they have a good attitude, but I was really disgusted with the way the Church shoved its beliefs down our throats through the school system. It's well and good to have beliefs, but not to show disrespect for other people's, like the Church did to ours."

"Yes, I have a pretty hard time with Christianity myself," said Crystal. "I was raised United Church of Canada, which is one of the more liberal and humane Churches in this country, but I really couldn't hack all those traditions about sin and hell and an angry God."

"I never came across an angry God," said Kerry. "I mean, I've met people who believe in one, but God always seemed to me to be such overwhelming love, I couldn't relate to the belief some people seem to have in a God who is like a vengeful little policeman in the sky."

"Well," said Elaine, reverting to an earlier thread of conversation, "I can certainly imagine some of my white feminist friends taking a negative view of gender reassignment, like that nun you met. But not all of them would. Anyway, we're holding a talking circle tomorrow night, and it's open to both men and women, so feel free to come to that if you're interested and if you feel either that you could learn something or contribute something."

"What's a talking circle?" asked Kerry.

"It's where we all sit in a circle and pass round a talking stick, and only the person with the stick can speak, and nobody's allowed to interrupt, and when they've finished, they pass the stick on to the next person and that person can talk uninterrupted, and so on. So often, people carry wounds inside them when all they need to do is speak about them and know that people are listening with respect and sympathy, and they work out their own solutions to their problems as they speak."

"Talking stick…?"

"Yes, it's a stick decorated with little symbols of Mother Earth – a little rock, a bird's feather, a bit of moose hide or buffalo fur, some sage, a piece of wood – things that symbolise the winged creatures, the four-legged creatures, the trees, the grasses, the Earth herself, because they all have something to teach us."

"That sounds beautiful."

"One of the great things about Native culture and spirituality," said Crystal, "is that it's so holistic. Our white tradition cuts things up into little bits and analyses them apart from each other. Native tradition sees things as a whole."

"Well, there's a place for both approaches," said Elaine. "But I find that, even among our white allies, there's a tendency to pull things apart and not see the relationships between things. You get someone who works only on pesticides, say, or only on oil, or only on mining, and sometimes they get so focused on what they're doing that they can't even see the value of what other people are doing, or they forget that human beings also need laughter, and music, and dancing, or they know absolutely everything about some subject but they can't share their knowledge easily with people because they've forgotten how to relate to anyone who isn't interested in the same stuff they're interested in, or they want to save the environment but they don't care about human beings, or they care about human rights but they don't see the point of working on climate change or stopping deforestation, all because they've forgotten that the connections between things are just as important as the things themselves.

"In Mother Earth Healing Association, we try to take this approach where we work on healing ourselves as well as the Earth, human society as well as the ecosystems that humans rely on. So we do our youth work, our publications on the environment, our talking circles, our legal work, our protests and blockades, our sweatlodge ceremonies and our campaigning. It all goes together."

"That's an awful lot of work," said Kerry.

"It is," agreed Elaine, "and we do rely on very white friends like dear Larry, who can focus totally on some historical or technical matter to the exclusion of virtually anything else, and then we weave what he finds out into the greater whole. We need people like that, the researchers as well as the connectors, but in the end we do have to keep in mind the relationships between things. Larry gets so interested in things he kind of disappears into them, then he can go on about them for hours if you let him, and it would bore the pants off any normal human being, so you just have to shut him up sometimes. Poor old Larry. We give him a hard time.

"Now," she went on, "here's one of the most ridiculous things about this white capacity to cut things up and define things and pigeon-hole them: that's the way the Canadian Government defined us Native people. First of all, they defined 'Indian' people differently from 'Metis' people – that's people of mixed Indian and white ancestry who had formed their own distinct group with its own culture. In actual fact, the boundaries between Indian and Metis society were much less definite than the Government made out, but they made a clear difference between the two, then gave different rights to each. Then, if you were a Native woman who married a white man, you lost your Native status. On the other hand, if you were a white woman who married a Native man, you gained Native status. Under treaties signed between the Government and Indian Bands, we were all entitled to free education up to and including university. But if we took up a university education, we lost our Native status. Native men also lost it if they joined the armed forces, which many Native men did during the World Wars.

"They didn't ask us about all this, about how we understood ourselves. They just imposed their own definitions on us and gave or removed various legal rights as a result.

"Then there was a big campaign among Native people for those who had lost Native status one way or another to get it back again, them and their children. Now, take our family. We've got some white ancestry, that's how come we're Macdonalds. But we never really functioned as part of Metis society, because we were Crees, we spoke Cree, we lived as Crees with other Crees. But the Government decides we're Metis. Then my dad joins the army in the Second World War and loses his Native status. Then, after all the campaigning, the Government passes Bill C-31, which allows us to reclaim

342

our Native status. So we all claim the Indian status that the Government never gave us, but instead, the Government gives us Metis status, and we appeal. At one stage, my mom and dad were classed as Metis, two of my brothers were Indians, one brother was white and me and my sister were white. Then we all got Indian status. Then the Government withdrew the Indian status, but only from the brothers who had been recognised as Indians first. Can you believe it? They're telling us who we are, and then changing it according to their bureaucratic whims!"

"What are you now?" asked Kerry.

"We are, and always were, Crees," said Elaine, "but now, the Government actually recognises it at last!"

Elaine sighed. "Jeez, I feel tired now," she said. "I think I'm going to go to bed. I'm just going to nip over to the toilet block by the laundromat. See you guys in a minute."

When Elaine had gone out, Crystal said, "That woman truly is a hero. She had such a hard time when she was younger! When her marriage broke up, she had three kids to look after and nowhere to live. So she went down to the city housing office and camped out there till they agreed to house her. She wouldn't shift even when they threatened her with the police. Then, when she and her kids had got housing, she organised all the other Native women in the city, so they'd get what they were legally entitled to get but were being denied because of racism and tight-fistedness. The city council really hated her. But they ended up respecting her, because she just would never take no for an answer.

"Now she's helping organise a whole bunch of Native communities against expansion of tar sands, logging and mining throughout Athabasca. She just never stops, never gives in. She's one of the founders of the Aboriginal Ecological Coalition too. And after all that she's had to put up with from white folks and from men, there's no bitterness in her. She can be pretty scathing, but she's never mean. The woman's all heart.

"On top of that, she realised that, growing up in the city, she'd missed out on a lot of her Native culture, and that was partly because her parents' generation were so keen to make sure their kids could function in the white world that they often didn't teach them the language or a bunch of other stuff. So she went looking for all that, too – travelling up into the North to learn from the elders in her parents' home area and elsewhere, and now she's teaching Native culture and spirituality in the Catholic school system – despite her pretty negative view of the Church. She never ceases to amaze me, that woman. She's one in a hundred million."

The camper door opened and Elaine climbed back in. "Jeez, that bathroom's pretty gross. I guess it's unisex. Why do men have to pee on the floor, for goodness' sake? It stinks in there."

Kerry assumed that the question was rhetorical and did not require an answer based on her own life experience. In any case, she was not sure that she could have answered. If she remembered correctly, there was no intentionality in it. It just happened, for lack of sufficiently accurate urinary targeting. She hadn't really noticed the smell before. Of course, now she had been made aware of it, she would. Knowledge could be a burdensome thing.

Two: Kerry makes a new friend and encounters an old one

About fifty people gathered in the community hall on the Saturday morning to prepare for the action at the Deep Lake blockade. Milton decided to stay on for the morning, to learn more about what was going on.

There were a dozen or so Native activists from all over the US West and Midwest, all members of the Aboriginal Ecological Coalition. The others were non-Native supporters, of varied ethnicity, from a variety of groups. Elaine invited each group to stand up and say who they were and where they were from. There were people from direct action environmental groups, solidarity groups campaigning for Indigenous rights, various church groups, and even four from the Vancouver Gender-queer Eco-activists' Collective – a group whose members' appearance made Kerry feel rather staid but whose acquaintance she was eager to make because of her own personal history.

Elaine then asked everyone to choose someone they had never met before and spend ten minutes with them, introducing themselves, explaining what brought them there and hearing what the other person had to say. She pointed out that there was a great variety of people in the room and asked that everyone keep some ground rules of respect for others there, since they were all involved in a common work and needed to focus on what united them rather than on anything that might divide them.

Kerry took the opportunity to approach one of the Vancouver group, a tall, strikingly beautiful woman with Chinese features and straight, waist-length black hair, who wore a figure-hugging ankle-length lavender dress, slit to the thigh at the sides. Engaging her in conversation, Kerry discovered that Zoe was not entirely as she seemed, having been born male and having breast implants upon reaching adulthood, but not the surgery that Kerry had undergone in Brazil. She had moved to Canada from Hong Kong to find work, but found that such was the prejudice against people like her, that to make a living, she had had to join an escort agency, through which she had at length met her husband, Leif, for whom she had left the agency and devoted herself full time to environmental work, which was his vocation. Together they had founded the Gender-queer eco-activists' collective.

Kerry was amazed at Zoe's fearless openness, her matter-of-fact description of circumstances which Kerry found considerably more disturbing than her own recent experience. She felt her heart burning within her as Zoe spoke. She felt a bond with this woman, who was not quite as other women were, a desire for friendship with another human being who would understand something of her own being from the inside.

Kerry summarised her own history for Zoe, and the bond was complete. Zoe embraced her warmly, kissing her cheek and calling her 'my sister'. Ten minutes was not enough: Kerry wanted to spend much more time with this woman, to build a friendship with her. And she wanted to know more about Zoe's husband, Leif, a plain but very manly man, to whom Zoe clearly felt an immense devotion, and about their companions, Hank and Marlon, who were both evidently cross-dressers.

Kerry wondered what her erstwhile companions at the seminary might think of such a gathering. She was aware, for instance, that the Catholic tradition strongly censured the practice of transvestism. Though how the Vatican could maintain such a position, while its male officials swathed themselves in vestments which to most westerners might appear the apotheosis of femininity, was a mystery to her. Perhaps it was the case that, as Father Duddleswell asserts in Peter De Rosa's *Bless Me Father*, 'one of the great things about the Catholic religion is that everything's forbidden until it's compulsory.'

She also wondered at the power of a cause that could draw together such a cross-section of humanity as was present in that room: people who might otherwise never have encountered one another or, if they had, might have been both suspicious of and unsympathetic to each other.

The ten minutes set aside for these introductions stretched to fifteen, but Elaine called the gathering to order again and asked for two minutes of complete silence so that people could gather their thoughts and, if they were so inclined, pray silently in whatever way was meaningful to them. Elaine explained that, out of respect for the tradition of Kropotkin, she would not perform the Native ceremony with which she would usually open such a gathering. Once the supporters had reached the blockade, she explained, they would notice that everything there was rooted in prayer, and that there were frequent ceremonies of one sort or another, and she asked that people respect that, even if they could not personally relate to it.

When the period of silence was completed, Elaine explained that Native Peoples throughout the Canadian North had treaty rights, which meant they retained an interest in lands they had agreed to share with the Canadian Government back in the late 1800s and early 1900s. The Government carried on as if Native Peoples had given up all their lands apart from the tiny pockets they were allowed to keep, the Indian Reserves. But Native Peoples had been told by the Government's treaty negotiators that they would still be able to hunt and trap and fish on the lands they had agreed to share. Now the Government was allowing the oil industry to destroy treaty lands irreversibly, so that Native communities could no longer rely on the land for sustenance. There was virtually no other way of living in the isolated Native communities in the northern forests, unless you got work in the very industries that were destroying them – oil, mining and logging – and the best paid jobs in these industries relied on a level of education that few Native people had. So what remained for most Native people, when their ability to live from the land was taken away, was debilitating poverty, based on a welfare system that sapped the spirit and provided no hope of a better future.

Native communities had not been given an opportunity to learn about the impacts of the proposed tar sands extraction. The Government had sold licences to dozens of oil companies to extract the sands, and then company officials had turned up in Native communities to tell them what they were going to do, and they had called this process 'consultation', when it was nothing of the kind. So some Native communities had understandably decided there was nothing they could do to stop the tar sands development, and tried to get the best financial deal that they could out of the companies, through roads, school buildings, sports centres, jobs. But their people were getting sick, along with residents in the communities that refused to co-operate with the industry.

Elaine said that the United Nations had issued a Declaration on the Rights of Indigenous Peoples that recognised the right of all Indigenous Peoples to free, prior and informed consent, before any project could go ahead on their land. But Canada, along with the United States, had first of all refused to sign it and then signed it, but with so many reservations that it might just as well not have bothered. Canada, with its global reputation for respecting human rights, was systematically violating its own Indigenous Peoples' rights in favour of extractives industries, which were making those Indigenous people sick, causing huge ecological destruction and hastening climate change.

As for the Athabasca Provincial Government, based in her home city of Strathcona, there was virtually no distinction between the Government and the oil and logging industries. The Government administered the Province on behalf of industry and kept the overwhelmingly urban population happy with bread and circuses, while the land over their urban horizons was torn to pieces and the minority Native communities devastated, because most non-Native people couldn't care a red cent about Native people in Canada.

Elaine had to stop for a while and sit down as her tears overwhelmed her. Her audience of activists applauded her warmly while she sat. She recovered herself, and stood up again.

"I guess that's probably enough on that for now," she said. "Now, before our mid-morning break, we're going to hear from Larry about tar sands extraction and the plan to mine uranium and use nuclear power to provide energy for it."

Larry explained at some length the environmental and health impacts of tar sands extraction and the uranium cycle. When he finished, and they broke for coffee, Kerry's head was reeling with all the information presented. She felt sick. It was not simply the quantity of information: it was the utter horror of it. She needed fresh air. While Will greeted his many acquaintances in the community hall, and her new friend Zoe spoke with her companions, Kerry went outside into the sunshine. Others wandered around outside, looking punch-drunk.

The ten minute mid-morning break stretched to half an hour. Kerry went back inside, got herself a coffee and a doughnut and returned outside. Milton joined her, coffee in hand. "Kind of depressing, ain't it?" he commented.

"It's awful," agreed Kerry. "I don't understand how people can think they're doing the right thing when they're causing so much destruction."

"Some people are so cut off from the planet, they don't even see it as destruction," said Milton. "They see it as creating prosperity. They genuinely think they're doing us all a favour."

Crystal leaned out of the door of the meeting hall and asked people please to come back in so they could get on with the second part of the agenda. People drained their coffees, finished their cigarettes, and filed back indoors.

The second half of the morning was more inspiring. Elaine explained what the people of Deep Lake were doing to prevent the destruction of their area; the environmental hearings, the court proceedings, and finally, the blockade. The blockade had continued throughout the winter, despite temperatures sinking to minus thirty for several weeks in a row. The Royal Canadian Mounted Police had eventually been sent in to end the blockade, but the AEC had obtained an injunction, preventing them from using force to end it before a decision had been made on the treaty rights issue, and the police had withdrawn. But both levels of Government had now appealed against the injunction, and it was likely that they would win the appeal. That was why the call had gone out to activists all over North America to join the Defenders and protect the blockade. The aim was to make it both physically and judicially difficult for the authorities to proceed. They would have to remove so many people blocking existing logging roads or locked on to trees, and so many structures built among the trees, and would have to make so many arrests, and all the while have to counter the bad publicity that their efforts would gain them. The protestors would not counter police violence with violence, and the moral imbalance would become ever clearer.

When Elaine finished speaking, Milton, genuinely perplexed, asked her, "Why the non-violence? I've fought for my country. I don't see why people shouldn't fight if they're attacked or if they're defending what's dear to them."

"Well," replied Elaine, "there are several reasons. One is purely practical. These are a few Native people and their allies up against the armed power of one of the richest countries in the world. There are US and British economic interests involved as well. In any armed confrontation, the other side would win – no question about it. Linked to that, suppose us Crees decided to take to guerrilla warfare in the woods. How long would that last? What would happen to our communities? They'd be wiped out. We're not in central Asia here, far away from our opponents' homeland. We right here in the middle of it. It wouldn't take them long to get rid of us.

"But there's a moral point involved as well. The Elders up there at Deep Lake are influenced by our own traditions about respect for human life and by the version of Catholic Christianity that they've been taught, which, for all its faults, speaks about the value of human life and the seriousness of taking it. We're fighting for the life of Mother Earth and of our People, and we want to fight in a way that respects everyone's life. The Elders are clear that they want their fight to be non-violent. I can't stress that enough. If people here don't feel able to work within the limits set down by the Elders, I respect your views, but I ask you not to come up to Deep Lake with us, because we want to make sure we win without ceding the moral high ground. We have to be willing to get injured without inflicting injury. Please, if you think you can't accept non-violence, you'd help us more by going home."

There was some further discussion of non-violence, and it became clear that some people were realising that, whatever their intentions, they might be unable to accept injury without at least attempting to inflict it. Elaine reminded them that the whole afternoon, and all the next day, would be spent in non-violence training, and urged people not to withdraw before they had had the opportunity to undertake the training.

Milton seemed deep in thought. Kerry herself felt a combination of fear and exhilaration. She had at least experienced not only violent confrontation, as Milton had on so many occasions, but the self-discipline of a non-violent community response. She had stood with the people of San Martin de Porres in the dignity of their non-violent resistance to eviction. She knew she had it within her to face whatever they may have to face at Deep Lake. But the people of San Martin had been defeated. She did not relish the prospect of a second such defeat. Nor did she look forward to the police violence that may precede it.

Her mind wandered far from the community hall in Kropotkin to the debates she had witnessed at the seminary years before, between her dear friend Peter, the would-be revolutionary, and that other friend, Francis Neale, so saintly, so committed to the ideal of non-violence. Peter's opinions had inspired her to commitment to the cause of justice, while

Francis' purity of life and thought had made her feel uncomfortable. He seemed to have attained a level of goodness which left her feeling morally flaccid, but at the same time, he seemed to Kerry to lack the clarity of thought which made Peter able to analyse and understand the precise nature of the injustices which necessitated the practice of charity in the first place. She wondered what Francis would have made of the struggle of the Crees of Deep Lake; would he understand their political struggle and participate in it because of their principled non-violence, or would he avoid engaging with it and limit himself to that interpersonal charity of which he was so outstanding an example?

It was as Kerry wondered about these things, that the door to the community hall opened and a tall, thin, grey-haired, elderly Native man entered the room, accompanied by a man dressed in black and wearing a clerical collar. It was Francis Neale.

"Ivan!" Elaine called out joyfully, interrupting her answer to one of the many questions. She greeted the Native elder with a warm embrace and then shook Francis' hand. "Well," she said, "I'd like you all to greet Ivan Silver, one of the Elders from Deep Lake, and Father Francis Neale, who's the Catholic priest in that community and who's been a good friend to the people in their struggle."

Kerry felt herself blushing at the thought of introducing her new self to her estranged friend. She felt more nervous about that, than about the possibility of being beaten up by the RCMP. She decided that the best way of dealing with this feeling of unease was to introduce herself to Francis without delay.

Elaine suggested that they break for lunch, so Ivan and Father Francis could refresh themselves before the afternoon workshop began. Kerry made straight for Francis, who was conversing with Elaine. Elaine immediately included her in the conversation. "Ah, Father, here's a woman from your own country, my friend Kerry." A look of surprise and confusion crossed Francis' face. Kerry decided to curtail it.

"We know each other," said Kerry. "We studied at the seminary together. When I was still a man."

"Oh, Jeez!" exclaimed Elaine. She laughed. "Then you've got some catching up to do! I'll leave you guys to it." She moved away to join Ivan in conversation with Will.

Francis looked utterly amazed. "Kerry?" he questioned.

"Yes," said Kerry. "The same person, but I had gender reassignment surgery, as you can see."

"Goodness!" said Francis. "Do you mind if I sit down? I feel a bit…shocked, I suppose."

"That's okay," said Kerry. "I'm sorry I didn't stay in touch with you. Then you'd have known."

"Well, I didn't stay in touch with you, either," noted Francis.

Kerry looked at Francis. Francis was looking at the floor.

"I'm sorry if I've made you feel uncomfortable," said Kerry.

Francis looked up. "No need to apologise, Kerry. But it's strange to see someone you knew as a bloke turning up as a woman." He was quiet for a while, and Kerry said nothing. Then he asked, "What made you do it?"

"Do you disapprove?" asked Kerry.

"I don't know, is the honest truth," replied Francis. "I mean, the Church teaches you shouldn't change sex, or rather, that you can't, even if you have the surgery, which means, I suppose, that according to the Vatican, you're still a bloke." He laughed nervously. "But you make a pretty convincing woman."

"Thanks."

They were both silent again, enclosed by a wall of human noise.

"Do you really want to know why I did it?" asked Kerry.

"Only if you want to tell me," replied Francis. "It's none of my business, is it?"

"If we're all related, as my Native friends keep insisting, then everything is everybody's business," said Kerry.

Francis laughed. "That could get a little uncomfortable, couldn't it?"

Kerry sat down next to Francis. "I do want to tell you," she said, "but you're tired from your journey, aren't you? Don't you want to eat?"

"You tell me whatever you want to tell me, then we'll eat," replied Francis. So Kerry told him, and Francis listened. Kerry summarised, so it only took a few minutes.

"Oh," said Francis. "I see."

"Do you still disapprove?"

"Well, it's not up to me to approve or disapprove, is it?" said Francis. "It's probably not the most common reason for blokes changing sex, is it? I suppose most people who change sex do it because they have a deep feeling inside them that they're in the wrong body."

"I think so, yes," said Kerry.

"Well, you've done what you've done for a reason, and it sounds like the reason you're happy now is different from the reason you had when you made the change, and since I've never been in the same situations you've been in, I can't judge, can I? So, give me a bit of time to get used to it, and then, whatever my views on the subject end up being – and I can't say I've thought about this much before now – you'll be my female friend, Kerry."

"I don't want to make you feel uneasy, given that what I've done is against Church teaching."

"So is judging other people. Any pastor worth his salt has to acknowledge that sometimes people get into situations where they can't keep the Church's rules, and help them make the best of that."

"What do you think Jesus would do?"

"That's the only question that really matters! He'd put compassion and human well-being above every other consideration."

"Shall we have some lunch?"

"Good idea. I'm starving."

"Then will you tell me what on earth you're doing in Kropotkin?"

Francis laughed again, much more easily this time.

"Yes, of course! And when I've told you, will you introduce me to your fiancé?"

So, as they ate their lunch, Francis explained how, after two years as assistant priest at Stonegate on Sea, he had read an appeal from the Apostolate of the North, an organisation established by the Missionary Society of St Jean-Marie Vianney to enable diocesan clergy from other parts of the world to commit to a few years of pastoral work with Native people in Northern Canada. He realised that he either had to do this or leave the priesthood. If he stayed where he was, he would go mad. His parish priest refused to leave the mental confines of the 1950s, attempting to run the parish as though the Second Vatican Council had never happened. That very day he went to see the bishop and told him he wanted to take a few years out to join the Apostolate of the North, and when the bishop began his standard reply, that this was not the kind of thing that we do in this diocese, Francis told him it was either that or leave the priesthood. Only that morning, the bishop had been forced to accept the loss of two young priests, one of whom had run off with his housekeeper, a woman who did not fulfil the 1910 Code of Canon Law's requirement that priests' housekeepers should be 'over forty, and of hideous countenance', and he did not wish to lose a third. He gave Francis his permission, and Francis applied and was accepted by the Apostolate.

Arriving in Deep Lake had been a bit of a shock. He could speak no Cree, he was experiencing an utterly different culture and environment, and he was the only priest for hundreds of square miles around, responsible for pastoral care for eight widely scattered Cree communities centred on Deep Lake itself. He had never been so happy in his life.

There was a great deal of poverty in Deep Lake, but most families survived by hunting. There were still plenty of moose in the surrounding forests. There were plenty of wild berries as well. But the whole ecosystem was threatened by the planned uranium mining. People in Deep Lake were worried about it. Francis could not be an effective pastor, if he did not take into account this mortal threat to his parishioners' way of life; nor would be have felt at ease if he had allowed such destruction of God's creation to go ahead without challenging it. So, he had become involved with the Elders in their campaign to stop the mine, and had spent a lot of time with them at the blockade.

Francis was particularly inspired by Ivan Silver. Ivan was in his seventies, but remained fit and strong after a life spent hunting and trapping in all weathers. Ivan was a pipe carrier, conducting sacred pipe ceremonies according to his people's traditions and passing on to others the spiritual teachings of his ancestors. He was also a devout Catholic. He never missed Mass and he constantly read the Gospels, which he frequently discussed with Francis. He was unyielding in his resolve to stop the mine and he had managed to maintain absolute unity in the community through the strength of his own self-disciplined commitment. He and Francis had been travelling around to preparatory gatherings for the blockade expansion. That morning, they had driven all the way from Dunkeld, and on Thursday, they had been in Strathcona.

Will found them and introduced himself to Francis. Kerry was glad to see that they immediately hit it off with one another. Things were not as awkward as she had feared they might be. She knew it would be disconcerting to Francis to discover that she had become a woman, and even more so, to meet the man she loved. But it looked as though Francis did not need Will's course in planning for spontaneity.

Kerry suddenly remembered that Milton was to leave at lunchtime. She looked around, but could not see him. "Has Milt left?" she asked Will. "I didn't say bye-bye."

"No," replied Will. "Now he says he'll stay the rest of the day. He's squared it with his wife and daughters. He won't come up to Deep Lake with us, but he's interested to learn more about non-violence. Wonders will never cease."

Now Crystal was asking everyone to take their seats for the afternoon session. The noise subsided as people sat down and prepared to pay attention once again.

"I never used to think much about hell," said Francis. "It didn't mean much to me, and to the extent that I thought about it at all, I saw the whole idea of it as a kind of blasphemy against the loving God that I believe in.

"Then the Provincial Government invited me to visit the tar sands development. They asked the Elders as well. The companies involved in the tar sands and the companies that want to mine the uranium and build the nuclear plant to power the eastward extension of the tar sands development were worried that people were being misled by propaganda from environmental extremists from outside the area. So, they asked the Provincial Government, as a supposedly neutral third party, to show us the tar sands to the west of us, and the existing uranium mines to the north of us, and explain everything, so we would have a correct understanding of what's being proposed for our area. Then we'd presumably drop our opposition to the whole project.

"The first thing they did was fly us over the whole area, so we could see the mines from above. Then they were going to take us to visit on the ground and speak to the mining engineers and the people working in environmental mitigation. But we never got that far. Once I saw the tar sands from above, I had no difficulty believing in hell. There it was. I wept. The scale of the destruction was greater than I could ever have imagined possible; mile after mile of huge pits and enormous settling ponds full of toxic waste. They wanted us to think how small the area of so-called development was in comparison to the size of the forest. But, in fact, we were all horrified at how big it was. I'm told you can even see the tar sands from space. And that whole area used to be forest, full of plants and animals, somewhere healthy and beautiful. Now, it's just wrecked, ugly, poisonous. I don't know if any of you have read *Lord of the Rings*, but the tar sands is just like what I imagine the land of Mordor is like.

"Then on we flew to the uranium mines in the north of the province. Again, huge pits gouged out of the forest, great dead scars on the land, productive forest turned into a poisonous wasteland, and from what I've learnt since, a wasteland that will go on producing deadly radiation and dangerous acid mine drainage for thousands and thousands of years.

"So none of us wanted to meet the engineers and scientists, because we all decided right then and there in that little plane that we would never, ever allow the land round Deep Lake to be carved up to fuel this project."

"Yes," agreed Ivan. "We're not going to sit back while our land is destroyed and our treaty rights violated. We're not going to let these companies poison Mother Earth. We've seen what they're doing. They don't understand the land. They see it as a dead thing. We know it's alive. We understand that everything is connected to everything else. You can't destroy one area, and think it won't affect the rest of Mother Earth. They don't understand you have to think about the impact of what you do on your great-great-great-great-grandchildren. Who's going to speak up for them, if we don't? The moose, the bear, the marten and the mink – they don't speak our languages, so who's going to speak up for them? These companies don't think about them. They don't plan for them. The animals have been planned out of their plan. The trees have been planned out of their plan. We saw those mines – not a tree left on them, not a single tree, not an animal in all that black, poisonous wasteland.

"That's why we set up the Defenders of Mother Earth. We're going to stop all this destruction before it goes any further, before we're all poisoned and we all get sick and die, like our Native brothers and sisters are getting sick and dying around the tar sands to the west of us. We need your help because there are few of us. I want to thank you for being here, thank you for helping us protect this land. We call it *our* land, but we're doing this for everybody. It's in everybody's interests that we save this bit of Mother Earth.

"I guess Elaine already told you we have our way of defending the land and that we want to defend it without violence. Soldiers are brave men and women, but you have to be even braver to confront the enemy without weapons. You have to be ready to accept injury without inflicting it. That's what we want to do. If the RCMP come at us with guns, maybe some of us are going to get hurt. I don't blame you if you want to turn around and not come up to Deep Lake, because things might get a bit hot up there in the next few days. We don't want any of us or any of you to get hurt, but we don't know what the RCMP are going to do, so we can't guarantee anything. But we do want to guarantee that we won't use violence against them. We're going to spend the rest of today and all of tomorrow explaining this so we can all be calm if things get difficult. We don't intend to lose this battle. We just want to win it our way. We don't want to keep our land and lose our soul. We want both."

Three: Kerry attends a talking circle

The time had now come for participants to break up into small groups and move off to various houses around the village to learn about the practice of non-violence. But Kerry was suffering from mental indigestion. She felt she could not take in any more information in one day.

Will was preparing to lead one of the workshops, and it looked as though Milton was going to spend the afternoon learning from his old military friend. But Kerry said, "Will, I've just got to get out. I'm sorry, I can't take in any more. I've got to get some fresh air, clear my head."

Will looked concerned. "Don't worry about it, honey. You've already heard what I have to say a dozen times. Why not take a walk? I'll see you later. Don't get lost."

So Kerry walked out into the bright afternoon. The air was crisp, but a warm breeze was blowing gently from the West. She walked in that direction, towards the breeze, feeling the mild warmth of the sun on her left cheek. When she reached the houses closest to the community hall, she turned, for no particular reason, up the lane to the right, and followed it, through various whimsical twists and turns – which reminded her rather of the staggering gait of a drunkard – to the edge of the settlement. A narrow lane led straight ahead, through open country. A small sign read, 'Nottard: 6km'.

She decided to walk over towards Nottard. She was wearing stout shoes, warm jeans and a warm jacket. The sky was clear. Six kilometres should take not much more than an hour. If she got bored or tired she could turn back before she got there.

The streets of Kropotkin were paved, but the lane to Nottard was made of gravel. To the right were bare, ploughed fields, waiting for spring sowing. The land sloped gently down hill towards the East, and in the distance, it seemed to level out and run flat as a table top to the horizon. To the left, beyond a fence, the land rose slightly. Grasses, yellowed with winter, were beginning to turn green. The meadows were scattered with small purple flowers and a number of other plants, which Kerry did not recognise. Once in a while, plaintive, unfamiliar birdcalls broke the silence. Here, in this glacier-scoured flat land, she missed the familiarity of the plants and birds of southern England and even, for that matter, Yellowstone State.

After half an hour or so, the ploughed fields ended at a small creek, flowing down from the higher country to the West. There was a bridge over the creek, and beyond it, the land rose slightly. It was unfenced and uncultivated, filled with a profusion of plants, including sizeable bushes and numerous small flowers. Now, familiar clumps of sagebrush filled the air with their clean, refreshing scent.

After a further quarter of an hour, ploughed fields began again, much smaller fields than those close to Kropotkin, and in some of them, she could see people at work, sowing seed by hand. Before long, Kerry could see the cluster of small houses that was Nottard.

She turned around and began, more slowly, to retrace her steps. She had done what she had come to do. She had cleared her head. Now, she needed to return to the task for which she had come here.

The first person Kerry encountered, when she entered the hall once more, was Francis. He was standing just inside the door, looking troubled.

"I caused a stir," he told her. "I didn't mean to. I asked Eric Smith if there was somewhere in Kropotkin where I could celebrate Mass with Ivan tomorrow, since it's Sunday. Eric said that, because Kropotkin is an atheist community, they've always had a policy of not having any religious celebrations of any sort there, which is why Elaine hasn't been opening each session with prayers. So I said that was fine, and that I was sorry to have asked, and there was no problem, I respect the community's tradition. But there were a couple of other residents there, and they said they thought they should discuss my request at their community meeting tomorrow morning, because they were concerned that the community was keeping this old tradition without thinking about it properly, so they asked me not to withdraw my request, and to let them give me an answer after their Sunday morning meeting."

"Well, that's alright, isn't it?" said Kerry.

"Well, I feel a bit embarrassed now. If I'd known it was such an issue, I wouldn't have asked. We could have gone and sat in a field outside the town, or driven somewhere and sat in the truck and celebrated Mass. I don't want to cause people offence."

"I don't suppose you've caused offence. They don't have to discuss it if they don't want to. You haven't demanded anything."

"No, that's true. Well, we'll see what happens tomorrow morning."

After everyone had eaten, and while the community hall was being rearranged for the social – which, of course, would involve dancing – Elaine announced that she was about to hold a talking circle in the lounge at the Kropotkin guesthouse. Kerry was talking to Larry at the time. "Are you going to go?" she asked.

"Oh, maybe not," said Larry. "I've been to a good few in my time. I guess they're helpful for a lot of people. I just get the feeling that, at some stage, people need to stop talking about their troubles and get on with life. There's one guy up in Strathcona who's been going to the Mother Earth Healing Circles for a couple of years now, and every time I go he's talking about the same troubles. I started thinking that maybe I should set up a Father Sky Getting-Your-Act-Together Rectangle." He smiled to himself. "Maybe that's just because

I haven't suffered like some people have. I don't know. I just think that unless the talking really does lead to healing, and helps people move on, it can get a bit self-indulgent."

"Yes, I see what you mean," said Kerry. "I think I might go, though, just to see what it's like."

When she arrived at the guesthouse, she found another dozen or so people gathered in the lounge, sitting on the floor with Elaine. Zoe and Leif were there; and, to Kerry's immense surprise, so was Milton. She caught his eye, and he smiled rather self-consciously.

Elaine, who was holding the talking stick, said, "Well, I guess we'd better begin, unless any of you know someone else is on their way." Nobody spoke. Elaine called for a minute's silence, and then explained the talking stick and the need to respect whatever anyone else said; not to interrupt or make negative comments on it, and to keep the information in the room. She asked if everyone was willing to abide by these rules, and everyone gave their consent. She explained that the talking stick would be passed around clockwise, like the movement of the sun in the sky, and that only the person holding it could speak. When each person had said all they wished to say, they should say "hai-hai," "thank you," and pass the stick on to the next person.

As the talking stick was passed around, Kerry was surprised at the frankness with which people spoke of difficulties in their lives – of health, or upbringing, or relationships – in this *ad hoc* company of strangers. At first, she wondered what possible comfort they might gain from what struck her as a typically North American form of emotional exhibitionism. But, as the stick approached her, she began to understand. The atmosphere in the room reminded her of that room in Stella Coelho's house years ago, when she first began to attend the parish prayer group meetings. There was an air of deep peacefulness and great kindness. People were being listened to, without being judged. Perhaps that was it. As each person recounted their tale of woe – and it was mostly woe, as people clearly felt little need to share their joys, only their sorrows – nobody was jumping in with unhelpful exclamations such as "Tell me about it!" or "You think *you've* had it rough!" or "Oh, I know! I've had *just* the same experience!" People were actually listening to one another, and there was something deeply reassuring in simply being heard.

Zoe spoke about the difficulties of growing up with a male body and a female identity; about her move from Hong Kong to Vancouver, and the immense difficulty of finding any work other than sex work; and about her leaving that work when she at last met a man who genuinely loved her for who she was. Leif spoke even more movingly about his search for love and his finding it only when he had abandoned hope and sought out a prostitute to fill the aching void. And there were no disapproving looks, or smirks, or sharp intakes of breath; just quiet listening.

So, when it came to her own turn, Kerry was not afraid to summarise her own recent history. She did not feel an especial need to speak of it for her own sake; it was more an act of respect towards those others who had bared their souls to her.

But, she was taken aback when the talking stick reached Milton, the last in the circle before Elaine. Milton was no more given to emotional self-disclosure than she was. She assumed that he considered it unmanly – and he was such a manly man. But the day's proceedings had moved him deeply, he admitted, and caused him to reflect on matters that he had kept stored away in the back of his mind, because he found it too painful to dwell on them. The birth of his daughters had brought him the most amazing joy that he could ever imagine, and that very joy had stabbed him with a kind of painful guilt – though he had not realised it was guilt until today – about the many people he had killed when in the marines. In no way, he said, did he wish to criticise his brave comrades in the service, but that did not alter the fact that he, in seeking to serve his country, had become a killer many times over. He had never felt at ease with that, though he had never before admitted it even to himself. Killing other people is not a natural thing for men to do, he said. You have to force yourself to do it. You have to force yourself to fix some other human being in your sights and squeeze the trigger. Then, when you've killed them, you feel terrible, but you have to numb your feelings and move on to the next engagement. It builds up like mental scar tissue. We weren't made to kill each other but to help each other, he said. He did not want to kill children's fathers any more than he wanted to kill children like his own. He didn't know, he said, whether war was always wrong or whether the wars he had fought in were right or wrong – though at the time he had believed they must be right or the President would not have sent Americans into battle – he just knew what it felt like to be killing people, or to have killed people, and it didn't feel right, and he wanted a world where nobody ever did that ever again.

His voice broke, and he fell silent, and began, quietly, to weep, and after a while he said, "Hai-hai," and passed the talking stick to Elaine.

Elaine placed the stick across her lap, and a deep silence descended. Kerry lost track of time as the silence continued, but felt no restless need for it to end.

Eventually, Elaine spoke again. She thanked everyone for the honesty and mutual respect they had shown. She reminded them of their undertaking not to speak of the matters they had heard within the circle. She exhorted them to treat everyone around them with the honour that they hoped for themselves, and to keep in mind the examples of people they knew who had inspired them in some way, who were for them the equivalent of Native Elders. She said she wished to honour her own elders and ancestors and show respect for every living being, and again there was a silence, briefer this time, while, Kerry supposed, Elaine prayed privately. Then she said, "Hai-hai," and everyone replied, "Hai-hai," and the talking circle was over, and it was time to dance.

Kerry contrived to walk back to the community hall with Milton. "Are you okay?" she asked him, quietly.

"Yeah, thanks, Kerry," he replied, somewhat subdued. He looked at her. "Thanks. I appreciate your concern."

"That's okay," she said.

Then Milton spoke of the weather, and the pleasing quality of the sunset, and asked her whether she would dance that night.

Late that night, when the music ended, and everyone began to drift off to their sleeping places, Zoe invited Kerry, Will and Milton to join the Vancouver group at the guesthouse in Nottard that night, rather than sleep on the community hall floor among the food crumbs and spilled beer. So Larry was able to get a more comfortable night's sleep again in Elaine's motor home.

Kerry was deeply impressed by Milton's ability to take his new acquaintances in his stride. She suspected that he found it rather difficult, given the rather garish frocks in which Hank and Marlon were dressed. But perhaps, she thought, Milton admired their bravery in asserting who they were, rather than accepting who they were expected to be. In any case, she thought, he had already accepted her.

Four: Kerry witnesses a momentous decision

Milton told Will and Kerry on the Sunday morning that he was coming with them to the blockade. He'd squared it with his wife and daughters. So they could ride in his truck.

That same morning, Francis' request was considered at the community meeting. Out of courtesy, Francis was invited to observe the relevant part of the meeting, and to bring along any other visitors he wished to accompany him – but as they were not members of the community, they would not be able to participate in the discussion themselves. Francis asked Ivan and Kerry to go with him, and they took seats in the corner of the community hall.

Eric opened the discussion, because it was to him that the request had been made. He simply reported what Francis had asked, what he, Eric, had said in response, Francis' consequent withdrawal of his request, and the suggestion by Nate Bardwell, Jeremiah Tate and Felicity Green, who had been present at the time, that the request should be discussed by the community. Then, Eric sat down.

Martina Sedgewick was chairing the meeting. She invited Nate, Jeremiah and Felicity to explain why they had made their suggestion. Nate spoke first.

"Three reasons," he began. "The first is, if we're going to be true to the anarchism that drew this community together over a century ago, we have to avoid getting mired in traditions. We can respect those who went before us, but we don't always have to do what they did. If we stick to what they decided, just because they decided it, we're mirroring one of the things about religion that they rightly rejected: the power of tradition. We have to be free to decide whatever we want, as long as it's not going to hurt those who come after us.

"The second is, as I understand it, that the main reason the founders of this community decided that religious people could not live here, was that they believed that religious people would cause division by carrying on as though they had the whole truth, that everyone who didn't share their religion was wrong, and that they had to convert everyone to their belief system. But over the years, at least over the ten years or so since I came to adulthood, we've had a good many people visit here who profess some kind of religion, whether they're Native people following their traditions, or Jews or Christians participating in the kinds of activities that we all support, like challenging capitalism or working against war – and not one of them has ever carried on like they knew everything, or tried to convert other people to their religion. I guess maybe there are plenty of bigoted religious people in the world, but all I can say is that none of the religious people I've met here have been like that. I've met some pretty scary religious types away from here, and especially down in the States, but the fact that we get some religious types turning up here, who are not like that, shows it's clearly not a necessary element of being religious.

"The third reason is what really made me think and made me want to have this respectful request discussed here. That other British guy who was here in the week, that academic or journalist or whatever he was, the one on the kind of atheist pilgrimage here, was the most bigoted guy we have ever had here in this community, without exception. The guy's got some kind of superiority complex. He was totally supercilious about religious people, and yet, he didn't seem interested in any of the kind of work or the kind of causes that we support and where we encounter allies who happen to be religious. And I thought, well, here's living proof that atheists can be just as narrow-minded as the worst of religious people.

"I mean, what brought our forebears together to found this community was not primarily atheism. It wasn't even primarily rejection of religious bigotry or religious institutions. It was a desire for equality, justice and freedom. They rejected religion because they saw religion as an enemy of these three great values. But my experience suggests it isn't always the case. Some of our allies are religious. Some of our opponents are atheists. I don't have a religious thought in my head – I have no understanding of what a religious worldview might feel like – but I would trust my life to some of our religious allies. We don't even have to change our rule that religious people can't come and live here with us. But we could soften our rule that visitors can't even have their prayers while they're here. Francis made his request in a really respectful manner, and I think we should show him a similar level of respect by letting him do his ceremony, without having to sneak around like a thief."

Nate sat down. People maintained a respectful silence while they considered his words.

Martina asked Jeremiah and Felicity if they had anything to add, but they said that Nate had already expressed everything they could have said.

Martina asked if anyone else had any comments.

Some worries were expressed. Nobody doubted Francis' good intentions, but allowing a religious ceremony to take place at Kropotkin would set a precedent, and who knew where it might lead? At two of the communities that had been founded by dissenters from Kropotkin over the past hundred years – Kinnard and Wellard – they'd built churches, and already, there were Fundamentalist preachers installed there, talking the kind of nonsense that the people of Kropotkin had always rejected. The community at Kropotkin had kept their tradition for a purpose.

On the other hand, people took the point that having a tradition was not very anarchic. Someone also suggested that telling visitors what they could or could not do was not very anarchic either. People should be free to do what they wanted.

Ah, said someone else, but what about that time when those young Californians had had that all-night open-air nude love-in, one midsummer night back in the early 70s? Hadn't the community decided to ask them to leave? People were worried it might scare the horses, or upset the children. So there were limits to people's freedom, weren't there? Wasn't it the same with religion?

Someone objected that an indoor religious ceremony was unlikely to scare the horses and that, anyway, the horses could be confined to their paddocks while it was going on.

But, asked another, was this not an unjustifiable restriction of the horses' freedom of movement?

Martina suggested that the discussion was perhaps going off on a tangent. She pointed out that the horses were quite often put in the paddocks and that nobody had ever raised the issue of their freedom of movement before.

Well, said someone else, the impact on children was the important thing. She had read that teaching children about religion was a form of abuse. It could corrupt their young minds and lead them astray. They might end up worrying about going to hell.

Nate spoke up again, saying that although this was a serious issue, the fact was that as far as he remembered, none of the religious people who had visited Kropotkin had ever talked in that way.

In that case, someone interjected, Nate had a very short memory, as he'd been in the community hall the day before, when this very same Father Francis had mentioned hell.

Well, yes, said Nate, but it was perfectly clear that he was using an image drawn from his religious tradition to put across the horror of the tar sands development and motivate people to struggle against it. He was certainly not using this imagery as a way of scaring children into accepting religious dogmas or making them feel guilty about their bodies.

Hmmph! It was the thin end of the wedge.

"Was that 'hmmph!' with two 'm's or three?" asked the minute taker. This did not go down too well. The maker of the remark felt that the question was flippant.

Martina suggested that the meeting spend two full minutes in silence, considering the various points that had been made.

The silence was punctuated by the creaking of old wooden chairs and periodic exhalations of breath. One of the older men belched rather more loudly than he had expected. Several of the children giggled.

"Well," said Martina, "I think that, before long, we should move on to other business. I am not sure that we have reached a consensus on this. Would anyone object to us voting on it?"

Nobody objected.

"In that case," said Martina, "could we have a show of hands? The proposal is that, at some time today, the Catholic priest, Father Francis Neale, be allowed to celebrate the religious ceremony of Catholic Mass here in the community and, I think, for others to attend this ceremony as they wish. Is that right, Nate?"

"That's right," said Nate. "And I further propose that we allow him to use the community hall, since the non-violent direct action workshops will be held in houses all over the village, and the community hall won't be in use between lunch time and supper time."

"But the proposal is about this one individual celebrating this one ceremony on this one occasion, without establishing a precedent?" queried Martina.

"That's right," confirmed Nate.

"Okay, then," said Martina. "Votes in favour, please?"

A forest of hands went up, hands attached to brains imprinted with the disagreeable memory of the visit by that distinguished British academic – or journalist, or whatever he was – earlier in the week.

"Oh, my," said Martina. "Votes against?" There was one vote against, that of the woman who had said 'hmmph!' with two 'm's.

"Abstentions?"

There were half a dozen.

"Well," said Martina, "I think we've made history. I suppose we could say it's a victory for anarchist tolerance."

There was a respectful silence as people considered the decision that they had collectively made. Then they moved on to the spring agricultural work rota and the need for repairs to one of the washing machines in the laundry.

Five: Kerry attends Kropotkin's first Mass

Word of the community's decision, and the consequent plan for Francis to celebrate Mass in the community hall at 4pm, travelled fast. Kerry was surprised to see quite a gathering of people there. In addition to Francis and Ivan, and Milton, Will and herself, there were a fair few of the activists from the gathering, including Hank and Marlon, who, it turned out, were both Catholics. Leif and Zoe attended out of affection for their friends. Elaine attended out of solidarity with Ivan and Francis. And the three young people who had suggested that Kropotkin allow this innovation also came, out of a mixture of curiosity and respect.

Francis invited everyone to bring chairs and sit in a circle, and in front of his own chair, he placed a small table on which he set a ceramic chalice and plate, small glass containers of wine and water, and two white candles, which he lit. He placed a brightly coloured stole over his shoulders, fell silent for a few moments, and then began.

"Thank you all for coming to join Ivan and me in this Mass," he said. "And many thanks to our hosts here in Kropotkin for their broad-mindedness and generosity in allowing us to celebrate this ceremony here. I really appreciate that." He fell silent again for a while, then made the sign of the cross, beginning the Mass in the Name of the Father and of the Son and of the Holy Spirit. He invited those present to call to mind God's infinite love for them and to consider the ways in which they had failed to respond to that love – how they may have fallen short in their love for other people and for the Earth which God had created. Then, he asked Ivan to bless the assembly with sweetgrass. He explained that sweetgrass was a sacred plant, whose smoke carried prayers to the spirit world and invited the good spirits to be present to those gathered in prayer; and that the braid of three bunches of the grass symbolised the unity of body, mind and spirit.

Ivan took a braid from his pocket and lit it at one of the candles on the altar. He moved around the circle of people, wafting the sacred smoke over them. Francis and the Native people present held their hands in the smoke from the burning braid and wafted it over their heads and down over their bodies in blessing. When Ivan had completed the circle, he set the smouldering sweetgrass down in an abalone shell on the table. Then Francis pronounced the words of forgiveness, offered a prayer and asked Ivan to read the first Bible reading.

The reading was from the tenth chapter of the Acts of the Apostles. The Apostle Peter overcame his distaste at entering the house of a man of different ethnic and religious origins from his own, and thus enabled the Christian community to embrace people of non-Jewish as well as Jewish origin.

Elaine, despite her feelings about the Catholic Church, consented to read the second reading, from the fourth chapter of the first letter of St John. The writer called on his readers to love one another, asserting that if they did not love, they could not know God, who is love.

Francis asked Kerry to read the Gospel reading. Kerry, conscious of the fact that according to the Church's rules this task belonged exclusively to ordained clergy, felt deeply moved to be asked. She understood it as an affirmation of her old friend's respect for her and of the value of the path she had followed since she had left the path to priesthood, which they had once walked together.

The reading was from the fifteenth chapter of the Gospel according to St John, part of Jesus' speech to his disciples at the Last Supper, in which he implores them to love one another. She handed the lectionary back to Francis, who smiled at her, and took her seat again. Francis looked down at the lectionary open on his lap, and there was a brief silence.

"What appropriate readings these are!" exclaimed Francis, looking up again. "They're the regular readings for the sixth Sunday of Easter, but how well they address our gathering today and the task that we are undertaking in the days to come!

"It was very difficult for Peter, a devoutly religious man, to overcome his taboo against associating too closely with people of other religious backgrounds. Going into the Roman Cornelius's house was a big deal for him. He would have worried about becoming ritually unclean. But he realises that God wants to break down the barriers that people set up between one another. He realises that this was part of what Jesus was about. He's already had a vision, where God tells him to eat ritually impure food. When he gets to Cornelius's place, he realises God was telling him he had to change his attitude to people who weren't part of his own group. So he's willing to accept non-Jews into the community of those trying to follow the way of Jesus, who later on came to be known as Christians. If he hadn't done that, we wouldn't be celebrating Mass here today, because the followers of Jesus would have been limited to members of the Jewish community, whereas in fact Jesus meant his way for everybody.

"I think I've learnt something too, today. It's really only come to me as a result of hearing these readings in this company. This reading isn't only about breaking down the barriers between Jews and non-Jews in the early Christian community. It's about breaking down the barriers that we continue setting up between us. I look round at you, my brothers and sisters, and I see several broken barriers. There's the fact that we have Native people, white people, black people and Asian people here. Perhaps that's the least significant thing today, because we're used to that now and the Church is used to it. But I think I'm not revealing any secrets, if I say we've also got gender identity variety here as well, if I can put it that way. To be honest, I don't know what are the best terms to use, because I'm only just now beginning to learn. I think it's true to say that not everyone at this gathering fully identifies with traditional gender roles. But I'm beginning to realise that even if the Book of Genesis says that God created human beings male and female, we don't have to understand that as meaning that God created everyone to be all one or all the other. There are obviously gradations in between.

"Peter says in this reading that 'anybody of any nationality who fears God and does what is right is acceptable to him', and I suppose that, before now, I would have assumed, without really thinking about it, that 'doing what is right' included conforming to certain forms of behaviour which meant that all men had to behave in one kind of way and all women in another, and that if you were born one way, you were stuck with it. I think maybe I was wrong about that, that God's creation is more varied and more interesting than that. I think this is another barrier that God wants to break down.

"Now, I suppose people of a conventional mindset might say, the Christian tradition is clear about what's right and what's wrong, and that means people do have to keep to certain ways of doing things and avoid others, and I think that what hearing this reading today has helped me to see, is that this is just what Peter had to unlearn, if you see what I mean. He had to unlearn a cultural tradition which he associated with God, in order to be faithful to what God actually wanted, and God continually surprises us. I think, actually, that the real key to what 'doing what is right' means, is to be found in the other two readings, from St John.

"There's one other barrier that I think we are in a certain sense surmounting today as well, and that's the barrier between believers and unbelievers. I welcome those of you, my brothers and sisters, who find faith, religious belief, concepts of God, forms of worship, incomprehensible or even offensive. I think that we Catholics, we Christians, we religious people of whatever tradition, have done plenty to justify people feeling negative about us and about what we stand for. In fact, we've done a great deal to make sure that people can't see what this is all about at all. I'm really grateful to all of you from Kropotkin, who have kindly allowed us to celebrate this Mass, and I hope that you'll find some meaning and use in what we're doing here this afternoon. Actually, I think we can break down this barrier through finding unity in the pursuit of 'doing what is right'.

"What is right, then? Well, doesn't St John's letter, and today's reading from John's Gospel, make it crystal clear? That reading from the letter of St John begins, 'My dear people, let us love one another, since love comes from God and everyone who loves is begotten by God and knows God. Anyone who fails to love can never have known God, because God is love.' Notice he says that *everyone who loves* is begotten by God and knows God. Not 'everyone who believes the right religious doctrines'. Not 'everyone who's had a religious conversion experience'. Not 'everyone who's been baptised'. Not 'everyone who lives a respectable life'. No. He says that *everyone who loves* comes from God and knows God. Anyone who doesn't love, however religious or respectable they are and however much they think they are friends of God and however much they shout about Jesus, doesn't know God or who God is, and that's because the nature of God is love. So doing what is right means loving, and if we fail to love, we are not doing what is right.

"I think we could probably also say, that if we haven't experienced God as love, we haven't experienced God at all; just as if we haven't experienced Christ as liberation, we haven't experienced Christ.

"In the Gospel reading, Jesus makes clear what loving implies. He doesn't simply tell his disciples to love each other. He says, 'love one another *as I have loved you.*' This love isn't something you do when you feel like it, or once every other Thursday. It's the total giving of your whole self for the wellbeing of others, whether or not you feel like it, whether or not you like the others whom you're called to love, whether or not it's convenient. It's a love that's willing to make the ultimate sacrifice for others. Jesus says, 'a man can have no greater love than to lay down his life for his friends,' and then goes on to make clear that the people he is talking to are his friends, and then he goes ahead and lays down his life for them.

"It's also a love which is necessarily non-violent. I can see how people come to the conclusion that loving people might involve violence against those who perpetrate injustice, but I don't see that in the example of Jesus, so I think we have to say that violence is a departure from the path of Jesus, whoever is doing it to whomever, and for whatever reason.

"Now, as we all know, there's the possibility that the situation up at Deep Lake might get a bit unpleasant and a bit scary. I think there's precious little chance of anyone having to lay down their life – this is Canada, not Cortesia – but there may be difficulties, there may be arrests, there may even be injuries. If we're going up there, we have to be ready for all this. We can take courage from each other. We can also draw strength from Jesus. In today's Gospel reading he says, 'you did not choose me, no, I chose you, and I commissioned you to go out and bear fruit, fruit that will last'. We believe that we have been called to go up to Deep Lake and bear fruit that will last, the fruit being the protection of Mother Earth from the destruction caused by uranium mining and tar sands development.

"And this is where we can find our unity, you see. Whatever our ethnic, religious or gender identity, whether we've got a faith or not, we are called to love one another, and we find our unity in that loving, and in this instance, we find our unity in a particular work of love, which is to save the part of Mother Earth around Deep Lake, with all her life forms, including human beings, from destruction."

Seven: Kerry and companions depart for Deep Lake

Early on the Monday morning, vehicles began leaving Kropotkin for Deep Lake in the distant north. Nearly a hundred people were making for the blockade, residents of Nottard and Kropotkin, people who had attended the weekend gathering, and others who had visited the blockade before and wanted to offer their support again. Thirty vehicles set out in groups of three, at intervals, so that there would be safety in numbers but without attracting the attention that a large convoy would attract. Each group included at least one person who knew the way well, and each group took different routes to Deep Lake.

It would take them a good four hours to reach the Athabasca provincial border by whatever route, and at least another five hours from there to the Deep Lake blockade. The latter part of the journey would be on gravel roads, and the final stretch on unsurfaced logging roads.

Kerry, sitting, as before, between Will and Milton, surveyed the countryside. As they drove north, the grassy plains began to give way to more varied land, with here and there a clump of spindly poplars or an outcrop of red willow. Great river valleys, running vaguely west to east, split the land from time to time. Towns were few, and small.

In front of them, Eric Smith led the way in one of Kropotkin's four-wheel drives. Behind them came their new friends from Vancouver.

By the time they crossed the provincial border into Athabasca, they were driving through continuous poplar forest. Further north, the poplars were joined by great stands of birch and jack pine, then spruce. Here and there, fields had been hacked out of the forest. More frequently, logging operations had clearcut large areas which had been replanted with spruce seedlings.

Around five o'clock, they turned off the main gravel road, on to a winding logging track that took them along a creek valley, between tall conifers. After several more turnings, they emerged into a small area of clearcut surrounded by jack pines. The track crossed the clearcut, which sloped down gently towards the North, and joined a wider track, just before it crossed a small bridge over a creek. Beyond the creek, a barrier had been set up across the track, and behind that was a large, low wooden building. Smaller structures were visible among the trees, and aerial walkways linked structures in the treetops. A large sign on wooden posts in front of the main building announced: 'Defenders of Mother Earth blockade.'

The barrier was lifted and the vehicles directed up a small track branching off to the left and running up among the trees. A couple of hundred metres behind the barrier, a small clearing had been created, and vehicles were parked in it. Kerry could see numerous colourful tents pitched among the trees on the far side of the clearing, the side away from the front line.

They parked the truck and made their way to the main building, which was full of people. Food was being served at one end of the large room, and Kerry joined the others there. They were weary from so much travel, and hungry with it.

New arrivals were shown around the site as soon as they had eaten. Ivan's son Vincent acted as guide for the latest arrivals from Nottard and Kropotkin. He pointed out the ceremonial site behind the main building, where a small mound had been fenced off with a white picket fence, and then took them into the woods.

The forest here consisted almost entirely of mature jack pine. It was light and airy and easy to see a long way through it because, unlike spruce, the lowest branches of the jack pine were quite high up on the trees' trunks. The blockaders had occupied a large quantity of land on the north side of the clear cut. Tree houses and aerial walkways had been set up over a distance of around five hundred metres along the creek bank. At either end of these constructions, felled and fallen timber had been piled into fences running back for some tens of metres away from the creek bed into the woods. The land rose gently away from the creek. Scattered among the trees, as far as Kerry could see, were tents of varying shades and sizes. Vincent suggested that they pitch their tents wherever they could find space. It was fine to pitch them beyond the edges of the current area of occupation, as long as they realised that any assault by the police might reach them first. He recommended they pitch their tents straight away and told them that there would be a briefing at about nine o'clock behind the main building.

Will and Eric chose a site at the edge of the settlement, close to the northern end of the western timber fence. The ground was flat, the soil dry and sandy. Those who had travelled together from Kropotkin pitched their tents in a rough circle around a large jack pine. Kerry hoped that if the police did come, they would not wreck Will's tent. They had bought it in a store in Cottonwood Creek, and it had been rather expensive. Will wanted something which would give them the maximum protection against the northern cold.

A couple of hundred metres away, outside the fence and back down the gentle slope towards the creek, was a collection of half a dozen impressively painted tipis, detached from the rest of the camp, arranged in a circle among the trees. One of the tipis bore the words 'Warriors of Mother Earth'.

"I guess they're the group from back east that people have been worried about," said Will. "There's been a bit of tension, because they're not too happy with the Elders' commitment to non-violence."

"D'you know 'em?" asked Milton.

"Only by repute," replied Will. "Maybe I'll check 'em out tomorrow."

By the time the light was failing, and the new blockaders had gathered for the briefing, there must have been nearly five hundred people in the camp. Ivan and Elaine ascended the small sacred mound and Ivan spoke, with the help of a loudspeaker system powered by a small bicycle generator operated by two of the more energetic blockaders.

Ivan thanked everyone for coming, especially those who had travelled furthest. He reminded everyone that they expected that within the next few days the police would move in to evict the blockaders, and that it was the Elders' wish that the resistance should be non-violent. He exhorted everyone to remember the training that they had received, so that they could maximise the inconvenience caused to the police, while minimising the possibility of people being hurt. He said that members of the Defenders of Mother Earth and their helpers in the Aboriginal Ecological Coalition would be taking responsibility for different areas of the blockade camp to help people with problems, answer people's questions and ensure that the Elders' wishes were respected. He said that, if no action had been taken within a week, nobody should feel compelled to stay, though they were welcome to do so. If anyone had to leave before the week was out, they should feel free to do so. The Elders, with the help of the Aboriginal Ecological Coalition and the contributions brought by new arrivals, had stockpiled enough food and water for the whole camp for a week. After that, he said with a smile, the non-native people could go shopping while the Native people went hunting moose.

Ivan told them that the blockade was being supported by a number of other actions around the country and the world: the Indigenous tent embassy outside the Houses of Parliament in Ottawa, a resolution in Parliament, which was gaining increasing support, the judicial action against the Federal and Provincial Governments for violation of Indigenous treaty rights, several judicial actions in Canada against North Atlantic Mining and its contractors, campaigns against the company in England and against its major investors in a number of other countries, resolutions by several state governments in the US to avoid purchase of oil from the Athabasca tar sands, and a growing international boycott of tourism to Canada. The blockaders were not alone, he said, and the battle was not lost, even if they were evicted. Then, he called on Elaine to share news about the latest legal developments.

Elaine said that a verdict was expected the next day on the appeal against the injunction, which the blockaders had obtained to prevent a forced eviction. It was very likely, as everyone knew, that the injunction would be lifted and that the RCMP would move immediately to evict. They would probably send officers first to serve a notice of eviction and give the blockaders twenty-four hours to leave. Then, they would probably return in much greater numbers to remove everyone by force. The other legal actions were at different stages and although they might delay or even ultimately halt mine construction they could not prevent a police action. She urged the blockaders to make sure that at least one person in each group attended briefings after each meal time in the main building, and to remember that the blockade was called at the behest of the Defenders of Mother Earth, whose wishes should be respected in the way the blockade was conducted. That included not only the approach to the authorities but respect for other blockaders. Elaine asked that unless there were specific events planned, people should avoid making excessive noise anywhere after ten o'clock, and avoid making any noise at all around the tents where people were sleeping. Then she asked for a period of silence, while she and Ivan smudged with sweetgrass and prayed for the blockaders and for the assistance of the Creator, the Grandfathers and Grandmothers.

After the prayers, most people dispersed quickly to their own sections of the camp. A rather sombre atmosphere had come upon them, of apprehensiveness exacerbated perhaps by travel weariness.

Will was acting as one of the organising team, so before he rested he walked around the section of the camp surrounding the tents which he and Kerry and their friends had pitched, in order to acquaint himself with their neighbours. Some time after ten, he returned to the tent which he and Kerry were to share, removed his outer clothes and lay down in his sleeping bag beside her. She was still wide awake.

"Do you have to do anything else, Will?" she asked.

"Not tonight," he replied.

"Good," she said. "Maybe I'm being selfish, but I want you all to myself just now."

He kissed her tenderly on the lips, his hair falling over her face.

"What's brought this on?" he asked.

"I don't know," she said. "I suppose because you've been so busy the past few days, whenever we've been alone together, you've been exhausted. It's been as if your mind's been elsewhere."

He embraced her tightly. "Well, my mind's here, now," he assured her.

"Good," she said. "I feel safe with you around."

"Are you worried?" he asked.

"Yes. I mean, I can't imagine it'll be any worse than what happened at San Martin de Porres, but I don't look forward to being pushed around by the RCMP."

"It'll be okay," he said. "You know what you have to do. Just stay sitting down until they come along and pick you up and move you, and don't struggle when they do."

"Kiss me again."

He kissed her. She sighed deeply. "Can your sleeping bag zip up together with mine?" she asked.

"Of course," he said. "That's why I bought them."

"Do it, then."

For some reason, the very act of rearranging their sleeping bags ignited a physical passion which surprised them both –a passion which, out of consideration for travelling companions well with earshot, and on account of their own natural modesty, and the hardness of the ground on which they lay, they felt constrained to express with the utmost delicacy.

Eight: Kerry encounters an unwelcome acquaintance

As Elaine had predicted, the police arrived the next day. Three police four by fours crossed the clearcut around noon and came to a halt in front of the bridge across the creek. They were followed by an expensive Range Rover, bearing the insignia of North Atlantic Mining plc. As news of their arrival spread through the camp, blockaders began to gather along the creek bank to observe what might take place. Kerry and Will, who happened to be in the main building at the time, finishing their lunch, were among the first, and stood right next to the barrier across the track.

Ivan Silver and Elaine went across the creek bridge to talk with the police. Chief Superintendent Raymond Hawrylak, commanding officer of the RCMP detachment, climbed out of the leading vehicle with a file of paperwork. He was a decent man, convinced of the legitimacy of the Canadian State and the need to defend whatever that State, democratic as it was, had decided to do. But he preferred to do it, as far as possible, with the minimum of humiliation or suffering for those who stood in its way. He had always managed to do so, and he was approaching retirement now and eager not to blemish his humanitarian record.

He was straightforward, without being aggressive. "Ivan, Elaine, I have the legal paperwork here, lifting the injunction against forced eviction and giving me permission to evict you guys without further notice," he announced. "You know we'd prefer to avoid force, so we intend to give you guys twenty-four hours to leave. I strongly advise you guys to do so, because you've run out of legal options and you guys know you're not going to be able to hold on for long once we get started, and we really don't want any injuries to anyone, you guys or us."

Ivan was slightly taller than Chief Superintendent Hawrylak and he pulled himself up to the full height of his septuagenarian Indigenous dignity. He looked at the officer squarely in the chin, carefully avoiding eye contact, which would, for him, have been aggressive, implying that the officer was lying. "We're grateful to you for your consideration, Chief Superintendent Hawrylak," he said, "but you know we're not moving. This is treaty land and we're going to defend it."

"I kind of thought you'd take that line," replied the police officer. "I've brought along some people from the company, because I figured, maybe if you guys could talk to them, you'd maybe realise you've no need to fear this development – it could even help you guys."

"Jeez!" exclaimed Elaine. "We already talked to those guys I don't know how many times!"

"Well," replied Chief Superintendent Hawrylak, "they're a conscientious company and they've brought over a new guy from London to head up their Athabasca community relations operations. I think you'll like the guy, and maybe he can persuade you guys you won't lose out if they go ahead with this mine."

The commander turned and beckoned to a shadowy figure in the back of the company Range Rover. The door opened and a well-groomed, slick-suited man in his early thirties strode confidently towards the bridge, borne on expensive, fashionable grey suede walking boots. Kerry was at first surprised, and then not surprised at all, to notice that it was Tony Conwell. A colleague climbed out of the back of the Range Rover and began to follow him, but Conwell waved him back.

North Atlantic Mining's Athabasca Community and Public Relations Department Head of Operations walked straight up to Ivan Silver, grasped his hand and looked him straight in the eye. "Good to meet you, Ivan," he said, with a cheerful smile, slapping Ivan's right shoulder with his left hand while shaking the Elder's right hand firmly. "I'm Tony Conwell from North Atlantic Mining. Please call me Tony. Elaine, good to meet you," he said, turning slightly to face her, but finding that her hands were firmly by her sides, unshakeable, without a lunge that might appear too eager or too aggressive even for Tony Conwell. Arrested in his stride for a fraction of a second, his gaze passed momentarily over Elaine's shoulder and he made direct eye contact with Kerry. A look of confused recognition passed across his face, as though he was sure he had seen her before but had no idea where. "Hi!" he said, with a smile.

"Hello, Tony," said Kerry.

Tony Conwell smiled at her again, but turned his attention back to the petty power brokers before him who needed to be won over quickly if the company were to avoid the expense of contributing to the cost of a forced eviction.

"Ivan, Elaine," he said, "I know you're all busy right now, but I'd be really grateful if you could spare a bit of time to talk. At least so we can understand each other and maybe all come to a deeper understanding of the other's point of view."

"I'm not sure there's much to talk about," replied Ivan. "You guys want us to move. We won't."

"I'm sure our positions are much more nuanced than that," responded Conwell.

"Ours isn't," said Elaine.

"Well, why don't we at least talk, and see if there are ways of going forward together as friends instead of foes."

"You're welcome to come and have a coffee with us, if there's new things you want to tell us," said Ivan. "But don't expect us to change our position. This is treaty land, and we're defending our rights. This is Mother Earth, and we're defending her."

"Well, you know," said Tony Conwell as he took Ivan by the arm and led him towards the main building, as though he were the host and Ivan the visitor, "I think when we talk we'll discover that our positions are not so different as you may think. North Atlantic is determined to carry out this mining in a way that respects your treaty rights, the integrity of Mother Earth and the needs of the generations to come."

Chief Superintendent Hawrylak looked concerned as Tony Conwell moved away from the bridge towards the main building with Ivan and Elaine, and the blockaders, led by Will and Kerry, began to follow them, cutting Conwell off from his RCMP escort. Chief Superintendent Hawrylak called out, "Tony!" and Conwell turned round and smiled in a carefree manner, indicating with a dismissive wave of his hand that there was no problem. Chief Superintendent Hawrylak, feeling uneasy, followed the crowd, indicating to the three other officers from his own vehicle that they should accompany him. The eight other officers from the other two vehicles stepped out of their vehicles, but Hawrylak gestured to them to stay put. They stood by their vehicles, looking on in dark-glassed impassiveness.

Inspector Kowalchuk stood bolt upright beside the second vehicle. He would be in charge if anything unpleasant happened to Chief Superintendent Hawrylak.

Elaine told Kerry all about Inspector Kowalchuk later. The Chief Superintendent's second in command was cut from different cloth from his superior. Kowalchuk was more ambitious than his boss and less concerned about the impact of his decisions on opponents of the State. Whereas Hawrylak felt uneasy whenever he had to work with CFIS – the Canadian Federal Intelligence Service – Elaine suspected that there was nothing Kowalchuk felt happier about. It probably made him feel important. She felt sure CFIS would have agents among the blockaders, though she did not know who. Hawrylak preferred everything to be open and above board. He had worked on Ivan's Reserve when he was a young officer and he felt a deep respect for the man, even though he thought he was mistaken. Kowalchuk thought the Indians were a bunch of savages who stood in the way of progress. Hawrylak rarely wore dark glasses, and then only when he was driving in bright sunlight or walking on snow. Kowalchuk wore them as frequently as possible, to cut himself off from the public, especially the Indians, and deepen his inscrutability.

Ivan allowed himself to be led into the main building and then asked one of the blockaders on kitchen duty for a coffee for Mr Conwell.

"Tony, please," Conwell reminded him. Elaine rolled her eyes skywards.

"Take a seat," Ivan urged him, and the three of them sat down at one of the tables in the eating area, while as many blockaders as could do so crowded into the room, and the RCMP detachment pushed their way to the front of the crowd and gathered by the table. Will and Kerry stood behind Ivan's chair, with Larry Randall right behind them. Conwell, facing them, looked up at Kerry once again and smiled, looked down and then suddenly looked up at her again as if some vague memory had stirred.

"Look," began Conwell, in a tone of voice that he had learnt from politicians in his homeland and which communicated simultaneously a declared intention to be disarmingly frank and a psychological incapacity to transcend an unalterable mendacity, "to be honest with you, I can understand your reservations." 'Honest?' thought Kerry. 'The man has no inkling of the meaning of the word.' Then, delighted by the sharpness of his own wit and eager to impress his audience, Conwell laughed abruptly, saying, "Ha! 'Understand your reservations!' I mean your misgivings – although I *do* understand your Reservations, as I've spent the last few days visiting many of the Reservations in this part of Athabasca."

"In Canada they're called Reserves," Elaine corrected him, stonily.

"Ah well, I'm still learning," replied Conwell, still pleased by his own wordplay and entirely oblivious to the fact that he was the only one laughing, since even the RCMP officers had enough cultural sensitivity to know that his oafish joking around would cause irritation rather than amusement.

"The point I want to make, is this," continued Conwell, donning his serious face once more. "This project truly is a win-win situation. The Province and the country prosper; the company, of course, profits. But you guys prosper along with us. Your communities get jobs, roads, schools, sports facilities, medical clinics, housing. Ivan and Elaine, you two know well that the benefit-sharing agreement we're offering is in advance of anything so far proposed for any mining project anywhere in North America. It's state of the art. It sets the standard for others to follow."

"That's such a crock of shit," commented Larry to himself, loud enough for Kerry to hear, but not loud enough to disrupt the conversation and cause Ivan offence.

Elaine began to say something, but Ivan spoke up and she fell silent. "Mr Conwell, you people still don't seem to understand what we've been telling you from the beginning. We don't want your money. We don't want your benefits. We want our treaty rights respected and we want Mother Earth protected from nuclear waste and tar sands waste and greenhouse gases and all the rest of it. We know full well that around uranium mines and nuclear plants and tar sands developments the land and the water get sick and then the animals and people get sick. There's not enough money in the world to compensate for that. We want us and our grandchildren and their grandchildren to have clean air, clean water, healthy plants and animals. The only way to avoid a conflict is for your company to pull out. You've consulted us many times, and we've consistently said, 'No'. We don't want your mine. We want you to go home and leave us alone. What part of that is not clear to you?"

"Ivan, Ivan," scolded Tony Conwell, affectionately, "the point I'm trying to make is that your people are not going to suffer these problems that you mention. Our mine is going to be state of the art. State of the art! You're not going to have the kind of problems that have occurred at uranium mines in the past because the industry's moved on."

Larry could not restrain himself. He leaned forward and touched Ivan on the shoulder. Ivan turned his head, nodded, and said, "It's okay, Larry, I'll deal with it." Then, turning to Tony Conwell, he said, "Mr Conwell, I don't think North

Atlantic Mining has the power to change the half-life of uranium or its so-called daughters. You can't stop radioactive substances being radioactive. You can't shorten their half lives. You're not God. The only safe place for uranium is in the ground, and that's where we're determined to keep it."

"Ivan!" chided Conwell, "this is just the kind of misapprehension that we need to clear up. The trouble is – and I'm not blaming anyone – people get taken over by emotion when these things get discussed, and most of us aren't scientists. We don't always understand why it is that things that have caused problems before won't cause problems again because we're moving on, we're going forward, we're learning the lessons. We can't understand all the ins and outs of the science, but I'm asking you please to trust the scientists who are assuring us that the problems that have occurred in the past simply *cannot* happen now because of changes in the technology."

"What about all the scientists who are telling us exactly the opposite?" asked Elaine.

"Well, this is one of the problems with the whole consultation process," replied Conwell. "As you know, Canada's a signatory to the United Nations Declaration on the Rights of Indigenous Peoples, and under this Declaration Indigenous Peoples have the right to Free, Prior Informed Consent before any development goes ahead on their land. So, number one, the fact that the Federal Government has approved this project shows that it *does* have the consent of any Indigenous Peoples whose *legally recognised* land, and I must stress that, *legally recognised* land, is affected. Because, otherwise, we'd have to question the good will and even the legitimacy of a democratically elected government, and I can't imagine any of you would want to do that. Number two, for the UN Declaration to be kept, Indigenous Peoples have to have their right to accurate information respected, and that must mean – *must* mean – that pressure groups and so-called independent scientists, and who knows what, should stay out of the whole process of informing Indigenous Peoples. That process must be strictly controlled by the companies concerned and the Government, otherwise Indigenous Peoples are just going to be confused by all the one-sided misinformation that all these campaigning groups throw at them. I'm not questioning their good intentions, you understand, but these groups have got a vested interest in making companies look bad, and Indigenous Peoples have a right – a *right* – to be protected from them."

It was impossible for the blockaders to restrain themselves any longer. There were cries of "Horse shit!", "Baloney!", "Rubbish!" and "Go fuck yourself, asshole!" Ivan stood up from the table and motioned for calm. Elaine caught his eye. He sat down again "Go ahead, Elaine," he said.

"You've totally twisted the facts into the opposite of what's going on," she said, making an effort to restrain her anger. "The UN Declaration means virtually the opposite of what you've just said, and the fact that Canada signs it and then lies about what it means simply proves what we already knew, that you can't ever trust the Canadian Government, not that its approval of a project means that Indigenous Peoples support it. How much clearer can we be? We're saying, 'No'. What part of 'no' don't you people understand?

"And what's with this 'legally recognised land' baloney? We know where our ancestral lands are. We know what lands we agreed to share by treaty and what rights we retained over them. We haven't been given any rights by some settler Government. Our rights were here before any of you guys sailed across from Europe. Our lands are where we say they are, not where the Government says they are.

"As for information, we have the right to inform ourselves from whatever sources we choose, and we absolutely refuse a process controlled by the Government and its corporate allies. You've asked us so many times what we think, we feel like we're being consulted to death. We've said, 'no'. We mean, 'no'. We'll go on saying, 'no'. There's nothing more to be gained by consultation and discussion. Our answer's, 'no'."

Tony Conwell, whose insensitivity was of a truly heroic level, maintained his cheerful and self-confident smile. He began to stand up, as if to address the crowd, but Chief

Superintendent Hawrylak grasped his shoulder and exerted firm downward pressure. "I think anything further may be counter-productive," he said in a low voice, and Conwell sat down.

There was an uneasy pause as Ivan consulted Elaine, and then he stood up again and addressed the crowd.

"I want to thank Mr Conwell for his courtesy in coming to speak with us today," he said, "and I regret that we can't send him on his way with the result that he hoped for. Elaine and I have decided we want to do two things before Mr Conwell leaves us. The first is to restate our position with regard to the mine, the nuclear plant and the tar sands expansion. I'd ask our non-Native friends to remain silent, and only the hundred or so local Native people present to answer the three questions I'm going to put to you now. Question one is, do you agree to a uranium mine being built on land on which we retain rights under the treaty our ancestors signed with the Crown in right of Canada?"

"No!" shouted a hundred voices.

"Do you agree to the construction of a nuclear power plant on our treaty lands?"

"No!"

"And do you approve of the expansion of the tar sands development?"

"No!"

"I think it would be difficult to be any clearer than we have been," concluded Ivan. "But now, to show that our opposition to these projects isn't anything personal, and that we don't hate the people involved, just what they're doing, I'd ask the hand drumming group to play us a round dance, and I invite Mr Conwell, Chief Superintendent Hawrylak and their colleagues to join us in a dance of friendship. Let's go outside and dance between the building and the bridge."

Now it was Tony Conwell's turn to be led, and he followed Ivan and Elaine outside, a cheery if slightly bemused smile fixed to his face. Kerry, leaving her fiancé's side, pushed through the blockaders until she was next to Tony Conwell.

"Hello, Tony," she said again, and Conwell, hemmed in by the press of the crowd, half turned his head towards her. "Oh, hi!" he said.

"I see you haven't changed," she said.

"Oh, thanks!" he replied. "Yes, I suppose I weather pretty well. I still feel about twenty, to be honest."

"Honest?" she queried. "That's what I'm talking about. You still seem incapable of honesty."

Conwell, assuming for a moment that the woman must be one of the many one-nighters that he had humped and dumped, said, "Look, I'm really sorry if there was any misunderstanding between us. You know I never promised a commitment, and I was under the impression that we were singing from the same hymn sheet on that one."

The moving tide came to a stop and Elaine called out, asking people to press themselves back to form a circle. Kerry and Conwell stood side by side and began shuffling backwards as a space opened up in the middle of the crowd.

"You don't even remember me, do you?" asked Kerry.

"Of course I do!" replied Tony Conwell, looking sideways at her. "How could I forget a beautiful face like yours? Just remind me when it was we first met. Things get hazy sometimes now I'm so busy."

"We met when we were singing from the same hymn sheet every day."

"You've lost me."

"At the seminary."

Conwell turned and looked her full in the face. "Oh God! Was it you whose husband…"

"No, Tony, I was one of the students. Kerry. Kerry Ahern."

Conwell looked thunderstruck. "Well, how the hell did you get through the medical? They certainly weren't ordaining women when I was a student. I mean, not knowingly. But then I suppose you never got ordained, or you wouldn't be here."

"No, I was asked to leave after sheltering your girlfriend in my room. Don't you remember?"

"No, no, that was a bloke! What was his name, now?"

"Kerry. Kerry Ahern."

"Yes. Yes, that's right. Well, who the hell are you, then? Come to think of it, he looked a lot like you. Are you his sister?"

Kerry decided not to persist in her attempts at self-revelation. She was wasting her time.

"Yes. Yes, that's right," she said.

"But you just said your name was Kerry as well!"

"No. Kiera."

"And what brings you out to this neck of the woods, then, Kiera?"

"Oh, it's a long story. I'm doing my bit to protect the environment."

"Yes, same here," Conwell assured her. "We can make a massive reduction in greenhouse gas emissions once we get this mine and the nuclear plant up and running." His smile returned. "Well, Kiera, we must get together some time and talk about the old days. Here's my card." He reached into the inside pocket of his slick suit and pulled out his business card, contriving to brush Kerry's left breast with his hand as he passed it over, which left Kerry feeling mildly nauseous. "We must certainly get together."

"I'm on the other side," Kerry reminded him.

Conwell laughed. "Oh, we're all on the same side!" he exclaimed. "Remember, when this project goes ahead it'll be a win-win for all of us."

The circle was complete, though a large number of blockaders were still milling about outside it. Elaine, speaking at the top of her voice, asked everyone to hold hands and keep an eye on the Native dancers present if they did not know how a friendship dance worked. She called to the drummers to begin, and a line of young Native men standing outside the circle began to beat a lively rhythm and to sing a chant which sounded very different to Kerry from those she was used to from the Whispering River Reservation. Elaine led off, dancing sideways with a simple step that even confirmed non-dancers could follow. Kerry could not see Elaine from where she was standing, but followed the dance steps of the people opposite her in the circle. She thought the dance was just like walking sideways with a little bounce in the step. She stepped firmly with her left foot and let the right foot land more daintily.

She wondered where Francis was, and whether he had made himself known to Tony Conwell. She could not see him in the circle of dancers. Elaine was holding hands with Ivan on her left and Chief Superintendent Hawrylak on her right; he had willingly joined the circle while his subalterns had remained outside, despite repeated invitations to join in. They stood looking shifty and embarrassed. Chief Superintendent Hawrylak was holding hands with an elderly Cree woman from Ivan's village. To her right was Tony Conwell, then Kerry, then several more local people before Will and Milton.

As the circle of dancers moved round, Elaine broke off from Ivan and began leading the dancers inside the existing circle, spiralling gently in towards the centre point. This enabled more people to join what was now becoming the outer circle, and as Elaine continued to lead the dance round and round inside the circling dancers, more and more people joined the outside end while Elaine was dancing in an ever tightening spiral. After some minutes, Elaine, the Chief Superintendent, the elderly woman from Ivan's village, Tony Conwell and Kerry were dancing round more or less face to face in a tight knot in the middle of the tightening spiral, and Kerry feared that the pressure of the other dancers moving inwards from outside would crush them. But Elaine, smiling broadly, called out loudly, and stopped moving, and gradually the whole dance ground to a halt and everybody was laughing and breaking away and going to find places to sit down.

Kerry immediately went to find Will, and they embraced warmly. She felt a strong need to be close to him again after her unpleasant encounter with Tony Conwell. She saw Conwell walking back towards his Range Rover, and noticed that Francis was following him. The two of them reached the vehicle at the same time, and Conwell turned to face his former colleague. They conversed for a few minutes, while Kerry explained Conwell's history to Will.

"It's at times like these that I'm tempted to regret my commitment to non-violence," said Will.

"Can I go and stick his head up his ass and make him walk around like a pretzel?" asked Milton.

"I thought you'd been converted," replied Will.

"I could be backsliding," answered Milton.

"Well, better leave it for now. It would set an unhelpful precedent."

They watched as Conwell shook Francis' hand and turned towards his vehicle. Then Francis walked back towards the main building, while the police and company men climbed inside their four by fours and headed off across the clearcut. Kerry left Will's side and hurried over to speak to Francis.

"Did he remember you?" she asked.

"Oh yes," said Francis. "And he was as patronising as he ever was."

"What did you say to him?"

"I tried to be polite, but I probably wound him up anyway. I told him his company should get out, and that our people here would never give up the struggle, and he gave me a whole load of platitudes about win-win scenarios and such like old tripe, and I told him he never did know the difference between truth and falsehood and that I was available any time he felt the need to go to confession. He told me that at least he'd stopped believing all that religious bollocks, and that he wasn't surprised to see a priest mixed up in this sorry business, because religion's all about emotion, and religious people can't understand science and technology and need to get out of the way so the world can be run by people who know what they're talking about."

"Like him?"

"I assume so."

"My goodness. If Tony Conwell counts as one of the people who know what they're talking about, there's no hope left."

"Well, there isn't any hope left for that kind of world, is there? That's why we're working for one run along the lines of Indigenous wisdom, isn't it? Given a choice between the world of Ivan Silver and the world of Tony Conwell, there isn't a choice, really, is there? It's a choice between collective sustainability and collective suicide."

Nine: Kerry witnesses Will's courageous self-sacrifice

That evening, Kerry did not attend the briefing, because Will was to represent their whole section of the camp. He returned to their encampment, just after the sun had set and the temperature was beginning to drop towards freezing.

"Ivan's worried about those Warriors of Mother Earth guys," he said. "They've stopped participating in discussions, they didn't attend briefings the last couple of days, they've voiced opposition to the involvement of non-Indigenous people in the blockade, they've questioned the Elders' line on non-violence, and yet they don't seem to want to leave. He's told them that if they don't agree with the way the Elders are running things, they don't have to stay, but they don't take the hint. He's asked me to talk to them. I said I'd do it in the morning."

At the morning's briefing, Ivan explained that the eviction operation was expected to begin at noon, as soon as the twenty-four hour deadline expired. That would give the RCMP plenty of hours of daylight to complete the operation. Those who had opted to lock themselves on to trees or occupy the tree houses should be in position half an hour in advance.

Ivan, the other Elders and Elaine would occupy the mound behind the main building and would spend the morning in prayer. They would eat shortly before noon and return to the mound to remain in prayer during the eviction operation. Those responsible for good order in each section of the camp would supervise activities in their areas and campers were asked to respect their requests. Ivan reminded everyone that nobody had the power or the inclination to force anybody to do anything, but that the Elders would like everyone to remain respectful of the principles on which the blockade had been established and respectful of one another. If anyone was hurt, a report should be made to the section supervisor if he or she were still at liberty, or to the Elders if not, but in the latter stages of the eviction there may well be nobody other than people's immediate neighbours to report to.

Elaine introduced two young Cree women from the Aboriginal Ecological Coalition, Darla Vendredi and Amy Desjarlais, who would be filming the eviction. They would be broadcasting live to the Internet, so that people all over the world could see how the Canadian State treated Indigenous people defending their rights. Campers were asked not to be disturbed or distracted by their filming, but if they saw anyone else filming, they would probably be from the police.

Will visited the Warriors' encampment. He told Kerry that they were courteous to him as a fellow Native warrior, and they assured him they did not intend to do anything to disrupt what the Elders were planning to do, but that they were fundamentally opposed to the presence of non-Indigenous people on Indigenous land and had withdrawn to their own camp when the new blockaders began arriving, as this had tipped the demographic balance. They said that there was now a majority of white people in the camp, and they could no longer co-operate. Will asked them what they intended to do, and they told him that, like everyone else, they would do what they could to resist removal. Will asked them if they were committed to non-violence, and they told him frankly that they were not, but that they respected the Elders and their wishes in the matter. Will urged them to follow those wishes. The Warriors pointed out that they had been accompanying the Elders for some weeks now, whereas Will had only just arrived. So, although they wished him no ill, they did not believe he had the right to urge them to do or not do anything. Will left, hoping that the Warriors' respect for the Elders would prove stronger than their own beliefs about strategy.

Back at their encampment, Kerry and Will and their colleagues discussed what each was going to do. Hank and Marlon were going to be occupying one of the tree houses near the creek. But all the others were just going to remain in their tents, until such time as the police physically removed them. They would attempt, by going limp, to make removal difficult, but they would not struggle.

Around eleven thirty, the two Vancouver eco-activists gathered their equipment together, including a supply of food and drink, and went off to ascend into the trees. Kerry noted that in their small group, it was the two cross-dressers who proved the most daring on this occasion. Perhaps this was not surprising. One had to be brave to dare to wear clothing that excited the strong irrational disapproval of so many others.

Will walked round his section, to check that things were well. He returned, and suggested that they all eat without delay, in case the siege proved to be protracted. They all ate the lunches they had prepared and drank from their flasks of coffee.

Noon came and went. The afternoon wore on. The police were nowhere to be seen. The Elders and the AEC had clearly been mistaken.

Around six o'clock, word was sent out by the Elders that people should come section by section to the main building and eat some supper, starting with those furthest from the building. They were no longer sure what the RCMP had in mind, but they thought it likely that they were waiting until dawn, to give themselves a full day to undertake the task. It was now too late in the day for them to begin. Everyone should rest well overnight but be ready at first light.

Will and Kerry did not make love that night. They were distracted and on edge. But they fell asleep embracing and spent the night entwined with one another.

Well before dawn, Kerry was awoken by shouts. She was suddenly wide awake, completely alert, her heart thumping. She could see nothing in the utter darkness, but she immediately knew Will was awake because he asked her if she was.

"Where did it come from?" she asked.

"Couldn't tell," replied Will. "As soon as I was awake enough to judge where it came from, it stopped."

But then there were more shouts, not far away from them, just to the North, further into the woods. Will slipped out of his sleeping bag and unzipped the tent. A draft of shockingly cold night air flowed in and Kerry shivered. Milton's voice came from close by. "You awake, Will?"

"Yeah. What's going on?"

"Can't tell. I only just got out of my tent. Some commotion off in the trees there. Can't tell whether it's campers or not."

"Maybe the police came early."

"Guess so."

Will stepped out of the tent, reached back in for his sweater and jacket, and quickly dressed himself. Kerry pulled her clothes on and emerged from the tent. The others were all now also awake and beginning to leave their tents.

Without warning, a gunshot rang out from the direction of the Warriors' camp.

"Oh, Jeez!" exclaimed Will. "Dang! They've got a gun! I'd better try and stop 'em shooting."

"I'll come with you," said Milton.

"Don't! It'd be like a red rag to a bull."

"Be careful!" urged Kerry, unnecessarily.

In what little starlight filtered through the trees, Will hurried round the end of the timber fence and started to run down the slope towards the Warriors' encampment. Suddenly, a beam of dazzling light shining from the woods to the north of the camp stabbed through the darkness and began dancing among the trees towards the Warriors' tents. It briefly illuminated Will's running form and then he was in darkness again. Immediately, a volley of shots was fired from the direction of the spotlight, followed by complete silence.

Kerry thought her heart would burst her ribcage. She began to run towards the Warriors' camp, trying to avoid the spotlight. The light danced around as if its source were itself in motion, and now Kerry could hear shouts again, and heavy footfalls, and the breaking of small fallen branches as men ran. The light caught her just as it picked out the fallen body, and rested on it as Kerry sank to her knees beside it.

Will lay motionless on his back by a tree. Blood flowed freely from the gunshot wound in his side and from a jagged wound across his forehead where he had hit the tree in falling, turning as he fell. "Will!" she said. She lay her left hand on his head, touched his chest with her right, then moved her left hand under his head and went to feel his pulse with her right. She felt nothing.

"Move away from the body!" demanded Inspector Kowalchuk, pointing his handgun at Kerry's head. She looked up at him. Two other officers joined him, then three more, then the one carrying the spotlight, which he trained on Will's body. Behind them came Milton. One of the officers swung round and trained his gun on him. "I'm unarmed," said Milton, raising his hands.

"Move away from the body!" Inspector Kowalchuk said again. Kerry stood up slowly and took a pace back. One of the other officers moved around the body and took hold of her arm roughly. Inspector Kowalchuk stooped down, felt Will's pulse, put his ear to his chest, felt for breath. He stood up. "Dead," he said, flatly. Then, to his officers, he said, "Find his weapon."

"He was unarmed," said Kerry.

"A shot was fired and he was clearly seen running," said Inspector Kowalchuk.

"He was running down to the tipis there to stop the guys there from firing," said Milton.

Inspector Kowalchuk sneered. "Find his weapon," he said again, and three of his accomplices began poking around on the forest floor back towards Will and Kerry's tent while the other two guarded Kerry and Milton.

There was now a great deal of light and commotion as RCMP officers swept through the camp from the North, floodlighting the whole area, moving campers from their tents and arresting any who resisted, pushing everyone down towards the officers who were now gathering across the creek in the clearcut.

Up the slope from the Warriors' camp came half a dozen officers, led by Chief Superintendent Hawrylak, carrying a rifle. "You can call your men off, Kowalchuk," he said. "Here's your weapon. I arrested the guy a couple of seconds after he fired."

Kowalchuk replied angrily, "Sir, there could be any number of weapons in this camp. I advise maximum caution. You can see they've already killed one of their own!"

Chief Superintendent Hawrylak regarded Kowalchuk with contempt.

"I already had his gun before you guys fired your volley. And I guess forensics will find an RCMP issue bullet."

Kowalchuk remained silent.

Chief Superintendent Hawrylak turned to Kerry. "Who are you, Ma'am?"

"Kerry Ahern," replied Kerry.

"And your relationship to the deceased?"

"I'm his fiancée."

"I'm sorry, Ma'am. And the deceased?"

Kerry could not speak now for her tears. Milton answered.

"Wilhelm Many Paint Horses, former Marine, peace activist, member of the North American Aboriginal Ecological Coalition, unarmed citizen of the United States of America."

"Shit," said Inspector Kowalchuk.

Under Hawrylak's command, the rest of the eviction was conducted almost apologetically. On hearing the news of Will's death a few minutes after it had happened, the Elders and Elaine called for an orderly abandonment of the camp, to avoid any further casualties. Those who had been detained, other than the Warrior arrested for firearms offences, were released without charge later that morning. The others were allowed to make their way, without harassment, to the Deep Lake Reserve's community hall and left to their own devices. A large detachment of officers remained at the blockade camp to prevent re-occupation, while contractors dismantled the dining hall, the aerial walkways and the other structures.

Darla Vendredi's footage of the killing, broadcast live to the worldwide web, with the RCMP officers' subsequent conversation clearly audible, thanks to Darla's state of the art video equipment, ensured maximum negative publicity for the Canadian authorities.

There were forensic and judicial procedures to be completed before Will's body could be released to his family and returned to the United States for burial. The day after the eviction, Chief Superintendent Hawrylak allowed Kerry and Milton to accompany the body, which was in the custody of the police, to the forensic pathology laboratory in the city of Prince Edward, some hundred kilometres away to the South. Billie, as his next of kin, was notified immediately and brought by air to Prince Edward at RCMP expense the following day. She left Missy with Vera Shoots Straight.

Billie formally identified the body. The three of them spent a dismal night in a local motel. Kerry found she could not stop crying. The others were too distressed themselves to be much comfort to her. The next day, for want of any practical reason to remain in Prince Edward while the autopsy was carried out, Kerry and Milton took Billie with them to Deep Lake.

Many of the blockaders had already left. Elaine was staying with her family there on the Reserve and helping organise the follow-up to the blockade with the Elders and with Darla and Amy from the AEC.

The Vancouver group had decided to wait until Kerry and Milton returned. They were staying at Francis's house, next door to the community hall. When Kerry and Milton arrived with Billie, Francis offered them hospitality as well.

Kerry learnt that, from the authorities' perspective, the eviction had been a disaster. Will's death had provoked strong and immediate diplomatic intervention from Washington. A mass demonstration in Ottawa had panicked many more wavering MPs into opposing the planned uranium mine and nuclear power station. Demonstrations outside Canadian Embassies and High Commissions in several other countries had deepened the Federal Government's embarrassment.

The next day, Prime Minister Bugler lost a confidence vote in the House of Commons, and resigned. North Atlantic Mining's share price on the London Stock Exchange dropped fifteen percent in twenty-four hours as a result. The company's London offices were picketed, and a group of young activists locked on to the main doors, preventing anyone from entering or leaving the building except through the fire exit at the back. It was all on the breakfast time news.

Later that day, Darla read online that major institutional investors had made discreet contact with North Atlantic's Chair and Chief Executive. These investors' offices were also being targeted by protesters, and critical letters had been published in British newspapers.

By the evening, the company had announced that it was pulling out of the Deep Lake uranium project, because its painstaking Environmental and Social Impact Assessment procedure had revealed what had not been clear before, that the project lacked a clear 'social licence to operate'.

Darla learnt from AEC colleagues that both Tony Conwell and Inspector Kowalchuk had lost their jobs.

Before any more activists left, it was decided to hold a memorial service. Chief Superintendent Hawrylak gave them his permission to return to the blockade site to do so.

A great number of people set out from the Reserve, not only the couple of dozen remaining blockaders but the majority of the community as well, who wanted to honour the brave Indigenous warrior who had given his life in solidarity with their struggle.

Francis Neale ascended the prayer mound at the blockade site, together with Ivan and Elaine, and the people gathered round, covering the mound and surrounding it.

Ivan and Elaine spoke of Will's dedication, his purity of spirit and his bravery, and invited others to share memories of him.

Milton spoke once more about how Will had saved his life when they were on active service in Cortesia, and of his bitter regret that he had not been able to save his friend's life in return.

Kerry tried to speak about Will's love for her and hers for him, but found herself unable to do so, for the strength of emotion that overwhelmed her.

Elaine lit a braid of sweetgrass and passed through the congregation so that all could smudge themselves.

Then Francis, at the request of the Deep Lake Elders, celebrated a Requiem Mass there on the hill. And when it was over, Ivan offered the sacred pipe, so that all who wished to smoke in honour of their departed friend could do so.

Milton had to leave the next day to return to his family, and Leif and Zoe, Hank and Marlon left the day after. Kerry deeply regretted each departure, undertaking to keep in touch and to make sure that they all met again some time. But it was another two weeks before Will's body was released. Billie remained at Francis' house with Kerry. Both were able to accompany the body on its flight back to the United States, accompanied by Chief Superintendent Hawrylak.

On the way to the airport at Prince Edward, the news on Hawrylak's radio informed them that the Supreme Court had given judgement in the case of First Nations of Athabasca versus Crown in Right of Canada and Crown in Right of Athabasca. Both the Provincial and Federal Governments had violated their treaty obligations to the First Nations of Athabasca. The uranium mining project was dead.

EAST

Kerry ascends into heaven

Both Billie and Vera urged Kerry to stay – at least for a while. She had, after all, renewed permission to remain in the United States for three months.

Hannah was distraught. The death of Kerry's beloved refreshed the guilt that Hannah felt for having provided the motive for her friend's ill-judged gender reassignment operation. Again and again, Kerry urged her not to blame herself, but Hannah found it desperately difficult not to do so.

Perhaps it was this more than anything else that led Kerry to conclude, after Will's desolating burial on the hill behind Grandpa Jimmy's house, that a swift return to England was the least of evils. In any case, it was over three years since she had been in her homeland. Whatever was to happen in the future, she should re-establish a connection with her past.

It was not until she reached her Aunty Liza's old house in Westhampton, and telephoned her beloved spiritual guide, Father Patrick, that she learned that he was gravely ill. He was now in St Luke's hospice in nearby West Wessex, south west of the seminary, near the foot of the Tor.

Kerry was uneasy in Westhampton, where she had spent her teenage years, and where so many people would remember her as him. She did not wish to court mockery and disapproval. She was not at all sure where she should go. But before she did anything else, she would go to visit Father Patrick.

The bus dropped her at the entrance to the drive leading down to the hospice. She walked down between hedges of beech and bay and asked for him at reception.

Father Patrick was asleep in his bed when she went into his room. His face looked pale and drawn and his lips were open. He was dribbling on the pillow in his sleep. Kerry sat in the armchair by his head and waited for him to wake.

More than an hour went by before he opened his eyes, exhaling loudly as he did so.

"Father Patrick?" said Kerry, gently. He turned his head towards her. A beatific smile lit up his face.

"My goodness me!" he said, weakly. "It's Kerry Ahern!" He observed her for a few moments, then said, "You know, you make a very good-looking young woman."

Kerry blushed. "Thank you, Father," she said. "Thank you for not condemning me."

"What on earth would I do that for?" he replied. "It's not for me to judge you."

Tears filled Kerry's eyes. "Thank you, Father," she said. "Thank you for being understanding."

"Oh, say no more about it," said Father Patrick. "Now, you'd better tell me your news. What have you been getting up to over in America?"

"First, you'd better tell me what you're doing here, Father," replied Kerry.

"Oh, well, it's that blessed cancer, I'm afraid. Did I tell you about that? A rather rare one, apparently, in the fatty tissue round my stomach. They took almost all of it out a few years ago, I think probably the year you were off at the seminary, but they couldn't get it all. It slowly grew back, and now there's nothing much more they can do."

"You never told me about that!" said Kerry, accusingly.

"Well, there's no need to go on about these things," said Father Patrick. "You couldn't have done anything, anyway."

"I wish I'd known!"

"Well, I was alright until a few months ago, then I started feeling a bit poorly, you know, until I couldn't really work any more because it was as much as I could do to get out of bed. The Archbishop brought in a younger priest to take over the work for me and I had a nurse come in twice a day to help sort me out, but a few weeks ago it was all getting a bit too much for everyone, so I came in here. I thought Father Kevin had sent you a letter about it in America, but perhaps he forgot, or perhaps it never reached you."

"Oh, Father, I'm sorry. I was in Canada for a few weeks before I came back, and I never got the letter."

"Never mind," said Father Patrick. "Here you are now."

They were silent for a while. Then Father Patrick said, "Before I drop off again, which I'm afraid I do with disturbing frequency, you'd better tell me about your adventures in America."

"Oh, well, I don't want to tire you, Father."

"If I start getting tired, I'll either nod off or I'll tell you. Either way, you'll get the message."

So Kerry began, starting with the most recent events, and told him, with tears, about the death of her beloved.

Father Patrick was deeply moved. He reached out from his bed and Kerry took hold of his hand. It felt thin and weakened, but Father Patrick squeezed her hand gently. "I'm so sorry for your grief," he said. "And so soon after you'd found love, at last."

They sat in silence again.

After a while, Kerry said, "I don't want to lose you, Father. It would be too much."

"Oh, now, don't be thinking like that," said Father Patrick. "I'm still here today, and who knows how long I'll carry on? There's life in me yet. But nobody lives for ever, that's for sure. You're stronger than you think you are, you know. And you're never alone, you know that. We're all held in the loving arms of Christ. However catastrophic your loss, take hope in that."

Kerry squeezed his hand. "I don't want to tire you, Father. Do you mind if I come to visit again soon?"

"You come whenever you like," said Father Patrick.

"Do you get many visitors?"

"More than my fair share, I'd say. A number of parishioners have come down from London, and various clergy friends, and my niece comes every other day, all the way from Bristol."

"Well, I'm going to go now, Father, but I'll be back soon."

"It'd be lovely to see you, whenever you're free to come."

Kerry left the hospice feeling distraught. Her family in England were all dead. Her lover had been killed. Her best friends were all in the Americas. Her greatest guide and confidant was dying. She desperately needed some human warmth. She did not feel able to face her old friends Chris and Brett, and so, returning to her aunt's house, she phoned the only other person she felt she had left in England – Father Donald Black.

Donald was out, but she felt some comfort in hearing his voice on his voicemail. She left a message and asked him to call her back as soon as he could.

Then she began to concentrate on practicalities to take her mind off the sadness of bereavement. She would sell her aunt's house. She would rent a flat in London once again, but in some area where nobody knew her. She still had money saved from the sale of her mother's house, but she would seek out translation work again while considering what she really wanted to do.

Then she decided against that. She no longer wanted to spend her time putting other people's thoughts into different languages, because she now had too many thoughts of her own. Perhaps she could study anthropology. Or train to be a counsellor — something that involved understanding people. She wanted to do something that used her heart, that drew forth from her the love that she felt for other human beings. Perhaps she could become a Samaritan. Or even a nun.

She realised she also wanted to do something to challenge the injustice of the world. She had got used to that, spending time with Peter in Cortesia and Will in North America. Life would seem rather peculiar and flat if she were not doing something subversive.

She would need to find other people who had gone through gender reassignment, as she had, because life was going to be a lot harder than she had thought it would be. Now she was back where she started again, where everyone who knew her had known her as a him, and where not everyone would be as understanding as those she had told so far.

More than that, she knew she would need to find other Christians, other Catholics, who were in her position, because her spiritual roots were so important to her. She would need to find a church where she could be known and accepted for who she was. She wanted desperately to go to church now, even just to sit in one, as she had on that bleak day back in Boston, but she felt too embarrassed to go into the Catholic church in Westhampton, in case she were recognised, and rejected.

She wondered whether it might be possible to set up a Christian Gender-queer Eco-activist collective, but feared she might find it rather difficult to find members.

She had to do something; but what?

Donald Black phoned back the next day. He was teaching at the seminary that afternoon but could come by on his way back home.

And so it was, that the priest who had first enabled Kerry to find excitement in theology with his praise for the path of dark unknowing, helped her through the emotional desolation of her current dark night of the soul. He took her out to supper and listened to a good two hours of virtually uninterrupted monologue, making the odd comment, an affirmation here, a dry joke there, a question for clarification once in a while, until Kerry felt stirring in the depths of her being that most valuable of motivators, hope, and knew that, although she did not yet know what to hope for, she would know soon, and would have the strength to do all that needed to be done, and would find purpose and happiness again.

She also knew that she would find in herself the courage to face those who had known her as a man, and that if they rejected her for what she had become, she would rise above their prejudice and judgement and be the stronger for it.

Over the next two weeks, she made a trip to London to find accommodation. She met up several more times with Donald Black. She hired a lock-up for the few possessions that she cared for and made arrangements with the estate agent to take care of her aunt's house while it was on the market, because she was going away again.

Then she booked into a bed and breakfast in the small town by the Tor, and determined to remain there for as long as Father Patrick was in the hospice.

It was late in the afternoon of the 19th of June, when Kerry walked up from the town to the hospice. Father Patrick had certainly deteriorated in the two weeks since she had last seen him. His stomach was more bloated, his face and arms much thinner, his skin yellowed and hanging off him in loose folds. The air in his small, stuffy room, baking in the summer heat but still too chilly for him, had begun to smell of decay, catching in Kerry's throat as she breathed it.

Father Patrick was asleep, but there was a woman sitting with him, older than Kerry, perhaps in her late forties, Kerry thought. She stood up when Kerry entered, and introduced herself as Deirdre, Father Patrick's niece.

"I'm Kerry," replied Kerry.

"Oh, my uncle's told me a lot about you," said Deirdre. "He thinks the world of you. He says you combine gentleness with courage, and he feels great respect for that," she said.

"Well, I don't know about that," replied Kerry.

"He's going downhill, you know," said Deirdre. "I've been staying with him day and night the past week. Every time I go to get a cup of tea, or go to the loo, I wonder whether he'll be alive when I get back."

"You must be very tired," observed Kerry.

"I *am* rather," agreed Deirdre.

"Well, I'm happy to stay with him tonight, if you'd like a break."

"Oh, that would be ever so kind of you," said Deirdre, her eyes filling with tears. "I'd be so grateful to you. I don't want to leave him, but I could *so* do with a good sleep tonight. I don't want him to die alone, you see. I want to be with him if I can, but if I can't, I want someone to be with him who he feels close to. If you could do just this one night, it would give me the strength to carry on for another week — though I doubt he's got a week now, to be honest."

"I'll happily do that," said Kerry.

"He's sleeping most of the time now," said Deirdre. "It's the morphine. They've kept increasing the dose because of the pain, and it makes him very sleepy. But then he'll suddenly wake up and be quite coherent for a while before he drifts off again. When he's wide awake, he's still as sharp as ever."

"Well, feel free to go whenever you want to," said Kerry. "I'll make myself comfortable in here."

"Why don't you go and get yourself something to eat first, and I'll stay with him while you do that, and then I'll go. I'd feel happier that way."

"Alright," agreed Kerry. So she made her way back out of the hospice and ate an early supper at the nearby pub, returning to the hospice before seven.

Father Patrick was awake, and eating a light supper with the help of a nurse. His face lit up when Kerry walked in.

"God bless you, my dear child!" he greeted her, and held out his hand to her. She took it and gave it a gentle squeeze. It felt so thin, it made her want to cry.

"Well, I'll be going now, then," said Deirdre. "I've told uncle Patrick and nurse Flaherty here that you're going to stay tonight, and that's fine with them, isn't it, uncle?"

"Oh, it is, it is," said Father Patrick, and the nurse said, "You let us know at the nurses' station if you need anything. In any case, we'll be in from time to time to check on things in here."

"I normally pull the two armchairs together and put the little table in between them so I can stretch my legs out and put my feet up, and nurse Flaherty's given us some blankets to cover up with."

"That's fine," said Kerry. "I'll be quite comfortable."

"Have you had enough to eat?" nurse Flaherty asked Father Patrick.

"Oh, more than enough, thank you," he replied. "I haven't got much of an appetite these days."

"Well, I'll leave you now, then, Father," said the nurse, and she left with Deirdre, taking Father Patrick's supper tray with her.

"Would you mind saying Evening Prayer for me?" asked Father Patrick. "I do like to say it but I can't hold my breviary any more, and I can't see straight to read it, either."

"I'll read it for you, then," said Kerry, and she picked up Father Patrick's battered, well-thumbed prayer book from the bedside table, found the correct day with the help of his instructions, and began. It took her back to her days at the seminary. She almost felt as if Peter, Mario and Francis were in the room with them. When she finished, she looked to Father Patrick to give a blessing, but he had fallen asleep. She closed the book and put it back on the table.

She sat quietly, listening to the ticking of the bedside clock and the distant sound of music from a radio in the common room.

After an hour or so, Father Patrick stirred, and opened his eyes.

"Oh, goodness! I think I nodded off again."

"Never mind," said Kerry. "You must have needed the sleep."

He fell silent, and after a minute or two, Kerry saw that he had fallen asleep again.

Kerry sat quietly again, her mind at rest, as the long summer evening gradually faded into darkness. She began to drift in and out of sleep.

Suddenly, Father Patrick snorted, moved in his bed and said, "Oh! Am I awake?"

Kerry was immediately wide awake herself.

"Yes, yes, you're awake, Father," she said, reaching out to touch the old priest's shoulder in the dark.

"Oh, is that Kerry?"

"Yes, it's me, Father."

"Oh, good. I didn't know where I was for a moment there."

"Are you alright, Father?"

"Yes, I'm fine. I just had a most beautiful dream."

"Oh? What was it about?"

"Turn on the little light in the corner and I'll tell you about it."

Kerry switched on the bedside light and they both screwed up their eyes, which had grown accustomed to the darkness.

"I was in a wood. I always loved walking in the woods, when I could, on my days off. Where I grew up in Ireland, there were very few woodlands, and that's what I most loved when I came over here, especially in the spring when they were full of bluebells. I think there's nothing more beautiful than that, when all the air is full of their lovely scent.

"Anyway, there I was in this wood, and I sort of recognised it as a wood I used to walk in when I was in my first parish, down in Sussex, because I was sitting with my back to an old hornbeam that grew close to a little stream by a clearing where I once saw fox cubs playing. It was still dark, just before dawn. I was sitting there and the sound of the stream grew louder and louder, and the water was rising, and it was all full of horrible yellow foam, like you see where they've put too much fertiliser on the fields and it washes off and ends up in the streams. The water kept rising and rising, and I stood up to move away from the stream, but all of a sudden, the water was up to my knees, then my waist, then my neck, and I was being washed away down stream along with great pieces of wood and clumps of leaf mould and dead squirrels, and I couldn't see where I was going or how wide the stream had become, and I felt terrified."

"I thought you said it was a beautiful dream, Father," said Kerry.

"Oh, it was in the end, but we're coming to that," said Father Patrick. "Eventually, the current slowed and I was left like a piece of old driftwood at the mouth of a great river, on a beach of warm golden sand at the edge of a sparkling sea, calm and flat as glass. The sun had come up. I stood up and looked along the shore, and there, by the edge of the sea, was a grand piano, and sitting at the piano was my beloved father. He was a lovely, kind, gentle man, and I always wanted to be like him. He was a wonderful pianist and he taught me to play when I was a child, but I never carried on with it, which I regret.

"Anyway, I walked towards him and as I got closer I heard he was playing Beethoven's *Moonlight Sonata*, which I've always liked very much indeed. He looked up from the keyboard and smiled at me."

Father Patrick fell silent for a while.

"I'm having a bit of trouble getting my breath," he said at length.

"Perhaps you should rest, Father," suggested Kerry, her own eyes heavy with sleep.

"No, not yet," replied Father Patrick. "I would so like to tell you this dream, because it was so vivid, and I rather think that if I don't tell someone now, I'll forget it."

After a few minutes, he began again.

"Behind my father, this beach curved out towards a great headland which was really an enormous mountain, rearing straight up from the sea. There was a kind of causeway made up of sand and stones leading out from the beach. My father carried on playing, and I walked past him towards the headland. Then I saw there were lots of other people walking in the same direction, but I couldn't see where they'd come from."

Father Patrick's voice trailed off again, and Kerry, weary with the hour and the effort of listening to Father Patrick's thin, quiet voice, began to drift off again into unconsciousness.

Kerry could see Father Patrick at the foot of the mountain path which began at the far end of the causeway. Running to catch up with him, she woke suddenly.

"We started to climb up this path," Father Patrick was saying, "and as we climbed, the piano music disappeared behind us, swallowed up by distance and the sound of wind and birdcalls. The air was warm and the sky shone like summer in the Mediterranean."

He paused. The bedside clock ticked monotonously, and Kerry's eyelids grew heavy.

They climbed all morning with neither water nor weariness. At midday, they reached a plateau, like a saucer surrounded by crags and ridges, so they could no longer see the sea. Behind them, the path had led them through a narrow gully so they could no longer see the mainland either. It was clear to Kerry that the mountain was an extinct volcano, and they were in its crater.

They walked straight across this crater, and as they walked, the air began to vibrate with drumbeats like the heartbeat after vigorous exercise. Then a song began, and Kerry recognised the voice of Will's uncle Ben. It was his drum group playing a sundance song. She could see no source for the music, but it seemed to come from the peaks on the far side of the crater, towards which they began to climb.

It was hot climbing in the afternoon sun with no water. At times she lost the sound of drumbeats, but then it returned, as the freshening late afternoon breeze brought it back to her. The path began to level out as they passed above the tops of the surrounding crags and ridges, and she could see the sparkling ocean again.

They entered a stand of young birches, their leaves whispering in the wind. She lost the sound of drumbeats. Then, as they emerged on the other side of the small birch wood, she could see the final, steep ascent to what must be the summit, sharp against the blue sky, and now she could hear music again, coming from just beyond the peak, and now it was not drumbeats, but the stomping of the wooden soles of a great troupe of flamenco dancers. All at once, the earth shivered, and her heart too, with the cascade of a *rasgueado* of unimaginable wistfulness, and it was repeated, and then another song began, accompanied by castanets and clapping and wooden-soled dancing and the passionate playing of the guitarist, and she awoke once again.

"And as I reached the summit," Father Patrick was saying, "I saw the sun sinking over the purple sea, and the evening breeze took away the music, and I could hear nothing but a sound like gentle laughter in the distance, and above and around me there was only air, and the light fading, and the sky turning indigo, then black."

Kerry's head sank on her breast again and her eyes closed.

Then she heard a voice of absolute serenity. Perhaps it was just the sound of the breeze in the leaves of the birches below her, or the pounding of the blood in her ears after the final, steep climb. But it sounded to her like the voice of the Carpenter of Nazareth, the man who had walked with her since childhood and shown her the nature of the God that she believed in. It was a gentle voice, full of understanding and compassion.

"Turn around," said the voice, and she turned around, and all at once she was back in the crater of the volcano, with Father Patrick at her side, surrounded by a great crowd of people, all bathed in the light of the full moon climbing over the eastern ridges.

"I am alive in everyone and everything and the connections between them. I am the end of all oppression, and the struggle for it. I am the desperation of the poor and the way out of it. I am the protester against injustice and her bravery. I am the land and the love of it. I am the artist and her creativity. I am the misfit and his strangeness. I am the monk and his serenity. I am the wise woman and her wisdom. I am compassion, I am commitment, I am serenity and passion. I became flesh and in flesh you will find me."

Kerry looked at the people around them. There were her old friends Peter Steel, Mario Rankin and Francis Neale. There was Aristides, Juan Pablo Ramirez and Carmen, Dona Isabela, Gustavo, Chaio and Celia, Fidelia and all the villagers from San Martin de Porres. There was Ivan Silver and Elaine Macdonald and the Elders of Deep Lake. There was Gabriel Garcia Araujo, Patricio from the CCN, Bill Cowley, Sister Alison, Sister Patsy and Hannah. There was Milton, Leif and Sophie, Hank and Marlon and Eric Smith and others from the blockade. There was Vera Shoots Straight and Grandpa Jimmy and Uncle Eddy, Father Donald Black and Stella Coelho and Kerry's father and mother, people who encouraged and strengthened others through their wisdom and quiet compassion. And there was Kerry's most deeply beloved soul friend and lover, Will, who had shed his blood struggling for a better future in a world he would not see, but which he hoped to bequeath to generations not yet born.

She woke up again, lifting her head from her chest, trying to clear her head, fighting against sleep.

"And you were by my side, Kerry, and Deirdre, too," said Father Patrick, "and there were all my old parishioners, and the homeless men who used to come to the presbytery for sandwiches, and a whole lot of people who I just knew were so desperate or so depressed they never had the strength to do anything other than survive, and those who couldn't even manage survival and were beaten down and broken in body, mind or soul.

"And the voice spoke to me again, not in my ear but in my insides, and it said, 'Behold your God,' and suddenly I was back in the woods, sitting against the old hornbeam, and day was breaking, and the air in the wood was full of birdsong. And then I woke up."

"What a beautiful dream!" exclaimed Kerry.

"Oh, it was! Thank you for listening to it. I just needed to tell someone, so it wouldn't be forgotten."

He was silent for a while. Kerry struggled against the desire for sleep.

"Would you be so good…as to call the nurse," said Father Patrick after a few minutes. He sounded breathless. "I'm having a bit of…trouble…with my breathing."

Kerry hurried to the nursing station and nurse Flaherty returned with her.

419

"I think we'll need to put you back on the oxygen, Father," she said. "You're struggling a bit, aren't you?"

"I am," said Father Patrick, with some difficulty.

Nurse Flaherty turned on the oxygen supply and placed a breathing mask over Father Patrick's mouth and nose. His breathing began to become easier; but a look of pain crossed his face. He moved the mask to one side and said, "I'm afraid I might need a bit more morphine, sister. It's a bit painful down below."

"Of course, my love," replied the nurse. She adjusted the settings on the intravenous painkiller to deliver a stronger dose. "Better keep that breathing mask on for now," she cautioned. "I'll check on you in a while, but call me if you need anything." She left the room.

Father Patrick moved the breathing mask to one side again, and said, "Would you do one more thing for me, Kerry?"

"Of course, Father," replied Kerry.

"Would you read me a poem?"

"Of course. Which one?"

"It's called 'God's Grandeur', by Gerard Manley Hopkins. It's near the back of my breviary. If you would just read that." He replaced the breathing mask and relaxed back on his pillow.

Kerry found the poem and began to read.

"The world is charged with the grandeur of God.
It will flame out, like shining from shook foil;
It gathers to a greatness, like the ooze of oil
Crushed. Why do men then now not reck his rod?
Generations have trod, have trod, have trod;
And all is seared with trade; bleared, smeared with toil;
And wears man's smudge and shares man's smell: the soil
Is bare now, nor can foot feel, being shod.

"And for all this, nature is never spent;
There lives the dearest freshness deep down things;
And though the last lights off the black West went

Oh, morning, at the brown brink eastward, springs –
Because the Holy Ghost over the bent
World broods with warm breast and with ah! bright
wings."

Kerry closed the breviary and looked at Father Patrick. He had fallen asleep again, his breathing calm and regular in the flow of oxygen from the mask.

Kerry's eyelids were heavy, and she let them close, and slept again.

She woke with a start, and looked at Father Patrick, upon whose face was a look of absolute serenity. She listened to the sound of the oxygen rushing from the face mask, a constant flow uninterrupted by respiration. Alarmed, she reached for Father Patrick's arm. It was warm, but she could feel no pulse.

"Father?" she called out. "Father Patrick?"

He did not stir.

Kerry hurried once again to the nursing station and asked nurse Flaherty to come quickly. The nurse listened to the sound of the oxygen, felt Father Patrick's pulse, listened for his heartbeat with a stethoscope. She straightened up.

"I'm afraid he's dead, my love. I'm sorry."

She turned off the oxygen and the intravenous drip.

Kerry said nothing, fighting back tears.

Nurse Flaherty looked at her watch, took Father Patrick's notes from the pouch at the end of his bed, and said aloud – perhaps to ensure it was official – "Time of death, 2.15 a.m." She made a note, and replaced the papers in the pouch.

"I think I'm going to take a break," said Kerry. "I'll go and get some fresh air."

"I should get some rest, my love," said nurse Flaherty. "There's nothing you can do here. I'll phone Deirdre now, but really there's not much either of you can do until the morning."

"I'll be back in the morning, then," said Kerry.

"I'm so sorry, my love," said nurse Flaherty, putting her arm round Kerry's shoulders. "We did all we could to make him comfortable."

"I know," said Kerry. "Thank you."

She took up her coat and walked out of the heat of the hospice into the cool night air, and down the drive. She turned right towards the town, but instead of returning to her accommodation, she turned up the lane towards the bottom of the Tor. There was no moon, but the sky was clear and the starlight was sufficient for her to find her way up the path that led up the hill. The path was steep, and she was tired. She stopped frequently to catch her breath.

At last she reached the top, and passed through the arch of the great tower, and stood facing east towards the hospice and the coming dawn. She was glad that she was alone there. The next day would be the summer solstice, and the Tor would be filled with people eager to watch the sunrise from this ancient sacred place.

The sky was lightening, and a breeze began to spring up from the South West. Kerry pulled her coat around her, surprised at how cold it was at this time of night in mid-June.

From a hawthorn bush on the hillside, a single blackbird began to sing, plaintive and liquid and sweet.

And suddenly, there was with the blackbird a multitude of the avian host, praising the morning and singing; and in the East, the wispy clouds turned primrose yellow and pale pink; and at length, as Kerry watched, the golden sun rose in splendour over the wooded horizon to the North East, and the world was filled with radiant light.